Balls AND
INSTINCTS

Balls **AND** INSTINCTS

Michael Drosdowich

This novel is dedicated to my wife Teresa and my son Michael. Without them, I would probably be dead or have written this novel from prison.

THE DOUBLE WHAMMY...

The double whammy is being born too cute and too smart for your own good. I know that sounds like a good thing to most people, but during the time period that I grew up it wasn't. When I was a kid, no one liked a cute, quick witted, out spoken, highly emotional child. All those qualities got you when I was a kid is abuse from your parents, teachers, and peers alike. Add a little high-spirited sarcasm into the mix, and you got a kid just looking to be abused. And abused I was.

Little kids in the sixties were still supposed to be seen and not heard. Parents weren't supposed to praise their children unless absolutely necessary. It might make them too complacent, secure, or heaven forbid they might even grow up feeling good about themselves. We couldn't have that now could we? Hell, who wants a kid with a high self-esteem anyway? When I brought home A's from school on my report card my father never praised me. When I asked him why, he would always say, "Why should I praise you for doing what you're supposed to do?" There were no rewards or positive reinforcements given in my house for good behavior. The only time I received any special attention from my old man was when I was bad.

So what happens to a very bright child who only receives attention from his father for doing wrong? Hmm, let's guess. The child simply responds by doing wrong again. By the age of five my parents and teachers already labeled me a bad boy in the community. The negative social labeling of a five year old would be considered by most people today as child abuse in itself. Not back then though. It was routine. When this destructive power is used by the people that you love and rely on for guidance it becomes almost impossible to overcome.

Mom was my best friend, but she also would abuse me. It might have been because she was hooked on speed at the time and didn't know it. The local pharmacist, Mr. Rich, was selling black beauties to all of the housewives in the neighborhood as diet pills. His pharmacy was right next door to the first women's health club in the neighborhood called Elaine Powers. My mom was truly naïve and had no idea what was happening to her. I remember her blinking her eyes so much that I could actually slip by her without her even noticing me. When my dad finally found out about moms addiction he went to visit Mr. Rich at his store. Pops walked over to him and pulled him over the counter by his throat right in front of his customers. With his hands gripped tightly around his neck he assured Mr. Rich there wouldn't be a next time. Needless to say, Mr. Rich stopped selling speed to the housewives in the neighborhood. Things did get better with Mom after that.

My kindergarten teacher at P.S. 13 was named Mrs. Conti. She was an old, short, heavyset Italian lady with grey hair and a mustache. She always wore a navy blue dress, a white shirt, and black shoes. She looked harmless enough, except for maybe the mustache, but looks can be deceiving. This woman used to grab me by the back of the shirt and the seat of my pants and throw me behind her piano. Then the old broad slapped me around a little for good measure before she started playing sweet little sing along songs for the rest of the kids. What was my terrible crime? I was talking when I wasn't supposed to. Back then in the sixties a lot of the parents told the teachers to discipline their kids as they see fit, so even at five years old I would take any beaten a teacher had to offer. That was a lot better than letting my old man find out I had been misbehaving in school. If he did, he would have beaten me again. Then he would have punished me by not letting me go out and play with my friends. Beatings were nothing compared to being kept indoors. I remember some nights my mom would give me a bath. While she was washing my hair, she would find bumps and tiny bald spots on her little boy's head. She would then ask me, "How did this happen?" Of course, I would lie and tell her it happened while I was playing rough with my friends. As the years passed by the physical and mental abuse would get much worse. Even though I was just a child, I took it like a man.

My fifth grade teacher Mr. Caregine had his own personal and special brand of sadistic behavior. This guy was only about five foot seven, but he weighed in at around two hundred and fifty pounds. Mr. Caregine always wore a suit and tie. To the world, he was respectable. To us kids though, he was a sadistic and perverted monster. For talking in class, Mr. Caregine would make the young culprits stand in front of the room facing the blackboard. With our backs facing the class, he would casually walk around the room continuing to give his lecture. Mr. Caregine would then turn his college ring around so the gemstone was in his palm. Then when you least expected it, he would brutally whack you across the back of your head. This would cause a little cut and a very painful bump on the back of your skull. Truthfully, the worst part about this punishment was you never knew when it was coming. I remember one faithful day in fifth grade when I made a tragic mistake. I forgot a book I needed for another class I was changing to, so I had to go back to Mr. Caregine's class and ask him if I could retrieve the book from my desk. I knocked on the door and politely asked permission to come in. Permission granted. I asked if I could retrieve my science book from my desk. Mr. Caregine answered this seemingly harmless request by throwing me violently to the floor. He then kicked me repeatedly across the floor until I was huddled under his desk. Mr. Caregine would then sit at his desk with his crotch right in my face while he conversed perversely with young girls. This became his favorite way of abusing me. When he was in a good mood, Mr. Caregine would just throw me in his closet. He wouldn't even let me out for lunch or to pee, so I would pee in his coat pockets. The fucking pervert must have liked it because I never heard anything about it. There is a particularly special place in hell for men like Mr. Caregine. One time when Mr. Caregine called my house Dad happened to be home. This was really unlucky for me because my old man was hardly ever home. Usually my mom would get the call and then never tell my father because she wanted to protect me. I truly and deeply loved my mother. She saved me from my father's wrath. Mom would keep anything from the old man that might get me in trouble. She also undermined Dad's punishments for me by letting me go out and play when I was grounded. Mom also threw herself between me and my father when I was getting a beating. She risked life and limb doing that for me, so I did the same for her. I was the only one of my siblings brave enough to take that risk. Anyway, Mr. Caregine told my dad I had been disruptive in class, so the same teacher who abused me daily in school calls my father so I would be abused again at home. Pops was in a creative mood that day, so instead of beating me he decided take me to the barbershop. I had beautiful shoulder length hair. When he got there, he told the barber to give me a crew cut. In 1970, every kid in the neighborhood had long hair. No one had a crew cut, so now when I went to school or outside to play I was cruelly teased and ridiculed by my peers. I was told only mongoloids and retarded kids get crew cuts because they put food in their hair when they eat. Parents in the neighborhood told their children not to play with me. The worst part about having all of my hair cut off really wasn't all the teasing. I could handle that by kicking someone's ass. The worst part about it was no one wanted to be seen hanging around with me. I was all alone. That's when I first became a thief and stole from my father. I took a bunch of his silver dimes he was collecting. I took them to the candy store around the corner to play pinball. I treated the other kids to free games so they would hang around with me until my hair grew back. This type of repeated abuse just hardened and toughened me for what lied ahead. That fifth year at St. Dennis would be my last. I was thrown out of school that April for bringing booze to school with my classmates. Three of us were thrown out for bringing it in, and nine others were suspended. Somebody in the gang snitched. We never knew whom. I had to study on my own for my finals, or I would have been left back a year. Being the genius that I am, I aced all the tests. None of the other boys even passed and were left back, so next year it was on to public school.

THE GAUNTLET...

White kids got three choices going to school in my neighborhood. The first and most obvious choice is to simply not go to school. Now this choice is okay for those white kids who have oblivious or alcoholic parents. Parents with no clue where their kids are or what they're doing. The second choice the white kids have growing up in my neighborhood is to succumb to the constant intimidation being doled out by the blacks and Puerto Ricans. They just got done burning down their apartments in the Bronx and are looking for new prey in Yonkers. This means giving up your lunch money and your manhood on a daily basis. The third choice is the one for the white kids who are blessed with extremely mean, very violent, and streetwise fathers. Men like my father who had become legends in their neighborhoods. The kind of men everyone looks up to and respects, but most of all fears.

My dad is a fireman in Yonkers. A real life superhero that has saved many lives in our city, but being a fireman wasn't his only job. Now let me explain what I mean about being blessed for having my kind of father. Knowingly or not, my father gives me the skills and mindset I need to survive. The neighborhood's landscape is changing rapidly and becoming increasingly more violent. Pops teaches me the 'Old School Rules.' I am taught to always defend myself and never be a bully. My father teaches me bullies are cowards. All I have to do is stand up to them and punch them right in their nose. "Let them taste their own blood," is what my dad tells me. I am also taught that the only thing worse than a coward is a squealer. Fear is truly the great motivator in this life, and my father makes me fear him more than anything else.

I learn a lot from public school kids right away. Like if a teacher hits you, you hit them back and they won't try it again. If they call your home, you slash their tires and they won't call again. Things really begin to get interesting the next year when I enter 7th grade at Hawthorne Junior High School. Hawthorne Junior High School is located right smack in the middle of the worst neighborhood Yonkers has to offer. Here is where I first realize I am born a predator and not prey.

As the white kids are trying to get into the school, there are large groups of black kids waiting for them at the doors. One by one as each white kid tries to get into the school they're being shaken down by the black kids. "Come here white boy! What's that I hear jingling in your pocket? Did your momma give you some money for lunch today? Give it up punk! It's my money now!" The black kids start rifling through all of the white kid's pockets. Some of the white kids try to resist by pulling the black kids' hands out of their pockets. That causes them to be thrown to the ground and stomped. I hear them frantically screaming, "Leave me alone! Leave me alone! Somebody, please help me!" What these kids learn quickly is no one is coming to help them. The teachers at Hawthorne Junior High School are hiding in their classrooms hoping to leave in one piece every day and not have their tires slashed. I need to think quickly because I'm close to being next. There is NO WAY on God's green earth I can go home and tell my daddy I let some kid take my lunch money! When it's my turn to enter the gauntlet, I reverse the roles on them. I say, "Hey black boy! What I hear jingling in your pocket? You got some money for me?" When I went for the black kid's pockets, he cried out to his boys to help him. "Yo, I got some crazy motherfucking white boy over here! Help me out bros!" Once I knew this black kid is scared of me, I go

7

through his pockets just like he did to the white kids in front of me. There are lots of 'left backs' in those days, so his friends are all older than me. I figure I'm in for a major ass kicking, but it didn't happen. When the older black kids see how I turned the tables on their boy they all begin laughing at him. Then the oldest and biggest black kid of the gang walks over to me and says, "You got big motherfucking balls for a white boy. What's your name?"

"Michael Drosdowich," I boldly reply.

"Michael what the fuck you say?"

"Drosdowich, Michael Drosdowich."

The brother lets out a huge laugh and says, "Drosowitz, you're a fucking Jew boy?"

"Fuck no. I aint no fucking Jew boy, I'm Russian. Just call me Droz for short. That's what my father's friends call him."

"Well Droz it is." He smiles and slaps five with me. He turns to his boys and says, "This here's Droz. He's one crazy motherfucking white boy, and he's alright with me."

That day I learned black kid's aint that bad at all. In fact, they are pretty cool and funny. You just need to stand up to their intimidation. I do feel bad for the other white kids though. All they had to do is make a stand, but they are too scared. Most of the white kids growing up where I live are born prey. It reminds me of the Time Machine movie when the guy travels way into the future and those half humans living underground are eating everybody. Nobody cares who is being dragged away by the monsters as long as it aint them. That's how it is at Hawthorne Junior High School. As long it's not them being robbed they can care less about anyone else. Like my father always says, "You can run forever, or you can make a stand and never run again."

LOOSE JOINTS, NICKEL BAGS...

I didn't know it at the time, but my first day at Yonkers High School changes my life forever. There are over 3,000 kids at this school, mostly black and Puerto Rican. As in Hawthorne Junior High School, a lot of the white kids just didn't go. When the school bell rings, I watch hundreds of kids walking through the parking lot trying to get into the school. All of a sudden, I hear someone yelling, "Loose joints nickel bags!" Out of the corner of my eye, I see a black kid holding up what looks to be at least a hundred joints. They are bound together by a rubber band. By the time he reaches the end of the parking lot, the joints are gone and he's counting money.

Boom! A light bulb goes off in my head! Why can't that be me? As I start walking towards this guy, I quickly notice I know him. I'll be dammed if it isn't Toby selling the weed. Toby is the black kid from Hawthorne Junior High that tried taking my lunch money. Over time, we had become friends. Toby looks like he's moved up from lunch money shakedowns to pot dealing.

I tap Toby on the shoulder and boldly say, "Give me your money boy!"

Toby turns around quickly and is relieved to see that it's me. He laughs and then hugs me saying, "Droz, what's up man?"

"You're up Toby. Look at you man. You're getting fucking rich out here."

"This aint all mine Droz. I wish the fuck it was, but it aint." Toby laughs.

"Well who's the fuck is it then?"

"It's Shayne's man. He fronts me weed and I sell it for him."

"Where does Shayne get his weed Toby?" I ask coyly.

"I don't know and I don't want to know. What the fuck you care for Droz? You want some bad ass weed to smoke I'll sell it to you."

"I want to smoke it Toby, but I don't want to buy it. I want to make money on it and smoke it."

"Well then I can't help you Droz," Toby replies as he is walking away.

"Wait a minute Toby."

"I got to split Droz and go give Shayne his money. He's an impatient motherfucker and I damn sure don't want to piss his ass off."

"Well Toby when you hand him his money tell him I'm interested in selling weed too."

"Why the fuck would I do that? I may like you're crazy white ass, but I sure aint looking to compete with you."

"I don't want to compete with you Toby. I want to be like Shayne, but in my neighborhood."

"Look Droz I aint asking the motherfucker shit. If you want to ask his ass you're going to have to do it yourself."

That night I take a big fucking risk and go to the projects to see Shayne. Shayne is the meanest and toughest motherfucker in all of the projects in Yonkers. He stands about six four and is built like a Greek fucking god. No one and I mean no one fucks with Shayne. As I approach his building two black guys jump out from the shadows. One's about my age and my size. The other guy is bigger and older than me. The older one barks out, "You fucking lost white boy?"

"No I aint fucking lost motherfucker. I'm looking for Shayne," I indignantly reply.

Both guys look at each other. Now the younger one plays dumb and says, "Looking for Shayne? Who the fuck is Shayne? I don't know any motherfucker named Shayne."

Stiffening up my tone, I look this kid square in his fucking eyes and say, "Just go tell Shayne that Droz is here."

My bold persistence really pisses this kid off, so he grabs his dick and angrily replies back, "How bout I make you my bitch instead!"

"How about you motherfucking try!" I shout back.

The kid makes a move towards me, and I drop him like a sack of fucking potatoes. Shocked by my power and fearless aggressiveness the older guy hesitates for a second. That's all I need to plant a hard swift kick to his stomach. Both guys quickly recover and pull their knives out on me. I reach into my pocket for my own knife, and then I hear Shayne yell, "Put them motherfucking blades down! Droz is cool with me. He gets a pass down here, you dig?"

Both guys put their knives back into their pockets and reluctantly nod their heads agreeing. I hold out my hand in a gesture of friendship and both of them give me skin. Luckily, the ruckus worked to my advantage and causes enough commotion to attract Shayne's attention. Shayne extends his hand out to me for some skin and says, "If it aint the crazy motherfucking white boy Droz."

"What other white boy could it be Shayne?" I proudly reply.

"Hearing your ass arguing out here sure didn't sound like a motherfucking white boy. You sounded like some uninvited nigger from another project looking for trouble." Shayne lifts his shirt showing me the cold dark steel of his pistol. Now he asks, "So what brings your crazy white ass down here?"

"Business."

"What kind of motherfucking business?"

"Weed business Shayne. I saw Toby today at school making money and I want to do the same."

"I already got Toby Droz. What do I need you for?"

"No disrespect Shayne, but not every white motherfucker wants to buy from a nigger and I think you know that. They are either afraid, prejudiced, or both."

Shayne laughs mightily at my boldness and then replies back, "You got big motherfucking balls talking to me like that Droz, but you're right. I could make more money having a white boy dealing for me too. Follow me upstairs."

I follow Shayne into his building and up to his apartment. When we walk inside Shayne's place, there are a bunch of little kids playing board games on the floor in the living room. He takes me to the kitchen where there's an old black lady humming softly cooking at the stove. Whatever she's cooking smells delicious!

"Meet my granny Droz. She takes care of all these kids while I supply the money. My father's never any help and my momma died giving birth to little Leona here."

Granny looks at me with a gracious smile and bids me a kind hello. Then she asks, "What's your Christian name son?"

"Michael, Granny. I was baptized Michael John."

"That's a mighty strong name, Michael the Arch Angel and John the Baptist. I hope you make your parents proud and do it justice."

"Well I hope so too Granny. Whatever you're cooking on the stove Granny sure smells delicious. Do you mind if I ask you what it is?"

Smiling proudly, Granny replies back, "Oh no, not at all Michael John. This here's smoked neck bones, smoked ham hocks, ox tails, and collard greens. I simmer it in some onions, some garlic, some sugar, and a little vinegar. Would you like to try some?"

"Love too Granny," I enthusiastically reply.

"You better watch out white boy. You may walk out of here a lot darker than you started!" Shayne laughs.

Granny and I laugh too as she fixes me a plate. Granny then pulls an old cast iron pan out of the oven and cuts me out a big piece of cornbread. I go through that plate of food like Grant went through Richmond! Man was that fucking good! Watching me enjoy that meal the way I did put a big smile on both Shayne's and Granny's face! After I'm finished sucking the last bit of juice out of them bones, Shayne invites me to his room.

Shayne takes a key ring out of his pocket and opens up his door. He locks the door behind us and opens his closet showing me what's inside. There's a rifle, a shotgun, two pistols, and eight garbage bags full of weed. Shayne picks up the pump shotgun, looks at me and asks, "You ever seen one of these Droz?"

"I sure have Shayne."

Seeing Shayne's guns makes me think of my Uncle Richie. He's my father's younger brother. Uncle Richie is an Ex-Marine Korean War Veteran and biker from the fifties. My uncle left Yonkers for the country because he wanted to become a mountain man. He bought some land up in the Adirondacks and built a cabin. When my parents wanted to get rid of me, they shipped me up there to him. My uncle taught me how to hunt, fish, trap, and use all kinds of weapons. He's a forest ranger. When I stay with him, he takes me out on his nightly patrols. One night out on patrol, he abruptly cuts off his headlights. Then he makes a quick turn into a field. When the car stops, he opens his glove box and hands me a snub-nose 357 magnum pistol. He looks me in the eyes and calmly says, "Michael, if anybody but me comes out of those woods and approaches this car, you shoot them." Uncle Richie then gets out of the truck with his 44 magnum strapped to his side. I become very nervous watching my uncle disappear into the woods. I know I'm supposed to be this tough city boy, but I'm only 13 and scared shitless! After about ten minutes or so, I hear gunshots. I can tell some are rifle shots and others are pistol. Now I'm really fucking scared! My heart is pounding so hard my tee shirt is moving. After about five minutes which feels like a fucking lifetime, my uncle comes back out of the woods. He hollers out, "I'm alright!" and disappears again into the woods. When he comes back out this time, he's dragging a body. Then he goes back in and drags out two more. It turns out these three guys were poachers. That was their first mistake. Their second mistake was firing on my uncle, which proved to be their last. Killing these three men didn't phase my Uncle Richie one bit, so I took heed and learned from his example. There are lots of firsts for me up there in the mountains.

One Sunday at the church picnic, I meet a beautiful girl named Melissa. Even though we are from totally different worlds, we get along instantly. It's puppy love at first sight. That night my uncle wanted me to get the fishing gear ready for the morning while he goes on patrol. While I'm putting everything together, I hear a knock at the door. What do you know, it's Mellissa holding a blanket! Standing there with a smile that could melt an iceberg, she asks, "Hey Michael, it's a beautiful starry night. Would you like to take a walk with me?" First thing that crosses my mind is not finishing what my uncle asked me to do. The second thing is that Mellissa is the preacher's daughter! Trouble on both ends! Needless to say, my hard on throws caution to the wind and I leave with Mellissa. We both lost our virginity under the stars that night. It was a bit clumsy at first, but the natural chemistry brewing between us soon took over. We were in love! Well at least we thought we were.

After I tell Shayne about the times I spent with my uncle, he knew I could handle a gun. Now he asks, "Have you ever smoked weed before Droz?"

"Hell yeah Shayne, but I don't know shit about selling it."

That night Shayne teaches me everything I needed to know. I walk out of his apartment with two hundred fifty joints and fifty nickel bags. He tells me to be back with his half of the money in three days or less. The other half of the dough is mine to keep.

The next day is Saturday, a perfect day to start my new business. After mom cooks me up some bacon and eggs for breakfast, I head for Pelton Park. Shockingly my first customers are some of the girls I go to school with. They're ecstatic that someone they are comfortable with is selling weed. Next, I hit up all the guys my age. When everyone starts hunting me down for more, I know Shayne's weed is better than what they were getting. With such positive feedback, I approach the older guys in the park. I light up a couple of joints with them so they can try it. They fucking love it! Shayne's weed moves me right up the totem pole! By Sunday night, I'm heading back to Shayne's apartment for more weed! Shayne gladly stocks me up with as much weed as I need. Soon I began to branch out. I set some white kids up selling weed in North Yonkers. Either the cops are oblivious to my business or they just don't give a shit about people selling weed. My biggest problem now is converting all of the small bills I get from dealing into hundreds. This way I can more easily hide my drug money from my father and mother.

Two years pass by, and Shayne and I are like brothers. We share everything in our lives together. I'm selling so much weed now that Shayne's connection wants to meet me. Shayne picks me up in his car at Pelton Field the very next morning. Shayne drives a cool fucking car. It's a 1966 purple Coupe Deville. "So where are we heading Shayne?"

"We're meeting my guy at a warehouse in Brooklyn. It's a long motherfucking ride, so spark up."

"Sure thing Shayne," I reply as I reach into my sock for a joint.

I light up a bone and take a few pokes then pass it to Shayne. He tells me to pop his Parliament Mothership Connection eight track into his boom box. I love George Clinton. I love getting high to Parliament and James Brown records. As Shayne's Cadillac pulls into a warehouse district in Brooklyn things look all too familiar. This is where my old man keeps his casino equipment. My dad has a partnership with old man Rose. Old man Rose is a big time Jewish gangster in New York. He made his first million during prohibition. My dad and old man Rose have a legitimate business together. They rent casino equipment and train casino workers to charitable organizations. They would put on casino nights for these so called charities in New York, Chicago, and Florida. Of course, it's nothing but a front for their illegal gambling racket. Before midnight, the dough goes to charity. After midnight is a totally different story. That's when the high rollers and celebrities come to play. They also rent all the equipment and men for bazaars. Every church and synagogue within a hundred miles of New York uses their service. They even supplied the prizes you win at the bazaars. Old man Rose was Jewish, but he's like Santa Clause to me. Every time my father takes me to his warehouse, he would give me a choice of any prize I wanted. Back in 1971, my old man took to me Florida with him. He was putting on one of these so called charity events at the Boca Hotel. One afternoon he took me to a giant warehouse located in Hialeah. It turns out that old man Rose had partnered with the Cubans during prohibition smuggling rum out of Cuba. Over the years, their partnership built into a deep friendship and my father became a part of it. Instead of smuggling liquor, they're building casino equipment. Inside the warehouse, I saw dozens of Cuban men hard at work. These men were building Black Jack tables, Baccarat tables, Dice tables, and Roulette tables. My father would get the silkscreen coverings for the tables and the Roulette Wheels directly from Vegas. This is where I first met Willie. He's the son of my old man's contact down there, and Willie and I became great friends.

So now I'm really fucking worried. I turn and say, "Hey man this aint fucking cool Shayne. This is one of my father's places."

"Your old man is hooked up with Howie Rose?" Shayne asks in a very surprised tone.

"Howie Rose. That's old man Rose's son Shayne. He's your connection?"

"Hell yeah he is, and a motherfucking good one too. Howie's hooked up real tight with some of them Italian Mafia motherfuckers. So what do you know Droz, your old man's a fucking gangster. You told me he was a fireman."

"Well, he is Shayne, but he also has a casino business with old man Rose. I got to tell you something Shayne. Old man Rose and my father hate fucking drugs. Howie's taking a big fucking risk doing this, especially fucking here. I'm telling you Shayne something inside of me is saying that this just aint fucking right."

When we pull up to the warehouse, I see Howie standing outside. Howie is a tall skinny kid with glasses. He always dresses nice. That's probably because his mother makes him. His mom is the typical dominating Jewish mother. Whenever she's around you could hear old man Rose saying, "Yes dear, okay dear, whatever you say dear." I only see Howie when our families get together on holidays or outings, so we aren't really close friends. I never would have dreamed he had the fucking balls to deal drugs. We park and get out of the car. When Howie sees me, he shits a fucking brick. He looks at Shayne with panic and says, "You got to be fucking kidding me Shayne! Georgey Droz's son is your main man? The way you fucking described him I thought he was black."

"Well he is Howie, on the inside anyway," Shayne proudly replies.

"You never told Howie my name Shayne?"

"I just called you my main man Droz. Nobody needed to know your real fucking name. I looked out for you like a brother."

I nod my head to Shayne and then turn to Howie saying, "You know we're fucking toast Howie if either one of our fathers find out."

Howie hugs me and says, "Our fathers are partners for life Droz and now we are too."

When we walk into the warehouse the hair on the back of my neck stands up. My instincts scream at me to get the fuck out of there. Howie throws on the lights and sure enough there's old man Rose staring right at us. He always looked like a kind and gentle man, but today he looks like a killer. Howie immediately starts apologizing to me while four men come in the door behind us grabbing Shayne. I go to help him, but get knocked to the floor. As I'm getting up old man Rose grabs me by the scruff of the neck and says the magic words, "You want me to tell your father Michael?" I was putty in his hands. Old man Rose knew how much I feared my father. As tough as Shayne is he's no match for these men. They take out blackjacks and mercilessly beat him to the ground. Shayne is a bloody mess when they tie him up and gag him. The four men then drag him out the door, and I knew right then I would never see my best friend again.

After it's over a couple of old guys come in to clean up Shayne's blood. Then old man Rose sits me and his son down for a little chat. "I know the two of you are good boys at heart. You were just being influenced by these black hoodlums that have taken over parts of our city. What you saw happen here today will happen to the both of you if you continue to go down this path. If you boys need money, just ask. There is no need to get involved in such a dirty business." Old man Rose then turns to me and says, "Michael, I was at the hospital with your father on the day you were born. It was a beautiful fall afternoon, and I had never seen your father happier. It would break his heart to find this out. If you promise me you won't get involved with these kinds of people again, I won't tell your father. You promise?"

"I promise Mr. Rose," I sedately reply.

"Good. Now let's all go down to Abramowitz's Deli and get some lunch. I don't know about you kids, but I'm starved."

When I get home, my mom tells me Pops decided twenty-three years on the fire department is enough. He's retiring. The house will be going up for sale and the three of us are moving to Florida. Gee, why aint I surprised? My father knew all along what I was doing with Shayne. That's why old man Rose's men didn't grab me too. He wanted me out of Yonkers and away from my friends. Mom says my brother and sister decided to stay behind. The both of them are involved in relationships and don't want to move. They're old enough to do what they wanted. Now I'm really bummed out!

I accumulated a little over thirty six thousand dollars dealing weed with Shayne. That's a lot of money in 1977. Before I leave Yonkers, I visit Shayne's granny. Granny knew Shayne's gangster life finally caught up with him. She told me that it will catch up to me too if I didn't quit. Shayne was the sole provider for granny and all of the kids. With Shayne gone, things were going to get tough. I hand granny a bag with eighteen grand in it, kiss her on the cheek, and begin walking away. As I'm walking towards the door granny shouts, "What's wrong with you Michael John? Don't tell me you're going to leave old granny standing here without fixing you one last plate?" I turn around and see granny with her hands on her hips and tapping her foot on the floor. Tears run down my cheeks as I sit down and have my last meal with granny. She breaks out some pictures of Shayne as a little boy and tells me nice stories about him.

The old man sold the house with everything in it wanting to start off totally new. All mom and I are allowed to take is clothes and my boom box. In there I carefully hide my last ounce of premium 'Colombian Gold' weed. I stash eighteen grand in hundred dollar bills deep into my suitcase. We throw everything into Pop's Lincoln and hit the road for our new life in Florida.

"Exactly where in Florida are we heading to Pops?" I inquisitively ask.

"We're going to live in a brand new city Michael called Coral Springs."

"Whereabouts is that pops?"

"It's about twenty two miles from Ft. Lauderdale Beach and only eleven miles from Pompano Beach."

"I hope I like it dad."

"You'll love it, and if you don't, tough shit. Your mother and I will love it, right honey?"

"You better hope so Georgey, for your sake. I'll make you miserable if I don't."

"You'll find a way to make me miserable either way LuLu." My father laughs.

"Aint that the truth pops," I quickly add.

"The both of you better shut up. We aint gone five minutes and the both of you are already giving me a fucking headache."

"I bet you have to pee too, don't you mom?"

Mom's head turns around like the girl in the Exorcist movie. She looks at me evilly and yells, "You little son of a bitch, you're the devil's seed! George, I'm telling you! This kid is just no fucking good! Why don't we just leave him on the side of the fucking road somewhere? We'll both be happier without him."

My father and I both start laughing. One of our favorite things to do together is tease my mother! This trip to Florida may be more fun than I thought!

THE TRIP...

Pops says he wants to visit an old Navy buddy in North Carolina. The ride to Coral Springs will take us about four days. Mom actually stops her bitching along the way and I knew why. My old man was hardly ever home, and I'm always out running the streets. Having us in the same car with her meant she didn't have to worry about us and that made her happy.

Dad pulls off an exit in North Carolina named Mt. Airy and I ask, "Is this where your Navy buddy lives pops?"

"Yes it is son. Mt. Airy, North Carolina. Remember watching the Andy Griffith show?"

"Of course I do Pops."

"Remember the town in it called Mayberry?"

"I sure do dad."

"Well Mt. Airy is the real life Mayberry where they filmed the show."

"Wow, aint that a trip. You got friends in Mayberry?"

"I guess you can say that Michael." Dad chuckles

"I'm not looking forward to this Georgey. After that movie we seen, you shouldn't be either," Mom says worriedly.

"What movie?" Dad replies.

"I think Mom means Deliverance Dad."

"Of course I mean Deliverance! What other movie shows hillbilly queers butt raping men from the city? This place could be full of hillbilly queers that are just licking their chops waiting for a New Yorker!"

"Michael and I will be fine. We can take care of ourselves. You're the one that better watch out LuLu."

"Me watch out? Why should I watch out? Hillbilly queers want men."

Dad raises his eyebrows replying in a serious tone, "Women hillbilly queers. I hear they wait in the ladies' rooms at gas stations for unsuspecting tourists. Didn't you say a few miles back you needed to pee? There's a bumpy road ahead LuLu. Oh, look honey. There's a gas station on the left. We'll pull in."

"Go fuck yourself Georgey! I'll bust a fucking kidney before we stop! You just get us where we're going and fast!"

Out of mom's reach, I laugh my ass off in the backseat. We go up and down mountains and around turns that scare the pants off me. Mom is getting nervous, so she shouts out, "Just admit it Georgey! You're fucking lost! Men never want to admit when they're lost and I really got to fucking pee now!"

Pops smiles, and in about another minute or so we come to a large fenced in pasture. I saw horses grazing on the grass. I look straight ahead and my eyes open up wide at this big ranch house at the end of the road. Dad says, "We're here."

"Thank God!" Mom shouts.

We pull up to this humongous ranch style house and stop the car. We all get out and stretch a bit. This place is big, and I mean really big. This house looks like something straight out of a movie. We walk up to a giant wooden double door that has huge iron rings for knocking. Dad takes hold of one of them iron rings and bangs it on the door. We hear a big dog barking. This triggers mom to cry out, "Oh shit Georgey! They have a dog! I'm scared." Dad smiles and puts his arm around mom reassuring her he will protect her from any danger. From behind the giant door we hear a lady in a strong but elegant southern accent say, "You hush now buster! Get on out the way boy and let me open the door! Go on now boy! Get!" The dog quiets down and a beautiful older woman answers the door. She has long auburn colored hair, blue eyes, and is wearing a colorful flowered dress. Standing behind her is a pure white bulldog. Mom quickly ducks behind dad. The woman now greets us, "Hey Georgey, we have been a waiting on you! Come on in!"

We walk in the door and mom is still hiding behind dad as he introduces us. "Hi Elizabeth, this is my son Michael and my wife LuLu."

Mom cautiously peaks around dad and politely states, "I'm scared of dogs Elizabeth."

"Oh don't you mind old Buster here LuLu. He's just a big old mush puppy," Elizabeth replies.

"Look at the mug on that dog Dad. He's cute!"

"Just pet him LuLu and let him smell you," Pops says.

Mom cautiously reaches down and pets Buster and he takes a liking to mom right away. So while rubbing Buster's head mom says, "He is kind of cute Elizabeth. "

"Why thank you LuLu."

"Listen honey. We've been driving for hours and I'm about to burst. Point me to the ladies room," Mom says desperately.

Empathetically, Elizabeth waves her hand. "Oh, I know the feeling LuLu. Men just don't understand when they take us on their little trips."

"Tell me about it." Mom rolls her eyes with her hand on her hip.

"Just walk down the hallway LuLu and make your first right. The bathroom is on your left."

"Thank you Elizabeth." Mom walks to the bathroom and Buster follows right behind her like he just found a new friend.

"Well Georgey, I know you want a beer! Michael, I just made some sweet tea. How about I get you some?"

"Sure Elizabeth. That sounds great."

"Good. Just follow me into the kitchen."

We follow Elizabeth through the house to the kitchen. The house is unbelievable! The entire inside is made out of wooden logs. There's a giant stone fireplace in the living room, and a bear skin rug lying right in front of it. The kitchen is tremendous, bright, and airy. Giant bay windows opened up to an incredible view of the mountains. Dad gets his beer and I get my sweet tea. Boy is it good!

Here comes mom and Buster. In an excited tone mom says, "I was lost when I got out of the bathroom, so I just followed Buster and he led me right to you. Elizabeth, your home is stunning! Right out of a magazine! The view is to die for!"

"Why thank you LuLu."

"Mom, you got to try some sweet tea. It's delicious."

"Would sweet tea be okay for you LuLu, or would you like something else?"

"No, sweet tea would be great Elizabeth. Thank you."

We all hear the big front door open and close. Then in a deep manly voice with a big southern accent we hear, "I see that New York plate Georgey, I know you're here!" Buster darts out of the kitchen to meet his master. A tall strongly built man with dark hair wearing faded jeans and a red flannel shirt walks into the kitchen saying, "You all made it! Now introduce me to your lovely family Georgey."

"Gladly James, this is my wife LuLu and my youngest son Michael," My father says proudly.

James looks at my mom and then turns to my father. "I'll tell you Georgey, your wife's pictures just don't do her justice! She's one fine looking woman!" Then he hugs her gently in his big strong arms.

My mom starts bubbling all over. "Why thank you James."

"LuLu, old Georgey Boy here has been head over heels for you since we served together in the Navy."

Mom still bubbling over James's flattery replies, "Well I must say James that I was head over heels for my cutie pie too. I couldn't wait for him to come home to me!"

"So this here's your youngest boy Michael."

I stand up and shake James's hand. James has a hand the size of a bear and a grip like a vice. Pops always taught me to look a man straight in the eyes and shake his hand firmly. So that's exactly what I do.

"Fine strapping young man you got here Georgey." James says as he stares deeply into my eyes.

Reading James's eyes, I know right away he likes my steady eye contact and strong grip. After the handshake, we all go out into the living room to get better acquainted. It aint long before James and my father disappear leaving me alone with the women. While they're talking, I start looking at all the pictures hanging on the wall. When Elizabeth sees me, she walks over with my mom and says, "Those are some old pictures of our daughters Michael. The first one is Teresa Sue. The next two are Rebecca Joe and little Sally. They're all much older now."

I start thinking to myself, "How much older?" I didn't have to think long because Elizabeth tells us. "Teresa Sue is 17, Rebecca Joe is 14 and Little Sally is 10." I wonder how Teresa Sue turned out I think to myself.

My mom and Elizabeth continue to hit it off while I twiddle my thumbs waiting for the girls to come home. Then bang! The front door bursts open and I hear all kinds of feet running up the stairs. The girls are even too fast for Buster to react!

"Now you girls come down here this instant! We have company!" Elizabeth shouts.

"Not now momma! We're all filthy dirty from riding! We need to get in the shower before we meet company!" One of the girls yells back in her southern accent.

"Okay girls. I understand. Well you all hurry up now. We got work to do in the kitchen! The girls are always behind in their time LuLu. I told them we would be having company and I needed them to help me fix dinner."

"Come on Elizabeth, I'll be glad to help you," My mom says.

"I won't hear of it LuLu. You're my guest!"

"Please Elizabeth. Let me help. I've been sitting in that damn car all day. I need to move around."

Elizabeth touches my mom's shoulder and gladly obliges her. It wasn't long before I start smelling dinner. It's fried chicken! One of my all-time favorites at home! Now I hear the girls running down the stairs laughing and giggling all the way. There they are standing still right in front of me with big smiles on all of their faces. And still giggling!

In unison the girls say, "Hi Michael!"

"Hi girls," I reply with a big grin.

All three of the girls are beautiful. However, the oldest one, Teresa Sue, has the kind of looks you only see in a magazine. She has long, fiery, auburn hair and big, blue, sparkling eyes. Her clothes melted to her sexy curves. Our eyes lock on to each other's right away.

"Girls! Get in this kitchen right now!" Elizabeth shouts.

Rebecca Joe and little Sally run to the kitchen. Teresa Sue and I stand there mesmerized staring into each other's eyes. It feels like time has stopped and we are the only two people left in the world. Love at first sight! At least I'm hoping so anyway!

"Teresa Sue! Get in here this instant!" Her momma yells again.

This breaks our trance and Teresa Sue quickly shouts back, "Coming momma!"

As she is running into the kitchen, I get my first glimpse of her perfect round ass. Right after that my old man and James walk back in the house. "Smells like its dinnertime," James says smiling. "Are you hungry Michael?"

"I'm starved. My stomach's been growling for an hour smelling all that food cooking."

"Good. That's good," James says patting me on the shoulder. Then he tells me to follow him. When we reach the dining room, it's a sight to behold. The table is beautifully set with a red-checkered tablecloth and freshly picked flowers. Man size plates are on this table.

"Teresa Sue! Bring us all a nice cold beer. It's alright if your boy has a cold one with us, right Georgey?"

"I'm sure it aint his first James."

Teresa Sue quickly brings us all a cold beer. When she hands me my beer she gives me a big bright smile. She then quickly turns around and slowly struts back into the kitchen. I fully appreciate the show and stare at her ass the entire way back.

"Put your eyes back in your head son," My father says.

"Awe, that's alright Georgey. Hell a fire. What kind of young man would he be if he didn't look?"

My father smiles and lifts up his beer. Then he taps it to James's like he's proposing a toast. "The kind we wouldn't be having a beer with."

"You got that right Georgey." James lets out a big laugh. Then both men take a slug of their beer. Men of that generation didn't tolerate snitches, cowards, or faggots.

Here comes Elizabeth, Mom, and all three girls carrying food. First to be set down are two giant platters of golden brown fried chicken. Next, the girls bring out a platter of homemade biscuits and a giant bowl of homemade potato salad. There's also a big bowl of garden salad filled with ripe, juicy, red tomatoes. Last but not least out comes a platter of corn on the cob and a tub of homemade butter. What a feast! Before we dig in James says grace and thanks the Lord Almighty for the bounty on our table. After devouring one of the best dinners I have ever eaten, out comes coffee and dessert! "Fresh baked pies anyone? We have pecan pie made from the pecans grown on our tree and peach pie from our peach tree," Elizabeth boasts.

This is all too good to be true. I fall in love with a beautiful girl and fall in love with her momma's cooking! Man, I sure am enjoying this southern experience! After dessert, the women clean up while my Dad and James disappear again. I sit there at the table full to the gills and listen to the girls chattering in the kitchen. This is light years away from my world and I liked it!

When the girls are done cleaning up Elizabeth asks Teresa Sue to show me around the ranch. I needed to pinch myself after hearing that. With a big smile Teresa Sue replies, "Sure Momma, we still got a few hours before sunset. Are you ready Michael? Or are you just too stuffed to move?" She pokes at my belly and giggles.

"No, no, I aint too stuffed Teresa Sue. Let's go," I reply while pushing her hand away.

When we get outside, she walks me over to the stalls where they keep their horses. I count twelve horses. Using her extremely sexy southern accent and mannerism, Teresa Sue asks, "Have you ever ridden a horse before Michael?"

In a not too confident tone, I reply, "Well, not really. Unless you count pony rides when I was a kid."

Teresa Sue tries to hold back her laughter, but she couldn't. She gently touches my arm and teasingly says, "Okay city boy. I guess I'll just have to teach you."

I know I'm way out of my element here. This can quickly go really, really, bad for me I think to myself.

Teresa Sue smiles. "I'm going to let you ride Sam. Sam's really good-natured, so there's no need to be afraid of him. Okay Michael?"

I quickly point to my chest. "What, me afraid? I'm not afraid. Just show me what to do."

Teresa then shows me how to properly saddle a horse and mount him. So far so good, I think to myself. I didn't fall off the other damn side! Teresa and her horse named Buck lead the way. Luckily for me, Sam follows right behind. Teresa tells me her dad's ranch is over two hundred acres. The property has gentle rolling hills and beautiful green pastures. What a wonderful place to live and grow up in I think to myself. As we're riding through a wooded trail, I hear the sound of rushing water. When we come to a clearing, I see a beautiful waterfall crashing into a lake. "Isn't this pretty Michael?" Teresa Sue asks.

"It's absolutely gorgeous Teresa Sue."

"This is my favorite spot on the entire ranch Michael. I can't tell you how many times I just come out here to sit and think. You want to sit by the lake with me?"

"Why sure Teresa Sue, I would love it. This is hands down the most beautiful place I have ever seen."

"How come your daddy never brought you and your momma to visit us before Michael?"

"We never knew he came here. It was a surprise to both of us that we even stopped here."

"Don't you work with your daddy Michael?"

"No. He's a fireman. I'm too young to do that."

"I mean with his other job Michael."

Okay. Now I get it I think to myself. My old man and her old man are in the casino business together. "So you know about the casino business?"

"Of course I do Michael. Your daddy and his friends have been coming down here four or five times a year since I could remember."

"Wow, I never knew that Teresa. I wish he would have taken me. As far as my mom goes, he never tells her anything. Where do they put on gambling nights in Mt. Airy anyway?"

"They mostly set up bazaars at our fairs. Not too many casino nights in Mt. Airy. Your dad mainly comes down here to get moonshine and cigarettes from my father. He supplies all of your private clubs up north. Your daddy and his friends bring back two truckloads every time."

"So your dad tells you and your mom all of this?"

"Sure, why not?"

"Well things don't work that way in our family Teresa. I feel lucky to know what little I do. My mom is never told anything. I guess that's why my father always says 'Telegraphs, tele wire, tell LuLu'."

Teresa laughs real hard at that one. Then in a really serious tone says, "Since your daddy aint told you nothing about this Michael you need to promise me not to let him know I told you."

"Of course Teresa Sue, that goes without saying. My lips are sealed girl."

"Are you sure Michael?"

"Absolutely Teresa, you don't know me yet. I'm a hardcore keep my mouth shut kind of guy."

"Well, we'll see about that Michael. I'll sure find out soon enough if I can trust you."

I look her straight in her pretty, blue eyes now. "Don't worry. You can trust me. Just like you can trust me when I say you are the most beautiful girl I have ever laid eyes on."

My flirtatious advance catches Teresa Sue totally off guard. She blushes from ear to ear and replies softly, "Well thank you Michael. You're kind of cute yourself."

"I'm only kind of cute Teresa?" I ask coyly.

"Okay Michael. You're really cute, but I think you already know that. So don't be a jerk and let it go to your head," She reluctantly replies.

With that said, our lips meet for a long, soft, wet kiss. When we stop and open our eyes we are both star struck. Teresa gives me another soft wet kiss and then says, "We need to get back to the house Michael before it gets dark."

Every inch of me wants to keep her hot ass right there and try to go all the way with her, but I don't. I learned my lesson with the preacher's daughter. I knocked her up, embarrassed my uncle, and disgraced her family. The preacher packed up and moved away because of what I did. I never heard from or seen Mellissa again. I want this to be different. I want her family to respect me and I want Teresa Sue to know I respect her. When we reach the stables, she shows me how to unsaddle the horses. Walking out of the barn, I put my arm around her and she reciprocates. I tell her again how beautiful she is and she embraces me for one more long juicy kiss before we go inside. This time I press my bulging hard on up against her. She presses back letting me know it's welcome.

When I'm alone in my room, I jerk off fantasizing about her. Then I picture her playing with herself and I jerk off again! The next morning we all awake to a king's breakfast. My dad and James disappear again right after we eat. Teresa Sue and I seize the opportunity to return to the lake. There we make out passionately and clothes fuck all morning until we had to return to the house for lunch. After lunch come the dreaded goodbyes. We're both heartbroken. Our parents see it in our faces. My dad rubs me on the head and Teresa's mom holds her close. I'm deeply depressed and sleep all the way to Georgia. My parents wake me up after we park at a Georgia peach stand off one of the exits. I'm sad and blue, but these Georgia peaches manage to put a smile on my face. Georgia peaches are the sweetest and juiciest pieces of fruit I have ever eaten! Three dollars for an entire bucket of heaven! You need a bib when you eat these babies!

In about another four hours or so we reach Daytona Beach. The smell of the ocean fills my nostrils as I take in the breeze coming off the surf. Pops takes a left turn following the car in front of him right onto the beach. Boy this is cool, cruising along the shoreline! That is until we get stuck in the sand. My old man isn't used to making mistakes, so this aint boding well for him. We all get out of the car to take a closer look. My mother and I watch Pops grimacing as he assesses the situation. Mom takes her cigarettes out of her purse and lights one up. She takes a big drag and puts her hand on her hip while looking out at the ocean. She exhales and turns back to my father sarcastically saying, "Gee George. It looks like the tide's coming in. What do we do now? Swim the rest of the way?" Then mom and I bust out laughing together! Needless to say, the old man doesn't think it's funny and starts chasing us around the car. Luckily, we have a head start. All of a sudden, he loses his footing and falls face down in the sand. This makes things even more hilarious because now he's chasing us with sand all over his face! To make matters worse, people are snapping pictures of us! Fortunately, now some of the locals come to our rescue before my old man can catch us. They put boards under our tires and help push us out. One of the tourists walks up to my father and hands him a couple of Polaroid pictures. Pops looks down at the pictures and just starts laughing. He thanks the man and shakes his hand for taking the funny photos. My father hands each guy a double sawbuck for helping us. With that, we continue on our journey to Coral Springs. We arrive there in about another four hours. It would have been a lot sooner if Mom didn't have to stop so many times to pee! Pops pulls into a condo complex on Sample Road and says this will be our temporary home until our new house is finished being built. The place is brand spanking new. We turn the air down to a comfortable 70 degrees and unpack. After that we are all dead tired, so we hit the showers and go to bed.

JOHNNY SANTORI...

I wake up bright and early the next morning before my parents. I'm anxious to take a look around outside in the daylight at my new home. I put on my jeans and wife beater tee shirt. Then I lace up my purple converse and head out the door. Holy fucking shit this place is desolate! Not one car going up or down the road! This must be a part of my old man's plan to keep me out of trouble. I must say, it is a clean and pretty place to live. Newly paved litter free streets and lots of beautiful palm trees. It's a stark contrast from the traffic laden dirty streets of Southwest Yonkers. My tranquility is shattered by my mother yelling for me off the balcony.

"Michael! Michael! Where the hell are you?"

Answering mom back right away is never any fun. I like to make her sweat a little before I answer. This always makes the next time she yells a lot more theatrical. Now I hear her yelling at my father.

"Georgey, Georgey! Get up off your ass and go look for your son!"

I know my father aint budging. This will make mom even madder. "Look, I'm telling you now Georgey! If you don't go look for your son and he gets eaten by a fucking Alligator, you'll burn in hell!"

Just as mom finishes saying that I strut back into the condo and excitingly say, "You should have seen mom! There was a giant alligator in the parking lot! And he almost got me!"

"You little son of a bitch, he should have fucking gotten you!"

With that being said, our happy little family heads out the door for our first breakfast in our new town. Pops drives west down Sample Road to University Drive. On the northwest corner there's a Publix and a small drug store. The drug store has a sign that reads breakfast and lunch. The waitress warmly welcomes us to town and the owner gives us a free pitcher of fresh squeezed orange juice! I never had fresh squeezed OJ before, but it's something I definitely can get used to. After breakfast, Pops says he and mom need to go finish some paperwork for our new house being built. Then they say what I want to hear most. I don't have to go with them! Finally, I'll have some time alone to smoke a joint and relax without them. Outside of smoking the joint part, they probably both felt the same way too. Pops hands me a twenty-dollar bill and a key to the condo. I don't want to send up any red flags, so I take the twenty. This way my old man doesn't suspect I'm hiding any money. Pops tells me there's a small park with a basketball court about a block east of the condo. He says there's also a 7- Eleven close by in case I want a soda and some chips. I say, "Cool Pops and thanks for the twenty." He smiles and mom gives me a kiss before dropping me off at the condo. I run up the stairs, go inside, and head straight for my stash. I roll myself up a nice fatty and go out on the balcony to smoke it. Coral Springs is really peaceful. It's so fucking quiet it's deafening. My ears are used to the constant sounds of sirens and traffic. I didn't smoke for a few days, so it doesn't take long to catch a really good buzz. I still have about a half a joint left, so I put it in my sock for later. Now it's time to go explore! I lock up the condo and head towards the park. No signs of people, but I do see lots of different types of birds flying about. I'm hoping to see an alligator in one of the canals along the way, but I didn't. As I approach the park, I see a brand new blue Coup De Ville parked next to an old pick-up truck. When I get to the park, I see two big guys shoving another smaller guy around. "Some things never change," I think to myself. "There are bullies wherever you go." The two big guys talk with a strange type of southern twang. It was nothing like the pretty southern accent that I had learned to love in North Carolina. As I get closer, I can't believe my ears when one guy shouts out, "I thought I told you New Yorkers to stay clear of this here park!"

"No Yankee scum allowed! Boy!" The other guy shouts.

Do people really talk like this? I don't see any cameras, but it's like a movie is being filmed. The smaller guy they are shoving around has GQ Magazine kind of looks, and he even dresses the part. He's average height with jet black hair and a slim build. He must have a good tan because he's pretty dark for a white kid. He's got on a fancy watch and a big gold chain. Dangling from the chain is a large gold crucifix. The other two guys are every bit of six feet and are both strongly built. They're both wearing old jeans with no shirt and no shoes. Both guys have long brown hair and are wearing bandannas. They got them on their head Aunt Jemima style. They keep knocking the fancy dressed kid to the ground and he keeps getting right back up! I got to hand it to him, but I'm starting to hope he would just stay down. He doesn't and hollers back at his attackers in a New York accent that I aint familiar with. "Fuck you, you redneck cocksuckers! Why don't you go home and fuck your sister for a while! Tap your old man on the fucking shoulder and tell him it's your turn!"

I thought what he said was pretty fucking funny, but the two bullies didn't see any humor in it at all. That's when things start getting really ugly for this poor kid. The two guys are punching him for real now. I'm a street guy and like to mind my own business, but I hate fucking bullies. Pops always taught me bullies are pussies. When I was twelve years old, my old man bought me a set of weights, a speed bag, and a heavy bag. He taught me how to use all three. I stand five feet nine and weigh in at about a hundred sixty five pounds. Muscled and ripped, just like my old man wanted me to be. These two guys are a lot bigger than me, but we look to be about the same age. I can't stomach watching this kid take any more of a beating, so I throw caution to the wind and yell out, "Leave the motherfucker alone! You proved your fucking point! Now back the fuck off!"

They both turn around simultaneously to see who could possibly be yelling at them in this manner. They both eye fuck me for a moment and then burst out laughing. The kid on the ground sees the diversion and tries to get up, but to no avail. One of the bullies quickly knocks him back to the ground. Then he jumps on top of him and pins him there. His partner turns to his buddy and says, "Well I'll be damned Butch! Today's our lucky day! We got another one of them there New York faggots to beat on! And this one here Butch talks just like a nigger!"

"Hell Josie. Look at them purple sneakers he's a wearing. Only a nigger would wear purple sneakers!" Butch replies back sarcastically.

"You two pussy motherfuckers done running your mouths yet?" I respond indignantly.

"Yeah, were done talking to you white nigger," Josie replies back with contempt.

As Josie approaches me, he rears back for a haymaker. I easily block it and like a bolt of lightning counter him with a straight left right left. I open up a nice juicy gash over his left eye. Josie staggers back. He's furious now! Wiping the blood away from his left eye, he comes at me swinging again. This time I kick him in the stomach knocking the wind right out of him. Butch flies off the kid on the ground and charges me. I move aside and step on the back of his knee taking him down to the ground. Before Butch can get back up, I kick him solidly right on the bridge of his nose. I hear it crack on impact. Josie catches his breath and comes at me again. The other kid gets off the ground and tackles Josie from behind. Then he starts wailing away on the back of Josie's head. I go to finish off Butch, but he's already done. His nose is busted and pouring out blood. He had enough. My father always taught me to let a guy give. If he tries to trick you and still fight, then you beat him even worse. My old man said that he has seen fights where one guy wanted to give and the other guy didn't let him. The guy that wanted to give then got so fucking mad he turned the fight around and killed the other guy. I can tell Josie had enough too, but he won't give. I pull the other kid off him anyway. Josie vehemently curses us both out. Then he and Butch retreat back to their pickup truck. Peeling out of the parking lot, Josie yells out his window, "This aint over!"

The other kid and I both yell, "Fuck you!", and give him the middle finger as he speeds away.

The kid I saved shakes my hand and thanks me for helping him. He introduces himself as Johnny Santori. I tell him my name is Michael Drosdowich.

His immediate response is, "Are you Jewish?"

"No. I'm Russian and Italian." I smile.

"Russian and Italian, that's a pretty fucking wild combination. Maybe that's why you fight so fucking good."

"Well after I evened up the odds for you Johnny, you didn't do so bad yourself."

"Yeah, but nothing like how you fucking fight. You're one hell of a fucking streetfighter. Me, I just wing it and hope for the best. Where are you from in New York Michael?"

"My friends call me Droz, Johnny."

"Okay Droz. Where are you from?

"I'm from Yonkers"

Johnny gets a shocked look on his face. "Yonkers? I thought fucking Yonkers was a nice suburb. How the fuck did you learn to talk like a ghetto nigger and fight like that living in fucking Yonkers?" Johnny points down at my sneakers laughing and says, "And I aint never seen a fucking white guy wear a pair of purple fucking Converse."

I laugh along with Johnny. "I'm from Southwest Yonkers Johnny. It's about a half mile from the Bronx. I was a fucking minority in my neighborhood. You either kicked ass as a white kid or the niggers and spics took everything you had. How about you Johnny? Where in the fuck are you from in New York wearing those fucking fancy clothes and sporting gold jewelry around your neck? That necklace wouldn't last five fucking minutes in my neighborhood. Plus you talk funny."

Johnny laughs really hard pointing to his chest replying back proudly, "I grew up in Bensonhurst, Brooklyn. Back there it's mostly Italians and a few scattered Jews. There aint no fucking niggers or spics in my neighborhood. They stay far the fuck away. If they know what's good for them that is."

"Well that's cool Johnny, but my best friend back in Yonkers was black. He taught me a fucking lot about the streets."

Looking down at my sneakers, Johnny sarcastically says, "Gee, I guess he taught you how to dress too."

I laugh along with Johnny shoving him. "We were like fucking brothers Johnny. I trusted him with my life"

Johnny gets a perplexed look. "You trusted a fucking nigger with your life? What are you fucking crazy? If shit broke out between you and one of his nigger friends, you're telling me he wouldn't choose his own over you?"

"Being able to trust someone with your life Johnny goes a lot deeper than the color of his fucking skin."

"You got a point there Droz. Why don't you come home with me and meet my family. We're barbecuing hot dogs and hamburgers for lunch. Not those fucking redneck hotdogs they sell down here either. My old man gets Sabretts shipped to him from his friends back in New York."

"You mean you can't get Sabretts down here?" I ask stunned.

Johnny waves his hand at me and in his Italian Brooklyn accent says, "Forget about it! You're in the middle of fucking nowhere down here! This is redneck fucking heaven! Your parents fucked you real good by bringing you down here Droz. You must have really fucked up bad in Yonkers to deserve this fucking place."

I snicker. "You're probably right Johnny. This place is night and day from where I grew up. It kind of reminds me of when Dorothy in the Wizard of OZ says, 'Toto I have a feeling we're not in Kansas anymore'."

Johnny belly laughs and slaps me on the shoulder. "You got that fucking right, we sure as hell aint in fucking Kansas anymore!"

"So what the fuck did you do to deserve this place Johnny?"

"Well probably everything, but my old man's a building contractor and he needs me to work with him. He's putting up houses all over this fucking town. So are you coming home with me or what?"

"Sure Johnny. I'll come home with you."

"Great, take my keys. You're fucking driving. I'm still fucking dizzy from the beaten them rednecks gave me."

Oh shit I think to myself. He wants me to drive? I never drove before! I play it off real cool like and get in the caddy. I start it up and put in reverse. I hit the gas, but way too hard, spinning the tires. Then I hit the brakes even harder! This sends Johnny crashing into the dashboard!

"Mother of God, you never fucking drove before!" Johnny exclaims.

"Does it show?" I sheepishly ask.

"Yeah it fucking shows, you almost put me through the fucking windshield!" Johnny looks at me smiling now and says, "Well Droz you couldn't pick a better place to learn. The only thing you're going to run into on the way to my house is a fucking alligator. Just give it a little gas. You'll get the feel. I hope."

We both laugh as I drive off. It doesn't take long to figure out how to use the gas pedal and the brake. Steering the car itself is pretty fucking easy. Johnny tells me to make a right down a road with some really big houses. I'm gawking at the one with a tennis court, and all of a sudden, Johnny says, "Pull in here."

I slam on the brakes sending him once again flying towards the windshield!

"Holy fucking shit Droz! Didn't I get beat up enough today?" He cries out.

"Sorry Johnny. I'll pay better attention next time. Wow, what a fucking house! Don't tell me this is yours Johnny!"

"Yeah, it will do for now," Johnny replies in a cocky tone.

"I guess builders make a ton of fucking cash."

"Down here they do. From what my old man tells me this is just the start. That's why my father brought us to this fucking outpost."

When we get inside Johnny's house his mother is standing in the living room waiting for him. She's a pretty little lady with short nicely styled black hair and big brown eyes. Johnny's mom is about five foot two and has a very nice figure. She takes a closer look at Johnny and immediately does the sign of the cross. With both hands over her heart she shouts out dramatically, "Oh my God, what happened to you? Did you go to that park again? I told you not to go to that park! Angelo! Angelo! Come in here right now and take a look at your son!"

After a few seconds, Johnny's old man casually walks into the room. Johnny's father is a good-looking man built exactly like Johnny, except for his little potbelly. Angelo had perfectly trimmed, short, jet black hair and stood about an inch or two taller than his son. Surprisingly his skin tone was actually darker then Johnny's. He stood there silently in amusement, like my father would, as his wife continues her rant.

"It's your fault Angelo! You know that, right? I know you're the one that keeps telling him to go to that stupid park! I tell him not too, and you make him go! These people down here aren't even civilized! In fact, they are all animals! I told you I didn't want to move to this Godforsaken place, but you didn't listen! You made me! Now these inbreeds are going to kill my son!"

Angelo takes a good look at his sons face and a closer look at his knuckles. He then nods his head up and down. Then Angelo pats Johnny on the back and consolingly says, "I can tell they are still getting the best of you son, but I'm real proud of you for continuing to stand up to them. It won't be long before you're all friends."

"I tried Pops, but I couldn't keep them off of me," Johnny says apologetically.

Then with a burst of emotion Johnny says, "If it wasn't for my new friend here Pops, it would have been a lot worse! You should see him fight! He took care of both of them at the same time! Kicked one of the rednecks in the face and broke his nose! He comes from a really bad neighborhood near the Bronx in Yonkers."

Angelo slowly looks me up and down trying to size me up. Then he nods his head and says, "There's an old saying. It's not the size of the man. It's the size of the fight in the man."

Turns out Johnny's old man is 'old school' just like mine. He makes Johnny keep going back to the park. Angelo must figure standing up to these rednecks fist to fist will gain their respect. After hearing the hatred in Josie and Butch's voices I knew it aint happening. They look at us the same way Italians in Johnny's neighborhood look at niggers and spics. We're a threat to their way of life and need to be exterminated. Just like Josie said, this aint over.

Johnny's father extends his hand out to me. I reach out to shake it and he pulls me closer. He kisses me on the cheek and whispers, "Thank you." Angelo then steps back asking, "What's your name son?"

"Michael Drosdowich."

Angelo lights up like a Christmas tree and cheerfully says, "Well that explains how you fight so well! You're Georgey Droz's boy, a chip off the old block! I'm Angelo Santori. I'm the contractor building your father's new house in Ramblewood."

"The one with all of the floor safes Pops?" Johnny asks.

Johnny's old man frowns at him like he shouldn't have said that. I think to myself, "What does my old man need floor safes for?"

Angelo changes the subject, "Johnny, go and get Mikey a bathing suit while I light up the barbecue. Let's show him how we live down here."

THE TALK...

I have a great time at Johnny's house. It turns out he doesn't have any brothers or sisters so we form a bond pretty quickly. Their pool is humongous and it even has a diving board! I don't know if I'll ever get all of the water out of my ears. We get so stuffed on barbecued hamburgers and hot dogs that we both fall asleep like two old men by the pool. It's starting to get dark by the time we wake up, so I tell Johnny I need to get back to the condo. He lets me drive the caddy back. When I pull into the parking lot, I see my mother out on the patio smoking a cigarette. Johnny and I shoot the shit for a while and agree to get back together the next day. After he pulls away mom starts yelling at me. "Who said you can drive!"

"He did."

"And who the fuck is he to say you can drive?"

"My new friend, his name is Johnny Santori. I had lunch at his house with his family."

"Georgey, isn't that the name of the man building our new home?"

"It sure is LuLu. Come on up here son and tell me all about your day."

I run upstairs and tell Pops how I beat up the redneck bullies and met Johnny. The old man is thrilled I am adjusting so well. As a reward, he says he will take me crabbing. Excited and surprised, I ask, "Crabbing? There are blue claws down here?"

"Of course there are son, and a lot more then in Yonkers!" Dad exclaims.

"We got nets and bait?"

"Yup, I bought the nets this afternoon when I was out with mom. We'll pick up some chicken wings and beer on the way down to the spot I found."

This makes me very, very, happy. Some of the best times I ever had with my father were when he took me crabbing. Occasionally he would take me to his River Rat Club on the Hudson River in Yonkers. This is an ultra-exclusive member's only club. Instead of a watchdog at the River Rat Club, they have a watch rooster. They kept him chained by the ankle during the day. At night, they let him loose, so he could kill the rats. The rats by the Hudson River are so fucking big they hunt stray cats for dinner. This is also where I first learned how to swim. One summer day when I was six years old my dad and his friends were standing on the dock drinking beer. Out of nowhere, one of Dad's friends asks him if I can swim. My father shrugs his shoulders and throws me in the River! I remember going under and popping back up like a cork in a bathtub. I kicked and swung my arms for all I was worth making it back to the dock. All the men laughed and congratulated me. I felt fantastic because I made my pops proud. Mom would have killed my father if she seen it.

I wake up the next morning totally excited. Mom cooks us breakfast and then we head out the door to go crabbing. We stop at a grocery store off A1A to get the bait and the beer. Then dad drives the car to an old abandoned boat dock. It's a perfect place for crabbing. I quickly bait the nets while Pops cracks open a beer. Then we tie them to the dock, throw them in the water, and sit waiting for about fifteen minutes for the crabs to find the bait. As we were waiting, Pops begins talking to me. "Today Michael I am going to share with you some things about my life. By the time I was twenty, we already had your brother and sister. Times were really tough for your mother and I back then. Even working two jobs, I could barely keep a roof over their heads and food on the table. One winter when your brother and sister were still in diapers, they got very sick. I had no money for doctors or medicine, so Mom volunteered to go waitress for a little while. I'm strongly against it, but for our children's sake, I had to give in. Mom worked for three days waitressing before I found myself a third job. Thankfully, we were soon able to pay for the doctor and the medicine. Things start going pretty good for us for about a year. Then one Sunday morning there's a knock at the door. It's a man dressed in a suit. He said we owed a thousand dollars in back taxes from Mom's waitressing. I tell him he's crazy. Mom only worked three days, so it's impossible to owe that much. He hands a piece of paper to me and says, "Sorry Mr. Drosdowich. That isn't what our records indicate and we're never wrong." Then he told me that the penalties would be added if I didn't pay up by the end of the month. He said if I didn't pay the penalties I would be arrested.

After he's gone, I go for a long walk to think about things. That's when I remembered what my Navy buddy James Pritchard told me after our discharge. He said that if I ever needed money his daddy had a way for me to make it, so I gave James a call and he kept his word. He told me to get a truck and come see him. James filled that truck with tax-free cigarettes and moonshine. I came back home and started up a new business. Two weeks later, I paid the IRS in full. Soon the tax-free cigarette business led me to old man Rose, who sold as many as I can get. Then old man Rose offered me a job running his gambling operation. Later, I became a fireman Michael because it made me feel good to help people. It also let me show a legitimate income to the pricks at the IRS, who I fucked every chance I got. Your mother is in the blind about all of this, so let's keep her that way. I love her dearly, but she got a big mouth and worries too much."

I'm ecstatic my father is sharing all this with me! So I quickly reply back, "No problem Pops. Mom will never find out anything from me. Can I work with you?"

"I'll make you a deal Michael. If you can stay out of trouble and finish high school you can work with me, okay?"

"Sure Pops! It's a deal!"

After our heartfelt talk, I feel closer to my father than I ever felt before. We catch a ton of blue claw crabs. Every time we pull up our nets there are two or three crabs in each one! We go home and have ourselves a feast.

THE SCHOOL…

The next week my parents take me to register at the newly built Coral Springs High School on Sample Road. It's about a quarter mile east from where we're staying. As we pull into the parking lot, the first thing I notice is the school has no real windows. The place looks like a fucking prison! They march me inside the guidance office and register me. Thank God, it's easy and painless. On the way home Mom turns to me smiling and says, "You will have the honor of being in the first graduating class of Coral Springs High. Isn't that wonderful Michael?"

"Yeah Mom, that's just dandy," I roll my eyes and unenthusiastically reply.

My dad quickly responds to this lack of enthusiasm angrily, "You better hope you graduate smart ass because you won't like the alternative."

After my dad's tough response, I use my brains and sit there quietly until we get home. First thing I do when we get back to the condo is call Johnny. I want to ask him to pick me up for school Monday morning. Johnny's response is both shocking and depressing.

"What are you fucking crazy Droz? You won't be seeing my Brooklyn ass in that fucking redneck school."

"What do mean Johnny? Don't your father and mother make you go?"

"Fuck no. My old man needs me working with him and learning how to be a contractor. He says when the time comes, if I want, I can get a GED."

"Damn if you aint fucking lucky Johnny, my old man wants me to go. Mom's all excited about me being in the first graduating class of Coral Springs High."

"That school's full of fucking rednecks Droz, so there's a better chance of you being the first fucking kid to get kicked out!" Johnny laughs.

I laugh heartedly along with Johnny and he wish's me good luck as we hang up the phone.

Monday morning comes fast. It's 6 AM when my alarm goes off. I look out the window, and it's still fucking dark out. I jump in the shower while Mom cooks me breakfast. I huff down my bacon and eggs and brush my teeth. It's only a quarter mile to school, so I tell my old man I'll walk. He agrees and hands me another twenty. They both wish me good luck, and Mom gives me a big kiss goodbye.

When I get to school, I immediately realize Johnny's right. I stand out like a sore fucking thumb. By the end of first period, I'm already getting the cold shoulder from most of the other kids. They make snide nigger remarks about my purple converse. After third period, I hear rumors about payback for what I did to Butch and Josie. After growing up the way I did in Southwest Yonkers I surely aint afraid of any Florida rednecks.

When lunchtime rolls around I make my way with everyone else to the cafeteria. I get in the lunch line with the rest of the kids and pick up a tray. The food smells alright, and it doesn't look too bad either. I get a chicken quarter, green beans, mashed potatoes, and gravy. I also buy two chocolate milks and two chocolate chip cookies. As I'm looking for a place to sit down, Josie, Butch, and two other guys approach me. The four of them block my path and Josie says, "I got six stitches because of you boy, and you broke my best friend's nose. I told your white nigger ass it aint over."

With that said, I don't hesitate. I throw my tray of hot food right into Josie's face and kick him in the balls. One down, three to go, so I grab a chair and start swinging! I hit Butch right in his broken fucking nose! Fresh blood splatters all over his face. I give the other two a couple of shots with the chair, and they run off like pussies.

The kids in the cafeteria start panicking. Some of them holler out, "He's crazy, he's crazy! Call the police! Call the police!"

Three teachers run into the cafeteria. Two of them grab me by the arms. I snap at them, "You guys got about two fucking seconds to let me go!"

The teacher that's not holding me gets in my face and yells, "I am the principle! You will not use foul and disgusting language in my school!"

"Why aint you grabbing the other fucking guys Mr. Principle! They're the ones that fucking started it!"

After hearing me curse again, the principle loses it. He rears back and slaps me really hard on the left side of my face. My reflex response is kicking him in the nuts just like I kicked Josie. I stomp the foot of one of the teachers holding me, so he lets go. Then I punch the other teacher in the stomach. He goes down, and I make a mad dash for the door! I burst through it and right into the arms of two policemen! I know better than to resist, so I just give up. They cuff me and bring me back to the principle.

The principle is hunched over. He's still trying to recover from me kicking him in the nuts. When he looks up, he's relieved the police have me in custody. Now the douche bag puts on a show and frantically starts yelling, "That's him! That's the hoodlum that assaulted four students with a chair and two of my teachers! You got him officers! This derelict even had the audacity to kick me in the testicles!"

Both cops are doing their best not to laugh at the principle's animated account of what happened. Now one of the officers turns to me and asks, "What's your name son?"

To my pleasant surprise, the cop has a New York accent! "Michael Drosdowich sir," I reply with confidence.

"You must be Georgey Droz's son?" The officer asks smiling.

"Why yes sir," I proudly respond. I think to myself, "Everyone knows my old man!"

The officer sits me down in a chair and asks me my side of the story, so I tell him everything starting with my first encounter with Josie and Butch back at the park. I also tell the officer the teachers held me while the principle slapped me in the face. The officer observes the hand print on the left side of my face. He turns his attention to the principle now and asks authoritatively, "Is that true Mr. Backman? Did you slap this student in the face while he was being held by two teachers?"

The principle stutters and nervously answers, "Well, why, yes officer. I did. We had to control this animal somehow. He was behaving like a lunatic, and the language he was using towards me was absolutely intolerable."

The officer turns to me and kindly asks, "How old are you son?"

"Seventeen," I reply boyishly.

The officer nods his head. Then he tells his partner to go round up a few witnesses. Now he asks the principle, "May I speak to you in your office for a moment Mr. Backman?"

Mr. Backman grimaces at me and then begrudgingly obliges the officer. The officer tells me to stay put until he comes back. I'm handcuffed, so I aint going anywhere.

After about half an hour, the two officers and the principle walk back over to where I am sitting. The officer asks me to stand up and turn around. To my relief he unlocks my handcuffs. The officer says my story checks out with other witnesses. I did indeed act in self-defense and will not be arrested, but the school can punish me as they see fit. The principle says he wants me off school grounds, so the officers escort me out of the building. As soon as we get outside, I asked the officer how he knew my dad.

"I retired from the Yonkers Police Department about a year ago Michael. Your father and I have been friends for many years. He saved a lot of lives when he was a fireman. Your old man is a hero back in Yonkers. All of us police officers respected your dad and his crew. Cops with families living in your fathers dispatch area felt extra safe when working the night shift. You ought to be real proud of your father."

With my head held high, I say proudly, "I am."

"I'll give you a ride home Michael. Let's see if I can maybe soften the blow for you with your old man."

"That will be deeply appreciated." I reply thankfully.

When we arrive at our condo I can see my mother on the balcony smoking a cigarette. She sees me getting out of the cop car and immediately starts yelling at me, "First day of school and you're already in trouble! Your father is inside on the phone talking with your principle!"

The officer gets out of the car and tips his hat. "Hello LuLu," he says cheerfully.

"Tom! I wondered what happened to you! Georgey doesn't tell me anything! How's your wife Tom? And how do you guys like it down here?"

"Shirley's fine. I love it down here LuLu. The Coral Springs Police Department made me an offer I just couldn't refuse, so I retired up in Yonkers and took this job. Shirley's another story. She seems to be having a hard time adjusting. This is my partner Bobby Dumbrowsky. He's a retired cop from Jersey."

"Glad to meet you Bobby. Why don't you boys come upstairs while I put on a pot of coffee?"

We all make our way upstairs and into the condo. There I see my old man on the phone in the kitchen. He isn't talking. He's only listening. Then I hear him say, "So there isn't anything I can do to change your mind Mr. Backman? I see Mr. Backman; well that's your opinion."

My dad hangs up the phone with a saddened look. When he sees Tom, his frown turns into a big smile. Both men embrace in a hug. Then Pops says, "Maloney, I was meaning to look you up, but my wife and I have been real busy trying to get settled down here."

"That's perfectly understandable Georgey. I had no doubts when the time was right you would find me. This is my partner Bobby Dumbrowsky. He's a good man. I recruited him from the force in Jersey."

"Pleased to meet you Bobby, it would have been nice of course to do it under better circumstances."

Both men shake hands as Bobby replies, "Your reputation precedes you Georgey Droz, even over in Jersey. Just for the record Georgey, your boy acted in self-defense and was damn good at."

My dad smiles as Tom adds, "These rednecks down here don't like us one damn bit Georgey. I get an earful out of them every time I pull one over. Your son did the right thing throwing these redneck kids a beating. Two teachers held your kid by the arms while the principle slapped him in the face. Your boy returned the favor by rearranging his family jewels. I told the principle if he didn't press charges for assault I wouldn't arrest him for striking a minor."

I feel a little relieved as all three men laugh. My mother walks out of the kitchen with a fresh pot of coffee and blurts out, "Those dirty no good bastards. I'll put an Italian curse on all of them for hitting my son!"

My father looks sadly down into his cup of coffee and says, "They don't want Michael back Tom. The principle says that he is a danger to the other students. Is there anything you can do?"

Tom silently puts two teaspoons of sugar into his coffee and stirs. He slowly brings the coffee cup to his lips and takes a sip. Then he calmly replies, "Nothing legally Georgey. There are other ways of course."

"Let me think it over Tom, and I'll let you know," My father replies nodding his head.

"You do that Georgey. I will always do whatever I can for you."

"Me too Droz," Dumbrowsky adds.

My dad nods his head again and then all of a sudden Maloney gets a call over his radio. It's about an alligator taking over somebody's swimming pool! We all start to laugh. Except for my mother of course, she sits there speechless with a frightened look on her face. When my father notices he tells her, "Don't worry LuLu. Our pool will be screened in."

"I like these calls a lot better than ones I got back in Yonkers Georgey," Tom says smiling.

"I like them way better than Jersey too," Dumbrowsky adds with a smile of his own.

Both men quickly finish their coffee. Then they graciously thank my mother for making it and kiss her on the cheek. My mom and dad thank them both for looking out for me. After they leave my father turns to me and says, "You're going in the service Michael. I don't care which branch you pick, but tomorrow morning you pick one. Or I'll pick it for you."

Mom stays eerily silent as I obediently nod my head. I am surprised and relieved I'm still standing there in one piece. I really thought my old man was going to kill me after they left. The service aint a bad idea, I think to myself. All I need to do now is decide which one. My father was in the Navy and his father was in the Navy. Why not make it three generations? If there were a war to fight, I would become a Marine like my Uncle Richie. Being a Marine with no war is no fun, so why not see the world! At breakfast the next morning, I give Pops my decision. I tell him I decided to join the Navy. After breakfast, he drives me to the recruiting office. Luckily, the recruiter tells me I don't need a high school diploma to join the Navy. All I need to do is pass their ASVAB test and a physical. My ASVAB score turns out to be one of the highest in the country. The recruiter wants to me to sign up for Nuke School. He says I will come out of school a third class Petty Officer. However, after reading the details of the enlistment I quickly decline the offer. If I accepted, I would have to sign up for six years and be stationed on a submarine. I don't want to do that. Luckily, my dad didn't force me. I sign up to be a regular sailor. If I like it, I will go for what he suggested later. After passing the physical, I get a date to report for boot camp. On the way home in the car Pops tells me the house will be finished before I leave. He also says he's throwing a big house warming party. I wonder if the party is for the house, or for getting rid of me!

BEFORE I LEAVE...

That night after dinner, I call Johnny to tell him what happened to me at school. I don't even get a sentence in before he stops me. "You beat up four rednecks with a chair and kicked the principle in the nuts!"

"How the fuck did you know Johnny?"

"Coral Springs is a small fucking town Droz. Word travels fast here. My mom was playing tennis at the Coral Springs Country Club and got the low down from one of the other ladies. She told me and my old man when we got home. Mom was trying to be serious, but the fucking story put me and the old man in stitches! I laughed so fucking hard my sides still fucking hurt! If you think my father liked you before, he fucking loves you now! You aint here a fucking month and you're already becoming a legend in this town!"

"Yeah well, you can add being the first kid kicked out of the new Coral Springs High School to my legend too," I somberly reply.

"No shit? I told you that would happen. Personally, I think it's a good thing getting kicked out of school."

"How can you say getting kicked out of high school is a good thing Johnny?"

"I can say it because now you can work with me and my father in the construction business. I know he would love to have you."

"I wish I could Johnny, but I can't. My father wants me to go into the service. He told me to pick any branch I wanted, so I picked the Navy."

"Your father wants you to join the fucking service? Why would your old man tell you to do that when you can work with us? Or for that matter, you can work with him at his new club, right?"

"What club Johnny?" I ask surprised.

"You mean you don't know?"

"If I knew I wouldn't be asking you what club Johnny."

"Damn it! Now I'm in fucking trouble! My old man's going to kill me for opening up my big fucking mouth."

"Fuck trouble Johnny. Just spit it out."

"You're right Droz. You saved my ass. I fucking owe you. The least I can do is tell you what the fuck is going on with your own father. My old man is building your old man a private social club here in town on University Drive."

"My old man is building a social club? What the fuck is a social club Johnny?"

"Man Droz, you really don't know anything about anything do you? A social club is a fucking place to eat and gamble for the boys."

"Damn it! I really fucking blew it Johnny. Pops promised to let me work with him if I finished high school. All he wants me to do now is go in the service. The social club will have to wait until I get out."

"Yeah, you did fucking blow it. Listen. Cheer up. Tonight I'm going to tell my old man you're going in the Navy. Then I'm going to tell him I want time off so we can have fun together before you leave."

"You think he'll go for that Johnny?"

"Sure he will. My father loves you Droz. He thinks you got some big fucking balls coming down here and standing tall the way you did."

"Yeah, I got big balls alright Johnny and look where they fucking got me. They got me going to fucking boot camp and then God only knows where else."

Johnny laughs. "Listen, you don't worry about a fucking thing Droz. I'll come by in the morning to pick you up. Then we'll have a fucking blast together until you leave."

"That's music to my ears Johnny." After we hang up the phone, I go to bed feeling really good about my new friend Johnny Santori.

The next morning Johnny is a man of his word and picks me up in his Caddy. I ask Johnny to turn on the tunes while I reach into my sock for a nice fat stogie. When Johnny sees the stogie he happily shouts, "Alright Droz! You brought some shit down from New York! The weed down here aint that fucking good, but it's cheap. Open up my glove box. I got a bag of weed in there you can take a look at."

I open up Johnny's glove box and pull out a baggie with about a half an ounce of weed in it. I open it up to give it a smell and a feel. Johnny's assessment is right, so I tell him, "Yeah, you're fucking right Johnny; this here's regular weed for sure. You're going to love this fucking weed though. I'm sparking up some primo Colombian Gold for us."

I light up the joint and take a nice big hit. Then I pass it on to Johnny. As he's taking the joint off of my fingertips he excitedly says, "Oh yeah Droz. I can smell the sweetness already." Johnny takes in a deep hit and starts smiling. He holds down the smoke for as long as he can before coughing it out. Johnny's eyes half close and turn red. He takes another huge poke and passes it back to me. Struggling to speak, he says, "This is the shit right here boy. That's some good fucking weed Droz."

I take another big toke. I hold the smoke down as long as I can. Then I blow it out and cockily reply, "This used to be my business back in Yonkers Johnny."

"Cool Droz. Why not continue it down here?"

"Lost my connection," I reply as I pass the joint back to Johnny.

Johnny looks ahead at the road and then takes a hit off the joint. "He got pinched?"

"Worse Johnny, he's fucking gone, if you know what I mean. He was the black guy I mentioned to you at the park."

"That fucking sucks Droz. You not only lost your fucking weed connection, you lost your best friend too."

We both stay quiet after that and finish up the joint listening to tunes. By the time we reach the beach, the both of us are good and stoned. Johnny parks the Caddy and says enthusiastically "First stop, Ft. Lauderdale Beach!"

I cheer up as soon as we get out of the car. Ft. Lauderdale Beach is fucking gorgeous! Clean and pristine is how I put it to Johnny. We walk along the beach for a while making sure we check out all the pretty girls in bikinis before we leave. After we leave Ft. Lauderdale Beach the next stop on Johnny's tour is Pompano Beach. We get the munchies, so Johnny takes me to a place called Lums. He says they make a fantastic hot roast beef sandwich, and he's right. What's really cool is that you don't need to wear a shirt or shoes to do anything down here. The streets are so clean you really don't mind going barefoot. Try that shit where I came from and your feet would be cut to ribbons by all the broken glass. After Johnny gives me a guided tour of Pompano Beach we head north down A1A to Deerfield Beach. Before Deerfield Beach there is a stretch of A1A Johnny called 'Millionaire Mile.' It's lined with big mansions with their front yards on the Intracoastal where they dock these huge yachts. Their back yards are the beach and the ocean. What a way to live I dream to myself.

After we park at Deerfield Beach Johnny wants to take me out on the pier. I say cool and bring another joint to smoke. At the end of the pier, there is a nice place to sit. The deep blue sky is filled with big puffy white clouds. I gaze out over the sparkling aquamarine beauty of the Atlantic Ocean and light up the joint. As we're getting high and talking, Johnny's big mouth gets ahead of him again. "I shouldn't be telling you this Droz, but my old man is a very important guy in the mob."

Impressed by this, I reply in a fascinated tone. "Wow Johnny that sounds really fucking cool."

Chuckling proudly to himself now, Johnny says, "It sure fucking is Droz. Not for nothing I hear your old man aint no fucking slouch either."

I reply just as proudly now back to Johnny, "Yeah, he's got a gambling thing going on back in New York with some Jewish gangsters. He's also in business with his old Navy buddy selling moonshine and tax-free cigarettes. Since your father's Italian he's a 'made' man in the Mafia, right?"

Johnny snickers at my question. "Some of our people like to play that game. My father and my Uncle Rocco teach me different. They taught me that the Mafia, mob, or whatever you want to call it is made up of people from all walks of life. Not just Italians."

I think for a second and then nod my head. "You know, that makes a lot of sense Johnny. But the fucking movies tell a different fucking story."

Johnny waves his hand at me. "Forget the fucking movies Droz. They're just that, a fucking movie."

I'm really interested in what Johnny is saying, so I edge him on. "So there's no such thing as the five families, the commission, and the Godfather?"

"Don't get me wrong Droz, they definitely exist. They just aren't as powerful as they're being portrayed in the books and the movies."

Johnny looks from side to side and then moves closer to me. He lowers his voice and says, "Now this I definitely shouldn't be telling you. My Uncle Rocco is feared by fucking all of them. He's what's closest in the movies to being the 'Godfather, Boss of Bosses,' but to tell you the truth Droz, that would be grossly under estimating his power. That's all I'm going to say. I've said enough already. You got to promise me you'll keep your mouth shut."

"Of course I'll keep my mouth shut Johnny. My lips are fucking sealed. It's just way too fucking cool you have an uncle like that!"

Johnny smiles from ear to ear. Then he points to his chest with his thumb proudly boasting, "He's not only my uncle. I'm his fucking godson!"

"All I can say Johnny, is it must be cool to be you!"

Johnny comes down off his cloud replying, "Let me tell you Droz, it aint all a bed of fucking roses. In fact it really sucks in a way."

Taken back by Johnny's change in demeanor, I ask surprised. "How you figure that Johnny, how could it suck to have such a powerful father and uncle?"

"Easy Droz, I would like to see you try and live up to their fucking standards. Nothing I do is ever good enough for them. Everything I think, do, or say, is always being put under a fucking microscope. I am always being measured to see if I could ever possibly walk in their fucking shoes. It's like living inside a fucking pressure cooker. I'm telling you, I can't take it sometimes. Truthfully Droz, between me and you, I fucking hate it."

I let out a big sigh and empathetically tell him, "My old man aint no fucking picnic to live up to either Johnny, so I know where you're coming from, but having a fucking uncle like the one you just described could be worth the effort. I would love a fucking chance to impress him."

Johnny stares out at the ocean and chuckles for a moment. Then he looks at me and pats me on the back saying, "You already did. My uncle heard all about your escapades from my old man. He thinks you got some set of fucking balls on you, just like my father does."

Inside I'm glowing, but I sense a bit of jealousy in Johnny, so I give him a halfhearted smile and humbly reply, "It seems to me Johnny that all my big balls do is get me in trouble."

I quickly change the subject asking, "Since we both get high Johnny, how do your old man and uncle feel about weed? My father is against all fucking drugs. Weed included."

"My father and uncle were against weed too. Until Uncle Rocco's wife got cancer and died. While she was fighting her cancer, marijuana was the only drug that made her feel better. After witnessing marijuana's medical benefits first hand, both of them approve of it. They don't think we should go around smoking it all day, but both of them do want to see it made legal. My uncle blames the government and the drug companies for weed not being available as a medicine. He is always cursing them saying, "If the fucking drug companies could put a patent on marijuana it would be legal. But they can't because everyone would be growing it in flower pots."

I laugh whole-heartedly at that statement. "You know Johnny, I never thought of it that way. But he's fucking right! It's all about the fucking money!"

"You can say that again Droz, but narcotics are an entirely different fucking story. My Uncle's only child named Bobby tragically died of an overdose back in Brooklyn. Anyone working for my father or my uncle will be killed if they're caught dealing narcotics. I think they would even kill me if I was caught selling it. After my cousin Bobby died, Uncle Rocco has been on a quest to build drug free cities like Coral Springs all over the country. He wants Coral Springs to be a model town for families to bring up their kids in. He figures if we do this one right and keep out the drug dealers, we'll use it as a model for the rest of the country."

In a sad tone I say, "Man Johnny, that really sucks. Your poor uncle lost not only his wife, but his only son too. I can understand why he is so against narcotics, and I applaud him for it. My best friend and partner in the weed business, Shayne, also hated narcotics. About a year ago on a beautiful summer night Shayne threw a block party for everyone living in his project. He was cool like that. Shayne had fifty-gallon metal drums torched in half and made grills out of them. You got no idea Johnny how good the chicken and ribs were coming off them fucking barbecues. People living there made homemade potato salad, coleslaw, molasses baked beans, and corn on the cob. It was all fucking delicious Johnny. The projects have some really hot looking black girls, and it was summertime baby, so the way these black chicks were dressing didn't leave much to the imagination. It didn't take long before I locked eyes with a really cute young black girl."

"Was she like light black, or really fucking black?" Johnny inquisitively asks.

"She was more on the really black side Johnny. Does it matter?"

"Well, kind of. I guess. I don't fucking know. I never fucked a black chick. What kind of body did she have?"

"Believe me Johnny. A hot chick is a hot chick no matter what fucking color she is. I don't care if she's fucking purple. This bitch was fucking booming! She was wearing a tiny white bathing suit top and these little super tight candy red shorts. Her big titties and nipples were busting right through her top Johnny. The candy red shorts she was wearing clung to her perfectly like fucking skin, especially around the crotch. They wedged up between her pussy lips letting you see the entire outline of her snatch, and she had a nice plump one too Johnny. I was licking my chops because I knew it would be juicy!"

Johnny abruptly interrupts me now and excitedly says, "You're right Droz. Fuck what color she is. This chick is fucking hot!"

"See what I mean Johnny? Now one of my favorite songs starts playing loud, B.T. Express 'Do it Til You're Satisfied.' This song is fucking perfect for me. So I slide on over to where this little cutie is standing and politely ask her to dance. She smiles and starts grooving with me right there."

Johnny looking confused interrupts me again, "You can dance to that shit Droz?"

I snicker and reply cockily, "Of course I can dance to that shit Johnny. I love funky music! You're looking at a white boy with fucking rhythm baby! Black people say it just aint fair for a white boy to move the way I do. So as we start bumping and grinding to the music together I get a raging fucking hard on. I aint fucking shy about it either Johnny. I start rubbing that bad boy up and down on her pelvis to the beat of the music. Her eyes open wide when she feels the size of my bulge. Then she kind of gives me a shy little smile. I take this as a greenlight, so I grab a whole of her ass and we start dry humping to the music together. We weren't the only ones doing this kind of dancing, so it was cool."

"Oh man! That's fucking hot Droz!"

"Yeah it was. Until I get a tap on my motherfucking shoulder. I turn around and it's fucking Shayne holding a Louisville Slugger! I quickly get all kinds of fucking paranoid thinking I'm humping on the wrong bitch! Shayne sees he freaked me out and laughs at me. That's when I knew everything was cool. I breathe a sigh of relief and Shayne asks me to follow him. Begrudgingly I excuse myself and follow his ass. We turn down an alley where there are five black men standing in a circle. Without saying a motherfucking word Shayne took a Mickey Mantle swing right across one of these guys' heads. Pieces of his fucking skull with afro hair on it flew all over the fucking sidewalk. The fucking guy's brains slowly dripped down the side of the fucking building. They kind of looked like grey fucking jelly to me. The other four men ran for their fucking lives. As they're running away, Shayne yells, "Let me see who the next motherfucking fool is to come selling that shit around here!" Shayne goes through the pockets of the headless man's quivering body. He pulls out some small bags of powder and scatters them all around the dead fuck. Shayne now looks me in the eye with a hard ass motherfucking look saying, "You best learn from me white boy. When you kill a motherfucker, whether he's dirty or not, always leave some powder on the scene. This way the motherfucking police will treat it as another drug related homicide. It gets put on a pile with all the motherfucking others.""

"As we're walking away my buddy Shayne reveals the truth to me about his mother and father. He had told me when we first started doing business together his mother died giving birth and his father disappeared. The truth was his momma died of a heroin overdose. His father was the one that hooked her. When his old man came home and found out she overdosed, he hung himself. That's when Shayne swore he would do whatever he could to keep narcotics out of his neighborhood."

After hearing this, Johnny nods his head up and down for a moment in silence. Then in a very serious tone asks, "Did you go back to the barbecue and fuck that black chick?"

I laugh with a big smile. "I fucked the shit out of that girl Johnny! I fucked her every which way but loose! Right in the back of Shayne's motherfucking Caddy! The backseat of his car is so fucking big we did 69 and fucked doggie style without my head hitting the roof, how's that!"

We both stand up high fiving each other!

I didn't tell Johnny, but Tamicka and I actually went steady for a while. We were developing a fantastic relationship on every level until her father found out. He thought white people were devils and didn't want his daughter dating one. My parents were cool with our relationship. I asked Shayne for advice and he told me it was best for me to back off, so I respectfully did.

Johnny and I spend the rest of the week beach hopping and getting high. Being Sicilian, Johnny's skin is already dark, but the Florida sun makes him even darker. I'm half Italian, so it wasn't long before my skin color got almost as dark as his. We have a great time and by the end of the week I aint looking forward to leaving. Our new house will be ready to move into next week and mom's already getting everything ready for the party. My father says a lot of people are going to be there. I will be seeing Willie again and Teresa Sue! The old man says James and his family are spending the week down by the beach. Pops takes me to get my driver's license so I can drive to see her. We go and ask for a guy named Gus. Gus smiles when he sees my father and tells him he'll take care of everything. I was out of there with my license in less than half an hour.

The next day, James calls to let us know they arrived. My old man tells James he's making reservations for all of us at the

Captain's Table in Lighthouse Point. He gives James directions and we will meet them there at 6 PM. As we're driving down to the restaurant Mom starts on me. "I'm telling you right now Michael. You better behave and not embarrass us when you see your little girlfriend again. No playing kissy face in the restaurant. You understand?"

I roll my eyes. Before I can even come back with a wisecrack, Dad says. "Leave the kids alone LuLu. Don't you remember me and you playing kissy face behind our parents back?"

"Of course I do Georgey. After Michael's gone into the Navy we could play kissy face all the time." Mom giggles.

I can't stand hearing this mushy shit from my parents, so I say, "Mom, we're going out to eat. If you keep talking like this I'll lose my appetite."

Mom quickly scowls at me and replies meanly, "Don't you worry Michael. You'll be out of my hair soon enough. Then your father and I will be free to do as we please."

"That's nice Mom, and so will I."

Luckily, we make it to the restaurant before things get worse between me and mom. The restaurant is right on the Intracoastal Waterway. When we check in, the hostess promptly escorts us to our table where the Pritchard's are already seated. When Teresa Sue's eyes and mine meet no words need to be spoken. We are in love!

"How was the ride down here James?" My father asks as the hostess hands out the menus.

"Not too bad Georgey boy. We made good time getting here."

Elizabeth raises her eyebrows and gives James a disapproving look. Then she slowly turns to us saying, "He made good time alright. He speeded the entire way. I have no idea how we didn't get pulled over."

In a humorous and sarcastic tone James replies, "Yup. Elizabeth is right Georgey. I'm guilty as charged. I was speeding faster than I would if I was hauling a trunk load of moonshine. That's what four cackling women in a car will do to you."

Everyone laughs except Elizabeth who gives James a slap on the shoulder. Then she fires right back at him. "You hush James. How do you think us girls felt being trapped in the car while you passed wind for eleven hours?"

We all laugh real hard now. James not being embarrassed one bit by his wife's comment laughs along with us. Then he replies, "Well I won't mention any names, but I wasn't the only one lifting a leg on the way down here."

In unison, all three girls point a finger and shout. "It wasn't us! It was Mom!"

Hearing that is almost too much to handle. We all start laughing again while Elizabeth turns three shades of red and shouts back, "Girls, how could you!"

I find it incredibly refreshing to be around real people! Luckily, for Elizabeth the waiter comes over to our table and asks for our drink order. My dad and James order beers. Both moms ask for iced tea and us kids order cokes. The conversation between our folks becomes boring, so the girls and I strike up our own. I ask about their horses and they ask me if I have seen any alligators. While we're talking, my hand finds Teresa's under the table. When we touch, I feel a warm glow inside.

Dinner was fabulous! Outside the window, you can see large schools of fish swimming around the dock. My dad tells me they're bait fish called mullet. There are so many it looks like you can walk on their backs across the water. After dessert, James calls the waiter over and asks for the check. The waiter politely informs him it's already been taken care of. James gets visibly upset and says, "Dang it Georgey! Let me at least leave the darn tip!"

"Don't you remember James? It's my turn?"

"That lines getting pretty old Georgey boy," James shakes his head replying.

My father waves his hand at James and says, "Don't worry James. The way our two kids keep looking at each other, your time is coming."

Teresa Sue blushes and I smile while her two sisters tease her. Then Elizabeth chimes in, "Well I guess it won't be too soon. Teresa Sue starts college in the fall and I hear Michael has a date with Uncle Sam."

"Aint that nice Georgey," James says, "your boy's going in the Navy just like us. You must be awful proud of him."

"I sure am James. Time will tell if these two little love birds will keep their feelings for each other," Dad replied.

"The feelings between us and our girls grew when we left home Georgey. Maybe theirs will too," James adds.

Both wives and Teresa Sue smile. As we're leaving the restaurant, my mom and Elizabeth put their arms proudly under their husbands. Teresa Sue and I hold hands.

The next morning I can't wait to ask my dad for the car. He says okay because James is picking him up. With Mom downstairs by the pool, Dad spills the beans to me about his social club. I give him a big hug and thank him for telling me. Then he gives me directions to the beachfront motel where the Pritchard's are staying. My father walks with me downstairs to his car. As I'm getting in, I see Mom walking towards us. With a diabolical look on her face she begins waving her finger at me and talking meanly, "You better not wreck the car Michael. And you better keep your paws off Teresa Sue!"

"You know what Mom?"

"What's that?"

"How about while I'm groping Teresa Sue I wreck the car? I bet that will make you happy!"

Oh boy, this agitates Mom real good! She rants, "Why you little son of a bitch, you think you're funny? Georgey! Did you fucking hear him! Take the car away!"

My father shakes his head and says, "Goodbye son, and have a good time."

"Thanks Pops," I reply while smiling at mom and pulling away.

Luckily for Pops, as I'm leaving the parking lot James is pulling in. I get on the road feeling really good about life. My old man's being my friend, which is what I always wanted. I drive east down Atlantic Boulevard passing where Pops and I went crabbing. I get to A1A and head north to the Beachside Motel. When I get out of the car, I see a note hanging from their door. The note reads, "We're at the beach Michael!" I walk around back to the beach and oh my God! There she is, Teresa Sue in a fucking bikini! Her sisters are making sand castles and Teresa is by the shoreline calling me over. Elizabeth is nowhere in sight. I'm wearing blue jean cut offs and a wife beater tee shirt. I quickly pull off my shirt and throw it on her blanket. Then I swagger on over to her. Teresa Sue smiles and in her sexy southern accent says, "Are you ready Michael?"

"I'm always ready Teresa," I reply as I grab at her ass.

"I don't mean that! Run with me into the ocean, silly!" She slaps my hand playfully.

With that said Teresa Sue pulls me by the hand and we both run straight into the ocean! When we can't run anymore, we dive head first into a wave! The sun makes droplets of seawater sparkle on her beautiful face. Our eyes meet and we kiss and keep kissing till our hearts content. We spend the rest of the day exploring the shoreline and collecting seashells. A day I wish will never end.

THE BIG DAY...

The morning of the house warming party sure is a hectic one. Pops gave Mom a break and hired caterers. When they arrive, Mom is on them like white on rice. She has to oversee every little detail to feel comfortable. Our new home isn't nearly as big as Johnny's, but it's a lot bigger than the one we sold in Yonkers. The new house has five bedrooms and three bathrooms. My dad had it built with two master bedrooms so I could have one. Both master bedrooms have sliding glass doors and cabana baths that lead straight to the tropical pool area! The house is built on an oversized canal lot, so the pool and patio area definitely had to be screened in. This kept us safe from mosquitos, snakes, and alligators when lounging outside.

It's close to noon and some of the guests are starting to arrive. Johnny and his parents arrive first. I'm sure Angelo wanted to be the first to hear if anything is wrong with the house. My mother couldn't find anything wrong, which is a first. This means Johnny's old man is an excellent builder who pays attention to detail. Angelo, Carina, and Johnny are all carrying gift boxes. The logo on the outside of the boxes reads Tiffany & Co. We greet the Santori's with hugs and kisses. Johnny's dressed like a GQ model. Carina and Angelo's attire is more suited to Florida living. My mom and dad have nothing but praise for the fantastic job Angelo did building our house. As more and more guests arrive, Carina helps my mother show them around. I can't tell who they all are, but every one of them brings gifts. As I'm greeting new guests, out of the corner of my eye I see Willie and his family. They are also holding all kinds of gifts and trays of food! I help Willie and his mom put the trays of food on our dining room table. As soon as Willie and I are done, we embrace. Speaking in his strong Cuban accent, Willie exclaims, "Droz! You don't know how happy I am you moved here! We are finally together!"

Equaling Willie's excitement I reply, "Amen to that Willie! Listen, I want you to meet my new friend. His name is Johnny. His father built my house."

"Cool Droz. Any friend of yours is a friend of mine."

"That's good Willie. I knew you'd feel that way. Let me grab him away from his father. Then the three of us will dip into my room."

I go over to Johnny and tap him on the shoulder. When he looks at me, I give him a nod to follow me. When we get to my room, I quickly close the door behind us and lock it. "Johnny, I want you to meet Willie. We've been friends since I was eleven years old. I love him like a brother."

"That's cool Droz; you can never have enough brothers in this world. I am pleased to meet you Willie."

"I am pleased to meet you too Johnny."

Both guys shake hands and hug. The three of us immediately start telling stories about where we grew up. In spite of the fact we grew up in totally different environments, we still have a lot in common. For instance, all of our fathers are mean to us and do something illegal!

Willie's stories are the most interesting though. Willie proudly points to his chest and says, "My family runs the docks in Miami man. Nothing goes in or out of our port without my father or grandfather's approval. We help the Cuban people being held captive by that pig Fidel. My family makes money for our fight against him by selling containers of designer goods that disappear from the docks."

Johnny and I are impressed. Johnny now says, "My friends back in Brooklyn know all about shit disappearing Willie. We all spend a fucking fortune on designer goods. I am definitely interested in those disappearing containers. What about you Droz?"

"Count me out. I aint got no use for designer fucking anything. Anyway, I'm leaving for the Navy tomorrow."

This is the first time Willie heard this. Visibly upset, he says, "Navy? What are you loco Droz? Why the fuck would you go in the Navy when you can make money here with me and my family? Cancel that bullshit amigo and come live with me in Miami. I'll show you how to really live down here!"

"I told him the same fucking thing Willie." Johnny quickly adds.

Extremely disappointed I'm leaving tomorrow, I snap back, "Guys, I don't want to go in the fucking Navy. I got kicked out of fucking high school so my father's making me go. I'm totally fucking depressed about it."

Johnny and Willie see how upset I am over this. They nod their heads and quickly change the subject. Johnny now asks Willie, "So Willie, how about you hooking me up with some of them designer goods?"

"Since you're a friend of Droz that won't be a problem Johnny. Do you want to start out with a large container or a small one?"

Johnny looks at me and shrugs his shoulders. Then replies back to Willie, "I really don't know Willie. How much do they cost?"

A small container will run you fifteen grand Johnny. A large container will cost you thirty. Even if you sell the merchandise for half of retail, you will double your investment. It's a great deal, but you have to pay up front and I can't break up containers."

"Shit I aint got fifteen grand Willie. In fact, I'm in the fucking hole. I've been borrowing from my old man since we got down here. In about a year I'll be rolling in fucking dough, but right now I got my hand out."

Boom, a light bulb goes off in my head! I ask Willie, "Could you get containers with construction supplies?"

"I can't see why not Droz. Of course the cost of the containers will vary depending on what kind of construction supplies are inside."

Johnny gets really excited and shouts out, "That's a great fucking idea Droz! If the prices are low enough, I'm sure my father and his friends will kick us back something! That will help me get out of the hole!"

Breaking into Johnny's euphoria, I tap him on the shoulder and calmly say, "I got a better idea Johnny. Instead of relying on what your old man and his friends are going to kick us back, why don't the three of us go into business for ourselves? It's our idea and our connection, right?"

Willie and Johnny both nod their heads agreeing with me. Then Johnny asks, "That's a great idea Droz, but Willie just got done saying he needs the money up front, right Willie?"

"Unfortunately, that's true. No money, no containers. And don't look at me because I'm always broke."

"See? We're fucked Droz. Let's just set my father up with Willie and see what he gives us. "

I snicker at Johnny and casually walk over to my closet. I take out my suitcase and plop it up on the bed. I dig deep inside it and pull out three wads of hundred dollar bills wrapped in rubber bands. I toss them on the bed and say, "There's fifteen grand sitting on that bed. That should be enough to start our new business."

Johnny and Willie are shocked. Johnny scratching his head looks at me and says, "Geez Droz. I know you told me you sold weed back in Yonkers with your buddy, but I had no fucking idea."

Willie looks at me strangely and comments, "You must have sold a lot of weed amigo."

"I did Willie, but that's over. It's time to start something new. I'm leaving for the Navy tomorrow, but I'll be back. While I'm gone, I will trust you guys build our business."

Willie with every bit of sincerity he can muster says, "Droz, you know I love you like a brother. If something goes wrong I will pay you back every single dollar that is lying on your bed."

Johnny flying on cloud nine shouts out confidently, "This is a fucking homerun! Nothing can go wrong! The construction in this fucking town has only just begun! You two guys got no fucking idea how much supplies my father and his friends are going to need!"

"Willie and I are counting on it Johnny."

Then I reach back into my suitcase for my last three grand. I knew I could trust Willie, but I needed to see if I could trust Johnny. So I hand it to him and say, "There's three grand here Johnny. I can't take it with me to boot camp. I will let you know when it's cool to send it to me. When I do, make sure you send it as fast as you could. I may really need it."

"I'll be your bank Droz. You can count on it," Johnny replies and then hugs me.

"Thanks Johnny. Willie, you take the fifteen grand on the bed and invest it in the supplies Johnny says he needs."

"I will guard it with my life my brother," Willie picks up the money and puts it down his pants.

"Okay boys. Let's go get high."

I roll up a couple of bones for us to go smoke. I keep a few gold buds for myself to smoke later. Whatever weed is left I split equally between Willie and Johnny. They thank me and we head out.

Outside on the patio the party is at full tilt. Thankfully, no one even notices us leaving. When we get out the front door, I stop dead in my tracks and say, "Shit guys. Here comes my girl and her family."

Johnny shrugs his shoulders and Willie gives me a so what look. Then Johnny asks, "I hope this means we're still going to get high Droz."

"Of course we're still going to get high Johnny. Just give me a minute to be polite."

Both their jaws drop when they see the two older girls get out of the car. Willie leans over and whispers in my ear, "Which one is yours Droz?"

"The one with the long reddish hair," I softly reply.

As Teresa Sue turns around to help her parents get gifts out of the trunk, Willie whispers again. "Very nice Droz, you found yourself a white girl with a hot round booty."

Johnny, not being nearly as discreet, says, "Holy shit Droz. Your girl is fucking smoke. I don't think I could leave that."

With gifts in hand the Pritchard's walk up the driveway towards the house. James sees the three of us standing there and in his big southern drawl says, "Looks like you all got yourselves a little shin dig going on here, hey Michael?" I smile and nod my head yes. Johnny and Willie look at each other like where in the fuck are these people from. Then Elizabeth Pritchard exclaims, "Oh my James! What a beautiful house! I just can't wait to see the inside!"

I think to myself what a gracious comment coming from the woman living on the Ponderosa. Teresa Sue is glowing like sunshine in a bottle. She gives me a big smile and using her sexy southern accent says, "Hey Michael. Are these your friends?"

"They sure are Teresa. Let me introduce everyone to each other. Johnny, Willie, this is Mr. and Mrs. Pritchard. These are their daughters Teresa Sue, Rebecca Joe, and little Sally."

Everyone in their own way is cordial with their greetings. Then I tell Teresa Sue that I'll be back in about a half hour. She smiles and kisses me on the cheek. Then Teresa follows her family into my house. When we get into the car, Johnny and Willie are floored by how hot Teresa Sue is. Her southern accent is the icing on the cake of hotness to them. Johnny now asks, "How in the world did you meet them Droz?"

"Teresa Sue's father is my old man's old Navy buddy I was telling you about."

Johnny nods his head as I bring Willie up to speed on their business relationship. Now I ask, "How about you two guys? Do either one of you have a girlfriend?"

"It's against my religion to have a girlfriend," Johnny replies in a cocky tone.

Willie reaches into his back pocket and pulls out his wallet. He takes a picture out and hands it to me. As I'm examining his girlfriend's picture he proudly says, "This is my girlfriend Mizar. She's a Cuban princess."

"Wow Willie. She is fucking beautiful! Here Johnny. Check this chick out."

Johnny takes the picture and stares at it smiling and says, "She's a princess alright Willie. But are you sure she's Cuban?"

"Of course she's Cuban Johnny; just look at the size of the earrings she's wearing!"

"No shit Willie. The fucking earrings are as big as her head. It's the blonde hair that's throwing me off here. What did she do? Dye it?"

"No, no. Blonde Cuban girls are special Johnny. Mizar is a natural blonde, even down below."

Johnny and I nod our heads as I park the car in a wooded area just off of Atlantic Boulevard. Everything west of University Drive is wooded and desolate. We get high and bullshit about how rich we're going to get. I keep one eye on the clock and when a half hour approaches, we leave. Back at the house, we say goodbye and go our separate ways. I immediately hone in on Teresa and ask her to go take a ride with me. She says sure, but first she needs to tell her momma. I grab a blanket out of my room and out the door we go. I decide to give Teresa the same tour that Johnny gave me. Before I start up the car, Teresa Sue lifts the armrest and scoots right over to me. Needless to say, I get an immediate hard on. She sees the big bulge in my jeans and snuggles even closer. Then Teresa grabs a hold of it and alluringly says, "Is this car a stick shift or an automatic?"

"Stick shift," I quickly reply.

I start up the car and pull away as Teresa Sue shifts gears! She teases me all the way to Ft. Lauderdale Beach! I park the car and we walk hand in hand on the beach. I also take Teresa to Pompano Beach and Deerfield Beach. I show her millionaire mile and we both talk about what it would be like to live there.

At Deerfield Beach, I park on the southern side away from the pier. It's a lot more secluded there. No condos or people. We sit on my blanket by the water watching the waves roll up on the shore. We talk and laugh until the sun starts setting. As we snuggle closer reality hits. Neither of us knows when we'll see each other again. Instinctively now we both undress. Her body is exquisite. Soft kisses turn into gentle caresses as we explore our bodies. The sounds of the ocean blend perfectly with our passion. After making love we cuddle while gazing up at the moon and stars. The tide is rolling in, so Teresa suggests we head back to where she is staying. She wants to call her momma and let her know she's okay. The motel isn't far from where we are, so we get dressed and head back there. The phone is in the kitchen, and I go sit on the couch in the living room while she checks in. I overhear hear her say she's having a great time and she's okay. Teresa hangs up and walks back into the living room giving me a devilish grin. She slowly waves her sexy body back and forth erotically saying, "Momma told me that they won't be back for hours. She said they haven't even got to the coffee and cake yet."

With that said, Teresa Sue reaches her hand out to me. I take hold of it and she leads me down the hallway to a bedroom. Once inside we roughly tear each other's clothes off. This session is going to be a lot different from the one on the beach! Teresa Sue pushes me down on the bed and begins lustfully sucking on my cock. In a matter of minutes, she has me on the brink of orgasm! I don't want to drop my load in her mouth, so I pull her off my dick and start going down on her. Teresa quickly positions her hands on both sides of my head. Then she passionately rubs her pretty little pussy up and down on my tongue until she explodes all over my face! As I'm wiping her juices from my chin, she turns around showing off that perfect ass! When she shows me her world, I show her I know what to do with it. I'm used to wearing girls out, but that aint the case with Teresa Sue. The more hard cock I give her, the more she wants!

Time sure flies when you're having fun. We both know it's time to get dressed and go sit outside all innocent like. Neither one of us is the jealous type, so we both agree to see other people while we're apart. After all, I'm going in the Navy and she's going to college. How stupid would it be if we make promises to each other we couldn't nor shouldn't keep? We both agree to spare each other the stories though. A few minutes later, her family pulls into the parking lot. They all say they had a wonderful time at the party. Teresa Sue is bubbling over telling her family all about the guided tour I gave her. Then out of nowhere, she tells her family she's in love with me. I put my arm around her and proclaim the same. James and Elizabeth put their arms around each other and warmly smile at us. Teresa Sue's sisters tease her. I shake James's hand and hug Elizabeth goodbye, then they both wish me luck. Then I hug and kiss her sisters. After the goodbyes are said to her family, Teresa Sue and I walk hand in hand to my car. With tears streaming down both our faces, we share one final soft and gentle kiss then say goodbye. As I'm driving away, I look into the rearview mirror. My heart breaks into a million tiny little pieces watching my love wave goodbye...

BOOT CAMP...

I toss and turn the entire night. You don't sleep well with a broken heart. I also can't help thinking about whether I made the right decision trusting Willie and Johnny. I'm torturing myself with my own thoughts. 5 AM couldn't come soon enough for me. When it finally rolls around, I drag my ass into the bathroom for a cold shower. Damn it, I forgot! In South Florida, there is no such thing as a cold fucking shower. I get out of the shower, get dressed, and go in the kitchen. The recruiter's picking me up by six. The old man is already at the table sipping his coffee while mom cooks breakfast. As I'm eating my bacon and eggs, Pops assures me I'll do fine in boot camp. After breakfast, I make sure I have Teresa Sue and Johnny's contact info. When it's time to go, my mother starts balling. She hugs and kisses her baby boy one last time before I go out the door. As soon as I get downstairs, the recruiter pulls into the parking lot. When I get in the car, the recruiter looks and smells like he was out drinking all night. He babbles for a few moments about how easy boot camp will be. He says it's only eight weeks and will go by quickly. I nod my head. The only interactions we have after that is me poking him every now and then to keep him awake. The recruiter drops me off at a Greyhound Bus Station in Ft. Lauderdale. I walk over and join the other lost souls and exchange hellos before we board the bus.

We all began loosening up about an hour into the trip. Everybody is wondering what's going to happen when we get to boot camp. Talking makes the ride to Orlando go by quickly. We get dropped off at a bus terminal in Orlando where a Navy van is waiting for us. On the ride to our final destination, the guy driving the van cracks jokes. He's pretty funny, so we all have a good laugh until we see the front gates. When they close behind us, reality sets in. Everyone becomes very quiet. The van stops and a mean looking guy in uniform opened the door. He starts yelling at us to get out of the van. Then another man outside the van yells at us to follow a blue line. The first stop is the barbershop where they give us all a crew cut. Next stop is a building where they issue us clothes. You had to put your name on everything. Even your fucking underwear! That's simple for the Smiths and Jones of the world, but not for me. We also put our name and social security numbers on a sack. In the sack, we toss our civilian clothes and personal belongings. We're told we will get them back when we graduate. After all that bullshit, they march our asses to the chow hall. As we were marching past other recruits, they laugh at us and mock us. It's easy to tell they've been there for a while. Their hair has grown back a little and their clothes are faded. After chow, they march us to the barracks where we are assigned racks. Then they show us how to fold and stow our clothes away in our locker. The drill instructors watch us like hawks. They don't hesitate to jump on your ass if you don't follow instructions. After that bullshit, we all take a shower together and hit our racks.

I'm awakened the next morning by the sound of empty trashcans being thrown down the middle of the barracks. It's only 4 AM and our two drill instructors are yelling at us at the top of their lungs.

"Stand tall recruits!"

Most everyone quickly follows their orders and line up in front of our lockers. The guys that don't move fast enough catch holy hell! The drill instructors get right in their face's and call them every name in the book! I find it all pretty humorous until one of the drill instructors sees me smiling. I surely don't think it's a crime, but they do! One of the instructors is about six foot four and built like a tank. The other guy is about my height and pretty skinny. The smaller guy gets right in my face with his gorilla standing next to him. Chin to chin, he screams. "Do I fucking amuse you recruit!?"

"No sir," I quickly reply.

"Did you hear this piece of maggot shit say anything?" he asks the other drill instructor.

"I don't think so. Maybe the maggot shit didn't hear you?"

So now this prick yells at me even louder!

"I said, do I fucking amuse you recruit!?"

I get it now. It's a contest on who can yell the loudest. So I yell back louder. "No Sir!"

Now the big guy gets all in my shit and yells, "If you weren't amused recruit. Then why were you fucking smiling!?"

Now I'm getting confused, so I just yell out, "I don't know Sir!"

They both look at each other and grin. Then the smaller instructor looks back at me and yells, "Well I think I know recruit! I think you're some kind of fucking queer! Are you a fucking queer or a faggot recruit!? Which one is it!?"

"Neither one sir, I love pussy sir!"

"Oh I get it now, so you're a fucking pussy boy! What's your name pussy boy?"

I hear other guys crack up now but the two instructors stay concentrated on me. I know I must keep a straight face when I answer, "Seamen recruit Drosdowich Sir!"

The littler guy now bounces back in, "Drowsowitz? What are you, some kind of Jew boy recruit?"

"No Sir! It's pronounced Droz-do-wich! I am Russian sir!"

"Holy fucking shit Charles! We got ourselves a fucking communist! Get down and give me fifty you Ruskie bastard!"

I happily drop and quickly give them fifty good ones. They both crack a teeny bitty smile and move on to the next guy.

Right then I knew I was okay with them. They couldn't rattle me, and I'm in great shape.

Navy boot camp is filled with classes, exercise, and endless marching drills. They feed us really good and work us hard. By the end of each day, everyone is beat and ready for bed. You live for mail call. Teresa Sue writes often. She even sends me sexy pictures of herself wearing a bikini. Most of the guys' girls send pictures and we all enjoy gawking at them. Even if their girl is ugly, we make the guy feel great about her. In one of Teresa's letters, she tells me she earned a full scholarship to Wake Forest University. The college is close to her home, which makes her family very happy. She's also very happy because now she doesn't have to leave her horses. The weeks pass by quickly. Soon it's time to fill out our dream sheets. A dream sheet is a piece of paper with Navy Bases listed on it. We are supposed to check the box next to the base we hope we will be stationed at. Most everyone, including me, picks Pearl Harbor Hawaii as his first choice!

On graduation day my parents come to watch. They erupt with pride as I march pass them during the ceremony. Afterwards we take pictures and go get something to eat. Most guys take leave after boot camp, but I decide not to. It's bad timing for Teresa Sue because of college and she's the only one I really want to see, so I decide to save my leave until the timing is right so we can be together.

The most anticipated day of all is the day after graduation. This is the day we receive our orders. As the drill instructors call out our names in alphabetical order, I sit nervously awaiting my turn. Some guys walk away happy and others not so happy, but everyone will be glad to get the fuck out of here! When my name is called, I quickly walk up to the table and salute them. Both drill instructors chuckle and shake their heads when they look at my orders. I didn't know what to think!

"You're one lucky son of bitch Seamen Recruit Drosdowich. You are going to The USS Harrison. It's an oiler dry docked at

Subic Bay in the Philippines, and your home port is Pearl Harbor Hawaii."

I Jump for joy! I find out later that dry docked means my ship is lifted out of the water and being overhauled. I also find out that Subic Bay is right next to Olongapo City. The drill instructors describe Olongapo City as a modern day 'Sodom and Gomorrah!' Life is good.

Since I declined leave, I will be shipping out as soon as my travel arrangements can be made. I receive my itinerary the very next day. I leave Orlando International that evening for Dallas, Texas. Then I board a connecting commercial flight to Houston. From Houston I fly across the country to San Francisco. Then I board another plane to Los Angeles. From Los Angeles, I fly to Honolulu Hawaii where I board a military flight to Guam. After landing in Guam, I needed to catch another military flight to the Philippines. This will take almost two days, wow! The adventure is beginning!

Subic Bay...

Military flights are the true definition of flying 'no frills.' There's no food or drinks available, and sometimes you may not even get a seat. New recruits, or 'boots' as we are so fondly called, travel in their dress whites. Well, after two days of traveling my dress whites just aren't that white anymore. When I get off the plane at Clarks Air Force Base in the Philippines I find out what hot and humid is all about. I am told to get on an old yellow school bus parked way down at the end of the runway. I throw my duffle bag over my shoulder and start walking. When I make it to the bus, I'm totally drenched in sweat. As I get on the bus a sailor already seated says, "Welcome to the Philippines boot."

"Thank you," I reply as I throw my duffle bag on an empty seat and sit down.

A couple of more guys introduce themselves to me as Hutch, Yates, and Sanders. I tell everyone to call me Droz. A little Filipino man jumps onto the bus and hops into the driver's seat. It takes a few cranks, but by the third try the bus finally starts. As the little guy puts the bus in gear he glances at me and begins laughing. He continues this laughing even as we drive away. Curious, I ask, "Why's this guy laughing at me Hutch?"

"He sees you're a boot Droz. He knows you never took this ride before. The rest of us have."

"So not having taken this ride before is funny?" I ask inquisitively.

All three guys chuckle and Hutch replies, "You'll see boot. Just sit back and relax."

I decide to take Hutch's advice. It isn't long before all three guys start trading sailor stories. I listen attentively as their yarns take me on exotic adventures spanning the globe. Then we suddenly take a sharp turn onto a dirt road and straight up a mountain. All I can see on both sides of the bus is jungle. When we come to a clearing, I peek out my window and look straight down at the canopy below. That's when I notice there aren't any guardrails!

This shakes me up a bit. Well, more than a bit. Hutch now asks, "What's the matter boot? You look a little pale."

I manage a fake smile. Before I can reply back, the bus hits a big pothole sending it dangerously to the edge! While my knuckles turn white gripping the sides of my seat, the Filipino bus driver laughs his ass off! I sit there silently trying to reassure myself the military surely knows what they're doing.

After about an hour of gut wrenching, nail biting, twists and turns through the mountains, we mercifully stop at a small village. This is my first encounter with people of an impoverished nation. There are no houses in sight, just huts and little shacks scattered about. Everyone gets off the bus to stretch their legs. As soon as we do, we're bombarded by little children dressed in rags begging for money. The sailors on the bus give the kids hard candies and pesos. I only had American money to give the kids. When I reach into my pocket Hutch pulls me aside and says, "Can't hand out greenbacks to the kids Droz, it will cause a riot. A twenty-dollar bill is over 120 pesos. I'll give you a few pesos to give to the kids. This is a very poor country. You can get laid here for a pack of Marlboro."

"Geez Hutch thanks. I can see I have a lot to learn. I'll pay you back as soon as I can exchange some of my money for pesos."

Hutch shakes his head and pats me on the back. Then he says, "Don't worry about the pesos Droz, but if it bothers you, inside the hut you can exchange some money."

"Sure it bothers me Hutch; you just wizened me up out of your own pocket!"

"Listen Droz, we all have to look out for each other wherever we go. Come on inside the hut and we'll have a beer together," Hutch replies smiling.

I follow Hutch like a puppy into a small hut. Inside the hut there's a make shift bar set up and a cashier. I exchange a twenty for one hundred and twenty six pesos and pay back Hutch. Then I buy everybody a round of beers. The name on the bottle of beer is San Miguel. They keep the beers in a metal basin full of ice so they are ice cold. Hutch says when you drink too many San Miguel's you shit green. They call it the San Miguel shits. I thank him for telling me because if I started shitting green I would have thought I caught something! After downing a few cold ones, we all moseyed on back to the bus with a nice buzz. I don't know whether it's the buzz or I just got used to the ride, but I aint frightened anymore. After the guys tell a few more wild stories and the buzz wears off, we take a nap.

I am awakened by the sound of screeching brakes. The sun is high and bright, reflecting strongly off the bay. Through squinted eyes, I can see Navy ships docked all around me. We get off the bus and say our goodbyes. Then we all go our separate ways. Carrying my duffle bag proudly over my shoulder I approach a Chief Petty Officer standing on the dock. His face is darkly tanned and wrinkled. Probably from the countless days he had spent out at sea. I'll bet every wrinkle could tell a story. "Excuse me Chief, could you please tell me which ship is the Harrison?" I politely ask.

The Chief cracks a smile seeing me standing there in my dress whites. He points to the end of the pier and says, "You see that ship lifted up out of the water sailor? That's the old rust bucket down there."

"Thank You Chief," I cheerfully reply. With a hip and a hop, I begin the long hot walk to my new home. A tower of steel stairs confronts me when arrive at the ship. The stairs are widely set apart and go straight up to the gangplank. I take a deep breath and start my assent. Arduously, I make it to the top. I cross the gangplank and salute the flag. Then I salute the officer of the deck and say, "Seamen Recruit Drosdowich reporting for duty sir." The officer smiles and salutes me back. Then he says, "Welcome aboard sailor. I'm Ensign Reese. May I see your orders?" Ensign Reese is a tall skinny man. He has a kind face and a non-threatening demeanor. I take out my orders and hand them to him. He peruses them for a moment. Then he nods his head saying, "That was some trip you took to get here sailor. Nice to see you're still in one piece."

"Thank you, sir."

Ensign Reese turns to the messenger of the watch and says, "Jonesy, escort Seamen Recruit uh, how do you pronounce your last name sailor?"

"Just call me Droz sir."

"That will work. Okay Jonesy. Escort Seamen Recruit Droz down to personnel."

"Yes Sir. Follow me boot." Jonesy replies and salutes the Ensign.

Jonesy is a scrappy looking guy with a beard and mustache. I wondered how he could stand all that hair on his face with all of this heat! Ensign Reese hands me back my orders and I salute him. Then I throw my duffle bag over my shoulder and follow Jonesy. The ship is like a fucking construction site. The sound of pneumatic drills and hammers banging on the steel deck is deafening. Sparks from the welders torches rain down around me like Fourth of July sparklers. This ship is being torn apart from stem to stern. We make our way through the chaos and arrive at the personnel office. Jonesy knocks on the door and a squeaky voice from the other side replies, "Come in."

Jonesy opens up the door and says, "Goldstein. This is Seamen Recruit Droz. He's our new boot; you need to check his ass in."

"Not a problem Jonesy. Just take a seat Droz and I'll be with you in a minute."

Goldstein is a short chubby Jewish guy with glasses. He's clean-shaven and his office is neatly organized. He finishes up the paperwork in front of him and I hand him my orders.

He looks them and says, "Michael Drosdowich, so I guess everyone calls you Droz because they can't pronounce your name properly. Am I correct?"

"I guess you can say that."

"Well Droz, I got good news and bad news. Which would you like to hear first?"

"Give me the bad news Goldstein."

"The bad news is there isn't a rack available in your division. As you can see, the entire ship is going through an overhaul and your berthing compartment isn't completed yet."

"So the good news is I get to go home?" I reply seriously.

Goldstein laughs at my apparent attempt at humor and replies back, "No. Not quite Droz, but good try. The good news is today is Friday and I will do you the favor of not assigning you a duty section until Monday. This means you have the entire weekend off. You will not have to report back to the ship until 0700 Monday morning. Just sign the bottom of this form and I'll take care of the rest for you. You are assigned to the Deck Division. I will bring you to meet someone from your division who will find you a temporary rack in another compartment. Unfortunately the air conditioning isn't working down there, but you can grab a shower."

I'm thinking to myself, "You got to be fucking kidding me, no fucking air conditioning? We're in the fucking Philippines!" I quickly sign the form without reading it. I figure I'm fucked already, so why bother. Goldstein grabs a new combo lock out of his bottom desk draw and hands it to me. Then he tells me to follow him. He guides me through a maze of messes and sailors hard at work restoring the ship. I follow Goldstein down a couple of sets of stairs and through a number of hatches until he finds the sailor he is looking for. The sailors name is Gonzalez. He's a third class Petty Officer in the deck division. Gonzalez stands about six feet tall and is well built. He also has teardrops tattooed under his left eye.

"Gonzalez, this is Droz. He's your new boot for deck division. I want you to find him a temporary rack until your berthing compartment is done. I'm not assigning him a duty section until Monday, so he's free to hit the beach at knock off."

"No problem Goldstein," Gonzalez replies with a Spanish accent. Goldstein shakes my hand and wishes me luck. After he departs, Gonzalez looks me up and down for a moment before asking, "Where are you from boot?"

"Coral Springs, Florida."

"Coral Springs, Florida? Not with that fucking accent you aint."

"I'm originally from Yonkers New York. My family just moved to Coral Springs before I joined," I laugh.

Gonzalez nods his head. Then he smiles and says, "I guess you couldn't adjust from New York to Florida. You got your ass in trouble, so now you're here, right?"

I nod my head smiling. "That's about right. Where are you from Gonzalez?"

"I'm a Chicano from LA," Gonzalez responds in a cocky tone.

He offers me a handshake and asks me to follow him. It takes a while, but Gonzalez does find me an empty rack. There is no air conditioning just like Goldstein said. It has to be well over 90 degrees down here. I have no fucking idea how they expect anyone to sleep here.

Gonzalez now says, "It's close to knock off. Grab yourself a shower and change into your civvies. I'll meet you back here in about an hour and introduce you to some of the guys. Then we'll head out on the beach together."

"Thanks Gonzalez. I'll look forward to it."

"Not a problem boot. You're one of us now. You just do your job when I assign you one and we'll get along just fine. Remember to lock up your locker."

I nod okay and start to unpack as Gonzalez walks away. I didn't want to unpack everything because I knew this rack was just temporary, but it seems like I have to. The top of the bed opens upward. Inside there are various sized compartments to put my stuff in. When I close it down again there's a latch to put my lock on. After I finish unpacking, I put on my flip-flops and head to the showers. At least they're working! The water is warm, but it feels ice cold when it hits my sweaty body. My mind drifts off as I begin to relax for the first time since I left home. All of a sudden, I get excited about being in a foreign land. When I finish showering, I shave. Then I head back to my rack to put on my civvies. I throw on my favorite pair of worn out jeans and a wife beater tee shirt. Then I hear an announcement over the PA system, "Knock off ship's work." Guys start rushing from every direction to get to their lockers and into the showers. I hear guys complaining about how hard they are being worked. Other guys are talking excitedly about getting drunk and getting laid.

Now I hear Gonzalez's voice rising above all others yelling out, "Hey boot! Come on over here and meet some of the guys." I anxiously walk over to Gonzalez and he starts introducing me to his friends. Gonzalez is wearing jeans and a tight green tee shirt. It clings nicely to his physique. "This here's Manny Droz. He is also from LA." We both shake hands. Manny is a short and stocky Mexican guy. He has a jubilant smile and dark brown skin. He's dressed inconspicuously in baggy jeans and a big brown tee shirt.

"This is Marcus. He is from Atlanta Droz." Marcus and I shake hands. Marcus is a tall thin black man. He is well groomed and dresses himself neatly, but casually. His red shirt is pressed and collared. His jeans are creased perfectly.

"Last but not least, the big guy on my right is Tex, and of course he's from Texas. He's one tough hombre Droz, so you don't want get on his bad side."

Tex is fucking big alright. Big in all the right fucking places too! I'm guessing he's at least six foot four and probably weighed in at around 240 pounds. Tex is wearing worn out jeans like me and an old blue tee shirt, and of course, he's got on cowboy's boots! The big guy eyes me for a moment and I eye him right back. Then in his bold Texas accent, he says, "My buddy Gonzalez here told me you're from New York. Just so you know Droz I don't generally like New Yorkers. Especially big mouthed New Yorkers."

I think to myself that if I got a problem here I might as well get it over with quickly, so I reply back like a smartass, "Well that's strange Tex. I thought Texans like everything big." Gonzalez, Manny, and Marcus, all start laughing. Tex isn't laughing. He's standing there silently looking down at me with a blank expression on his face. I stare blankly right back at him. This is an all or nothing ploy on my part, so I know I can't flinch. Thankfully, Tex breaks the silence by laughing along with his friends, so I quickly join in the laughter too.

The big cowboy reaches out to shake my hand saying, "You got balls Droz and I like that. We might get along just fine."

Happy there was no trouble between me and Tex, Gonzalez shouts out, "Let's go party boys!"

We all head topside to leave the ship. You have to show your military ID, salute the officer of the deck, and then the flag, every time you leave or board the ship. Going down those fucking steep steel stairs wasn't any easier than going up them. In fact, it was actually fucking harder. The guys seem used to it, so I figure I will get used to it too. When we get out on the dock I ask the guys, "So what gives in this place? I was told it's like a modern day Sodom and Gomorrah. Is that true?"

All four guys laugh, and then Gonzalez replies, "Well let's just put it this way Droz, the town aint nothing but bars and pussy!"

"How am I supposed sleep on that fucking ship with no air conditioning?" I now ask.

"You need to get yourself a girl Droz and sleep at her place," Marcus answers.

"We have a good time with our buddies and then hookup with our steady bitches later," Gonzalez adds.

"If this place is like Sodom and Gomorrah, why the fuck would any of you guys have a girlfriend?" I ask.

Manny jumps in answering. "A good girlfriend will treat you like a king here Droz. She'll also keep your ass out of trouble. Olongapo City is a dangerous place.

"Come on Manny. You're telling me that it's more dangerous here than New York or LA?" I reply snickering.

Gonzalez quickly turns to me and speaks bluntly, "The first thing you need to get in your head boot is you're not in fucking New York or LA. They got their own set of rules here boot, and if you don't play by them, you could end up dead. There's martial law in this fucking city. If your ass gets caught out on the street after midnight Filipino soldiers will shoot you down."

"I get it Gonzalez. Thanks for cluing me in. I'm sorry if I came off cocky," I humbly reply.

Seeing that I'm a little sad, Tex puts his big arm around me and says, "Don't let old Gonzalez here scare you too much Droz. These soldiers are really bad shots. Sometimes I go out after midnight just for the fun of it."

Gonzalez shakes his head and quickly snaps at Tex, "He aint you Tex. He's just a fucking boot. So let's not get him fucking killed his first night out, okay?"

Tex laughs as we show our Military ID cards to the Marines guarding the gate. They check each one closely and then let us through. Once we're outside the gate, I feel like I'm in a movie. Bicycle rickshaws are flying up and down the crowded streets. We come to a small bridge over water and Manny says to me, "That's Shit River down there Droz. It's nothing but a big sewer."

I peek over the bridge and catch a whiff. "Damn Manny, it sure fucking is! What the fuck are those girls doing down there all dressed up in small boats?"

"Begging for pesos Droz, they either got the clap, or are just too dang ugly to work in the bars." Tex replies.

I nod my head and throw the girls some pesos. When we get in line at the money exchange booth Gonzalez schools me. "When you hookup with a girl tonight you need to know a few things. These Filipino girls may seem like whores, but most of them really aren't. They are being forced to work in bars to support their family. The girls are very poor, but they are also very proud Droz. Most of them will take you home and not even ask you for money. But if you like her leave her at least five or ten American dollars. She'll really, really, appreciate it."

"Sure Gonzalez. It sounds pretty sad, but I understand. Thanks for teaching me. How much money should I exchange?"

"A good old twenty should do Droz. It will be hard to spend more than that in a night." Tex answers.

"Well since I don't have to be back to the ship until Monday, I think I'll exchange sixty bucks for pesos."

"Well that's the spirit Droz!" Marcus exclaims.

After we're finished exchanging our money we continue walking further down the road into the heart of the city. The air smells like beer and barbecue. The streets are lined with all kinds of bars and street vendors. Each bar has a different theme including rock, disco, country, and soul. Vendors are hocking everything from watches to fortune telling. The barbecue cooking on the streets smells really appetizing, so I ask Manny, "What kind of meat are they barbecuing Manny?"

"Well they'll tell you that it's pork or chicken, but we learned different. It's really dog, cat, rat, and monkey, but it's delicious."

"I'm cool with that Manny. I'm fucking hungry. How about you guys? The food and beers are on the boot tonight."

My four new buddies cheer at my offer, so we all chow down on some Filipino barbecue. Manny was fucking right. The barbecue is delicious! You couldn't eat just one of these fucking things. After we're finish stuffing our bellies with whatever, we continue walking into Olongapo City. The music blaring out of the bars sounds great! The first bar we venture into is a Rock Bar. I'm shocked when I see a live band playing on stage. Hearing the Led Zeppelin tune 'Whole Lotta Love' from the street I would have sworn it was being played from the album! These guys don't only play like Led Zeppelin; they dress like Led Zeppelin too! Even the bar girls are dressed like hippies. The girls are all wearing hippy bandannas, flower child shirts, and bell bottom jeans! This is too good to be true, so I ask Gonzalez, "Is every bar this good?"

"Of course they're not Droz. Some are even better! Now buy us all a beer boot!"

After I buy the boys a beer, a bunch of cute little Filipino girls run up to our table. The girls ask us to dance and before I can say yes, Gonzalez shooed them all away. Then he tells me, "Look Droz, I'm not trying to be an asshole here. I just want you see each type of bar and all kinds of girls before you choose which one you like. If she's available of course, most of the good ones are already taken."

Manny chimes in, "The Marines have a base here and think who the fuck they are Droz. Hooking up with one of their girlfriends by mistake will lead to trouble. They run the brig in Subic Bay. The only redline brig left in the military."

"What's a redline brig Manny?"

"A redline brig is a jail that has no bars Droz, just a red line. If you cross the red line the Marines can shoot you."

I nod my head, and then Marcus adds, "You don't want these Filipino girls labeling you a butterfly either Droz."

"And what the fuck does that mean Marcus?"

"It means jumping from girl to girl like a butterfly does on flowers."

I nod my ahead again absorbing the knowledge. We finish our first beer and I order another round. Then Tex reaches into his boot and pulls out some type of contraption. He flips it one way and then flips it another. When he's done, it opens up into a 12-inch blade. He looks at me and says, "This here Droz is a butterfly knife. You butterfly on your girlfriend here and she butterflies on you with one of these."

"That sounds pretty fucking crazy Tex," I reply a little shocked.

Tex shakes his head and says, "No, no, Droz. It aint crazy. It's all good. Like my buddy here Gonzalez says, most of these girls aint whores. They're just nice girls with big hearts. You know, it might not be a bad idea for you to buy yourself one these butterfly knives. The main streets in Olongapo City are pretty safe, but the side streets can be deadly."

Gonzalez now elaborates, "Tex is right Droz. We all have one. There are some really hot girls that have been kicked out of the bars for getting the clap or robbing sailors. They still need to make money, so now they work the side streets. When you're really drunk, one of them may lead you by your dick down a side street to get jumped. Tex sometimes likes to go down a side street just for fun. I've seen him swing a Filipino by his feet and use him like a club on the rest of his gang."

Tex picks up his beer and chugs it down. Then he bangs the empty bottle down on the table proudly saying, "Yeah, sometimes I get in an ornery mood and need to blow off some steam. If it aint on a jarhead, it's on a gang of flips."

I buy Tex another beer. With a smile on my face I say, "You sound like a dangerous man Tex. What did you do back in Texas?"

Tex belches really loud. Then in a deep voice replies, "I rode Bulls."

That reply from Tex triggers Gonzalez to raise his hands saying, "Oh boy, here he goes. Order another round of beers Droz; this story may take a while."

I smile and gladly oblige. As a new round of beers hits the table, Tex rolls up his pant leg and asks, "See this scar Droz?"

"Damn Tex. That looks pretty fucking nasty. Looks like you had about a hundred stitches around that knee."

"Give or take a few. A two thousand pound bull stomped me pretty good on that knee."

"That must have hurt really fucking bad Tex."

"A trifle, but that aint nothing compared to these." Tex stands up and pulls off his tee shirt. Tex is ripped. When the bar girls see him without his shirt on they hoot and holler. Tex points to his shoulder and says, "See this one on my shoulder? That's where I first got gored. But that aint nothing compared to this baby." Tex turns to the side. On the right side of his body, he has a huge chunk of scar tissue covering up a big hole. He points to it and says, "Old Lucas gave me that one. He gored me real good right there. That bull's a legend."

"Damn Tex. You're lucky you survived. After wrestling bulls, no wonder you're such a fucking beast! If you could ride these bulls for a living, why did you join the Navy?"

"I kept getting in trouble. The judge gave me a choice. Go in the service, or go to jail. I chose the Navy. What about you Droz? Why did you join the Navy?"

"I kept getting into trouble too Tex, so my old man made me."

Gonzalez now chimes in, "I needed to get away from the barrio wars where I grew up. I lost one older brother to prison and another to the graveyard. I didn't want my mother to lose her last son. Manny and I grew up together, so we made a deal with the recruiter to stay together." Manny and Gonzalez toast to their friendship.

"I joined to help out my momma. My old man took a powder and left her with six kids. I'm the oldest and this was the best job I could get," Marcus says proudly.

I thought it was really cool for Marcus to step up like that. In a way, it reminded me of Shayne. Gonzalez says it's time to move on. The next bar we hit is a disco bar. It's incredible how great the band imitates the Bee Gees. This bar is John Travolta heaven! We have a few beers in there and then we hit the soul bar. Now this place is beyond fucking wild. All the flips have fucking afro's and the band imitates Kool and the Gang to the fucking tee! After a few beers in the soul bar, we leave. Marcus's girl works there, so he stayed behind with her. Last on the list is the country bar. Gonzalez and Manny stay for a beer and then go back to the disco bar. Now I'm alone with Tex. Of course, this is his favorite bar and where his girlfriend Tina works. I don't know any country music, so I can't tell whether the band is good or bad. Tex says they're great, so I believe him. The singers in the band imitate American country accents perfectly. The Filipino bar girls look so fucking cute wearing cowboy hats and boots. Looking around the room, one girl in particular catches my eye. She's hot as a pistol and sitting all alone not chasing any guys.

I watch one guy after another ask her to dance, but she refuses. This intrigues me, so I ask Tex, "What gives with that little cutie sitting all alone over there? She aint chasing anybody and when guys ask her to dance she refuses."

"You would like that one wouldn't you Droz. Her name is Angelina, and she's real picky. Tina knows her real good. She doesn't look it, but she's 24. That's ancient for a bar girl. They're usually all ragged out by twenty. Give it a shot Droz. If she shoots you down find another one."

"I think I will Cowboy."

I walk nonchalantly over to the table where Angelina is sitting. Without saying a word, I drink my beer and act more interested in the music than her. After about five minutes of ignoring her she leans over to me and abruptly asks, "Are you gay sailor boy?"

I don't know what I am surprised by more. What she just asked me, or her crazy fucking accent! Angelina speaks quickly with a lot of emotion. Startled by her curt manner, I gather myself a bit before replying, "No, I'm not fucking gay. And why in the world would you ever think that?"

"You no ask me to dance. You sit there like gay guy drinking beer. I know gay guy when I see one and you gay for sure."

"Oh yeah, let's just see if I'm gay. My name is Michael. Would you like to dance with me Angelina?"

Angelina's face lights up with a big smile. She puts her hands on her hips and cheerfully asks, "How you know my name sailor boy? I no tell you my name. Okay, I dance with you."

I take Angelina by the hand and proudly escort her to the dance floor. The other sailors gawk in envy. I also give Tex a wink on the way past him. I never danced to country music before, but I got rhythm, so I catch on quickly. Angelina and I are having a great time dancing together. Then all of a sudden, I get a tap on my shoulder. I turn around and some fucking marine starts yelling at me for dancing with his girlfriend. You can tell a jarhead from a squid by his high and tight haircut. I look behind him, and he's got buddies. Before I can even react, Angelina yells, "Go fuck yourself Joey! You know I'm not your fucking girlfriend!"

"Well if you're not my girlfriend Angelina, you're sure as in hell aint going to be some squid's!" Joey angrily replies.

Angelina gets really fucking pissed now. She stomps up and down pointing her finger at Joey yelling, "Fuck you Joey! Fuck you! You no tell me what to do! I do as I please!"

This girl is full of fire, and this really turns me on! Joey is frustrated and embarrassed by Angelina's verbal beat down, so he pushes me out of the way and grabs Angelina by the hand. He tries dragging her out the door and I try to rescue her. Joey's marine boyfriends step right into my path, so I bark out, "This is between me and your boy Joey!"

"I don't think so squid. You fight one marine, you fight them all," The marine blocking my path says calmly.

I go nose to nose with this guy and say, "I get it. Marines are fucking pussies and scared to fight one on one."

Joey struggling with Angelina to get out the door hears me call them pussies. This gets his goat, so he lets Angelina go and rushes me! Joey tackles me like a football player right on top of a table. The cheap bar table collapses and he pins me to the floor. This fucking marine is really strong! Joey rears back to punch me in the face, but rears too far. This gives me wiggle room to push out from under him and get back to my feet. Back on my feet, Joey rushes me again, but this time I'm ready. I back up while throwing straight punches just like my old man taught me. I bloody up his mouth and open up deep gashes under both his eyes. As hard as I'm hitting him, he still keeps coming. As I get close to the wall, I slip to one side and use Joey's forward momentum to throw him into it. He bounces off, and I connect again solidly with a left right combination. This finally sends his ass to the floor. I look up and here comes the rest of the marines. I put my back against the wall so no one can get behind me. I hold my own until they grab my legs. I'm finished if they get me to the floor. As I'm being lifted in the air, Tex decides to step in. He peels marines off me like he's peeling a fucking banana! One by one, he throws them across the bar. Tex is a one man wrecking crew! I jump back into the action with him. When a marine tries to get up, I whack him back down. We mop the floor with these mugs! This is the making of a great team, but what a fucking mess we made of the bar! Mamasan is hollering at the top of her lungs outside for the Shore Patrol, and soon we hear their whistles. Angelina and Tex's girlfriend Tina lead us out the back door of the bar. Outside there's a bicycle rickshaw waiting. Angelina tells us her cousin will get us safely out of there. Like thieves in the night, Tex and I make our getaway. Once safely away, Tex slaps my knee and says, "Well I'll be darned Droz. You sure handle yourself pretty good for a little guy. You got lightning and thunder in them punches boy!"

"Thanks Tex, but you're a fucking destroyer of men! Better late than never I might add."

"Well, I had to watch you for a while to see what you're made of. There was no need to worry shipmate. I had your back. Marines like a good fight and you earned their respect tonight Droz."

"What about you big guy, didn't you earn their respect too?"

"Hell Droz. They stopped respecting me a long time ago. Now they just hate me and can't wait to get me in one of their red line brigs," Tex laughs.

"So what do we do now Tex?"

"Well it's almost eleven and all the bars close at eleven. They have to so everybody can get home or back to the base before curfew. I'm going to have Angelina's cousin here drop me off at Tina's. I suspect that after what you did for Angelina tonight her cousin is taking you to her place."

"Well I hope so Tex, or I'm fucked out on these streets after midnight."

"Don't worry Droz; she wouldn't have bothered to save you if she wasn't going to bed you." Tex laughs.

After Tex gets dropped off, I get nervous. I'm all alone for the first time in a strange land. Even all the sounds and smells are strange to me. Angelina's cousin doesn't speak much English, but I understand him enough to know when we get to her place. He gets off his bicycle rickshaw and lets me in the front door. Once inside I'm shocked to see around twenty people sleeping on the floor. There aint even a light or a fan, just a fat white candle reflecting in an old mirror. Angelina's cousin leads me around a maze of sleeping people to a door. It's pretty damn dark, so he fumbles with the keys to find the right one to open it. He opens the door to a very pretty and clean room with electricity! I see a big fluffy bed with lots of pillows, and a bamboo ceiling fan turning above it. The room smells really nice too like a girl's room should, and it's decorated in pretty, soft colors. Off to one side there's a small bathroom with a shower. Angelina even has a radio and a small fridge. On the far side of the room, there is a comfy looking reclining chair and another entrance. I thank her cousin for everything with a sawbuck. He's beyond thrilled and can't stop thanking me. When I can finally get him to stop, he leaves and locks the door behind him. I'm locked in, but happy. When I look in Angelina's fridge, she has San Miguel's and cokes. I open up a beer and sit down in the reclining chair to relax. I slowly sip my beer wondering what the rest of the night has in store for me. I begin fantasizing about what sex will be like with such an exotic girl. It was a long day and I feel myself falling asleep. I'm startled by the sound of a key in the door. When it opens, there's Angelina! She quickly closes the door behind her. Then she smiles wide and says, "You one tough cookie sailor boy, Joey no easy to beat, but you beat him up good! Mamasan very mad, but I no tell her who you are. Mamasan know Tex and Joey. Tex she like, but Joey she no like, so Joey and his friends get picked up by Shore Patrol. You lucky I save you sailor boy."

I stand up and swagger over to Angelina. I place my hand gently under her chin. While gazing into her dark mysterious eyes I softly say, "I'm very lucky Angelina. I'm alone with you."

"You better believe it sailor boy," Angelina confidently replies. Then she quickly switches gears saying, "Now give me your clothes. I wash them for you."

"Wash my clothes? I don't want you to wash my clothes Angelina," I reply stunned.

"No argue, just take off clothes," She snaps back sternly.

She's very determined, so I shrug my shoulders and listen. Angelina grabs my clothes and heads out the other entrance into a small yard with a garden. There in the center of the yard is a large wooden barrel and scrub board. I can't believe my eyes; this crazy hot Filipino chick is hand washing my clothes in a fucking rain barrel! After Angelina's done she hangs them neatly on a clothesline. Then she takes me by the hand into the shower and strips down. I get an instant hard on! Angelina is petite, but has perfect little curves. She takes a bar of soap and begins thoroughly washing every inch of my body. When she's done, I gladly reciprocate. After washing each other, we dry each other off and jump in bed. Angelina lights up a blue candle and turns off the light. Her perfect little breasts and golden skin were aglow from the softly reflected candlelight. I become captivated by her exotic beauty. I begin slowly running my fingertips all along her sexy curves. Angelina purrs to my caresses. Then she guides my hand over her pussy to feel her wetness. I gently slide in a finger. She's very tight, but very wet. I remove my finger to taste her juices. Angelina alluringly asks, "You like how I taste sailor boy?"

"I love it Angelina."

Like a bolt of lightning, Angelina straddles my face! I'm in seventh heaven as she squirms above me. Before long, she turns around returning the favor! As I'm sucking her juicy pussy, she's moaning and sucking lustfully on my cock. Now I'm moaning! Not wanting to cum in her mouth, I quickly pull Angelina off my cock and position her below me. When I try to penetrate her, she stops me, softly saying, "You're too big Michael. Go slowly, so I can enjoy you."

I listen and take my time teasing her with the head of my cock. She places her hands on my sides and guides me in deeper. Soon our bodies move in perfect rhythm. Thrusting her pelvis up taking in every inch of my cock, she shouts, "Fuck my pussy Michael! Fuck me hard!"

Like a bull in heat, I fuck Angelina as hard as I can as she matches me stroke for stroke! She's so fucking tight and wet; it takes all the restraint I have not to drop my load! We passionately fuck the living daylights out of each other, slipping and sliding wildly in our own sweat. Angelina cries out, "Cum with me Michael, please cum with me!" Angelina's pussy contracts around my cock draining every bit of cum out of me! That's when she bites down hard on my cheek! Fearing I'll lose a piece of my face, I scream in panic, "Angelina! Angelina! You're biting my cheek off! Let go! Let go! "

Angelina doesn't hear me. She's still shaking and convulsing lost in bliss. I start thinking to myself that if I try to pull away she will do more damage. If she bites off a piece of my face, what do I tell my mother? What do I tell Teresa Sue? Finally, her orgasms are over and she let's go! I quickly feel my face for blood and hanging flesh. Thank God, there isn't any! Now I yell, "What are you, fucking crazy Angelina! You almost bit my cheek off!"

Looking surprised and confused Angelina replies in her wild Filipino accent, "What's the matter Michael, American girls no cum for you? When I cum, I cum!"

This girl is so fucking cute that all I can do is smile and kiss her. Angelina and I spend most of the night getting each other off in various ways, so consequently we sleep late the next morning. For breakfast, Angelina whips me up some sticky sweet rice cakes and coffee. Then we have a nice quickie in the shower and head out the door. Angelina's cousin is waiting for us outside with his rickshaw. She wants to show me around and do some shopping. I tell her whatever she needs is on me. Our first stop is the open market. This is where Angelina teaches me that everything is negotiable. From rice to fresh fish, Angelina negotiates the price. Going shopping with this girl is a very dramatic endeavor. If she doesn't like what the merchant is telling her, Angelina throws a hissy fit and walks away. Then the merchants chase her and drop their price. When the deal's done, the merchants act like they gave up their first-born. Angelina tells me to hand the merchant twenty American dollars, and I did. Then her cousin and I load up the rickshaw. Angelina says we bought enough food to feed all her relatives sleeping on the floor for a week. We head home to unload the groceries, and I am filled with joy watching all the happy faces put away the groceries. When the task is finished, I ask Angelina to help me buy a butterfly knife. Angelina immediately tells her cousin to take us back to town. She knows exactly where she wants to go. We stop at a merchant who has about every knife a man could wish for. Some of the butterfly knives look like swords. Angelina only shows me the ones that are made the best. I point one out to the merchant that looks a lot like Tex's. He takes the knife out of the case. Then he expertly opens it up and closes it again. The merchant then hands me the knife. I handle it a little and then try putting it in my back pocket. It's too big. If I move too fast, it'll fall out. I see a smaller pearl handed one, so I ask the merchant if I can see it. He gladly obliges me and again flips it open and closed. He hands me the knife and this one fits perfectly into my back pocket. I tell him I'll take it. Angelina haggles for a while and settles on eighteen American dollars. I tell Angelina it's a deal if he shows me how to use it. Angelina chuckles at my request and asks the merchant for the knife.

When he hands it to her she says, "This guy not too good with butterfly knife Michael, better you learn from me."

I raise my eyebrows and before I can reply, Angelina goes to town! I can't believe my eyes watching her! Then she asks the merchant for another one. He gives it to her, and oh my! This girl is deadly! Not only is she smooth with the blades, but she flicks them around like fucking lightning!

The merchant, who I didn't think spoke a lick of fucking English, waves his hand at me and says, "You got big trouble with this one buddy."

It takes Angelina about twenty minutes to teach me how to safely use a butterfly knife without chopping off any fingers. I need a lot of practice to use one like Angelina. When we left the store, I have a newfound respect for my girlfriend!

After touring the city in the rickshaw, our bellies start growling. Angelina suggests I try her favorite place for freshly prepared Filipino food. I quickly agree and she tells her cousin to take us there. When we get to the place, it looks more like someone's home than a restaurant. To me that's a good sign. As we walk in the door the first thing I hear is, "Yo Droz!" I look across the room and there's Tex with his girlfriend Tina. He's sitting at the biggest table in the house by a large window overlooking a beautiful garden. It turns out Tex just got there too, so we let the girls do the ordering. First, they try freaking me out with these baby duck in the egg appetizers. Angelina shows me how to eat one, so I give it a try. The little unborn duckling looks fucking gross, but once I sip that embryo juice I'm hooked! The flavors are fantastic. It has a nice spicy garlicky flavor to it. I peel the rest of the egg myself and scarf that little ducky down. Now a couple of servants start wheeling a cart over to our table. The girls giggle while Tex says, "Oh boy, I bet you never had this Droz."

"Had what Tex?"

"Live monkey brains," Tex replies with zeal.

I don't want to look like this bothers me, so I nonchalantly look over on the cart. I see little shaved heads poking out of the top of it. While the monkeys are still alive, the servant hacks the top of their skulls off. Tex says they gag the poor little monkeys so you don't hear them scream. Gee, isn't that considerate, I think to myself. The servant hands us all a spoon. I look down at the monkey heads and see little veins still beating! With my spoon in hand, I say aloud, "When in the Philippines you do as the Filipinos do." The live monkey brains are pretty damn good, but it isn't something I ever want to do again. After that act of animal cruelty, the food and Filipino delicacies just keep coming! I eat everything that comes out of that kitchen, and then gladly pay the bill.

When we leave the restaurant, the sun is starting to set. Angelina says she has a favorite spot to watch it from. It takes Angelina's cousin all of two minutes to get another rickshaw for Tex and Tina. Traveling to our destination, I witness the kind of impoverished neighborhoods I had only seen in the movies. It breaks my heart seeing the squalor these poor Filipino's are forced to live in. On the other side of the village, we come to a high hill. Our bicycle rickshaw drivers huff and puff to get up it. At the top of the hill, we are overlooking Subic Bay. What a contrast between the beauty of the sunset and the ugliness of the neighborhood I just passed through. As the sun dips below the horizon the shades of orange, red, and purple caress my spirit. Angelina and I cuddle lovingly. While over to my right Tina gives Tex a blowjob. After the last rays of sunset are over we head back down the hill. On the way back Angelina's cousin and the other driver start yelling at each other. Then Tina and Angelina start yelling at them, so I ask, "Is there something wrong Angelina?"

"Could be, not sure yet. No worry. They get us by."

"Get us by what Angelina?"

Before Angelina can even speak, my question is answered by six men on bicycles cutting us off. Both rickshaw drivers yell at the men and the men yell right back, "What gives here?" I quickly ask Angelina.

"Stupid men from village say you and Tex must pay toll because you are American. They say all Americans must pay toll to pass at night."

Tex hears this and jumps out of the rickshaw shouting, "I aint giving you flips one stinking peso! So move on out of the way before you make me mad."

Now Angelina and Tina jump right smack into the middle of the argument. Everybody's yelling at each other a mile a minute. I can't understand a fucking word, but my instincts tell me these guys aint leaving without getting money.

Feeling pragmatic, I say to Tex, "It might be a good idea to throw these assholes a few pesos and be on our merry way. After all Tex, it is their neighborhood, right?"

Tex scowls at me replying, "Listen boot. I don't care whose neighborhood it is. If you want to give these flips your money, go right ahead, but I aint giving them spit."

As the argument escalates, I reach into my pocket and take out my money. Then like a fish hitting a fucking lure, one of the flips runs at me and grabs my cash! The girls start really screaming now. The thief tries to get away, but I'm right behind him. I step on his heel causing him to tumble to the ground. He drops my cash and I pick it up. As I'm putting my money back in my pocket, his five friends whip out knives. The rickshaw drivers immediately get out of the way. The girls scream angrily at the drivers, but to no avail. They don't want any part of this fight. Tex sneers defiantly at the robbers, and then calmly says, "Stay out of the way girls. We'll handle it from here." Tex reaches into his boot for his butterfly knife. He flicks it open like he's been doing it all of his life. I reach into my back pocket and take out my butterfly knife. I open my knife carefully using both hands. Tex gives me a concerned look and asks, "Have you ever been in a knife fight before Droz?"

That question starts my adrenalin flowing. Now I get my mind into ghetto mode. Then I look at my blade with an evil grin and coldly reply, "I aint got no problem cutting up a motherfucker if that's what you mean."

Surprised by my alter ego, Tex raises an eyebrow and say, "Well then. If that's how you feel, let's go to work."

With that said, we go right at the motherfuckers! Like pussies, two of the robbers run away. This leaves four to fend off. Our fearless aggression freezes the other four. With a giant swoop of Tex's twelve inch blade he about severs an arm off one of the thieves. My two guys see this and run at me wildly waving their blades. I smoothly sidestep. Holding my knife upside down with a clenched fist, I punch across one of the guys faces. Blood splatters all over me as he falls to his knees holding his cheek. My right hand holding the knife is now by my left shoulder, so with a lunging motion I come back across my body and stab the second man in his chest. I pull my knife out and plunge it now deeply into his stomach. Then cut my way out sideways. His warm entrails spill out all over my hand and the ground. As he falls, his friend with half a face attacks me again. Lunging at me with his blade, I jump backwards out of reach. I quickly get behind him and shove him to the ground. Then I jump on top of the guy and stab him repeatedly in the neck until he's dead. Finishing my two guys, I look to help Tex but no help is needed. Tex gutted both men like fish. He's standing over their dead bodies using one of their shirts to clean off his blade. I copy Tex and do the same.

Through the entire fight, the girls remained calm and quiet. It's like they had already been through this shit before. Angelina speaks first, "Please forgive my cousin and the other driver. They are cowards. You two very brave, save us all. We must leave quickly before more men come."

Angelina's cousin and his friend are too ashamed to look us in the eye. Everyone stays quiet with their thoughts back to town. When we get to Tina's house, Tex asks me a question. "Where in the hell did you learn to fight with a knife like that?"

"My Uncle Richie fought in the Korean War as a Marine. He taught me." I take out my butterfly knife for a demonstration. "You see Tex; the last thing you want when you are in a knife fight is to have the knife knocked out of your hand or taken away. So instead of holding the blade pointed out towards your opponent like you do now, you clench the knife in your fist with the blade pointed down. With such a strong grip on the knife, it's almost impossible to lose it.

Gripping your knife like this also allows you to use multiple techniques for striking and defending. For instance, I can rest the blade of the knife across my lower arm and block another knife with it. I can also use my normal punching motion to slash with it and then plunge it in like dagger on the way back."

"Well I'll be darned Droz. You sure opened my eyes up to something new. So I guess that wasn't your first blood back there, or was it?"

"No Tex it wasn't, how about you?"

"Hell Droz, I grew up in a poor border town in Texas. I was only twelve when I first killed somebody. He was a drunken Mexican trying to rape my ten-year-old cousin. I bashed his skull in with a shovel. What about you?"

"I was fourteen. I grew up in a bad fucking neighborhood full of blacks and Puerto Ricans. I got along with most of the blacks. In fact, one black guy named Shayne was my best friend. Shayne was the meanest motherfucker in all of Southwest Yonkers. If it weren't for Shayne, I might not even be here today. The Puerto Ricans on the other hand didn't get along with anybody. They were always looking for trouble and especially hated whites. I started selling weed for Shayne in the white neighborhoods and did real well. I also sold it at the high school I went to. One day at school when I was making my rounds selling weed I got jumped by this guy named Jose and his crew. He ran the most vicious Puerto Rican street gang in Southwest Yonkers. They beat me up pretty fucking bad. Then they stole my money and my weed. I told Jose there would be hell to pay because I worked for Shayne. They laughed at me. Then Jose said I was Shayne's white bitch. He also told everyone I suck Shayne's dick and take it up the ass from his black friends."

Angelina interrupts me now loudly exclaiming, "You see, you see! I knew you were gay!"

The three of them belly laugh at my expense. I like a girl with a sense of humor, so I laugh along with them and then continue my story. "After the Puerto Rican gang leaves, I run to go see Shayne. As soon as Shayne sees me he says, 'Looks like Jose and his boys fucked you up pretty good.'

"I was shocked that he knew about it already, so I answer, 'How the fuck did you know?'

"He tells me, 'News travels fast Droz, especially when it's bad. I heard Jose's sissy ass was talking that homo shit again. The bitch likes that shit Droz. They turned his Rican ass out upstate in juvenile when he was a kid. I never liked that motherfucker. Now I've got a good reason to kill him.'

"I knew Shayne would have my back, but I didn't want him to kill Jose. I wanted to kill him myself, so I told him I want Jose one on one in front his crew. All I needed from him was to make sure his gang doesn't jump in. After I said that Shayne laughed right in my face and said, 'I knew you were a crazy motherfucking white boy Droz when I first met you, but I didn't think you were a suicidal one too. Jose is much older than your ass. He's more experienced too. He's killed motherfuckers before. He killed his fucking predecessor Manuel. I liked Manuel. He was a cool motherfucker that knew how to do business. He never fucked with another nigger's shit. So listen up, it will look really bad for me if I let your ass get killed. You dig?'

"Shayne showed absolutely no confidence in me Tex. I felt disrespected too, and that really pissed me off, so I told him about it. 'What about how it fucking looks for me Shayne? I'll look like your butt fuck white bitch for sure. Nobody on the street is ever going to respect me if I hide behind you!'

"Whether he liked it or not, Shayne knew I was right, so he laid his hand out for some skin and said, 'I got to respect that Droz. Jose will want knives. You cool with that?'

"I tell him, 'That's cool Shayne. I aint got no problem with knives.'

"Two days later, I get my wish. Shayne sets up the knife fight in the back of an A&P grocery store parking lot. It was a Sunday night, so it was deserted. I waited for Shayne to pick me up on the corner of Radford Street and South Broadway. When I get into Shayne's car, he introduced me to his cousin Roscoe. He told me that Roscoe did two tours over in Nam. I say what's up to the brother, but Roscoe don't answer. He just stared at me with cold dark eyes. This motherfucker had a real heartless look about him. He looked like the last guy on earth to give somebody mercy.

"Shayne now tells me, 'If you beat Jose, my cousin and I will make sure that you walk away clean. If you die tonight, you can rest assured that Jose and his boys will die too.' It was a good feeling knowing that if I died Shayne would avenge my death. Shayne lights up a joint. Then Roscoe puts the most perfect 8-track imaginable into the boom box, James Brown 'The Payback.' I'm psyched as a motherfucker when we pull into the A&P parking lot. Shayne stops the car and the three of us get out.

"When Jose sees us he yells, 'Did your little white bitch suck you and your friend's dick on the way over here?' Jose's entire gang laughs and high fives each other.

"Roscoe looks at Shayne with a cold hard look. You could tell he didn't like homo talk. Shayne doesn't even answer Jose. He just stared deep into my eyes saying, 'Kill this faggot motherfucker.'

"I was psyched already from James Brown, but when Shayne said that to me, it was like the leash being taken off a vicious dog. As I walk closer to Jose, one of his friends hands him a large switchblade knife. Jose takes the knife from his friend and then turns to me saying, 'You can still back out before I kill you.'

"That made me smile because Jose wouldn't have said that unless he was having doubts about the outcome. My smile pisses him off, so now he now he barks at me, 'Just so you know Droz. You're not going to be the first white boy I ever killed.'

"The more Jose talked shit to me, the more I knew he didn't want to fight. He thought I would be afraid but I wasn't, so now I reach into the front pocket of my jeans and break out the buck knife that my Uncle Richie gave me. Using my thumb I flick open the blade with a loud click. This was something that I had practiced many times in the mirror before this day. Then I looked Jose straight in the eyes and confidently said, 'I want you to know Jose. You will be the first person I ever kill.'

"Shayne yells out, 'I told you Roscoe! This white boy got big motherfucking balls!'

"Roscoe even broke a smile at my cockiness and high fived Shayne. Of course, this infuriates the shit out Jose, so he yells back at Shayne, 'I'm going to cut off his fucking balls Shayne and hand them to you!'

"Jose comes towards me now while he's still talking shit. He sees how I'm holding my knife and laughs at me. Then he quickly lunges at my belly. I side step and Jose swipes at me. The motherfucker gets me too. His knife ripped open my shirt and cut me slightly across my ribs. This gives me a fucking adrenalin rush. Jose smiles and lunges at me again. This time I time the motherfucker perfectly. When stepping aside I swing my knife across his shoulder and his chest. I cut Jose good. I cut him real fucking good. He was in motherfucking shock watching his blood pour out of the deep gashes I put into his body. I quickly take advantage and swing my knife back across again and right through his fucking throat. Choking on his blood Jose drops face first onto the ground. As he dies, Roscoe and Shayne whip out machine gun pistols. I find out later that they were Mac 10's. Seeing the machine guns, one of Jose's boys quickly hollers, 'Peace Shayne! Peace! Come on Shayne, Jose's dead! Let's go back to the way things were under Manuel!'

"Shayne hesitates for a moment. Then he nods his head okay. That's how it ended. I got cleaned up at Shayne's and went home. I slept like a fucking baby that night. My reputation on the street fucking skyrocketed after that."

The girls and Tex clap at my story. After bullshitting a little more, we go our separate ways. I don't know how Angelina did it, but she got all of the bloodstains out of my clothes. Monday morning I'm all fucked out when I report back to the ship for duty. Thankfully, Tex and I don't hear a word about what had happened. Tex says no one cares over here about Filipino lives. My job along with the other Boatswains' Mates is to bring the ship down to bare metal and paint it again. This is hard work. It's hotter than hell working on a metal deck out in this sun. Some guys keel over from dehydration. All I can think about every day is getting back to Angelina. When I get love letters from Teresa Sue, I feel guilty, but when I get back between Angelina's pretty little thighs, I forget all about it.

One day during lunch, I notice some guys lending other guys money for interest. I hear them call it slushing, so I ask Tex, "What's up with this slushing?"

"It's big business in the Navy Droz. Guys lend a twenty and get back twenty-five. Everyone gets paid onboard ship so it's easy to collect."

"Why don't you do it Tex? Afraid the officers might catch you?"

"Heck Droz, I'm one of their biggest customers. As far as the officers go, they borrow too," Tex laughs.

Boom, a light bulb goes off in my head. I'm going to slush too! I'll just get Johnny to send me my money. So now I inquisitively ask Tex, "Will the other guys that slush be mad if I slush?"

Tex gulps down the last drop of his bug juice and puts down his cup. Then he looks me in the eyes replying, "If you lend me money interest free, I'll guarantee you they won't say a word."

I smile and pat Tex on the back, "You got yourself a deal big guy."

Tex and I work hard all day during the week. After knock-off and on the weekends we fuck, drink, and eat. Once in a while, we do butterfly on our girls, but carefully! After about three months of this hedonism, the ship is finally finished and ready to set sail. Soon I will be leaving the Philippines. Most of the girls in Olongapo try their best to marry a sailor, but not Angelina. Angelina puts her family's needs ahead of her own. Leaving them for America isn't even an option she will consider. We do exchange contact information, so you never know what the future holds. She treated me like a king and I'm heartbroken leaving her. On the pier saying goodbye, Angelina does shed a tear, but it's I who is visibly heartbroken. Her heart is obviously seasoned. Mine is still in training. Standing topside as the ship pulls away from the Philippines, my empty heart soon fills with anticipation. Next stop, Pearl Harbor!

PEARL HARBOR...

The trip from the Philippines to Pearl Harbor is over five thousand miles. If all goes well we should hit Pearl in ten to eleven days. Life changes for sailors out at sea, and not for the better. When a Navy ship is underway everyone works a normal day, but some of the crew must also stand watches. The Boatswains' Mates stood round the clock watches in addition to their normal daily duties.

On our second day out Captain Fredrick catches us all off guard with a surprise announcement. The USS Harrison is being decommissioned. The Captain tells us we are all receiving a new set of orders. Right after the announcement, Goldstein and his boys from personnel set up shop on the fantail. The sons of bitches already had our orders before we left the Philippines and didn't tell us. I bet they were afraid some guys would go AWOL in Olongapo if they hated them. Awaiting my new orders brings back the anxiety I felt at the end of boot camp. When my name is called, I take a deep breath and walk up to Goldstein. He hands me my orders without comment. I walk back to where Tex is sitting and take a look. I read I will still be stationed at Pearl Harbor. Before I can read the rest, Tex grabs them out of my hand and says, "Let me see here. Hmm, you're going on the Polk. It's a Fast Frigate about six years old getting ready for a South Pac. Well how do you like them apples? Looks like you got lucky again Droz. "

Gonzalez now chimes in, "You did get lucky Droz. A South Pac is way more exotic than a West Pac. You got a really cool captain too. His name is Bill Keenan. They call him Wild Bill."

I snatch my orders out of Tex's hands and exclaim, "Wow! That's cool! Well, I guess it's cool. If you guys say so it must be. I hope you guys come with me."

The three of them laugh, and then Tex replies, "Welcome to the Navy Droz. Here today and gone tomorrow."

I hated hearing that, so I wait to see if my friends get the same orders as I did. Shit, Manny doesn't. He's happy though; he'll be stationed at Pearl, but on a cruiser. Wow! Gonzalez gets the same set of orders as Manny! I'm so happy the Navy keeps their promise! Shit, Marcus is heading to Norfolk, but he's thrilled. He will be closer to home now. It's Tex's turn. Oh, shit. He looks really fucking pissed. He walks over shaking his head bitching. "It just aint fair, I hate the Navy! As soon as we get to Pearl I'm going AWOL!"

Gonzalez, Manny, and Marcus stay quiet, so I bravely ask, "Geez Tex, how bad can it be?"

Tex grimaces at me and replies, "Oh it's bad Droz. It's real bad. I'm stuck with your sorry ass again!"

Gonzalez, Manny, and Marcus, bust out laughing. They were obviously all in on something here. I think Goldstein came through for the entire crew! I shout at Tex, "You dirty cock-sucker! I was really feeling sorry for you and you were just fucking with me! Don't drop the soap in the shower tonight big guy!" They all keep laughing, but that's okay with me. This is the best possible news I could get. Tex and I bonded in the Philippines.

As we get closer to the equator, the shellbacks start trying to scare us pollywogs. A shellback is a sailor who crossed the equator on a previous voyage. This means he already went through the 'Crossing the Line Ceremony.' Most guys on the Harrison are already shellbacks. They passed the equator on their West Pac. Gonzalez tells me that each ship is different on how they perform the ceremony. He says it all depends on the captain. Under Captain Fredrick's command, it's pretty mild, but he heard under Wild Bill's commands, it's off the fucking charts! I'm very happy to become a shellback on the Harrison!

The days out at sea pass by quickly, and now we're only a wakeup from Pearl Harbor. I get an eerie feeling as the ship sails into Pearl. The harbor is beautiful, but I can't help thinking about all the sailors who died here. We quickly moor the ship and make our last salutes. Some guys head to the airport and others right to their new ships. Tex and I have about a half a mile walk to the Polk. We throw our duffle bags over our shoulders and move on to our next adventure. Tex has spent a lot of time in Pearl Harbor already and says making friends with the local people, especially Hawaiians, is very important. Tex says even though there aren't many full blooded Hawaiians left they still run the islands. He also happily informs me the Hawaiians grow the best weed in the world. They call it pakalolo, and he knows where to get it. It's not cheap, but Tex says nothing's cheap in Hawaii.

As we get closer to the Polk, Tex and I admire what a beauty she is. A frigate is a lot smaller than an oiler and a lot cleaner. When we walk up the gangplank, we salute the flag and the officer of the deck. Then we ask permission to come aboard. Once onboard it takes about another hour to get checked in. It's Saturday, so only the duty section is onboard. The Boatswains' Mate on duty gives us a tour and then takes us to our berthing compartment. This ship is fancy. It has a crews lounge with a color TV. There are vending machines stocked with soda, candy, and chips. The bathrooms have private showers and doors on the toilets. That's a good thing because now you won't see guys spanking their monkeys! The berthing compartment is sparkling clean, and the air conditioning is ice cold. Wow, we even have new mattresses and pillows on all the racks! This place is a five star hotel compared to the Harrison. Apparently, the Polk is still adding on crew because there are plenty of empty racks to choose from. Tex and I both take middle racks across from each other as far away from the clanging doors that we can get. After we get unpacked, Tex suggests we head over to his favorite club called The Bounty. It's about five miles away and owned by the Hawaiians. All of the sailors go there because of the great food and entertainment. Tex tells me that Keoni and his sister Keona run the club for their father Keoki. They are Royal Hawaiian's, and that puts them at the top of the food chain. Tex brags Keoni and Keona are also his weed connection. This leads me to ask, "I guess their father is cool with weed then, right Tex?"

"Keoki turns a blind eye to weed Droz, but not narcotics. You get caught using coke or heroin in his clubs and you're barred for life. Get caught dealing those drugs and you'll end up as fertilizer in a pineapple field out in Waianae."

"That's cool with me Tex. The way Keoki feels about narcotics is just like how my friend Johnny's Italian family feels back in Coral Springs. So how many clubs does Keoki own?"

"I'm not sure. Rumor has it that Keoki owns most of the hot spots on all the Islands."

We show our ID's to the jarheads and walk out the gate. There are always cabs waiting right outside the base. We jump in one and arrive at The Bounty in no time. The entrance to the club is tropically landscaped with a beautiful cascading waterfall. Inside the club is like being inside a giant wooden pirate's ship. I like this place right away. It's what I call classy casual. We enter the lounge and secure ourselves a corner table by a big bay window. Almost immediately, a pretty little Polynesian waitress comes over and hands us a menu. She's wearing a colorful flowery loose fitting dress and has a white flower in her hair. She says, "Hello boys. My name is Lei and I will be your waitress this evening. May I get you both a drink while you look at our menu?"

"Why you sure can little lady, we'll have a pitcher of beer with two frosty mugs," Tex smiles replying in his big Texas accent.

Lei smiles back at Tex and goes to get our beer. As she's walking away I say, "Damn Tex, these local girls are fucking hot. I'm going to have to lay me a Lei real soon."

Tex lets out a smiling chuckle and says, "This aint Olongapo buddy .These local girls are friendly, but you're going to have to slow down your approach a bit."

"That's cool Tex. I can adjust. So what are you ordering?"

"Well Droz, I got a yearning for some Akule fish and rice. It's a local favorite here."

"Tex, I think I'm tired of local favorites. I had enough of that in the Philippines. I see here on the menu they serve American favorites too, so I think I'll have me a meatball sub. I aint had one of those since I left Yonkers."

After Lei comes back with our pitcher of beer, we make our order. We fill up our frosty mugs and wait patiently for our food. We arrived early, so thankfully it doesn't take long for our food to come out. Lei set our plates in front of us and we dig in. I take one bite of my meatball sub and spit it right back into my plate. Tex witnessing my displeasure cautiously asks, "What's wrong with the meatball sub Droz?"

Still cringing from the awful taste in my mouth, I slug down my entire beer. I give myself a refill before replying, "Tex, this is fucking horrible! It tastes like fucking Alpo mixed with oregano and drowned in ketchup!"

Tex is totally embarrassed by my outburst of displeasure. He looks from side to side to see if anyone heard me. Satisfied nobody did, he replies in a low voice, "Just calm yourself down Droz. All of us sailors have a good thing going here, so don't you go starting any trouble. Let me finish my meal and get us a bag of weed. Then I'll take you somewhere else to get a teriyaki burger or something."

Taking on an innocent tone, I reply back, "I aint going to start any trouble Tex. I'll be polite, but I have to say something." Tex tries to stop me, but it's too late. I already waved for the waitress. He shakes his head in dismay as Lei quickly comes over to our table. She smiles brightly and asks, "Is there something else I can bring you sir?"

"Don't take this personal honey, but the meatball sub is not what I'm expecting. Can you please take it back and bring me what my buddy is having?"

Looking disappointed, Lei asks, "Is there something wrong with the meatball sub?"

"To be kind Lei, let's just say it's not what I'm used to."

Looking very disappointed now, Lei bows her head. Then she hustles back to the kitchen with my plate. Tex looks at me like I just insulted the Pope. Now he starts scolding me under his breath, "Look at what you went and did Droz. You got the poor little girl all upset. Now she's going to go get Keoni and Keona. You aint on island three hours and you're already starting trouble with the wrong people. Worse, the wrong Hawaiian people, and I haven't even scored us any weed yet."

"Starting trouble with them? I don't think I'm starting trouble with them. Quite frankly Tex I think I'm doing them a favor by telling them how bad that meatball sub is."

"Please Droz pipe down and don't cause a scene. The waitress is coming back with Keoni and Keona. Do us a big favor and say it was a simple misunderstanding."

Keoni is a very good-looking man. He's about six feet tall and nicely built. He's dressed casually in kakis and a colorful Hawaiian style shirt. Keoni looks to be in his late twenties. Keona is absolutely beautiful. She's dressed in a knee high white form fitting dress with long jet black hair and large dark almond shaped eyes. She has a perfect figure, at least from the front. She's definitely younger than Keoni. Politely in a Hawaiian accent, Keoni directly addresses Tex, "Who's your new friend Tex?"

Tex puts down his fork and wipes his face with his napkin. Then he smiles and replies, "Why this here's Droz Keoni. He's new to Pearl, and he sure didn't mean to insult anybody, right Droz?"

"I don't need anybody to apologize for me Tex. I didn't do anything wrong, unless telling the truth is a bad thing around here?"

Keoni's sister Keona looks meanly at me and sternly says, "If you consider hurting our staffs' feelings as nothing wrong, I guess you didn't haole boy."

As Tex hurries to finish his meal, I look at him and kindly ask, "What's a haole boy Tex?"

Trying to swallow and talk at the same time, he replies, "It's all of us white people from the mainland."

"Oh, okay. But it's not like calling me a nigger or something, right?"

Tex chokes on his food while Keoni and Keona laugh. Keoni pats Tex on the back and then Tex replies, "No, no Droz, It's not that bad at all."

I nod my head okay. Then I politely reply to Keona, "Look Keona. Your chef is probably incredible at everything else he cooks, but I got to tell you something. When it comes to cooking Italian food, he's got a lot to learn."

Keona puts her hands on her hips and replies back sarcastically, "Oh really haole boy, so maybe you can teach him?"

I shrug my shoulders and cockily reply, "Well I wasn't planning on it Keona, but since you asked me, why not?"

I catch Keona and Keoni off guard. They look at each other for a brief moment. Then Keoni says to me, "Okay haole boy with big mouth. Let's go see if you can back it up. Follow us to the kitchen."

Keona and Keoni smile arrogantly at me. Then they turn around and walk towards the kitchen. Tex pats me on the back and says, "Well Droz, if you aint back out here in about twenty minutes I'll check the dumpster in the back for you."

"Gee, Thanks Tex. I knew I could count on you," I reply sarcastically.

When I walk into the kitchen, everyone stops working and gives me a dirty look. Keoki calls the chef out of his office. Just my fucking luck, the chef is a monster! Keona introduces me to him. "Chef Keanu, this is Droz. He's the haole boy who says you can't cook Italian."

The chef scowls at me and in his strong Hawaiian accent, he gruffly asks, "Is that true haole boy?"

I look the monster in the eye and calmly reply, "I'm sorry if it disappoints you Keanu, but it's true. You aint got a clue how to cook Italian."

Damn if my candidness didn't piss the chef off. He walks straight at me shouting, "You like beef haole boy."

I shout right back pointing to my chest, "Do I like beef? Not if it tastes like your fucking meatballs!"

Keoni is laughing his ass off as he rushes to get in front of Keanu. Keona is laughing too. Then she says, "Beef mean fight haole boy, not food."

I look at Keona and then back at the chef before saying, "I aint backing down from telling you the truth tough guy, so I'll fight you. You want to go right here, or you want to take it outside?"

I don't back down an inch. By the look on their faces, they like it. Keoni asks us both to cool down. Then he says to Keanu, "Haole boy stand up for himself, I like him. Keanu, maybe he shows you how he cooks Italian food."

Keanu grunts, but then cracks a smile. He offers his hand for a handshake and I gladly oblige. Then in a friendly tone he asks, "So braddah, how you make your meatballs?"

Relieved I gained their respect, I reply, "I'll tell you what Keanu. Tomorrow is Sunday and I don't have duty. Sunday is the traditional day for Italian families to eat spaghetti and meatballs. How about I come to your kitchen early in the morning and whip up an Italian feast for all of you."

The three of them look at each other and nod their heads. Then Keoni replies, "Sounds good braddah. Keanu, make a list of what Droz needs for tomorrow. I will make sure we have it here waiting for him."

Keanu reaches into his apron pocket taking out a pen and notepad. Then he says, "Shoot braddah."

"You guys got big pots, so let's go all out here. This way you'll have a lot of leftovers. We always eat the leftovers on the following Wednesday. First I need you to lay out seven or eight big sub rolls overnight to make stale bread."

"No need for stale bread haole boy. I have plenty bread crumbs."

"No, no, chef. Dry breadcrumbs make dry fucking meatballs. I soak the stale bread in water, and then drain it real good before I throw into the mix. This makes your meatballs nice and moist."

Keanu nods his head. Then he licks the point of his pencil and says, "Good idea haole boy. What next you need?"

"I will need lots of fresh garlic Keanu. I use it in the sauce and the meatballs. I will also need some fresh parsley."

Keanu gives me a surprised look and asks, "What, no fresh oregano?"

I put my hand sympathetically onto Keanu's shoulder. I shake my head a couple of times before replying, "This is going to come as a huge shock Keanu. Real Italians don't put oregano in their meatballs or their sauce." Keanu gives me a perplexed look and I continue. "I want five pounds of shoulder roast ground into chop meat to make my meatballs. I also need eggs and a lot of freshly grated parmesan cheese. For my sauce, I'll need some pork hocks and a nice fat pork butt to cut up. Also, five pounds of sweet Italian sausage and three pounds of hot, without fennel. 15 or 16 cans of Italian whole tomatoes, olive oil, fresh basil, and 8 boxes of thin spaghetti. That's it Keanu. Do you think you can get me what I need?"

Before Keanu can even reply, Keoni jumps in, "I will get you everything you need haole boy. You just make sure you show up to cook tomorrow."

"Don't worry Keoni. I'll be here, and so will my friend Tex to help me."

With a blank stare, Keoni nods his head. Then Keanu says, "List look good Keoni, I think haole boy know what he doing."

"After we go through the trouble of getting you everything you need Mr. Droz, you better know what to do with it," Keona adds sternly.

With a wink and a smile I reply back to her cockily, "Oh I'll know what to do with it Keona. You won't have to worry about that."

Keona raises her eyebrows and looks down her nose at me. I shake everyone's hand and we leave the kitchen. I walk out of there feeling pretty darn good about myself. All I have to do now is back up my mouth with my cooking. Tex sees me come out of the kitchen and says, "Well that's a good sign Droz. You're still walking."

I just smile at Tex while Keoni says, "Droz volunteer to cook for everybody tomorrow, and he says you will help him Tex."

With a confused look on his face, Tex turns to me and says, "I don't know what you got yourself into here Droz, but if you're relying on me to cook we got problems Droz."

"Not to worry Tex, I'll do all the cooking. All I want you to do is peel the garlic."

"Since you not happy with Keanu's Italian cooking Droz, how about you try his local dishes? The food will be on me of course," Keoni offers cordially.

"Sure Keoni. It would be my pleasure," I cheerfully reply.

"Before the food comes out Keoni, would it be alright if we grab something from you?" Tex asks.

"Of course Tex, Droz has never been to our Island. Our pakalolo will make him happy for sure. Go see Hani in the supply room."

"Thank you Keoni. I've been looking forward to this for a while," Tex replies.

I follow Tex to the supply room, and of course, it isn't really a supply room. It's a frosted sliding glass window. Tex taps on it and in about a minute a man opens it up, "Aloha Tex, long time no see my friend," Hani says with a happy smile. Hani is a jolly little Hawaiian guy with an infectious smile, probably because he's high all the time.

"It's great to see you again too Hani. This here's my friend Droz. Keoni knows all about him. We'll just take two bags for now Hani."

"No problem Tex."

Hani reaches down under the counter and exchanges two bags of pakalolo for fifty bucks. Tex hands me one and says, "You get the next one Droz, this ones on me."

"That's cool with me Tex."

I don't know how much is in the bag and I don't ask. What I do know is this weed smells like a skunk! We go outside to a pretty garden area where other people are getting high. Tex whips out a little pipe and puts a small piece of bud into the bowl. He hands me the pipe and says, "Aloha Droz." I put the pipe to my mouth while Tex lights the bowl. I close my eyes and draw in the sweetest smoke I ever tasted! In about two seconds, my lungs explode! I cough my hit out all over the place!

"It takes a bit getting used to, but you will," Tex says smiling.

As I hand the pipe over to Tex, I feel my eyelids shutting. Tex tokes up a big hit and handles it. While he's taking another hit, I look inside my bag at the buds. They're all perfectly trimmed nuggets. The buds are bright green and have long red hairs wrapping around them. When I pinch one of the buds it is very dense and sticks to my fingers. The pakalolo is as beautiful as the island. After another hit I feel a total body high. We float back into the club, and Lei escorts us to where Keoni and Keona are seated.

"My pakalolo make you happy haole boy?" Keoni asks grinning.

With my eyes half closed and a big wide smile I reply, "By far Keoni, the best weed I ever smoked."

Keoni and Keona smile happily at my delight. Keoni waves to Lei and out comes the food. First, we're brought fish and crab dishes, then kalua pig and turkey. Kalua means cooked underground. The meats are out of this world tasty, tender, and juicy. Keoki and Keona make sure that Tex and I get filled to the gills with their island favorites. Before I leave I go into the kitchen and tell Keanu how fantastic all his local dishes are. This makes him very happy. He even gives me a big Hawaiian hug. As much as we want to stay and party, we know we will be miserable in the morning if we get drunk, so we graciously thank our hosts and leave twenty dollars a piece on the table for Lei. As we're getting in a cab, Tex says, "I'm sure glad things worked out for you with Keoni and Keona. It would have sucked really badly for you if you got yourself barred the first day here."

"That's a fact Tex; I like the club and the people, but they're a little cocky. Don't you think?"

"They're a little cocky Droz?"

"Alright Tex, so we're both a little cocky. Maybe that's why we get along."

We take a few hits of pakalolo in the cab before we get to base. We show our ID's to get through the gate and then walk to the ship. In our berthing compartment there's a black sailor and a white sailor listening to strange sounding music on a boom box. The black guy is about six feet tall and slimly built. He is singing along to the music with a strange accent. The white guy is my height. He's a little overweight and has bright red hair. He looks Irish for sure. The black guy lowers the music when he sees us and introduces himself. "I'm Devan from Miami mon, and this is my friend Murray from Boston. Welcome aboard my friends."

"Why thank you Devan. I'm Tex and this here's Droz."

As we are exchanging handshakes I ask, "That's a strange accent Devan. Where you from originally, and what kind of music is that?"

"I'm from Jamaica mon, and my music is reggae. You are listening to Bob Marley, Rasta Man Vibration," He answers proudly.

Billy laughs and says, "That's why we all call him Rasta Man. You guys are cool right?"

Without saying a word, Tex takes out his pipe. Billy takes out his pipe too and fills it.

"I guess this ship's cool?" Tex asks.

"Yeah mon, pretty cool. Still some idiots you know, so we light a cigarette and spray some Ozium."

"This Hawaiian pakalolo is fucking great!" I exclaim.

"It good mon, but where I grow up in Westmoreland the ganja just as good ya know."

"So in Jamaica weed's called ganja?" Tex asks.

"Yeah mon, weed ganja in Jamaica."

That's' cool you live in Miami Rasta Man. I live in Coral Springs, Florida. When we get out maybe you can hook me up with some ganja."

"Where's Coral Springs?"

"About an hour drive north of Miami."

"Okay, cool then. When we home I hook you up for sure mon, no problem."

After shooting the shit and getting high for a while, we become friends. Then we both take a shower and hit the rack. Reveille is at 0700 on Sundays. Tex and I get up and head to the mess decks to check out the chow. "Oh boy Droz, they got it all on this ship," Tex says.

"You're right Tex; the guys ahead of us are ordering different kinds of omelets!"

Tex has pancakes and a few eggs over easy. I order a ham, bacon, and cheese omelet. The food is excellent. After breakfast, we go topside to toke up. We get high for a while enjoying the early morning breeze and then leave for the club. When we get there, Keoni is outside waiting. "Good thing you here braddah, me fadda is coming for your Italian dinner. Keona tell him all about your big mouth."

"Of course I'm here Keoni. Did you get everything I need?"

"Keanu has everything you asked for in the kitchen. What time should I tell fadda to be here?"

"Well it's almost nine already. So let's say one o'clock?"

"Okay."

Keoni leads us inside the club to the kitchen. Keanu greets us with a big aloha hug and hands us an apron. It's all on me now, so I put my head down and start cooking. Keona walks in as I'm taking out my first batch of meatballs and says, "Something smells ono!"

"Sounds like ono means good. Am I right Keona?"

"You right haole boy. Ono means good."

"Grab a fork Keona and stick it in one of those meatballs sitting on the platter. Take a bite and tell me what you think."

Keona grabs a fork and sticks into a meatball, and I watch her face as she takes a bite. She looks at me with wide, open eyes and says, "Onolisicious Michael! That means amazingly good! Keoni, Keanu, come try haole boy's meatballs! If everything else is this good fadda be happy we invite him."

While the three of them enjoy my meatballs, I quietly ask Tex, "Did you tell any of them my first name?"

Tex nods his head no. I go back to my cooking wondering how Keona knew. After he eats three meatballs, Keanu comes over and says, "Outstanding Droz, from now on I use your recipe in the club."

"Why thank you Keanu. A compliment like that coming from a chef means a lot to me."

Keona has Lei and some of the other girls help her set the table. Keanu pitched in too by throwing together a fresh garden salad. It's almost one o'clock and I'm draining the spaghetti when Keoki walks in. Everyone except me drops what they're doing to greet him. Keoki is a big man, and I don't mean fat. He's bigger than Keanu and Tex. Keoki is also a handsome man that has a strong aura about him. When Keoki sees me he walks right up to me with his hand extended saying, "Michael, it is a pleasure to meet you. I am Keona and Keoni's father Keoki."

I wipe my hands on my apron and shake Keoki's hand replying, "It is a pleasure to meet you too Keoki. Last night, Keoni treated my friend and me to traditional Hawaiian foods. Today I will treat your family to my family's traditional Italian Sunday Dinner."

"So I gather that your family traditions are important to you Michael?" Keoki brightly smiles and replies.

"They sure are Keoki. We have family traditions for a lot of things, especially the holidays. I was lucky to grow up half Italian and half Russian. My parents and grandparents on both sides made sure to teach me both."

"You are indeed lucky Michael. Are we ready to eat?"

"Sure are Keoki."

With that said Keoki sits down at the head of the table. The table is set beautifully with an array of fresh flowers. Tex, Keanu, and I, bring over the food. Once everyone is seated, Keoki asks me to say grace. "Thank you Lord for the food that we're about to eat, and thank you Mom and Grandma for teaching me how to cook. Amen."

Everyone replies, "Amen."

Keoki is the first to fill his plate with food. I wait for everyone else to take their portions before I do. They all look very happy, but Keoki is the first to speak, "Michael, you show your mother and grandmother great honor with this meal. This is the best Italian food I have ever eaten. It is truly onolisicious!" Now everyone starts saying, "Ono, Ono, and Onolisicious!"

There aint no slouches at this table, everybody eats like a truck driver! I'm glad I made five pounds of spaghetti. Through all of dinner, I sit and listen to Keoki interacting with his family. After dinner, the girls clear the table for fresh fruit and coffee. Keanu says the coffee is from coffee beans grown on the Big Island. They call it Kona Coffee, and I absolutely love it!

After coffee, Keoki says he has some business to attend to before heading home. He stands up and shakes my hand thanking me once more for such a wonderful meal. As Keoki is walking out the door he stops and turns to say, "Next Sunday Michael I would like you and your friend Tex to be my guests at my mother's birthday party. Keoni will let you know where and what time to be there."

This is a pleasant surprise I think to myself. Even if we're scheduled for duty, Tex and I will pay someone to stand in for us. Keoni now pats me on the back saying, "You back your mouth up pretty good Droz. I can tell fadda like you. Next

Sunday I pick you and Tex up here at my club. Say maybe, two o'clock island time."

"What's Island time Keoni?"

Keoni laughs and replies, "Island time never on time braddah. Tonight all of your drinks and Tex's are on me."

Tex and I thank Keoki. On my way out of the kitchen, Keona calls me back. I tell Tex I'll meet him at the bar. As I am walking over to Keona, she starts talking to me. "You impress fadda very much with the respect you have for your family and their traditions. Not too many haoles like that. Go tell Tex I want to show you some of our Island. Tell him Lei thinks he's cute, so he won't be lonely."

Before I can even reply Keoni says, "Keona, Droz only teenager. Maybe he not ready for island girl like you."

Keona lets out a big laugh and then replies, "Don't worry Keoni; I won't break your new friend."

I can't believe my ears; this is just too good to be true! I hurry to go tell Tex before Keona changes her mind. When I get to the bar Tex says, "I can tell by your smile Droz that something good happened. Spit it out sailor."

"Tex, you're not going to believe this. Keona wants to show me around the Island."

Tex tilts his head sideways and says, "Don't get me wrong Droz; the food you cooked was good but getting laid good? I don't know about that. Does Keoni know? Sailors won't even approach Keona because of her brother. Nobody wants trouble with Keoni. You better make sure he's okay with this."

"She asked me right in front of him Tex and he had no objections. Only maybe I was too young for her, but she said she won't break me."

"Oh my goodness Droz, don't break you?"

"Yeah, aint that a trip. Don't break me. I got some good news for you too buddy; Keona said Lei thinks you're cute so you won't be lonely tonight."

Tex smiles wide and takes a big gulp of beer before saying, "Now that is good news. You better rush along before Keona comes to her senses."

I nod my head and rush back into the kitchen, and I panic when I don't see Keona. Thankfully, Keanu tells me she's out back waiting in her car. Keanu laughs as I run out the door and nearly trip over myself. As I stumble to get my balance, I see Keona laughing at me. How embarrassing I think to myself! Keona's sitting in a yellow Corvette Stingray Convertible with black leather interior. As if the girl aint hot enough already! I hop in and she hits the gas sending me back into my seat. First Keona takes me by the big hotels on Waikiki Beach. As we're passing them by she says, "My fadda supplies most of these hotels with food and liquor Michael."

Nodding my head as I look at the beautiful hotels I ask, "How do you know my first name Keona?"

Keona stares at the road ahead. Then she punches me hard on the leg and says, "Just be happy I do."

"Okay, I guess I'll leave that one alone," I think to myself. After driving around Waikiki and seeing Diamond Head, Keona takes me to Hanauma Bay. Words cannot describe how pretty this place is. Then she takes me for a scenic ride across the Island to Waimea Bay on the North Shore. The waves are scary high breaking onto the beach. I don't know if I want to swim there. As the sun is getting low, Keona says she wants to take me to a special place only locals go to. She takes a left turn on a single lane road and then down a dirt one. We come to an opening where there are about a dozen or so parked cars. I see these beautiful high dark cliffs overlooking the ocean. A group of people are on top of them. Keona parks the car and reaches behind my seat. She pulls out a bikini and a man's bathing suit. Keona hands me the bathing suit and tells me to put it on. She says it's her brother's and will fit me just fine. I look at the bathing suit and I look at Keona. Then I ask timidly, "Here? You want me to change here in your car in front of you?"

Keona gives me a really dumb look while sarcastically replying, "Don't tell me you're shy haole boy." With that said, she pulls off her top. Keona unsnaps her purple lace bra and releases the most heavenly pair of breasts I have ever seen. She puts her bikini top on and without hesitation squeezes out of her jeans. Keona sees me watching her every move, so she teases me by slowly peeling off her purple-laced panties revealing a perfectly trimmed bush. Keona smiles seductively and asks softly, "You like what you see haole boy?"

I try my best to stay cool with my answer, so I reply, "What's not to like Keona? You seem to be perfect in every way."

"I know. Now put on the bathing suit and go cliff diving with me," She cockily says.

Cliff diving, I think to myself! This must be what Keoni meant by breaking me! The thought of cliff diving almost rids me of my hard on, but almost aint good enough. When I take off my clothes, my woody pops up like a Jack in the Box! No hiding from Keona I'm hot for her ass! Keona takes her time checking out my body. She stares right at Mr. Happy and says, "Well Michael. I guess there isn't anything average about you now, is there?"

As I'm putting on Keoni's swim trunks I reply proudly, "Well I guess we're both just blessed now aren't we Keona?"

She giggles as we get out of the car. I follow Keona up a trail on the side of the cliff. When we get to the top, there is a bunch of locals gathered. When the locals see Keona, they greet her as Princess Keona. This surprises me. I know Tex told me they were Royal Hawaiians, but I really didn't believe that shit. Keona introduces me as Michael, a friend of her family. Everyone warmly greets me by saying, "Aloha Michael." Now all the little children run up to Keona wanting hugs. Keona takes her time with them and graciously makes every child feel special. When Keona turns her attention back to me she says, "Moment of truth haole boy." She now takes me by the hand and walks me to the edge of the cliff. I look down and immediately take a step back. "You scared Michael?" She asks chuckling.

"What? Me scared? I don't think so Keona, but being curious by nature, how come I don't see anyone else jumping off this cliff? And also, didn't some wise man say that discretion is the better part of valor?"

Keona smirks at me. Then she walks me back away from the cliff. Now she looks me in the eyes and says, "To answer your first question Michael, not everyone brave enough to cliff dive. That is why you see no one else jumping. I am a Hawaiian Princess. I am born brave. The land, the ocean, and everything in it are a part of me. As far as the wise man who said discretion is the better part of valor, I bet he never fucked a princess." With that said Keona runs and dives off the cliff! All the locals cheer and clap for her! I feel like a real fucking pussy standing there. Not to mention I aint getting any pussy if I chicken out. Throwing caution to the wind, I run and jump off the cliff! Man it's a long way down! When I finally hit the water, I have no idea how far down I go. When my downward momentum stops, I thrust myself back up to the surface. I look around and see Keona treading water. She gives me a big happy smile. Right then I knew it was worth it. I swim over to Keona and say, "A guy must really like you if he jumps off a cliff for you." Keona giggles and spits a mouthful of sea water right in my face! Before I can respond, she turns tail on me and starts swimming like a fish towards the shore. Keona beats me to shore by at least ten yards. Then she runs as fast as she can down the beach with me in hot pursuit. Keona don't have a chance in a sprint. I catch up quickly and tackle her onto the sand. She fights and giggles trying to get away, but I won't let her. When I pin her arms to the sand our eyes lock. There's silence. I quickly become captivated by the princess's beauty. Instead of pouncing on her, I let her up. Keona's pleasantly surprised by my poise. Putting her arm under my own, we snuggle closely on the shoreline watching a glorious sunset. Absorbing all of the beauty around me, I thank Keona for taking me here. "It makes me very happy Michael to see you enjoy the beauty of my home. This is just one of many places I can show you. My family owns property on all of the islands," She replies.

"I would love it Keona. You sure are blessed to grow up and live here. It's dirty, crowded, and violent where I grew up in New York."

Keona stares out at the ocean for a moment. Then turns to me sadly saying, "My home is not without its problems Michael. There are parts of Honolulu that are just like what you described. We have street gangs of poor local youths committing violent crimes and dealing bad drugs in our neighborhoods. There are things happening right now in Oahu that threaten my family's existence."

"I thought your family is at the top of the food chain out here? What could possibly be threatening you and yours Keona?"

Forcing a smile, she replies, "It's getting dark Michael. Let's go home."

Obviously, Keona doesn't want to talk about it, so I drop it. Anyway, I'm much more intrigued with "Let's go home." Does she mean go back to the club or take me back to my ship? Or hopefully, home to her house. I figure not to ask. Let's just see where we end up. I keep my mouth shut as we walk hand in hand back to her car. It's a pretty decent walk from the beachhead we swam too after our kamikaze jump off the cliff. It's totally dark by the time we make it back to the parking lot. There's a bunch of local guys building a fire by the path to the cliff. They're drinking beer and smoking pakalolo. When they see us walking over to Keona's car, somebody shouts. "Hey Keona, you know haoles no welcome here!"

Keona looks at me sighs and says, "That's Kane and his gang of local boys. They love making plenny pilikia for haoles."

Kane is a rough looking dude standing about six feet tall. His body is ripped and covered with tattoos. He looks about twenty years old and his friends look even younger. I ask Keona, "What does plenny pilikia mean?"

"It means plenty trouble Michael. It's my fault for keeping you out here after dark. Don't worry, I can handle him." Before I can say anything, Keona yells back, "Haole boy is friend of my family Kane. You will respect that."

Kane laughs really loud and replies, "We all know your fadda no like haoles Keona. You do this behind his back for sure, so I got mo bedda idea. You tell panty boy go away and I no tell your fadda."

"Does he mean panty boy in a good way Keona? Like I get in girls panties a lot, or in a bad way like I wear them?" I ask nicely.

Keona laughs while putting her hand on my shoulder saying, "Kane mean you wear panties like a sissy boy Michael, but please don't try and impress me by doing something foolish. Kane has a bad reputation for hurting people, especially haoles. Like I said, I'll handle it. Kane will back down when I threaten him with my brother."

Keona pisses me off, so I brazenly reply, "Let me tell you something Keona. The only fucking person I care about impressing is me. I'll take care of fucking Kane; you just use your fucking threats to keep the rest of these assholes in line." With that said I turn to Kane and shout, "You talk a lot of fucking shit standing over there with your boys Kane. How about you bring your panty boy ass over here and fight me one on one."

Kane's boys hoot and holler. Kane the bully looks a little stunned as he shouts back, "Eh haole boy, you like beef with Kane!"

I take a few steps out towards Kane and grin. Then I grab my crotch and say, "I got your beef right here motherfucker! Come and get it bitch!"

Kane's friends start laughing their asses off as he runs full speed right at me! Keona yells, "If anyone jumps in they will deal with my brother."

Kane flies at me and I duck under him sending his body over me. He quickly gets to his feet. This time he approaches slowly. With a quick lunge, Kane hits me with a sidekick under my left arm sending me to the ground. He tries stomping my face, but I roll away and get back to my feet. Kane moves in again and I fire a quick left right. He dodges my punches and tackles me to the ground! He's on top of me and hits me with a glancing blow on the side of my face. As Kane rears back again, I use my legs to kick him off me. We both approach each other cautiously now. Kane throws a wild right and I duck inside landing a solid left hook to his body. I step back and follow it up with a front kick to his stomach and then another. Kane drops his hands to protect his mid-section, so I go up top with a barrage of punches. When he goes down, I jump on top of him and let loose until he gives up. He's face is a swollen bloody mess. I would have given up before taking such a beating. Some of his friends help him up and some of his friends shake my hand. When I swagger over to Keona, she raises one eyebrow and sarcastically asks, "So tell me pretty boy. Did you impress yourself?"

I silently laugh at her sarcasm replying, "Always"

Keona smiles and kisses me on the cheek. Then says, "Time I take you home before I break you like my brother says." While we're walking back to the car somebody yells, "Kane got a gun!"

Three gunshots ring out as we dive behind the car, and then silence. We peek over the hood and see Keoni standing over Kane's body with a gun. Keoni pumps three more rounds into him and then nods his head to the gang. They respond by running over and carrying away Kane's body. Keona shouts out, "Keoni you save us!" She runs up to her brother hugging and kissing him. Quickly changing moods, she pushes Keoni away asking, "Are you following me Keoni?"

"You can't fool me sista. You like haole boy, so now I know you want to see if haole boy brave enough to jump off cliff for you. Haoles not safe here after dark, so I check on you. You jump haole boy?"

"Yeah I jumped," I reply smiling.

"So sista, you take Droz home now?"

"Maybe," Keona replies coyly.

Using a sarcastic tone, Keoni says, "Give Droz break and bring him back to ship. First he lucky enough to survive cliff dive and then even more lucky to survive Kane. Maybe his luck runs out tonight and he doesn't survive you."

Keona shoves her brother really hard and replies, "Don't you have some blonde haole tourist girl waiting for you somewhere Keoni?"

"Not one blonde Keona, two blonde haoles," Keoni brags.

We all laugh and then I ask Keoni, "Aint you worried about all of those witnesses?"

"Kane disrespect my sister. Then he pull gun when lose fight. I watch whole thing. I see you fight with honor Droz. Everyone see Kane have no honor. They know he deserve to die. The local boys are embarrassed by Kane and proud to help Keoni. His body will never be found. Is that my bathing suit haole boy wearing?"

"Yes," Keona giggles.

Keoni takes a serious tone saying, "You betta wash real good sista, maybe haole boy leave stink stain when jump off cliff."

"You better tell me if you did Michael before you get into my car!" Keona exclaims.

I put both hands over my face and shake my head. Then I pull off Keoni's bathing suit and turn it inside out saying, "Look for yourselves."

They love my candor. Keoni wishes us a happy night and leaves. Pulling away Keona looks over at me and says, "Well Michael it's been an eventful day now, hasn't it?"

I place my hand on Keona's inner thigh and gently squeeze as I reply, "All's well that ends well."

"I'm glad you feel that way," Keona softly replies.

During the ride back I ask, "So your old man doesn't like haoles?"

"He really doesn't Michael. My father never wants me to date haoles, especially military ones. But fadda like how you respect your family and their traditions."

"Well that's good news. After seeing Keoni act with impunity I can only imagine what your father can do."

Keona gives no reply as she drives up a long secluded driveway. We park in front of a heavily landscaped old wooden house. The house is totally private with no neighbors. When we exit the car, I hear waves crashing onto the shore. When we get inside there's a giant saltwater fish tank built right into the wall. The tank is full of beautifully colored corals and exotic fish. The splendor of the aquarium spreads a cozy glow over the entire room. Fascinated by its brilliance, I turn to Keona and say, "This is without a doubt the most magnificent aquarium that I have ever seen."

Putting her arm under my own, she proudly replies, "My brother and I dived for everything you see in this aquarium. Some of the fish and corals are extremely rare."

"I believe it Keona. I've never even seen pictures of some of these fish."

"I'll grab a few things and we'll go outside Michael."

"Okay."

Keona grabs a big blanket and a velvet pouch. She hands me the blanket and leads me outside. Keona's yard is a tropical paradise lined with Tiki torches! She even has a Tiki bar! Just beyond that, there's the beach and the ocean. Keona and I light the torches together. The flickering flames make for a dreamlike setting. We lay the blanket on some soft grass and sit down. She takes one huge bud and a pipe made out of seashells from her pouch. The pungent smell of pakalolo fills the night air. Keona hands me the bud saying, "The pakalolo my brother and I smoke is not for sale Michael. It is grown in sacred volcanic soil from the seeds of a special strain of pakalolo. It is very potent."

I raise my eyebrows and nod my head. Then I closely inspect the bud. It is very sticky and very dense. The bud easily fits into the palm of my hand, but I would wager it weighs close to a quarter pound. The bud is almost black in color and has bright orange hairs running all through it. Keona hands me razor-blade saying, "Use this to shave some off the bud."

I carefully shave a few very thin slices of bud. Keona takes one of the slices and puts it in the pipe. She puts the pipe to my lips and lights it. I slowly draw in the sweetest smoke I have ever tasted. My lungs expand immediately, so I stop inhaling and hand the pipe to Keona. She smiles and then effortlessly takes in a big hit. Amazingly when I exhale I don't feel the high hit me like with the other pakalolo Tex bought from Hani. Keona takes another hit and passes me the pipe. I get ambitious now and draw in a really big hit. I try like crazy to keep it down, but I can't, and cough my brains out.

"Would you like some fresh coconut water Michael? It will soothe your throat and replenish your body," Keona asks. Still coughing, I can only nod my head yes. Keona goes over to the Tiki bar and grabs a green coconut out of a sack. Grabbing a machete from the side of the bar she begins methodically chopping layers off the top. She quickly does the same thing to another coconut. Then Keona walks back over to the blanket and hands me one. I down a few soothing mouthfuls so I can speak, "That was pretty impressive how you handled that machete Keona. You need to teach me that. The coconut water is sweet, soothing, and refreshing. Thank you Keona."

"You're welcome Michael. Hopefully we will need to drink another coconut together after our love making."

Well if that aint a fucking hint! As I'm downing the rest of my coconut water, the pakalolo finally kicks in. It's creep weed, and just like that I'm fucking wasted, but in a good way. My body and mind is full of happiness and energy. Keona must be feeling the same way, so I cozy up to her. Then I brush my lips across her cheek and neck. Her skin is smooth as silk. Keona moves her beautiful long hair to one side so I can do a thorough job. When I come back around our lips meet in a deep sensuous kiss. As we're kissing, I remove her bikini top and caress her breasts. Her nipples stand erect as little goose bumps pop out around her areolas. When our lips part Keona pulls off her bikini bottoms and I pull off my swim trunks. We begin kissing again and exploring each other's bodies. I reach between Keona's silky thighs and use her pussy lips to massage and jerk off her clit. She purrs like kitten as her clit swells between my fingertips. Keona gasps when I slowly slide my middle finger inside her. Her pussy is sopping wet and making squishy sounds as I finger her. Keona grabs ahold of my rock hard cock while I continue massaging her clit with my thumb and fingering her. Lustful moans slip from her lips as she firmly jerks my cock faster and faster. Her thighs begin quivering, so I quickly slip two fingers into her hot wet snatch and pump her hard. Clamping her thighs around my hand Keona moans loudly shuddering in orgasm. Smiling with wide eyes, she turns aggressive and pushes me down on the blanket. Impaling herself on my big dick Keona grinds her hips passionately back and forth. I spank her sweet little ass edging her on for more. The harder I spank her the harder and faster she grinds me. Keona's fucking me with an unbridled passion I have never experienced before! Sweat pours out our bodies along with our passion. As Keona begins shaking, I feel her pussy convulsing tightly around my cock. We explode together in an earth shaking mind-blowing orgasm! My cock and balls are drenched in her juices! Keona's body glistens with sweat in the torch light. She pushes her hair back from her face and I'm bewitched by her beauty. She smiles lovingly and kisses me. Staring deeply into my eyes, she says, "I feel like we have been together for a very long time Michael, perhaps even in another life, or a dream. Do you believe in such things?"

"Of course I do Keona, and I feel exactly the same as you do."

"Let's dream again," She whispers softly.

With that said. The walls of her pussy begin squeezing and contracting around what little was left of my hard on. It don't take long before Keona's pussy skills have me rock hard again! Accomplishing her task, she giggles like a schoolgirl and quickly rolls off me onto her back. "It's your turn," She says mischievously.

After a marathon session we drink a lot more coconut water, smoke more pakalolo, and then go right back at it again! We spend the entire night fucking and cuddling under the stars. Keona and I awake with the sun and swim naked in the blue surf of the Pacific. I feel like Adam and Eve in the Garden of Eden. There's still time before I have to be back to the ship, so Keona makes Akule fish and rice for breakfast. I wash it down with more coconut water. After a couple of hits of her magical pakalolo, she takes me back to my ship. Keona's father does business with the Navy so she has a base sticker on her car. This means she can drop me off at my boat. We share a juicy wet kiss right in front of everyone topside. They know who she is, and now they know I'm fucking her. Walking up the gangplank and hearing the chitchat makes me realize why Keona's father doesn't want her dating haole boy sailors.

Onboard, I rush down to my birthing compartment and put on my work clothes. After tying up my boondockers, I look up and there's Tex still in his civvies just getting back to the ship himself! As he hustles to get dressed before muster, he looks at me and cheerfully says, "Keona was right about Lei Droz. She did like me, so we spent the night together. She's a bit feisty, but that's right up my alley. I think we'll hook up for a while. How did things work out with you and Keona?"

"Real good Tex, I think we'll hook up for a while too."

We didn't have time to elaborate until later. When we did, I tell Tex everything. The ship is fairly new, so there isn't much work to do. We mostly all get high and tell stories. Both of us can't wait to get back to our girls. Keona is able to leave the club around ten, but Lei has to wait until eleven. Each night Keona shows me something new on the island. By the end of the week, I'm driving her Corvette around the island. When Saturday comes, Tex and I are more than anxious to go to Keoki's mom's birthday party. I remember Keoni said two o'clock 'Island Time,' so Tex and I aint picked up until a quarter to three. Keoni drives a blue Land Rover. He says it fits his lifestyle of surfing, diving, and hunting. Keoni sparks up a joint of his special weed for the ride over to his fathers. We're all fucking whacked when we get there. Keoni's father's house is more like a sprawling ocean estate than a house. I see a large main house and several smaller ones built on the property. All the homes have a tropical design and landscaping. I hear Hawaiian music coming from the back of the house. Keoni walks us around back where there's a full-blown Hawaiian Luau going on! The beach area is cut right out of a piece of paradise. Down by the ocean lots of children are playing in the water. When Keoki sees us, he calls us over to his table. He's sitting next to a woman who I presume to be his wife. Keoni says he needs to change clothes and excuse's himself. Tex and I walk over to the table where Keoki introduces us. "Miliani, I would like you to meet our new haole friends. Michael and Tex. Michael is the one who cooked us his Italian families' traditional Sunday meal. It was onolisicious."

Miliani frowns at Keoki sarcastically replying, "Yes it was onolisicious Keoki. Thanks to my thoughtful son I did have some that evening."

Like mother like daughter both stunningly beautiful and equally forthright in their manner. Miliani gracefully gets up from her chair and walks over to me. She looks me up and down before saying, "So, you are the Michael my daughter speaks so fondly of?"

"Well that's good to hear Miliani because I think the world of her," I smile replying.

Miliani, noticing that Keoki does not like my remark, comments, "Whoever my son or daughter decides they are happiest with makes us happy, right Keoki?"

"Well of course Miliani, but our ancestors may not be so happy," Keoki replies disgruntledly.

Miliani stares down her nose at her husband, and then turns around saying, "Here comes our son and daughter now with tutu. Michael, Tex, tutu means grandmother in our language.

They are all wearing traditional Royal Hawaiian dress. Some of the bird feathers in tutu's head ornament are from birds long extinct. Don't they look wonderful Keoki?"

"Yes my love. Since haoles come to our islands we have lost over twenty five species of birds and many native plants too," Keoki says gruffly as he grabs his camera and takes a few pictures.

Miliani smiles apologetically at Tex and I as Keona introduces us to tutu. "Tutu, these are our friends Michael and Tex. We invited them to share your birthday with you. Today tutu is 84 years old."

Tutu smiles brightly and reaches for a hug. We both hug the birthday girl and kiss her on the cheek. Keoki now says, "Time to Ai. That means eat my haole friends."

Sitting at Keoki's table, we're served all types of Hawaiian foods like at the club. Everyone is having a fantastic time, when all of a sudden someone yells, "The boat is sinking! The boat is sinking!" Keoki quickly leaves the table with Keoni and everybody at the party follows. When we get to the beach there's a big fishing boat anchored off shore sinking. To our left calmly walking up the shoreline are six Japanese men. Wearing only shorts and heavily tattooed, I see pistol grips in their waistbands. They all point at the sinking boat and laugh. Keoni and the other men move towards the intruders. The Japanese men draw their pistols while Keoki jumps in front of his people. The Hawaiian men have the numbers by far, but are unarmed. The women pull their children close to their bodies, but look more defiant than afraid. "They are dogs and have no honor!" Keoni yells angrily.

Keona looks at me and says, "This is exactly what I was I talking to you about Michael."

"It takes a real low life to do this kind of thing at a family gathering," I reply.

Keoki calms his son and then by himself walks towards the armed men. As Keoki gets closer, the Japanese men put their pistols back in their waistbands and bow. The man in the middle speaks to Keoki rudely and sarcastically saying, "We are all very sorry about your boat King Keoki." The men laugh as Keoki watches the rest of his fishing boat sink into the ocean. The Japanese men look like midgets standing next to Keoki, but the pistols in their waistbands make them giants.

"Boat does not breathe air. Nor does it have the blood of life flowing through its veins. Why have you gentlemen come to my home brandishing weapons?" Keoki replies humbly.

"We want to join the birthday celebration for your beloved mother Keoki. Maybe we can dance with your precious daughter and her friends. I think they will like Japanese men."

Like a pack of Hyena's they all laugh together. Now the Japanese man becomes belligerent shouting, "You know why we're here Keoki. It's time to decide to step aside, or die! So, which one will it be King Keoki? Give us your hotels and bars, or die today in front of your family?" With that said, the Japanese men pull out their pistols. The Hawaiians erupt in anger at the men. Keoki raises his hand silencing his people. Then he says to the man, "I wish to speak privately with you."

The Japanese man looks at his friends and nods his head. Then loudly and sarcastically replies, "Sure King Keoki. I understand. Your honor is at stake! You don't want your family hearing you humble yourself! So King, where shall we go?"

"Not far. Just out of the speaking distance of my family. The ocean is calm today, so we can talk privately in the shallows."

The Japanese men look at each other and nod okay. With pistols drawn, they follow Keoki into the water. When the water is at Keoki's knees, it's already at their waistlines. We see the Japanese man's lips moving, but can't hear what he's saying. When he's done speaking Keoki looks down at the water and nods his head. Then he raises his hands to the sky saying, "Aumakua, Aumakua." Pointing towards the ocean and smiling, tutu chants, "Aumakua, Aumakua." Now all the Hawaiians start chanting, "Aumakua, Aumakua," So Tex and I join in too. The Japanese men laugh and head to shore. Until they're path is cut off by sharks and stingrays! Their faces are riddled with fear as their leader shouts, "Enough of your Hawaiian bullshit Keoki, we die you die!"

Keoki bursts out in laughter and pats the top of the water. From the depths of the ocean two giant sharks appear! Keoki pets them and says, "You said you wished to celebrate and dance with my family. The stingrays and sharks are my ancestors and they wish to celebrate and dance with you too!"

The stingrays use their tales now to whip and sting the Japanese men! The six men scream out wildly in pain! In a desperate attempt to survive, they empty their pistols at Keoki, the sharks, and the stingrays. Now everyone is screaming! When the smoke clears, Keoki is laughing! Not one bullet pierces his skin, the skin of a shark, or stingray! Cut off from the beach by sharks, the six Japanese men beg for their lives! Keoki responds to their pleas for mercy with a sinister grin. Then he waves his hand motioning the two giant sharks to swim towards them. One shark grabs the leader and the other shark grabs the man to his right. Both men let out blood curdling screams as the giant sharks slowly and meticulously tear their bodies apart! Frozen in shock, the other four men watch their friends being eaten alive! Keoki turns to them and commands, "Go to your leaders and tell them what you have witnessed here today." As soon as those words leave Keoki's mouth, the smaller sharks nip and bite small chunks of flesh from the men's legs. They cry out in pain as Keoki slowly walks out of the water. Everyone bows to Keoki, including me and Tex. As Miliani, Keona, and Keoni hug their father, Tex looks at me and says, "Well Droz, if I didn't see it. I would never believe it."

"That's for sure Tex. If somebody told me they saw this, I would never believe them," I reply.

The bloodied waters soon become bright and blue again. The children resume playing in the surf like nothing ever happened. The celebration intensifies for the rest of the evening. The both of us eventually get around to asking Keoni and Keona if they knew their father had this power. They say, "Yes." They explain Aumakua to us as a family god, or gods, that can manifest themselves into almost any form in a time of crisis or festivity. They could even possess you and make you stronger, or better at something. We are also told they can judge and punish you for the bad things you may have done. I ask Keoni and Keona if they have the powers. They weren't sure. They do pray if their family ever needs it, the powers will come to them.

Keona and I sneak off after Lei shows up to be with Tex. Every weekend Keona takes me to one of the other Islands for a new adventure. We do so many romantic things together. In so many storybook places, that we fall deeply in love.

Time flies and soon we're taking on supplies for the South Pac. We all work hard to make sure the ship is in tiptop shape for the voyage. I write Johnny for my three grand so I can start slushing on the South Pac. It wasn't long before I get a package from him. To my surprise, Johnny sends ten grand instead of three! He says my idea sprouted wings! He wrote a detailed letter explaining everything. Demand for new homes in Coral Springs is sky rocketing. Johnny and Willie have become close friends. He says Uncle Rocco partnered with Willie's family on different business ventures at the Port of Miami and I'll get a cut. Johnny says Uncle Rocco will reinvest my cut for me back into the business. I'm excited about my future with Rocco Santori! I show Tex and burn the letter. I take half the money and buy four pounds of the best pakalolo Keoni will sell me. I give Keoni Johnny's address and ask him to send Johnny a quarter pound as a gift. The rest is for selling and smoking on the South Pac. I'll sell an eighth for twenty-five dollars cash. If you want it fronted until payday, it will cost you thirty. The other half of the money I'll use to start my slush fund.

We'll be pulling out of Pearl in two days. Needless to say, I'm beyond depressed. This is the third girl I have fallen completely in love with in less than a year and have to leave, and this fucking heartbreak feels worse than the other two combined! I figure it's because I spent more time with Keona then the other two combined. Keona knows all about my relationship with Teresa Sue. I know all about her father wanting her to marry a successful Hawaiian man, so before we can take our relationship to the next level we needed to reconcile these two things. Teresa Sue and I still exchange love letters, but we both agreed to see other people. So who knows if she met somebody special too? Leaving the Hawaiian lifestyle behind is almost as heartbreaking as leaving Keona herself. We kiss goodbye and cry like babies. When Hawaii disappears from sight, so do my tears. I quickly become excited with the thought, "What new and wild adventures await me over the next horizon?"

SOUTH PAC...

Everyone got their fucking rag on the first few days out at sea. Good thing I brought a bunch of pakalolo aboard to help everyone get their sea legs back. I feel the right thing to do is make Tex a full partner in both the weed and slushing business. After the South Pac, Tex won't have much time left on his enlistment. So I ask him if he would like to become part of what I have going on in Florida. He's delighted and very thankful for the offer. Now for the first time Tex opens up to me about his family. "Droz, you got no idea how bad things were for me growing up. For trusting me and making me your partner, I got your back for life. My grandma is the only family I know about left alive. As far as work goes, I guess I can try riding bulls again. My old man taught me how to ride bulls as a kid. For a while, he was the roughest toughest bull rider in all of Southwest Texas, but his injuries started taking a toll on him. Sometimes he couldn't even get out of bed in the morning without a few shots of whiskey and a handful of pills. It wasn't long before the liquor and the pills got the better of him. In a blink of an eye we became dirt poor, struggling everyday just to eat. Then we lost our house, our truck, and just about everything else we had to my old man's habit. Grandma put a roof over our heads by helping us rent an old trailer. My old man said it was handout and that just pushed him right over the edge. That's when he started beating on me and Mom."

"Wow buddy. I'm really sorry to hear that."

Tex shakes his head and somehow cracks a smile saying, "Oh, it gets worse Droz, it gets a lot worse. My father overdosed right in front of me and my mother. We tried to keep him breathing until the ambulance came, but we couldn't. After the funeral, my mom said she wanted to be alone for a spell, so she dropped me off at grandma's house. When she didn't answer the phone the next day me and Grandma drove over to the trailer. We went inside and found her dead in the bathtub. She washed down the rest of my old man's pain pills with half a bottle of whiskey and slit her wrists. Grandma brought me up after that. She cleaned houses for rich folk to put food in my mouth and taught me the Bible. She hated swear words, so that's why you don't hardly ever hear me use one. When I got old enough, I tried making money like my old man, but got drunk too much to stay on the rodeo circuit. I got a job as a bouncer in a low life titty bar until I got into too much trouble and ended up here."

Tex really looks like he needs a hug, so I give him one. He embraces me back for a few seconds and then roughly pushes me away saying, "I know what you're doing Droz. You can't fool me pal. Were out at sea a couple of days and you're already buttering me up for a blowjob. I'm telling you right now son it just aint a happening."

"After listening to that heartbreak story you should be giving me a fucking blowjob!" I reply and laugh.

Tex pushes me and says, "Enough of crying in my beer Droz, let's go get high."

"I'm right behind you buddy."

The Polk is three days away from the equator, so Captain Wild Bill calls a meeting of the Royal Order of Shellbacks. We gather on the fantail and no lowly scum of a pollywog is allowed topside. Here we formulate our dastardly plans for all the lowly wogs! Wild Bill says we'll fly the Jolly Roger honoring the pirate tradition. The shellbacks are instructed to make pirate outfits for themselves out of old clothes. The wogs will be ordered to wear their pants on backwards. Using a belt as a leash, the shellbacks will lead certain wogs around by their neck through a gauntlet of disgusting horrors we prepare for them. The shellbacks working in the kitchen will collect all of the table scraps from our meals and put them into plastic trash bags. The trash bags will be taken below deck to the boiler room where it's nice and hot. There the contents of the bags will be allowed to decompose and fester. The Captain wants pinholes put into dozens of eggs. Then store them in the boiler room too, letting them nicely spoil for the occasion. We will greet the wogs with a bombardment of rotten eggs as they crawl out onto the deck. The Chief Mess Cook brought aboard a pig head from a Luau. He put it into a plastic bag and stashed it in the boiler room to rot. The Captain commended the chief for his efforts and put him in charge of having every wog kiss the pigs head as they pass him by. We all make shillelaghs out of a cut up old fire hose. Then we soak them in seawater so they harden. The shillelagh will be used without mercy on wogs, whacking their asses as they crawl through the gauntlet. Captain Wild Bill just happens to have a medieval stock onboard. This will be used for bad wogs that revolt, or whine too much. Chief O'Rourke has the biggest Buddha belly, so he is nominated to play Neptune's baby. The chief will wear a towel as a diaper. His belly will be smeared with rotted butter and spoiled cottage cheese. An olive will be placed in baby Neptune's belly button. The wogs will have to suck it out while the chief rubs their faces all over his fouled fat belly! The doctor is a bit of a sadist himself. He's going to fill a large syringe with homemade hot sauce and inject it into the mouths of wogs that talk back.

The day before we cross the equator we hold a wog beauty contest. The winning wog becomes a shellback without having to go through all the torture. This ensures the wogs will do their best making themselves look as sweet as they can. They put on a spicy show for us, parading back and forth in front of the judges. The winner is decided by how loud us Shellbacks roar for their performance. Being true to the 'Line Crossing

Tradition' after dinner before we cross, brave but dumb wogs are allowed to attack shellbacks found topside. They can use fire hoses and rotten tomatoes as their weapons.

At 0500, all shellbacks begin their assault on the wogs! Dressed like pirates we bang on pots and pans rudely awakening all the lowly wogs! The wogs jump out of bed and put their pants on backwards. Select wogs are leashed. Select wogs are troublemakers and certain assholes of all ranks. First thing we make the wogs do is serve us shellbacks breakfast. Wogs can't have breakfast, and it's better off for them anyway. They'll just puke it up. Just about everyone on the ship hates the Chief Master at Arms. He's a Lifer Dog Chief Scumbag with over 20 years in the Navy, but this pansy ass never crossed the equator! The fucking prick loves sneaking around the ship at night trying to bust sailors smoking weed. Payback is a motherfucker, so we start whipping his ass real good! When wogs get hit with shillelagh's they're crawling on all fours through a maze of rotted garbage. It's forbidden for wogs to look back at who's hitting them. If they do look back, they have to start over from the beginning. We give it to this scumbag Chief so fucking bad the sissy bitch breaks down and cries! What the chief don't know is that a lot of the people he thinks are his friends beat him the most! Nobody likes a fucking rat. A couple of guys he busted for smoking weed and lost a stripe put him in the stock. They pull his pants down around his ankles and shove a giant frozen cucumber right up his rat ass! They take pictures of his shame so they can anonymously mail them to his family. The fun is all over by 0900. We hose off the wogs and the decks. The rest of the day we have off. It's a beautiful day too. A school of dolphins swims alongside the ship putting on an incredible show!

Our first Port of Call is American Samoa, then the Fiji Islands, and then Rora Tonga in the Cook Islands is up next. From there we'll set sail to Christchurch and Napier, New Zealand, Sumatra, Tasmania, and then Jakarta. Then six glorious ports in Australia! Now we get real lucky and a change in orders sends us to Karachi, Bahrain, Mombasa, Singapore, Honk

Kong, and Taiwan. Our final stop before heading home is Pattaya Beach, Thailand.

The morning before we anchor off the shores of Pattaya Beach, the Captain summons the entire crew above deck. Wild Bill informs us about the special dangers this port holds. The Captain reads the criminal penalties for drug smuggling and drug possession. If a sailor is caught with any drugs, or even drug paraphernalia, he will receive up to a twenty stroke caning. If a sailor is caught smuggling drugs, the penalty is death. The Captain says there's nothing he can do to help us if we get caught, so he pleads with us not to buy drugs. To deter us even further, he says every crewmember will be strip searched upon returning to the ship. Thailand possesses two of the world's most precious things. First, the hottest girls in the whole fucking Orient, and second, Thai sticks! Tex and I have already done a lot of very bad things on this cruise. We consider ourselves very lucky to be alive and not imprisoned somewhere. Pattaya Beach is our last stop before heading home to Pearl, so we decide to stay away from the drugs and just get laid.

The cabs are waiting in line for us sailors when our feet hit the beach. Tex and I quickly jump into one of them. I take shotgun and Tex gets the backseat. The cab driver has a thick scar running all along his neck. It looks like either somebody tried to hang him, or he had his throat slit. He's wearing a black tank top and old faded jeans. His arms are covered with beautiful tattoos of Bengal Tigers and Panda Bears roaming in jungles. A cigarette hangs precariously from his lips as he speaks in a cool Oriental accent, "So, you sailors here to play, or you want to make money?" I look back at Tex, he looks at me, and we both keep quiet. The guy laughs and says, "Let me guess. Your captain scared the shit out of you, right?"

I give the cabbie a cold hard look before replying, "Listen pal, there's a big difference between being scared and being fucking stupid."

The cabbie nods his head up and down a few times. This knocks a long ash off the end of his cigarette and into his lap.

Without taking his eyes off the road, he nonchalantly brushes the ashes off his jeans and assertively replies, "I don't like cops. I like money. You guys want to buy drugs? I can get them for you."

I think quietly to myself for a moment. I know this can be a set-up, but something inside of me tells me this guy is okay, so I go with my instincts replying, "We're not interested in narcotics, but we may be interested in some Thai sticks."

As the cabbie turns towards me to speak the smoke from the end of his cigarette rises into his right eye making him squint while replying, "How many do you want?"

Tex taps me on the shoulder and kindly asks, "What happened to staying away from the drugs and just getting laid plan Droz?"

"I got a good feeling about this guy Tex. I think he's on the level."

"Well you aint been wrong yet. I got your back buddy."

With that said. Tex whips out his butterfly knife and assures this guy that if we we're going down, he's coming with us. The cabbie is unfazed by Tex's threat. He just smiles and says, "I have a good feeling about you two too. So how many Thai sticks you buy today?"

Tex puts his knife back into his boot as I reply, "That depends on two things cabbie. One the price, and two, how do we get them onboard our ship? Our Captain is having everyone strip searched."

The cabbie takes another cigarette out of a pack from under his visor and puts it into his mouth. He lights it with what is left of the one he's already smoking. He takes a big drag and exhales before saying, "That won't be a problem; Mamasan show you."

The cab driver drives away from the city. The farther away from the city means the less likelihood of cops, but the bigger the chance of getting ripped off. Tex and I have virtually no chance against the police in the city, but I'll take our chances any fucking day in a rip off situation. Hell, if they try to rip us off we'll rip them off instead!

During the ride, we actually start making friends with this guy. His name is Chen and he fought as a Thai volunteer soldier in the Vietnam War. He got that wicked scar on his neck from a Vietcong booby trap in the jungle. He tells us some really cool stories about how some of the jungles are occupied by spirits. Chen says a spirit removed the snare from around his neck. His great grandfather was a forest monk, so he thought it was his spirit that saved him. After what Tex and I had seen in Hawaii, we don't doubt him.

It takes about an hour before we arrive at a farmhouse in the middle of nowhere. When we get out of the cab mama-san comes outside to greet us. She is a short and stout jolly old woman, with long grey braided hair. It's amazing how the mamasans run things in these countries. Men rely on them for their strength, wisdom, and leadership. She walks us over to her barn and opens the door. An overwhelming smell of really strong honey hits me. Inside the barn I quickly realize I do not smell honey! Bales of Thai stick are stacked up all around me! I look at mamasan with a bright smile and ask, "How much?"

"You want all?" She says politely.

I put my hands on my hip and chuckle before replying, "I wish Mamasan. I'm not sure yet how many. I would like to know how we get these on the ship first."

Mamasan gracefully smiles and waves her hand at me before saying, "You just follow me. I show you how. My family has been doing this for generations."

Tex and I nod our heads. Then the three of us follow the old woman into the house. Inside there's lots of very pretty young girls. They are all giggling and scurrying about the house. Tex and I know right off that dope isn't the only thing being sold here. I jokingly ask Mamasan, "I guess these are your daughters?"

She laughs and playfully shoves me. Then Mamasan replies, "Why, you want to marry one? All my daughters need husbands."

Now I know what's going on. This isn't a house of prostitution sitting way out here in the woods. These girls are purposely being kept away from the city and out of trouble. Mamasan is running a mail order bride service! Tex and I quickly tell Mamasan we're already spoken for. Mamasan takes us to another room where there are all different sizes of stuffed animals. She tells me how many sticks will fit into each one. The stuffed sea turtles hold one hundred sticks. They look like they'll easily fit in our stand up lockers. "How much for one hundred Thai sticks?" I ask mamasan.

"$100 for Thai sticks. Stuffed turtle ten more dollars. Sewing Thai sticks inside also ten dollars."

Light bulb goes off in my head. Throughout the entire cruise, sailors have been shipping things back to themselves at Pearl. Now I say to Mamasan, "I would buy a lot more Mamasan if you can ship them to me back at Pearl Harbor. Is that possible?"

"For the right amount of money Mamasan can do whatever you wish," She says smiling.

"How much for a thousand Thai sticks shipped to me at Pearl Harbor?"

"To ship 1,000 Thai sticks to Pearl Harbor will cost you $1,200."

Now I think to myself. I already made a lot of money on this cruise. Here I am in Thailand with a chance to either make a huge score, or lose a chunk of what I made. I make Mamasan an offer. "How about I give you $4,000 American dollars right now Mamasan for 5,000 Thai sticks shipped to me at Pearl."

Mamasan shakes her head and says, "No can do. You make it $5,000 and I will ship 5,000 Thai sticks in the finest hand-made bamboo trunks you will ever see. They will have false bottoms. "

I do some quick math in my head. I can just about break even on the five grand if I get two turtles aboard the ship. If the five thousand sticks make it to Pearl, they will be worth one hundred thousand dollars if sold at only $20 apiece. That's well worth the risk. So now I look Mamasan in the eye and say. "You throw in two turtles with a hundred Thai sticks apiece in them and I'll put five thousand greenbacks in your pretty little hand right now Mamasan."

Mamasan puts her hands on her hips and says, "Show me your greenbacks and we have a deal."

Tex and I cough up five grand for Mamasan. After Mamasan is done counting she smiles and says, "You no regret meeting Mamasan. Someday you come back and see me again. My girls will help count the Thai sticks. Also, you more than welcome to smoke if you like. But I must warn you. They are very strong."

We help the girls count out the sticks. As long as it's even close to a 1,000 in a bale we'll do just fine. We don't want to smoke until after we get everything squared away and the turtles safely onboard. One mistake because we're too fucking stoned could be our last.

Back inside the house, Mamasan makes us some herbal tea. The tea gives us both a real boost. It takes the girls about twenty minutes to finish sewing the Thai sticks into our turtles. I write down my shipping address for Mamasan and she gives me her contact information in return. Mamasan hugs and thanks us for trusting her. Chen then takes us back to the pier where we wait nervously to be picked up by one of our small boats. The longer we wait, the more nervous we get. We actually consider leaving the turtles on the dock and just hope the rest of the Thai sticks come through for us later. The moment of truth comes when the boat arrives. The sailor manning the boat is a third class Boatswains' Mate from our division. His name is Wally Spence, and he's a good old boy from Arkansas. As soon as he sees us, he gets a shocked look on his face and says, "Dang, I can't believe I'm picking you two boys up this early! What in the hell happened out there?"

Boarding the boat with our stuffed turtles, Tex replies, "This here's the last stop on our cruise Wally, and wouldn't you know it. The both of us knuckleheads done plum forgot to get our ladies something back at Pearl. You know how girls love stuffed animals and all, so we figured these two would do just nicely. What do you think Wally?"

"Hell Tex, I'm a glad you brought that up. I done plum forgot too! Them there turtles are awful damn cute. I think the girls will love them. In fact, I think I'll get me one for my wife Sally. Whereabouts did you boys get them?"

"We got them from a street vendor Wally. If you walk down the main drag you'll find him."

"Well I'll do just that when I get off duty. So, you guys ready to drop your draws for the Chief Master at Arms? If you aint, I suggest you throw it overboard now or suffer the consequences."

"We're good Wally. Thanks for the heads up anyway," I reply.

Wally pulls alongside the ship and I go up the cargo net first. Once I'm onboard, Tex tosses me the turtles. Then he climbs aboard. We salute the officer of the deck. Then the scumbag Chief Master at Arms orders us to strip. As we're taking off our clothes, the chief shakes and squeezes the turtles. They pass his inspection and so do we. We're home free baby! Mamasan knew what the fuck she was doing! This is a good sign I'll get my delivery at Pearl.

Tex and I stash the turtles in our lockers. Then we take a shower and change clothes before heading back out on liberty. This way, the Chief Master at Arms doesn't think we're just dropping off the turtles. Now that we can relax, Tex and I start having a great time bar hopping. We settle in with a couple of Thai cuties around 11 PM. These are some kinky little bitches too. They toss each other's salad doggie style and then beg us to fuck them in the ass. What a cute little pair of cum catchers!

The next day, we see Chen again and he offers to take us to Bangkok. It's only sixty miles away, so we say sure. What a rip-roaring time Chen shows us when we get there. Luckily, we don't have to report back to the ship the next day, so we spend another full day fucking and partying. Chen knows places off the beat and path to watch Thailand's infamous Muay Thai fights. Everybody seems to know Chen, so we feel welcomed. The fighters are absolutely incredible! Some of the fights are extremely brutal and bloody. Chen knows what fighters to bet on too, so we all make some money. Late that night Chen drops us off at the pier and we exchange contact info. Chen is one cool guy, and Tex and I will both miss him. We promised to one day see him again.

We pull up anchor to a beautiful fiery sunrise, and then off we sail towards Pearl. We have a long way to go, almost seven thousand miles. There's a rumor we may stop in Manila, so we weren't exactly sure how long it would be until we get home. First night out at sea we break into one of the turtles. We take out the sticks and toss the turtle overboard. We take Rasta Man and Murray out on the fantail for a midnight treat. This shit makes us so fucking high that in the middle of a conversation you can nod off into a fucking dream state. When you come back out of your dream world, you don't remember leaving the real world! Then crazily, somehow you will pick up your conversation right where you left off! The four of us slowly put the word out. By morning, Tex and I have to break into the other turtle. Everyone is so fucking amazed that we had the balls to smuggle them onboard! The stoner's on the ship are ecstatic they didn't leave Thailand without getting any Thai sticks! Tex and Droz came through! Of course, Tex and I kept quiet about our smuggling scheme.

Halfway to Pearl Harbor I'm called over the PA system to report to the Captain's cabin. Oh fucking shit! My mind starts racing a mile a minute! What the fuck is this about? It can't be good news, that's for fucking sure. Did somebody aboard get caught with Thai sticks and turn rat? Did the Captain receive a radio message from the authorities in one of the countries Tex and I did something really bad in? Or is it because half of the fucking crew is walking around like fucking zombies and the Captain found out I'm to blame! I knew it had to be one of these things, so now I'm really fucking worried, and so is Tex.

All our contraband is well hidden in case we get searched. Tex didn't need me to reassure him that I won't rat on him, but I did anyway. I tuck my shirt in real good and hustle on up there. When I get to his door, my heart starts pounding. I take a deep breath and knock. "Come in," the Captain says in a calm voice. I open the door, stand at attention and salute the captain saying, "Seamen Drosdowich reporting as ordered sir."

"Stand at ease Droz."

He calls me Droz. That's a good sign, I think to myself, but he looks really sad for some reason. There's an eerie silence before he speaks. "Droz, I've always liked you. You're what I call a throwback to the sailors of old. You're a great seaman. You love chasing skirts and you're as tough as fucking nails. You're going to need every bit of that toughness son for what I'm about to tell you. Both of your parents were killed in a car accident back in Florida."

My heart skips a beat and then falls right through the floor. My eyes cloud up as I stand there frozen in time. The Captain pulls out a bottle of scotch and a couple of shot glasses. He asks me to sit down as he pours us both a drink. We down our shots and the Captain quickly pours another while I bravely ask, "Do you know what caused the car accident Captain?"

The Captain downs his second shot before replying solemnly, "Sorry son. They didn't supply me with any details. You'll miss the funeral and there's nothing I can do about it. What I can do though is put you through immediately for a hardship discharge. This way you can go home and get together with whatever family you got left and then try to put your life back on course. If that don't work out for you and you want back in, I will help you with that too. There are no words to ease your sorrow son, but remember this, time heals all wounds." After the Captain says those words he pours us both one more shot. We both stand up and down it. Then Wild Bill hugs me like a son. He tells me I can call on him for advice any time after I get out. With tears streaming down my face, I salute Wild Bill. Then I about face and leave his cabin. When

I get outside the door, I'm devastated. I feel terribly alone. It's still during the workday, so I quietly walk to my duty station and pick up painting where I left off. I couldn't keep the tears back. Tex's duty section is right next to mine. He sees me crying and immediately walks over to me asking, "Droz, I know you aint crying because you got in trouble. So what in the hell happened up there?"

I suck up my tears and say, "The Captain said my parents were both killed in a car accident."

Tex bows his head and then looks me straight in the eyes saying, "You know I know how this feels Droz. I'm telling you now, you'll get through it. My grandmother helped me and I will help you. Let's go out on the fantail and say the prayer she taught me after my folks took their lives."

We both put down our paintbrushes and walk back to the fantail to pray. Looking out over the ocean Tex teaches me the Serenity Prayer. "God grant me the serenity to accept the things I cannot change; courage to change the things I can; and wisdom to know the difference."

Word must have spread because before long half the crew joins us on the fantail. Everyone is expressing their deepest sympathies. As bad as I'm feeling, I can only imagine how worse it would be without my shipmates supporting me.

GOING HOME...

When we pull into Pearl Harbor Tex takes control of the entire slushing and weed business. If and when the Thai sticks come through, Tex knew with the help of Keoni he will have no problem unloading them. I ask Tex, if he can, to mail me a hundred sticks to share with Johnny and Willie. Our slushing business grew from the initial five thousand dollars I started with to well over twenty thousand. Tex and I made a pretty penny for ourselves on that cruise, and if the Thai sticks come through, we're on easy street for quite a while.

The Captain sticks to his word about my hardship discharge. All of my separation papers are ready for me upon my arrival at Pearl. With all of the money I made on the cruise, I refuse the military's itinerary and fly home first class. Tex will be discharged soon. After a quick stop at his grandma's in Texas, he will fly to South Florida to live with me. We talk about getting his grandma out of her trailer and buying her a condo somewhere near us.

When we hit the Bounty Club, Keoni knew we were coming. He greets us with a big smile and open arms shouting, "Aloha my friends! We have all missed you! Come on in! Keanu has prepared a feast for us!" The three of us exchange hugs and walk into the dining area. When Lei sees Tex, she runs up to him and jumps into his big arms. As they both exchange smooches, I quietly say to Keoni, "I received some really bad news out at sea Keoni. Both of my parents were killed in a car accident back home."

Stunned and saddened, Keoni replies, "You have my deepest sympathies Droz. If there is anything my family can do, just ask."

"There's nothing anybody can do Keoni, but thanks for asking. The Captain got me a hardship discharge, so I'm going home a free man."

"You know you are more than welcome to stay here Droz and work with my family."

"I appreciate that Keoni and I hope that door is always open for me, but right now I need to go home and see what gives with everything my father left behind. By the way, where's Keona?"

Keoni looks at me with half a smile replying, "Unfortunately Droz, I have more bad news. When you were gone fadda set her up with a very well established older Hawaiian man. She told me to tell you that right now she cannot embarrass him or fadda by seeing you. If she came to work tonight, she knows what would happen. I have many employees and some of them know this man very well."

My face drops, my heart drops, and my cock shrivels up. I even tear up a bit. Now I wonder if Teresa Sue is going steady with someone too. Fuck it. There aint no use in worrying about it. Keoni sees I'm hurting, so he puts his arm around me and consoles me. Then he says, "Not to worry brah. I know my sista still loves you. Let her satisfy fadda for a while. Soon she will act sad and depressed all the time in front of the family. Madda and tutu will make fadda miserable and let Keona break up with him. In the meantime you go home and do what you need to do."

With a stiff upper lip I reply, "I understand Keoni. You tell her I love her too. I'll give you all my contact information. You guys can call me anytime. Also, I was hoping you can ship me a pound of Pakalolo each month. Is that cool?"

"No problem braddah. I will make you up a special Hawaiian package every month. I will also give you all of my family's contact information."

"Thanks Keoni. Tex will pay you in advance for the first few shipments."

"That will work for me Droz. Enough of business talk. Let's eat, drink and how you haoles say, be merry?"

I fake a laugh and hug Keoni. Then I ask, "I'll also need like a quarter pound to tide me over. Do you think you could seal it up in a way that it doesn't stink up the whole fucking plane?"

"Of course I can Droz. I have done this many times over the years and for many people. I will have it ready for you before you leave."

"I appreciate it Keoni. At least when I get home I'll have a piece of Hawaii with me to share with others."

"Ahh, nothing like spreading the spirit of aloha," Keona cheerfully replies.

The rest of the night, we spend doing just that. I tried my best on the outside to look happy, but inside I'm dying. I'm surrounded by friends, but feel terribly alone.

The next morning I make my travel arrangements. After they are set, I call Johnny. Johnny is happy to hear my voice. He does his best to try to console me. He tells me about all of the good things I have to look forward to. He says his mom and dad are waiting for me with open arms. I give Johnny my flight schedule and ask him to pick me up at Ft. Lauderdale Airport around eight o'clock Sunday morning. Johnny says he don't park, so he tells me to wait outside the terminal for him to pick me up. I say cool. The next day, Tex and I tie up any loose ends with the business. Then I pack my duffle bag and roll a few joints for the plane ride. Keoni actually picks us up on time to go to the airport. My quarter pound is about the size of a book and wrapped as a gift. You can't smell a thing. On the way to the airport, we toked up real good on Keoni's special pakalolo. When we get there, we're fucking toast! We say emotional goodbyes, and I head to the gate with tears in my eyes.

First class is nice. I mean real nice. My duffle bag squeezes in nicely up above me. I love my big comfy chair and fat arm rests. Drinks are served as soon as we takeoff. After downing a few cocktails, I stretch out to watch a movie and doze off. By the time I awake, we are landing in LA. I grab my connecting flight and cozy up in first class again. After we take off, I drink a couple of straight vodka's, and then head to the bathroom to get high. When I get back to my seat, I'm served a five-course meal. The people are all a bit snobby, so I keep to myself and watch movies. When I get bored, I sleep. The booze, the weed, and the food make it easy. This time I am awakened by the captain's voice over the intercom saying we had a tail wind and made great time. When we land, I jump up first and grab my duffle bag. I throw it over my shoulder and dart off the plane. I can't wait to see Johnny and I'm hoping he brought Willie with him. When I get outside, there's no Johnny. My flight arrived a little early, so I sit on top of my duffle bag and patiently wait for him. After about ten minutes, a black Lincoln Town Car pulls up to the curb with dark tinted windows. The passenger window rolls down and the trunk pops open. To my surprise, Johnny aint driving. A much older man is with short black hair and green eyes. He's casually dressed and strongly built. In a Brooklyn Italian accent he says, "Hey kid, put your duffle bag in my trunk and hop in the car. When you close the trunk, make sure you do it nice and easy. It catches a latch and close's itself automatically. But you got to be gentle, Capisce?"

What a fucking character this guy is, but who the fuck is he and where's Johnny? I casually look to my left and then I casually look to my right. Then I stare straight at this guy and bluntly say, "Listen pal, I don't want to be disrespectful or anything. But, who the fuck are you and where's my friend Johnny?"

The man genuinely laughs at me and replies, "Relax kid. Johnny's at home. I'm his uncle. Rocco Santori."

Without saying another word, I put my duffle bag into his trunk and make extra special sure to close it gently. I quickly get in his car and humbly say, "Thank you for picking me up Mr. Santori. I'm sorry for being gruff, but I was expecting Johnny. When he didn't show I figured something went wrong and you could be part of it."

Rocco waves his hand replying, "Perfectly understandable kid. You did the right thing. You never know what my nephew could have been caught up in. First off Michael, let me offer you my deepest condolences for your tremendous loss. I never had the pleasure of meeting your mother, but your father was a man amongst men. He will truly be missed. Second, please call me Rocco."

"You knew my father?" I reply shocked.

"Of course I knew your father!" Rocco cheerfully replies. I glow inside knowing Rocco Santori really respected my father. Rocco continues, "What happened to your parents was an absolute tragedy."

"Do you know what caused the accident Rocco?" I sadly ask.

Rocco takes a deep breath and uncomfortably says, "They were driving home from dinner and some old man in the opposite lane had a heart attack. The old guy veered into oncoming traffic and hit your parent's car head on. There was nothing anyone could do. Your mom and dad died on impact."

I start balling like a baby. Rocco reaches into his back pocket and hands me a handkerchief. He puts his arm around me to console me and says, "Let it out son. Cry all you want. It's important to grieve." After a good cry, Rocco rubs me on the head and jovially asks, "How about we go get some breakfast? I know a great little diner that serves up the best breakfast in South Florida. So what do you say kid?"

Rocco's enthusiasm starts making me feel better, so I smile and reply, "That's a great idea Rocco. I'd love some breakfast."

"That's good. You got to eat Michael."

We drive off. When we get to the diner, the waitress knows Rocco by name. She's a middle-aged woman with blue eyes and curly red hair. It may have been dyed, but who cares, the broad was pretty. A little bottom heavy, but I like that. She sits us down at a booth by the window and pours us some hot coffee. Rocco likes his coffee the same way I do, black with two sugars. Rocco stirs his without the spoon hitting the sides of the cup, so I mimic him. He raises his cup to his lips, takes a sip without making a slurping sound and then asks, "Good coffee, hey kid?"

I quietly take a sip too and then reply, "It sure is Rocco. A lot better than what we got on the ship that's for sure."

"Well kid, from here on out everything is going to get better for you. You don't know it yet, but that deal you set up with Willie's family has grown in many different ways for me. You know what that means right?"

"Hopefully it means that it's grown many different ways for me too."

"You're exactly right. It has, and it will continue growing for the both of us."

The waitress comes back to our table smiling and asks, "I know you don't order off the menu Rocco. So what are you in a mood for this morning?"

"I'll tell you what Mable. I'll have an omelet cooked soft, with ham, bacon, and cheddar cheese. Also, throw in a side of those wonderful homemade breakfast potatoes, and two lightly toasted English muffins."

Mable writes it all down. Then she smiles at me and asks, "How about you son, what would you like this morning?"

"That sounded delicious. Give me the same thing Mable."

The food came out fast and it is delicious. It's so good we don't even bother to talk while we're eating. Expect for the occasional with your mouth full, "Mmm that's good." After another cup of coffee, Mable brings out the check. I reach for it and Rocco slaps my hand saying, "Just like your father. It was always a fight to pick up the check, but I'm your senior son, so back off. There are too many people with deep pockets and alligator arms. Your father wasn't one of them, and neither am I."

I chuckle and nod my head. Rocco pays the check leaving Mable a big tip and we leave. As we're driving away Rocco says, "I have a condo about a half an hour from here; it will be a good place to talk. This may come as surprise Michael, but I already know a lot about you."

I look at Rocco and then back at the road before replying sarcastically, "Well if you know a lot about me Rocco, you would know to call me Droz."

Rocco snickers at my sarcasm and quickly replies back with his own, "Where should I start Droz? How about back in Yonkers with your friend Shayne? Or maybe we can talk about you and Tex's rampage through Australia? You guys got a little sloppy in Esperance, but overall things went pretty well for you, right? That story might take too long though. Wait, I know. We'll start with your favorite person in the whole wide world, Keoki in Hawaii."

Rocco definitely has my attention now, so I ask in a serious tone, "What do you know about Keoki?"

Without taking his eyes off the road Rocco replies, "The Yakuza should have known who they were fucking with. Before they sent them yoyos to try to shake him down the way they did. Like those street thugs in the Philippines should have known who they were fucking with, meaning you and Tex."

This is beyond fucking belief! How in the fuck does Rocco know this shit! Rocco sees me quietly staring out at the road ahead. Using a cutting tone, he now asks, "What's the matter Droz? Cat got your tongue? Or are you just fresh out of sarcastic comebacks?"

Not knowing what to say, I sit there quietly staring at the road. Seeing I'm subdued by his uncanny knowledge of my past, Rocco calmly says, "Take a deep breath kid. You're about to enter into a whole new life."

Rocco pulls up to the guard gate of a brand new building right on the ocean. The guard recognizes Rocco and quickly opens the gate. He backs his Lincoln into a reserved parking spot near an exit. We get out of the car and walk over to the elevator. Inside the elevator, Rocco pushes the button for the penthouse and asks, "Did you like sailing across the oceans in the Navy?"

My eyes light up as I reply, "I fucking loved it Rocco. In fact, I miss it. There's nothing like being out in the middle of the ocean under the stars alone with your thoughts."

Rocco seems to reflect for a moment before saying, "That's living kid, and don't let anybody tell you any different. I love the ocean too. We'll go out on my boat one day. I also love living down here on the beach. I get up every morning at the crack of dawn and take a five-mile walk. Well, when I'm in town anyway."

The elevator door opens, and as we are exiting I ask, "How old are you Rocco?"

Rocco puts his key in the lock replying, "Fifty years old kid, I'm half way home."

"Don't take this the wrong way Rocco. I aint no fag or nothing, but you look pretty damn good for your age."

"Thanks kid, and for the record, I know you aint no fag."

"So I guess that means you know about Angelina and Keona too?"

"Not only them Droz, but I also know about Teresa Sue. I've known her father for years. Not for nothing, she's prettier than both of them. I hear she's been dating some football hero up at Wake Forest."

With a wise ass smirk on my face, I cockily reply back, "So fucking be it Rocco, and my little fucking princess in Hawaii is dating some rich asshole. Let me tell you something, I aint the fucking jealous type. I care, but I don't fucking care, if you know what I mean. When they see me again their little fucking hearts will flutter and run right fucking back to me."

Rocco smiles and pats me on the back saying, "It's good to see a man who isn't ruled by jealousy. Way too many are."

We are talking so much I didn't notice what's right in front of me. Sliding glass doors leading to a wraparound balcony with a panoramic view of the ocean and the Intracoastal Waterway!

"This place is the deal Rocco! You mind if I go out on the balcony and take a look?" I turn to Rocco and ask.

"Of course not kid. You go check out the view while I go take a piss."

I open up one of the sliding glass doors and walk out onto the balcony. The view is absolutely stunning! It's a clear and sunny day, so you can see for miles in every direction. I take a deep breath of ocean air and think to myself, "I want a place like this."

Rocco's voice breaks me out of my daydreaming. "Come on in the living room kid. We got a lot to talk about. Leave the patio door open. I love the smell of the ocean and I always get a nice breeze up this high."

"Okay Rocco," I eagerly reply.

When I walk into the living room, I can't help but notice the pictures of his family hanging on the wall. Rocco sees me looking and before he can speak I say, "Johnny already told me what happened to your wife and son." Rocco bows his head and solemnly says, "The loss of my wife hurt me deeply Michael, but nothing can hurt a man more than the loss of a child. My son's death by overdose is part of my reason for bringing you up here." Rocco takes a moment to reflect and then asks me to sit down with him. I oblige and he continues. "I know my nephew said some things to you about me and what I do, so before we move forward I would like to teach you some history about what I will ask you to be part of. You are an incredibly intelligent young man. In fact, your test scores point to genius, so you shouldn't have any problems comprehending what I'm about to tell you. I just ask you let me finish before you ask questions, capisce?"

"Capisce Rocco."

"Good. In the mid 1800's the term Mafia came from a Sicilian-Arabic slang expression that means, 'Acting as a protector against the arrogance of the powerful.' The word Mafioso did not refer to someone who was a criminal, but rather a person who was suspicious of central authority. Unfortunately, over time leadership became corrupt and drunk with power. They started extorting money from their own people and dealing in narcotics. Some true Mafiosos decided to flee to America. They became patriotic and proudly fought for this country during World War 1. In 1924, Congress promised each veteran $1.25 for every day they served overseas, and $1 for each day served in the states. There was a catch though; fucking Congress said that we don't have to pay you until 1945. Well, lo and behold, the Great Depression hit. Now all of these veterans were out of a job and couldn't feed their families, so they marched on Washington. The newspapers called them the Bonus Army. Well over 15,000 veterans and their families camped out in various places close to the White House. They made shelters out of things left in an old junk pile. On June 17th, the Senate defeated the bill to pay them in a lopsided vote. The vets stayed in protest hoping that President Hoover would help. Former President Calvin Coolidge and prominent citizens like Henry Ford advised Hoover not to give in to the veterans. No one cared about their fate. On July 28th, 1932, America died. First the Washington Police tried to get rid of the veterans. When the local cops were met with resistance, they gunned down two veterans right in front of their wife and kids. Seeing that the local police couldn't do a thing, President Hoover ordered the army to clear them all out. The disgraceful task was given to Chief of Staff General Douglas the scumbag Macarthur. This prick called out the Infantry, the Calvary, and six fucking tanks to disperse the unarmed heroes of WW1. Major George the fucking traitor Patton led the cavalry. By dinnertime, troops were lined up and down Pennsylvania Ave. Thousands of Civil Service employees left work to watch. The veterans were really fucking naïve Droz. They thought that the military was there to honor their asses, so they cheered the sons of bitches. Then suddenly, Patton's Calvary turned and charged. The crowd watching was stunned and appalled by this hideous act of cowardice. They all began yelling, 'Shame! Shame! Shame!' They booed the troops as loud as they could, but it was to no avail. Next, soldiers with fixed bayonets took control of the streets hurling tear gas into the crowd of protesters. Our brave American heroes who survived being gassed by the German Army over in Europe were now being gassed again by their own army on their own soil.

"By nightfall, the protesting veterans had retreated across the Anacostia River. At this point President Hoover ordered General Macarthur to leave them alone, but the scumbag ignored it. Macarthur then led his infantry to the veteran's main camp where their families all were. By early morning, the 15,000 plus veterans along with their wives and kids were routed. Macarthur ordered his men to torch the camp destroying what little possessions that the veterans and their families had left. Two babies were killed and all of the nearby hospitals were soon overwhelmed with casualties. Both military and civilian men, on both sides of the conflict, swore on that very day that this would never happen again. From the ashes of our government's shame, the old Mafia was reborn. The Mafia, Michael, was never made up of all Italians. It is made up of people from every walk of life on this planet, people who are willing to risk their life and their liberty for common goals. Now you may ask questions."

I'm fucking stunned; I never would have imagined anything like this! So I have to ask, "Is this really fucking true Rocco? Our president ordered Macarthur and Patton to lead troops against our own veterans?"

"Well it's not common knowledge Michael. You surely aren't going to learn about it in school, but sadly, it's true.

I nod my head and now ask, "Tell me Rocco. How did things get to where they are today? All the things you hear or read about the Mafia are bad. Back then you guys sounded like good guys."

"Good Mafioso men weren't the only ones to immigrate to America Droz. A lot of bad ones did too. All Mafiosos, good and bad, made a fortune during prohibition. After it was repealed, the bad ones revved up their narcotics business. People like my father and the men spawned from the Bonus Army travesty went a different route. We only put some of our money into traditional organized crime enterprises like gambling, loan sharking, and unions. What we did with the majority of our fortune from prohibition was much wiser. We used it to gain a foothold into politics and our judicial system. Soon we were able to put the right people into the right places to serve our needs. We also began investing in large corporations both American and foreign. The other factions tried to do the same, but because their business was narcotics most corporations, judges, and politicians turned their backs on them. That's the part of The Godfather movie that rings most true. The Godfather said that the drug business would destroy them, and he was right. What he failed to point out was the drugs they were peddling would also addict and kill their own children."

Listening attentively, I nod my head agreeing. Then I inquisitively ask, "So how does the drug dealing factions of the Mafia survive? It sounds like you hold all the cards Rocco."

Rocco rocks his head from side to side and then replies, "Not all of them Droz. Unfortunately, our Government is also our worst enemy. They fund and protect scumbag rat fucking drug dealers all over the world."

Shocked hearing this, I interrupt asking, "Really Rocco, our own Government funds and protects drug dealers? Why would they do that? Last time I checked they were putting them in jail."

Rocco laughs at me and says, "You've got a lot to learn kid. The only large narcotics traffickers going to jail are the ones not working for them. The government uses the money from their drug dealing to fund illegal wars, political coups, arms dealing, and the assassinations of innocent people. The welfare of the American people doesn't matter one bit to our government unless it's election time. Otherwise, it's all about accomplishing their agenda. Our government creates wars for private profit only poor people fight. They tax you for everything and give you back a false sense of security. They allow the big drug companies to poison you and hook you on drugs. Instead, they should be giving us natural cures that exist all over the world."

Flabbergasted by everything I'm hearing, I say, "I am naïve Rocco. I would never have dreamt the things you just told me were true. I have no reason to doubt you. It will be an honor to help you. What would you like me to do?"

Rocco nods his head and says, "Ten years ago I would have never predicted two things. First, cocaine would become such a huge epidemic in this country. Second, South Florida would become the epicenter for its distribution. There are several Mafia families relocating down here to get into the construction business with my brother Angelo. Whoever gets involved with my brother knows they will be killed if caught dealing narcotics. I know it was somebody close to me importing the heroin that killed my son Bobby. I'm shocked no one turned him over to me for a favor. There's a fine line between loyalty and greed. This person's greed will not let them resist the opportunity in South Florida for cashing in on the cocaine trade, so this is what I need you to do for me Droz. I want you to hang out with Johnny's crew and get close to them. Then let me know if any of them are dealing cocaine. I know some of them may go it alone to make some extra cash, but others may be part of the bigger picture. I want you to report everything you find out to me no matter how small. It might lead us somewhere much bigger. It takes a small fish to catch a bigger one."

I am absolutely fucking appalled by what Rocco just asked me to do! I stare him straight in his fucking eyes and say angrily, "Listen Rocco, I thought you did your fucking homework on me. If you did you would have learned that Droz don't fucking rat, capisce?"

Now I start pacing back and forth like a lion in a cage. Rocco watches me pace for a while and then calmly says, "Sit down kid; you're starting to bother me."

I give Rocco a dirty look and reluctantly sit down as far away from him as I can get. Rocco now gives me a really mean look in return and bluntly says, "Quit being a drama queen. If I thought you were a fucking rat I wouldn't associate myself with you. So are you going to do this for me or not?"

Everything inside of me is screaming to swallow my pride and become Rocco's rat! "Sure Rocco, I'll help you, but I got to ask. With all of the fucking people you know in this world, why in the fuck did you pick me?"

Rocco stands up and proudly replies, "Why you Droz? I'll tell you why you. You got the two things money can't buy and I can't teach, balls and instincts. You show me loyalty, and I'll open up doors for you in this world you never dreamt existed."

"What kind of doors are we talking about Rocco?" I ambitiously ask.

Rocco grins like he has me in the palm of his hand and then replies, "Do as I ask, stay loyal, and you'll find out."

With that said Rocco extends his hand. I extend mine. Rocco grips my hand like a fucking vice and pulls me towards him. Staring deeply into my eyes, he says, "You are Georgey Droz's son; you have a lot to live up to." Rocco slowly let's go of his grip and hugs me. I hug him back, hoping he will fill the emptiness I feel in my heart by my father's death. When we sit back down on the sofa together I ask, "What about Johnny Rocco? Will he know what's going on?"

"No, and you must never tell him or anyone else. If there are things we share I want anyone else to know, I'll tell you. Everything else we talk about is to be kept between us. As long as you do exactly as I say I will protect you, and no jail will ever hold you."

"One important thing Rocco and it's not negotiable. I want my friend Tex to help me."

Rocco lets out a roar of a laugh and says, "I got to love it! You're just like your father! Loyal to a fucking fault! I know all about your friend Tex. So yes, you can tell Tex anything you see fit. Speaking of your father Michael, he didn't have to stay being a fireman. Georgey Droz had all of the money he wanted. Your father stayed being a fireman because he wanted to give back to his community and save lives."

Rocco gets up now and walks into his bedroom. When he returns he is holding a large manila envelope and carrying a black briefcase. Rocco sits down next to me and opens the manila envelope. As he's taking out papers, he starts explaining them to me. "Droz, here is all of the paperwork that legally gives you your father's estate. I changed all of the locks on your house and here are the new keys. Here are the two keys to your father's safety deposit box and these are the combinations to his floor safes. When you open those floor safes, you will see I'm right. Your father wasn't only a great man Michael, but a humble man as well."

Overwhelmed by all of this, I ask Rocco, "What about my brother and sister? And how did you do all of this without me?"

"As far as your brother and sister are concerned, they are more than happy with their settlement. How I did it without you Michael has to do with one of those doors."

I nod my head smiling and reply, "I'll play my part for you Rocco, and I'll be loyal. After I prove myself worthy I'll be looking forward to what you promised me about them doors."

Rocco places his hand on my shoulder saying, "I know I will never be able to replace your father Michael, but I want you to know from now on I'm here for you. Whether it's a problem with what you have been asked to do for me, or something personal. I will do everything in my power to help you, teach you, and console you."

With those words, I hug Rocco like I would have hugged my father. Whether I am being naïve to believe Rocco or not, I wanted too, and that's all that matters. Now Rocco says, "It's time for you to start getting settled, so let me take you home." As we are heading out the door Rocco pauses and says, "Hey kid, aren't you forgetting something?"

I think for a second replying, "No, I don't think so Rocco. I got my paper work and my keys."

"What about your briefcase?"

"You didn't tell me the briefcase was mine."

"I got it for you to put your important papers in."

"Oh cool, thank you Rocco."

I open the briefcase to put my papers in and I'm floored by what I see. It's loaded with stacks of hundred dollar bills! I look up at Rocco and say, "I think you gave me the wrong briefcase."

"That's your cut so far from the business I've been doing with Willie's family. Tonight at your father's club, Johnny's crew will have envelopes for you too."

As we're leaving the building, I think to myself, "I got the world by the fucking balls!" When we get into the car, I ask Rocco the question, "What's up with all of you wise guys moving down here to Florida? I mean let's face it Rocco, Coral Springs is in the middle of fucking nowhere."

Rocco smiles and replies with a sparkle in his eye, "That's what you think. It's actually situated in the middle of everything. Coral Springs is less than an hour from downtown Miami. It is only a half hour from downtown Ft. Lauderdale and the Ft. Lauderdale International Airport. We are also about a half hour from Deerfield Beach, Pompano Beach, Lauderdale by the Sea, and Ft. Lauderdale Beach. Large corporations like Westinghouse, Burroughs, and IBM are all expanding here creating great jobs. Jobs mean growth and growth means money. I caught wind of this place back in the early sixties from a corporate big wig who owed me a favor. I had put the word out that I was looking to build a city. Not just any city, but a prototype city for families to bring their kids up in. I wanted it to be a clean, safe place. A place with little or no crime and no fucking drugs. Make strict building codes to insure people's property values. Build great schools and lots of parks for the kids to play in. Your Cuban friend Willie and his family have been a tremendous help getting us those containers of building supplies. Willie's father explained to me how he is helping his people back in Cuba who are being oppressed by Castro. I have decided to join him in his humanitarian mission. Working together, we are making sure that the Cuban people receive necessary medicines, clothes, food, money, and other items they so desperately need to survive. While the Cuban people suffer under Castro's dictatorship the American Government does nothing. In fact they make matters worse."

"Damn Rocco! Chalk up another fucked up thing our government is doing!"

On the rest of the way home I make Rocco tell me stories about my father and the things they did together. When we pull up to my house there's a Lincoln Town Car that looks just like Rocco's parked in my driveway. "Is someone staying at the house?" I ask.

"It's yours kid. Consider it a bonus. The keys and title are in my glove box," Rocco nonchalantly says.

Slowly shaking my head back and forth, I open Rocco's glove box. I pull out an envelope finding a set of keys and a title with my name on it. I stare at my new Lincoln and turn to Rocco saying, "I just met you Rocco and you have already given me a small fortune."

"You earned it kid. Now earn my trust by doing as I ask and staying loyal."

"You will never regret trusting me Rocco," I confidently reply.

"I believe you Michael. Now go get some rest. Johnny will be over before dark to take you to your father's club; well, I should say your club now. Your father's two best friends, Billy and Georgie, will go over the splits with you."

Before I get out of the car, Rocco gives me his phone number and says, "I will be in touch with you one way or another when I need you. You can call me anytime. Use common sense over the phones and when leaving any messages, capisce?"

"I capisce Rocco, or how about I call you Uncle Rocco?"

Rocco chuckles before replying, "Whatever you want kid. Just remember from now on everyone will be jealous of our relationship. Some of my people will even hate you for it. Calling me Uncle Rocco in front of them is entirely up to you."

"Well I guess they'll just have to get over it Uncle Rocco."

Rocco chuckles again as we both get out of the car for a goodbye hug. Rocco pops open the trunk and I grab my stuff. He gets back into his Lincoln and tells me he'll see me tonight at the club. I put down my duffle bag and put my key in the door. He doesn't leave until he makes sure I get inside. It sure is an eerie feeling walking into my parent's house after they died. Everything is sparkling clean. I put down my stuff and walk into my father's den. His firemen's hat is hanging on the wall next to framed newspaper clippings of his heroics back in Yonkers. The smoky smell of the hat permeates the room. My emotions overwhelm me, dropping me to my knees. I begin crying like a baby. Suddenly a warm glow encompasses me. In my heart, I know it's my father's spirit comforting me. His presence leaves me feeling loved and protected. Physically and emotionally drained, I take a shower and jump into my parent's bed for some much needed sleep.

FIRST NIGHT AT THE CLUB...

I sleep long and deep in the comfort of my parent's bed. When I crawl out from under the sheets, it's almost dark. Johnny will be here soon. I dig into my duffle bag for clothes, get dressed, and head into the kitchen. Anything in the refrigerator must have gone bad by now, So I hold my breath and look inside. What a surprise, it's full of fresh groceries! Rocco thought of everything! I make myself a ham and cheese sandwich with mustard, grab a cold one, and sit down at the breakfast table to eat. As soon as I'm done scarfing down my sandwich, the doorbell rings. I rush over to the window to take a peek, and sure as shit, it's Johnny! I quickly open the door and we both yell out each other's names. Then we hug and kiss. I take a step back to get a good look at him and invite him in. Once inside my house, I exclaim, "Look at you, you cocksucker. Mr. G fucking Q!"

Johnny smiles proudly while grabbing both collars of his freshly pressed designer shirt, and replies cockily, "Yeah well, you know me Droz. I got an image to keep up. Speaking of images, I can see you're still keeping up yours too, wearing old jeans and wife beater tee shirt."

"I'm comfortable."

"Looks like the Navy did you good Droz. You look leaner and meaner than ever.

"Thanks Johnny. You look pretty damn fit yourself. Take a seat while I go get some buds."

As I'm walking back to my room, Johnny keeps talking. "I eat like fucking crazy, but I can't gain a fucking pound. The old man's working me like a fucking dog down here. I've learned a lot about building houses, and pretty soon I'll have my contractor's license."

I walk back into the living room and sit down next to Johnny. As I'm breaking up some weed I say, "Well that's good fucking news Johnny. Looking at that fat gold and diamond Rolex on your fucking wrist, I guess you're pulling down serious bread."

"I definitely am Droz, but it's all fucking relative."

I finish rolling the joint and hand it to Johnny along with a lighter. As he puts the flame to the tip I ask, "What the fuck you mean its relative?"

Johnny takes a hit off the joint and replies in a gargled voice, "I spend it as fast as I'm making it, sometimes faster. I love this fucking weed Droz. Willie and I are fucking hooked on it. Do you think you'll be able to get more?"

I take a big hit and hold it in as long as I can before replying, "I don't think it'll be a problem Johnny. I made good friends with the right Hawaiians."

I pass Johnny the joint and walk into the kitchen to grab some beers. When I'm walking back to the living room Johnny asks, "I guess you were surprised I didn't pick you up from the airport."

I hand Johnny a beer and sit down. I take a slug and say, "You can say that again. I actually got a little rude with your uncle before I knew who he was."

Johnny laughs and passes me back the joint. He takes a slug of beer and then replies back irritated, "Yeah well, I had no fucking choice in the matter. My father told me the night before my uncle wanted to pick you up. There must be a good fucking reason Droz, so what gives?"

I pick up on Johnny's tone and choose my words wisely before replying. "Everything's cool Johnny. He took me to breakfast and then over to his condo. What a fucking view! I wouldn't mind owning a condo like that myself someday."

Johnny takes another slug of beer before saying slyly, "With the money you're fucking making with my uncle I bet you can already buy one. How much fucking cake he give you?"

"I don't really know Johnny. I haven't counted it yet. How much cake did your old man give you?" I bluntly reply.

Johnny quickly realizes it aint his business, so he checks himself before saying, "I'm sorry Droz; it's none of my fucking business. I'm just pissed with myself for spending all my dough and gambling so much. Bennie the Bookie moved down here from Brooklyn and he's handling everybody's action. I'm into this Jewish prick for sixty large this week and I only have thirty. My old man has tons of closings coming up, but none before I have to pay. If my old man finds out I came up short with Bennie, he'll put me on a fucking allowance. That will be too fucking embarrassing for me. I hate to ask Droz, but can you bail me out? I'll pay you back in a few weeks. I'll even give you a vig if you want it."

I take a hit off the joint and a slug of beer. I hand the joint back to Johnny replying, "Sure Johnny. I'll lend you 30 G's without a vig. Do you want it now?"

"Thanks Droz. You're saving me a ton of fucking embarrassment. Sure, I'll take it now and pay the Jew bastard tomorrow. I'll pay you back as soon as I can."

I finish off my beer and think to myself, "This is a good time to see just how jealous Johnny will get." So I get up and go get the briefcase. I put it on the coffee table and open it. Johnny's jaw drops gazing at the stacks of hundreds his uncle gave me. He looks at me and says, "You took his fucking money Droz. He owns you now. Whatever he asks you to do, you got to do. You know that right?"

"He said I earned it Johnny, but I aint fucking stupid. I know I'm on the hook."

"I'm sure glad you understand because my uncle doesn't play games. So what did he ask you to do?"

Knowing I can't tell Johnny the truth, I smoothly reply, "Nothing yet Johnny, he's just happy about running shit through the Port of Miami with Willie's father."

Johnny nods his head and says, "Willie told me that his old man has been taking care of him better since my Uncle Rocco entered the picture. Let's count up what you got Droz and see how rich you fucking are."

Johnny and I count out forty stacks of hundreds. Each stack contains one hundred 100 dollar bills. That's a cool 400 grand. I hand Johnny three stacks of hundreds. He thanks me and then says sadly, "Not bad Droz, but I made twice as much on the housing alone since you were gone. The only problem is I blew it all."

I consolingly pat Johnny on the back, and then ask, "Give me the low down on my father's club Johnny. I know I'm supposed to see Billy and Georgie. I know all about them, but I don't know their roles at the club, or anything else about the club for that matter. Uncle Rocco also mentioned to me that your guys have money for me. What's up with that?"

Johnny takes a deep breath and unenthusiastically replies, "You're inheriting a fucking gold mine Droz. Your old man's club has great food and a full-blown Vegas style casino. There is also a separate billiard room, and a separate high stakes poker room. I mean, your old man thought of it all. You're one lucky prick you know."

I look at Johnny perplexed. Pointing to my chest, I reply sharply, "I'm lucky Johnny? I don't fucking think so. You still got both of your fucking parents. Mine are dead."

Johnny bows his head and takes in another deep breath. Regretful, he replies. "Forgive me Droz. That was pretty callous of me."

"Yeah it was Johnny. Now finish what you were telling me," I say gruffly.

"Your old man got all of his own people running things at the club. Most of them are retired firemen and policemen from Yonkers. Georgie handles the books while Billy oversees the rest. Billy is a brutal fucking bastard. I heard how he beat the shit out of a few wise guys down here from Brooklyn the first weekend the club opened. Nobody fucks with Billy anymore. He's got a lot of respect from my people."

I laugh replying, "Sorry they found out the hard way Johnny. Billy was known to be the toughest guy in Yonkers. He was my old man's 'Luca Brasi.' Billy never bragged, but Billy didn't have too. Everybody bragged for him. I'll tell you a little story. One night about four in the morning, Billy staggers drunk out of a bar in Yonkers. Three Puerto Ricans see him as an easy mark and try to rob him. One of the Puerto Ricans hits Billy right across the face with a tire iron. Bleeding profusely from his head and face, Billy takes the tire iron from the guy. Then he beats all three of the motherfuckers to death with it. My old man was on duty at the firehouse that night. His cop friends called him up to come hose the blood and brains off the sidewalk. I heard it was a grisly fucking scene. As tough as Billy is, he always said my dad was tougher."

"I don't doubt it Droz. I overheard stories about your old man. They refer to him as 'The Kingfish.'"

I smile and proudly reply, "Yeah, that's what all his friends called him at the firehouse. They engraved a nameplate with the name Kingfish on it and hung it above his locker. Now tell me about your guys Johnny. What should I know about them?"

Johnny shrugs his shoulders and replies, "My people all know the game. They have to kickback a certain percentage to you that was pre-arranged by my Uncle. It's based on how much construction supplies they take from the port. One of my uncle's guys collected for you while you were gone. Now that you're back, it's your job."

"That's cool. I can handle that. What time we have to be at the club?"

"I told my father and uncle we'll be there by seven, so we need to get going."

I put my money back into the briefcase and take it to my room. I grab my keys and we head out the door. Outside I'm absolutely floored by what I see. Johnny's driving a brand new red Mercedes Benz 450sl Convertible with black leather interior. I point to the car and ask, "And I'm lending you money?"

Johnny smiles, opens the trunk, and tosses the cash in. As he gently closes it he points to my Lincoln and sarcastically says, "At least I paid for mine. It's not like some rich uncle gave it to me or something."

I sneer at Johnny as I hop into his Mercedes and then ask, "How far are we away from the club?"

"Not far at all Droz. I'd say less than two miles."

With that said Johnny screeches his tires out of the driveway. On the way to the club, Johnny tells me Uncle Rocco has controlling interests in the two hottest discos in Broward County. He says he will be taking me to them at the end of the week. When we pull into the parking lot, it's full of Cadillacs and Lincolns. The outside of the club is very inconspicuous. It looks like a plain concrete building. "So this is my father's club?" I ask Johnny.

"Yup, my father built your old man just what he wanted. On the outside, it's a plain concrete fortress that won't attract attention and also survive a hurricane. On the inside, it's a first class Vegas style casino. Your old man paid cash for everything too."

We get out of the car and head towards the door where two men are standing. One guy is about six feet tall. He's totally bald and has a big grey Fu Manchu mustache. The other guy is about my size with a potbelly. He has reddish hair and is clean-shaven. His crooked nose tells me he's a retired Irish cop who's been in a lot of fights. As we approach them Johnny asks, "Do you recognize these two, or do I have to introduce you?"

"I don't know either one of them Johnny."

The men immediately recognize Johnny. "Who's your friend Johnny?" The Irish cop asks.

"This is Georgie Droz's son, Michael," Johnny happily replies.

The big guy extends his hand first and says, "You have our deepest condolences Michael. We both loved your father. My name is Ozzie."

The little guy jumps in extending his hand saying, "I'm Mickey. We are both retired policemen. If there's anything you ever need Michael, don't hesitate to ask."

"Thank you guys, I'll keep it in mind. In the meantime, please call me Droz."

"Okay Droz," They both reply and laugh.

Mickey opens the door and I'm astounded at what I see! The place is packed with men just the way my old man liked it. My father never liked bars with women in them. As Pops said, men go to bars to get away from women, not to be with them. I see a huge, beautifully handcrafted wooden bar with three bartenders. One of them is Mahoney, the cop that helped me at school. I don't recognize the others. The smell of tap beer and great food makes me hungry and thirsty. Off the bar is the dining room. Every table is occupied with merry men eating and drinking. Waiters and not waitresses serve the men. I say hello to a busy Mahoney and he too expresses his condolences. Johnny now leads me to a big wooden double door with large brass handles. He knocks twice and to my pleasant surprise, Billy opens the door! Billy's a big brawny dark haired Irishmen. Even with all of the battle scars he has on his face he's still good looking. Like a little kid, I jump into his arms for a hug! Billy laughs heartedly as he hugs me. After the hugs, Billy turns teary eyed and says, "Michael, I don't know what to say. You lost your parents and I lost my best friend. You know I'm here for you. Not just me either, there's Georgie and the rest of the boys too. Consider us all family. This club's yours now too and together we'll make sure to carry on your father's legacy. After you're done with Johnny, I want you to go see Georgie. He'll go over the books with you."

"How perfect," I think to myself, "to have Georgie in charge of the finances." Georgie had the rank of captain in the firehouse. He's a big hearted, funny guy with a ton of brains.

Georgie always let me use the pool table upstairs in the fire-house. That's where I learned to become a pool hustler. The room Billy's guarding does look like a Vegas Casino. There are blackjack tables, roulette wheels, baccarat tables, dice tables, and slot machines. Johnny is quiet watching my facial expressions as I absorb everything in. Looking around the room, I recognize other retired firemen handling the tables and roulette wheels. Everyone starts coming over to me and giving me their condolences. Tough guy after tough guy getting teary eyed when they mention my father's name. Their display of love and respect for my father has me glowing with pride.

Billy now shouts, "It's time for a toast!" He signals the bartenders and waiters. A case of Oban is put on the bar and opened. Shot glasses are passed around to everyone. Rocco Santori and Johnny's father Angelo come out of another room to join in. After the shots are poured, Billy looks up to heaven and shouts, "To the Kingfish!"

Everybody roars back, "To the Kingfish!"

After the teary-eyed toast, everybody gets back to gambling, eating, and drinking. Just like how Pops would want it!

"We got a lot more people to meet," Johnny whispers in my ear.

"Cool Johnny. I'm ready."

I excuse myself and follow Johnny to a private room. The rooms set up with large oak tables and a small bar. It looks looked like a meeting room. I presume it's Johnny's people seated at the tables. Everyone has a pot of black coffee and a bottle of anisette at their tables. Rocco stands up with Johnny's father saying, "It must be an incredible feeling, Michael, having so many men honoring your father."

I take a deep breath before replying, "Yes it does Uncle Rocco, and I only hope I can live up to his legacy."

There are mumblings and grumblings from everyone after I say Uncle Rocco. Johnny frowns at me and shakes his head in disapproval, while Rocco chuckles to himself, "Johnny, introduce Droz to your crew." Johnny's father says.

"As you know already, Me, Droz, and Willie set up a deal to get everybody containers of construction supplies. Droz provided the seed money to start this deal. A deal we all have been profiting on greatly. Then he had to go in the Navy. When he was gone, all of you kicked back a percentage each month to Rocco's pickup man. Now that Droz is back, he'll be handling it himself. Droz, I would like to introduce you to my crew. At this first table we have John Rannelli, along with his sons Joey, Michael, and Bobby." The father stands up and walks over to me. He shakes my hand and hands me a fat envelop. Then respectfully he gives Rocco and Johnny's father a nod. The Rannelli's are a rough looking group. They all smile at me as I thank them, so I guess they don't mind me.

Johnny moves on to the next table. "At this table we have John Leone, along with his sons John Jr., Michael, and Pauley." John Leone stands up, walks over, and gives me an envelope. Then he bows to Rocco and Johnny's father. I thank him graciously. I feel these guys are all right with me too.

"Behind the Leone's, Droz, are the Palermo's. All of them are led by their father Joseph Palermo. Joseph has seven sons and six grandsons working under him. The grandsons aren't here, but his sons are. This is his oldest son Richey. Then you got Joey Jr., Tommy, Peter, Johnny, Mikey, and Pauley." The father nods to his oldest son. Richey gets up and walks over to me with a real fucking attitude on his face. He slaps two thick envelops into my hand. I didn't get a warm cozy feeling from any of these fucking guys. Richey does show respect for Rocco and Johnny's father. I place the four envelops onto a table behind me.

Now Johnny says, "Last but not least we have the Carbucci family. They are led by their father Vincent Carbucci. This is his oldest son, Carmine. Sitting next to him are his younger brothers Frankie and Vincent Jr. The Carbucci's, Droz, employ about another forty men for us." Vincent nods to his oldest son Carmine. Carmine gives me a really fucking foul and mean look. This guy's a big ugly fuck. Carmine's so fucking big that

I can't even see the fucking chair he's sitting on. The big ugly fuck aint fat either. He looks solid as a fucking rock. Carmine's got a twisted fucking nose and various war scars around his face. He's balding and probably aint had any pussy since pussy had him.

Carmine gets up and angrily starts ranting away in his strong Brooklyn Italian accent. "My family came down here to this fucking swamp to work for the Santori's. We don't work for some punk fucking kid who's still wet behind the ears. Let him go get a fucking job because I aint giving him a fucking dime off my family's sweat. With all due respect, Rocco, this fucking half-breed aint even one of us. Yet he disrespects the family by calling you uncle. How about I throw him a fucking beating for the insult and we'll all move on."

Some people laugh, including Johnny. Carmine's father doesn't. He jumps up and starts speaking in Italian to Rocco. Carmine quickly interrupts him saying, "Please poppa. Don't humble yourself for me. I can take care of myself. You can hear a fucking pin drop in the room after Carmine says that. Rocco picks up his demitasse spoon and slowly stirs his espresso. He puts down the spoon and takes a sip. After Rocco places his cup back on the saucer he speaks Italian to Carmines father. Whatever he said put a big smile on Carmine and his old man's face. Rocco turns his attention to the entire room now and says, "If the Carbucci's don't want to pay Droz, that's Droz's problem. He will have to settle it on his own."

Just like fucking that, Rocco leaves me on a fucking island surrounded by sharks! Johnny won't even look at me as the other families talk amongst themselves. Rocco's response emboldened the beast Carmine tenfold. He looks at me now with total disdain and sarcastically says, "I thought he was your Uncle Rocco?"

I glare with contempt at Carmine, while Johnny and his crew laugh at me. Carmine now boisterously says, "Don't stare at me you little fucking punk. I'll kick your fucking ass. Your old man's reputation can't save you from a beating. You wouldn't even have this fucking club if it wasn't for him."

Billy must have been listening at the door because he barges into the room making a beeline for Carmine! Carmine about shits himself and nervously backs up saying, "I don't want any trouble with you Billy. This is between me and the kid."

Billy looks at me and asks calmly, "Is everything alright Michael? If this ape is giving you a problem I'll gladly take care of him for you."

"No thanks Billy. He aint nothing I can't handle," I reply confidently.

Billy nods his head as Carmine and his boys laugh. Carmine boldly says, "Before you bite off more than you can fucking chew little boy, take a good look at my face. I aint too pretty am I? I've been in a lot of fucking fights punk."

Everyone in the room except Billy nods their heads like they knew exactly what Carmine is talking about. Johnny struts over to me and says, "Carmine aint Jesse Droz, he'll hurt you bad."

I give Johnny a wise ass smirk and pat him on the back. Then with a thorn of sarcasm reply, "Gee Johnny. Thanks for the advice pal."

Carmine is still staring me down, so I run two fingers across both sides of my jawline. Then as arrogantly as I can most possibly be, say, "See this pretty boy face Carmine. It aint got a fucking mark on it, and I've been in a lot of fights too."

The entire room roars at my comeback! This enrages Carmine! He points his finger at me shouting, "Why you little fucking faggot! You better go look in the mirror and kiss your pretty boy face goodbye! I'll be waiting for you outside punk."

I don't say word as everyone follows Carmine into the parking lot. On his way out the door, Johnny says, "You know Droz; it isn't too late to back out."

I look at Johnny perplexed replying, "Back out? What fucking planet are you living on Johnny? I got a lot at stake here. I can't let this big fuck bully me out of my deal and disrespect me in my own club. Win or lose Johnny, I got to fucking fight."

Billy smiles and says, "That a boy Mikey. You're doing exactly what your father would do. Your old man would make mincemeat out of this big loud mouth. Just remember I got your back, just like I had your father's."

Billy's words boost my confidence. When we walk outside, it looks like the entire fucking club dropped everything to watch. The Santori crowd is standing behind Carmine and the Georgie Droz crowd is standing behind me. Rocco, his brother, and Johnny take a neutral position together. Carmine hands his shirt, watch, and gold chain to his father. I have nothing to take off, so I'm ready to go. We both step out, and all of a sudden, Rocco shouts, "I'll make Georgie Droz's boy a 2-1 favorite!"

The Santori crowd laughs and cheers, "You must be in a charitable mood tonight Rocco," Carmine says.

"That I am Carmine. So, do I have any takers?"

Johnny's crew gets in a frenzy trying to get their bets in. Rocco is overwhelmed, so he shouts, "Hold up guys! Hold up! Since you are all in unison here, let's sweeten the pot a little. How about we wager my cut on next month's construction business at 2-1?"

All of the fathers smile and quickly agree. Now Rocco says, "I have one stipulation gentlemen. If Droz wins, everybody shuts up and pays him as if they were paying me. If he loses, nobody has to ever pay him again. Agreed?"

Everyone quickly agrees and starts pumping up Carmine. I'm elated Rocco has so much confidence in me. Carmine looks at me like he's looking at a ham sandwich. "Are you ready pretty boy?" he sarcastically asks.

"Yeah, I'm ready tough guy. The question is, are you?"

Carmine answers by charging me like a raging bull! I easily side step him and deliver a hard blow to his kidneys as he passes. Carmine's dad yells out something in Italian and Carmine nods his head. Carmine slows down and tries to make me come to him now. I step in closer baiting him to swing so I can judge his speed. He swallows the bait and swings wildly at me. I back off easily. He's slow, so I approach again. Carmine surprises me and swings faster catching me on the side of the head! I get knocked to the ground and his followers roar! He tries stomping me, but I quickly roll away. I get back to my feet and feel a swelling on the left side of my head. His punches are heavy, but have no snap so I'm not hurt. Carmine is patient and waits for me to make another mistake. I step in again and he swings too hard, losing his balance. I get closer and deliver a blistering combination to his body! I quickly step back to see if I hurt him. I Didn't. All I did is make him mad. Knowing I can't hurt him, Carmine walks towards me with murder in his eyes. As I'm backing up, I throw straight punches up at his face. I connect solidly, cutting him under his left eye and bloodying his lip, but he keeps coming. Nothing I'm throwing slows him down! Carmine lunges at me with both hands trying to grab me! I dip behind him and jump on his back. Wrapping my arms around his neck, I begin choking him. Carmine goes wild trying to throw me off his back. I hold on for dear life as he rams me several times into a wall. After a few minutes, Carmine collapses with me still holding on. The crowd is silent. Carmine doesn't give up and I'm too afraid to let go. Thankfully, his father runs over and asks me. Right before I let loose of my hold, Carmine's body goes listless. One of the firemen runs over to give him mouth to mouth. Carmine recovers and then walks over to shake my hand. We become friends. Billy now says, "Mikey boy, your old man is looking down with great pride." My father's friends gather around to congratulate me. Then all of Johnny's crew congratulate me. As everyone is slipping back into the club, Rocco pulls me aside and says, "You know kid. It couldn't be any other way."

"I know Rocco. Hiding behind your skirt wasn't going to get your people to respect me. They would despise me even more if you saved me. I needed to standup and fight for what's mine."

"That's right kid."

"Just so you know Rocco. I specifically asked Johnny if there was anything I should know about his guys. He could have warned me, but he chose not to, and that hurts."

"I warned you about jealousy Michael. Tonight you found out my nephew may be the most jealous of all. It will be wise to watch your back with him."

"I will Rocco," I reply shaking my head sadly. As Rocco turns to walk away I say, "You sure showed a lot of confidence in me making me a 2-1 favorite Rocco."

"Like I said kid, I did my homework on you," Rocco replies smiling and then disappears into the night.

When I go back in the club, everyone's gone from the meeting room except for Billy. He's standing behind the small bar drinking a mug of beer. On top of the bar, I see eight envelops instead of four. The Carbucci's paid. Billy pours me a cold one and says, "Drink up Mikey. You earned it."

"Thanks Billy. I did work up a thirst out there. Good to see the Carbucci's paid me."

"They didn't only pay Mikey. They paid with a smile. You gained a measure of respect from everyone tonight. Let's finish up our beers and go see Georgie."

We chug down our beers and then Billy hands me a bank bag from under the bar to carry my money in. When we get to Georgie's office, he's busily banging away on an adding machine. He's got those funny looking half glasses on. Georgie is an averaged sized man who dresses neatly. He has greying short black hair with long sideburns. Georgie's my height and slimly built. Georgie is also a kind man, and I have always liked him. Billy taps lightly on the open door and says, "Look what the cat dragged in Georgie."

Georgie takes a second to finish writing down something and then gets up to greet me. His entire face lights up as he smiles and says, "You handled yourself well tonight Michael. We are all very proud of you. Come on in and sit down."

Billy excuses himself to go make his rounds as I hug Georgie and sit down. Georgie walks over to a filing cabinet and comes back carrying some folders saying, "Let me show you Mikey how we got to where we are today. Your father put up all the money for the club. He has already been paid back in full for it."

Georgie opens up a folder and shows me page after page of expenses. Before he can open up another folder, I stop him and say, "At the risk of sounding stupid here Georgie, let's forgo the past. I am willing to do business with you and Billy on the assumption my father wouldn't be doing business with you if you weren't honest with him. If you were honest with him, then I have no reason to believe you won't be honest with me."

Georgie looks at me silently for a second. Then bluntly replies, "You're not stupid kid. You're being realistic. If my intentions really are to fuck you, paper trails are the best way to do it, so here's what gives. This is a private club. Only open to members. We pay taxes on so called membership fees and the restaurant. Every quarter I give the government a handout to keep them happy. The rest we keep tax-free, so here's the breakdown. Billy and I run the club. For that privilege, your father gave us 30% a piece. He kept the other forty. The club kicks back Rocco 10% off the top for his protection and also for guiding all of his heavy hitters into our casino. The restaurant and bar after expenses has been bringing us in around $9500 per month. The casino, card room, and billiard room profits vary. You know the old saying, "Sometimes you win and sometimes you lose." Fortunately, the house always wins in the long run. Luckily, we have been raking in close to a hundred thousand dollars a month profit on average. It will only go up with all of the people Rocco refers to us. Last but not least, we also pull in another ten or twelve grand a month from a tax-free cigarettes business. This number has been growing steadily since Rocco's people are adding on new customers all the time. The splits are different for the cigarettes. The three of us split the profits from the cigarettes that we sell in the club equally. We sell them by the pack and by the carton. Rocco pays us a twenty percent markup for bringing the cigarettes from North Carolina to Florida and New York. I have your total take from last month sitting in the safe."

I sit in my chair quiet as a mouse hoping that all of this isn't too good to be true. Georgie gets up and walks over to a bank size safe and opens it up. He takes out a couple of banking bags like the one Billy gave me. He hands them to me and says, "Bring back the bank bags Mikey. We don't want to throw up any red flags ordering too many."

"Don't worry Georgie. I'll bring them back."

"Good. Now how about joining me for dinner? I'll order us up two nice, fat, juicy grilled Rib Eyes. We'll each get a big, salty crusted baked potato with butter and a fresh beefsteak tomato salad. What do you say Mikey boy?"

The description alone makes my mouth water! "Sure Georgie. That sounds terrific!" I enthusiastically reply.

Georgie walks me out front to the restaurant and has dinner with me. As the night goes on, firefighter after firefighter sits down with me for a beer. Each one of them shares a special personal story with me about my father. Life is good!

GETTING ACCLIMATED...

had no idea what time Billy dropped me off at home. All I know is that I wake up in a stupor when I hear the phone ring. Reluctantly I pick up the phone on the fifth ring and let out a faint. "Hello?"

"Put a load on last night, huh kid?" Rocco answers.

"I'm fine Rocco. I just got a little jet lag. What's up?"

"I'm picking you up at noon to go have lunch with someone."

"Not a problem Rocco. I'll be ready," I courageously reply.

"Good," Rocco says hanging up the phone.

I get out of bed and see it's already close to eleven. After taking a piss, I grab a towel and head out the cabana door to the pool. My father did an excellent job of landscaping the pool area for privacy, so I dive in naked. I swim a few laps to clear out the cobwebs from last night's binge. I get out of the pool to dry off and feel a nice refreshing breeze. I'm awake now, so I head into the kitchen to make myself some coffee. Walking back out on the patio with my coffee, I gaze at my kingdom. Small trees are growing all around my backyard. Knowing my mom and dad, I would bet they're different kinds of fruit trees. I see a Great Blue Heron down by the canal patiently looking for a meal. I also see Egrets in the backyard chasing little geckos around the shrubbery, and Ibises pecking at insects on the lawn. Coral Springs is truly a beautiful and quiet place to live. After daydreaming for a while, I go back inside and get dressed. Then

I grab the combinations to my father's safes from the envelop Rocco had given me. I take the briefcase full of money and go into my father's room. In the master bedroom closet under an area rug is a safe. My father has a floor safe under an area rug in every large closet in the house. Inside his safe, I find a large amount of neatly stacked wads of cash. I don't have time to count it, and truthfully didn't care to right now. All I want to do is hide my money. There is ample room down there, so I just empty the briefcase into the safe. What's in those envelops from last night should be more than enough for me to live on for now. Money, to me, buys freedom. Not objects of wealth. I close up the safe and head out front to wait for Rocco. I'm glad I did because he's early. Rocco pulls up sporting a big smile when he sees me waiting. When I get in the car, he pats me on the leg saying, "I hate people who are late, and so did your father. I see he taught you well."

"He sure did Rocco. If I was just one minute late he punished me. Pops said it is easier to be five minutes early then one minute late."

"No words truer spoken," Rocco replies as he pulls out the driveway.

"Who are we having lunch with Rocco?"

"A very unique and special woman named Ariella. She owns an orange grove. It's about a half hour's drive from here in Davie."

"Something tells me she does more than grow oranges, right?"

Rocco chuckles, and then replies, "Yes Droz, she does a lot more than grow oranges. Ariella organized and led various elite units inside the Israeli Special Forces. Ariella is one of the best strategists in the world at intelligence gathering and counter terrorism. She privately controls for me a worldwide network of highly trained covert operations personnel. Obtaining reliable and dependable information about the people and things you want to control is a precious commodity. She will be playing various unspecified roles in what I have asked you to do. You will not tell anyone about her except Tex."

"Wow Rocco. That sounds really fucking cool!" I enthusiastically reply.

Rocco makes a right down a single lane road. After about a mile, he slows down and makes a left onto a dirt road. We follow the road for a while until we reach a clearing. There I see a cute but modest wooden house, a large barn, and a fairly sized concrete building. There are orange trees as far as the eye can see. Rocco pulls his Lincoln right up to the house. Standing on the porch is a beautiful older woman dressed in army fatigues. She stands about five foot four with long dark curly hair and green eyes. Her army fatigues are old and faded like my jeans. They cling to her body outlining her sexy curves. She's talking on some type of portable phone with a long antenna.

"Dam Rocco, don't tell me that's Ariella standing on that porch."

"It sure is."

"She's fucking hot Rocco. Is she married?"

"No. Ariella isn't married Droz. Good luck trying to pick her up though."

"So it's okay if I try?"

"Be my guest kid, but you're not her type."

"Shit Rocco. I'm every girl's fucking type. They just don't know it yet," I cockily say.

"I got a C note that says you can't," Rocco replies slyly.

"You're on Rocco. I've picked up woman hotter than her all over the world."

"Okay kid. It's a bet."

We get out of the car and Rocco pops the trunk to retrieve something. Ariella sees this and quickly ends her phone call. She walks over to Rocco and he hands her a large paper bag.

Ariella opens the bag and smiles like a little girl saying, "How sweet of you Rocco, you brought me Challah Bread from my favorite kosher bakery." Ariella gives Rocco a great big hug and kiss. Then she says, "So Rocco, this must be Droz."

"Yes it is Ariella," Rocco smiles replying.

Rocco turns to me saying, "Ariella helped supply me with information about you and Tex when you were both overseas."

"Our escapades were pretty interesting, huh? What do you think Ariella? Should we write a book or what?" I smile cockily replying.

Ariella puts her hand over her mouth to stop herself from laughing. She glances quickly at Rocco and then back at me before replying, "If I were you and Tex, I would think twice before writing a book. Unless of course you both love each other's company so much that you wouldn't mind sharing a jail cell together."

The three of us laugh, and then I say, "You're right Ariella. A book may definitely lead to our demise."

"Is lunch ready yet Ariella?" Rocco asks anxiously.

"Yes it is Rocco. As soon as Katrina gets back from the orange grove and gets cleaned up we will all go in to eat."

Right after Ariella says that a jeep races out of the orange groves. It pulls up to the house in a cloud of dust. When the dust settles out jumps a much younger and even more beautiful woman than Ariella! This girl has short, cropped blonde hair and blue eyes. She's wearing a small pair of please fuck me now shorts showcasing her perfect little ass. Her thimble-sized nipples protrude proudly through her skimpy red bathing suit top. Katrina looks to be in fantastic fucking shape, but still has distinct feminine curves. After seeing this chick, I'm wishing I could change my bet to asking her out instead of Ariella! After dusting herself off Katrina walks up to Ariella and plants a big juicy kiss right on her sweet lips! Ariella pats her gently on the ass before turning to me saying, "Droz, this is Katrina. Katrina, this is Rocco's new protégé, Droz."

Stunned, I struggle to say, "Pleased to meet you Katrina."

"Pleased to meet you too Droz," Katrina smiles and replies in a sultry voice. Then she gives Rocco a hug and kiss before going to go get cleaned up. Rocco turns to me now and says, "Pay up kid."

Ariella and Rocco laugh together at my expense. I've been had, but I take it like a man. I reach into my pocket and roll a C note off my wad. As I hand it over to Rocco, I smile and say, "You're a cocksucker and you know it."

Grinning from ear to ear Rocco pats me on the back replying, "Yup, I sure am."

"I guess you'll never get tired of doing this Rocco. You must really have a soft spot for Droz to have only bet a C note," Ariella says.

"He's just a kid Ariella. I got plenty of time to get more out of him."

On the way into the house, Ariella notices me pouting, so she turns to me and says, "When I was younger Droz and still into guys I would have gone out with you."

That perks me right up, so now I turn to Rocco and ask, "You heard her Rocco. Shouldn't I at least get half my money back?"

"Not in this life," Rocco laughs and replies.

Inside Ariella's house, the mouthwatering aroma of a home cooked meal fills my nostrils. Her home is modestly furnished and decorated. Ariella's old wooden dining room table has a lot of character. It is set beautifully with fresh picked flowers in the middle. Ariella takes the Challah Bread into the kitchen and cuts it into thick slices. Then she places it into a pretty woven breadbasket. Katrina now walks into the room with her hair still wet from the shower. She kisses Ariella sensually on the lips before sitting at the table. I love the clean smell of a woman fresh out of the shower versus any type of perfume she puts on. We all hold hands while Ariella says what I believe to be a blessing in Hebrew. When she is done, everyone digs in. I don't know exactly what everything is I'm eating, but it's all delicious! After we're done, Ariella says another quick blessing. Then we all graciously thank her for such a wonderful meal. Ariella breaks out an old coffee maker and makes a pot of coffee. I don't know if it's the coffee, or the second helping of cabbage, but all of a sudden, my belly is growling. Oh no,

I think to myself. This could be embarrassing! So I try the old 'one cheek sneak.' Thankfully, it works, but, unfortunately, a fucking freight train of flatulence is right behind it! To my dismay, I let out a real ass flapper. I'd call it a 7.4 on the old rectum scale. Both girls put down their coffee cups and raise their eyebrows at me. As I'm excusing myself, Rocco makes it worse by saying, "You better go in the bathroom and check yourself kid. That sounded wet." The girls belly laugh as I turn three shades of red! Ariella now says, "Don't let Rocco get to you Michael. He's just overjoyed that it wasn't him this time."

"Don't jinx me Ariella, I aint left yet."

We all have a good laugh together and then walk out on the porch to say our goodbyes. On the ride home, Rocco reiterated that Ariella would be helping me without saying how. After he drops me off, I plop my ass down on the couch and pick up the remote. Before I can even put on the television, the doorbell rings. I peek out the window, and it's the mailman. He's holding a large box. I open up the door with a warm hello.

"Hello. You mind if I put this down?" He smiles and replies.

"Of course not, go right ahead."

The mailman places the box down and then extends his hand saying, "My name is Ted. You must be George and Lulu's boy, Michael."

"Yes I am sir," I shake his hand replying.

"Your parents spoke proudly of you being in the Navy. I only had the pleasure of knowing them for a short time, but they always brightened up my day. I offer my deepest condolences son."

"Thank you, Ted."

"The rest of your mail is on top of the box. You have a wonderful day Michael."

"You too Ted, and thanks again."

I wave goodbye as he walks back to his truck. Then I pick up the box and bring it in the house. I get excited when I see the return address is Hawaii! I put the box on the coffee table and take my buck knife out of my pocket. Flicking the blade open,

I cut open the box. On top are three beautiful ripe pineapples. I take them out and put them on the coffee table. Below the pineapples are three bags of Kona Coffee, two jars of home-made Lilikoi Butter, two jars of homemade Pineapple Coconut Jam, and two bags of Macadamia Nuts. At the bottom of the box is a shrink-wrapped pound of pakalolo and another shrink wrapped package holding my Thai Sticks! Bingo! God Bless Mamasan, she came through. Tex and I would now make about 100K for having the balls to make the deal. I sift through the rest of my mail and find a letter from Tex. I open up the letter and it's short and sweet. "Everything is going well. I will be getting discharged soon and will call you when I get to Grand-ma's." Well this pleasant surprise put me in a good mood. I sit down smiling and cut open both packages. My nostrils be-come filled with the pungent aroma of two very rare and exotic weeds. I make a mad dash to my bedroom and grab my roll-ing papers. In my room, I hear the doorbell ring once again. My heartbeat quickens wondering if the cops are on to me. Silently I sneak back out to the living room and peek through the blinds. It's Willie! I quickly open the door and hug him. Looking over Willie's shoulder, I see the neighbor lady across the street staring at us shaking her head. She's an average look-ing middle-aged woman wearing a lot of jewelry. She's dressed like she just got back from lunch at the Country Club. I whisper in Willie's ear, "Don't look now Willie, but the lady across the street thinks we're gay.

Willie turns around and stares back. He waves his hand at her like a fruitcake and begins really playing it up with me. Talking like a flaming faggot with his heavy Cuban accent he says, "My white prince you have finally come back to me from the Navy! My love! I have missed you so, so, much! Promise me that you will never leave me again!"

Following Willies lead, I reply, "I promise William!"

Then I pick Willie up in my arms and carry him across the threshold. I put him down, pat him on the ass, and wink at the lady. She clutches her chest like she's going to have a heart attack, and yells for her husband, "Howard! Howard! You are not going to believe this! The Drosdowich boy is a homo!"

Willie and I bust out laughing! After closing the door behind us Willie says, "Droz that was too fucking funny! Did you see her face?"

"Shit Willie. Wait until she sees all the hot chicks coming in and out of here. The nosey bitch won't know what to fucking think."

We laugh high fiving each other. Willie looks fucking great. Not an ounce of fat on him. He's dressed classy but not flashy. He's got on a nice pair of beige designer slacks and a black collared shirt. His shoes are real Cuban roach killers. They are the kind of shoes with a point on them so you can kill a roach in the corner. Willie parked a brand new Cadillac Coupe Deville in my driveway. It's gold with white leather. "Nice fucking ride you got there Willie. I don't know what looks better, you or the car. You're doing well," I happily comment.

Willie sways back and forth real suave like while replying, "You know how it is Droz. Look at that Lincoln you got parked out there."

"I guess you're right Willie. I do know how it is."

Willie looks down at the coffee table and says, "I knew I smelled something good when I walked in here. Looks like you brought back a piece of the islands."

"Not just the islands Willie, take a look at this." I reach down and pick up a few Thai Sticks from the pile. I hand them to Willie saying, "This is the real deal Willie. You're holding Thai Sticks from fucking Thailand my brother."

Willie's eyes bulge while he closely examines the Thai Sticks. He raises them up to his nose and says, "They smell like honey Droz. I aint never seen no shit like this. Let's spark one of these bad boys up!"

"I was just about to roll one before you rang the bell Willie. Take a seat. You want a beer?"

"Sure Droz, I'll take a beer," Willie replies as he sits down.

I walk into the kitchen and grab two beers out of the fridge. I sit down next to Willie and start breaking up a Thai Stick. As I'm rolling the joint, Willie takes a sip of beer and says, "Johnny told me his uncle Rocco gave you that Lincoln and a shit load of cash to go along with it."

I nod my head and take a sip of beer. Then I finish rolling the joint before replying, "He sure fucking did Willie. This guy Rocco along with your old man is going to make me a fucking millionaire."

I light up the joint and drag it gently making sure it burns right. As I am inhaling deeply I think to myself, "Man, I missed smoking this shit!" I take a couple of pokes and then pass the bone to Willie. Willie sniffs the smoke rising off the end of the joint and then takes a nice poke of his own. He struggles holding it down while nodding his head in obvious approval of its quality. He exhales, coughs, and says, "Droz, you got no idea how much Rocco is helping my family fight against that pig Castro. With the help of Rocco and his connections we're bringing more aid to the Cuban people than ever before."

"It makes me very happy to hear that Willie."

Willie takes another couple of whacks of the joint. I notice his eyes are already turning beet red. He hands the joint back to me and then in a very somber tone says, "My family and I are very sad about your parents. Poppa cried like a baby when he heard about your father. You know they have been friends for a very long time. He wants you to come live with us. I want you to come live with us."

I get all teary eyed as I hit the joint. I take big slug of beer to cool my throat before replying, "I mean no disrespect when I say this Willie. Right now, I want to live in my father's house. Tell Poppa his offer is both gracious and appreciated."

I hand Willie back the jay. He goes to take another hit and then hesitates for a moment, before replying, "I know if I lost my momma and poppa, I would want to live in their house too. I promised them tomorrow I would bring you by for lunch. That you have to do, okay?"

"Sure Willie; I don't have anything planned for tomorrow."

Willie takes a few more pokes off the joint and another slug of beer. He hands me back the bone and says, "That Thai weed got my whole body fucking tingling. You need to sell me a few of those sticks."

"Your money aint no good here Willie, just take a few," I gladly reply.

"Thank you Droz. Just so you know, Rocco gave Poppa the idea to make some of our relatives get contractor's licenses. Rocco said he will give them work building houses so they can employ the Cubans we help flee Cuba."

"That's a great idea Willie." I try to hand the joint back to him, but he waves his hand at it like he's had enough, so I take a couple of more tokes and put it down in the ashtray for later.

"Another thing you need to know Droz is that Rocco and my father are determined to keep narcotics out of the ports. Poppa says the government would love to break up our organization and take control of our ports by labeling us drug dealers."

"Rocco told me just about the same story Willie with regards to Coral Springs. So I gather there's a lot of that shit down here, huh?"

Willie almost chokes on his beer when I asked that question. "That's a fucking understatement Droz. Tons of cocaine comes in from Columbia and Peru every day. Heroin comes in from other places like Italy and Mexico, but in only a fraction of the quantities of coke. Now that we're on the subject of smuggling Droz, what are your chances of getting more Thai Sticks and weed?"

"I'd say really fucking good Willie. I have a trustworthy connection in Thailand and I'm in tight with the Hawaiians. My girlfriend over there is a fucking princess. Her name is Keona and I think I love her."

"What a dog you are Droz! What about that nice girl from North Carolina?" Willie shoves me exclaiming.

"Shit Willie. I love her too, but we're talking time and distance here man. I'm not naïve. Your woman's only your woman when you're with her Willie. I sincerely doubt either one of them is keeping their legs closed waiting for me. I do know when they see me again they will run right back to me."

"You're one cocky son of a bitch Droz, but so am I. I think you're full shit about fucking some Hawaiian Princess who gets you pot."

"It's pakalolo to them Willie, and don't bet me. I'll show you pictures of her and her family. They're all Royal Hawaiians and they fucking live like it too. I get the pakalolo from her brother Keoni. I can tell you stories about these people and the rest of my adventures that you'll never fucking believe."

"So the Navy was that cool?" Willie curiously asks.

"Not the Navy Willie. It's the luck of where the Navy can take you. Then it's up to you what you do when you get there. I made good friends with a guy named Tex. We did a lot of crazy shit together. When he gets out he's going to live with me."

"Tex? What is he, a fucking cowboy? You, the street thug from Yonkers made friends with a cowboy?"

I chuckle replying, "I know it sounds weird Willie, but weird shit happens in the Navy. This guy rides fucking bulls man. And he's got the scars to prove it."

"Now that's fucking cool Droz."

We hear music blasting in my driveway. We both peek through the blinds and see Johnny jamming away to the Jimi Hendrix song "All Along the Watchtower.' I turn to Willie and say, "Nice fucking car Johnny drives, hey Willie?"

"Poppa wouldn't let me buy a foreign car. Poppa says we live in America, we support America."

"I can't argue with that Willie."

The song ends and Johnny hops out of his Mercedes dressed to kill. Navy blue slacks, a rose-colored designer shirt, fat gold Gucci chain around his neck, and his flashy Rolex on his wrist. He casually struts up to the door in his $500 designer shoes and rings the bell. Willie answers the door and Johnny says, "Yo Droz, you hired a fucking butler? You speak any English there Poncho?"

Willie laughs giving Johnny a playful shove. He closes the door behind him saying, "Try those jokes when you're with me down in Miami you fucking dago. You fucking Italians think you're something special. How many times was Sicily conquered Johnny? Is that a tan, or Ethiopian blood running in your veins?"

We all laugh. Then Johnny says, "You guys look fucking whacked. Holy fucking shit. Look at all that fucking contraband sitting on the table."

"Take a seat Johnny while I get you a beer and roll you up a little Thai Stick."

Johnny sits down next to Willie and opens a bag of Macadamia Nuts. I hand Johnny his beer and sit down to roll up another joint.

"These fucking nuts are great Droz. Try a few of these Willie."

Johnny hands Willie the bag and I hand Johnny his joint. He puts a flame to the tip and takes in a big hit. He struggles mightily to hold it down, but loses the struggle. He violently coughs out smoke and little pieces of fucking macadamia nuts all over the fucking carpet!

"Damn Johnny, cover your fucking mouth! Look at the fucking mess you made!"

"Oh shit, I'm sorry Droz. Where's the vacuum? I'll clean it up," Johnny embarrassingly replies.

"Relax Johnny. Enjoy your joint and your beer. I'll take care of it." The fact Johnny felt bad and offered to clean it up was good enough for me. I grab the vacuum out of the hallway closet and quickly vacuum up his mess. Johnny's more careful now smoking the Thai Stick. After a few more hits he says, "Droz, this shit's fantastic. If you can smuggle this in weight we'll make a fucking fortune."

"You would already have a fortune Johnny if you didn't gamble so much," Willie says.

Johnny gives me and Willie side eyes. Then he replies, "Oh, okay. So the both of you cocksuckers have been comparing notes, huh?"

Willie and I look at each other puzzled. Then Willie asks, "Why Johnny, should we?"

"Maybe we should Willie. How much is Johnny into you for?"

Willie laughs as Johnny takes another hit off the joint and slugs his beer before saying, "I paid him back every fucking dime Droz."

"He did Droz, but it got to the point where I wasn't helping him by lending to him, so I stopped. How much did Johnny hit you up for?"

"Thirty grand," I reply with a smile.

Johnny takes a bigger slug of beer and places his bottle gently back down on the table before replying, "Look guys, I know my gambling is a fucking problem, and I'm trying to slow down. You think I like making this fucking Jew any richer than he is? Don't get me wrong, Bennie aint a bad guy, but he sure is cleaning up down here. I know he's kicking up to my uncle, so I got to keep things straight with him. I'm glad you both know and care. There shouldn't be any secrets between partners."

"That's right Johnny. No secrets between partners, right Droz?"

"It goes without saying, no fucking secrets," I reply.

What a fucking hypocrite I am. I think to myself. I'm the one keeping fucking secrets. Secrets about everything, especially being Rocco's fucking rat!

Johnny happily eats a few more Macadamia nuts and then washes them down with the rest of his beer. He goes to take another hit off the joint and then thinks twice about it. He puts it down in the ashtray saying, "I'm fucking ripped Droz. I don't need any more of that shit. Listen up. The reason why I stopped by is to make sure you're home later. I'm meeting up with a bunch of little hottie's that moved down here from my neighborhood in Brooklyn. After we hang out for a while I want to bring them back here for a little party, if you know what I mean."

"Sure Johnny. A little party with some Brooklyn booty would be a good change of pace for me. How about you Willie, you want to hang out here tonight?"

Willie looks at me all bright eyed and bushy tailed replying excitedly, "Hell yeah I'm fucking hanging. While you've been gone Droz, Johnny's become the ass master."

Johnny smiles proudly and gives a little tug to both sides of his shirt collar saying, "Well if you're going to be good at something, it might as well be fresh young pussy! So gentlemen, I'll be back around eight with the girls."

After Johnny leaves, I ask Willie, "I don't know about you Willie, but I'm fucking starved. How about we go get a nice, fat, juicy steak at the club?"

"Now that you mention it Droz, I got the fucking munchies bad. A juicy steak sounds real good to me." Willie rubs his stomach.

"Cool Willie."

I lock up the house, and off we go in my Lincoln to the club. This time when I show up everyone knows me and goes out of their way to say hello. Winning that fight with Carmine was important in a myriad of ways. Willie already knows most of the guys, and everyone seems to really like him. There's absolutely no reason not to. He's polite, upbeat and funny. We sit at the end of the bar where we can see everything going on. Billy and Georgie were engrossed in a conversation at a table nearby, so we didn't bother them. When they notice us, they both smile briefly and get back to their conversation. Mahoney walks right over to us with a big smile saying, "Good to see you Droz. You too Willie, what can I get you boys?"

"We're going to have dinner at the bar Mahoney. I'll take a draft for now please. What's your poison Willie?"

"I'll have a Bacardi and Coke please."

"Coming right up boys." As Mahoney walks away, he hand signals a waiter to come over to us.

Looking around the room, I see a lot of Johnny's crew enjoying dinner. They all nod to me. A young male waiter walks up to us and says, "My name is Jonathan. I'm pleased to meet you Mr. Drosdowich. Good to see you again Willie. Would you gentlemen like to see a menu?"

I cringe hearing Mr. Drosdowich, so I reply, "Please call me Droz, Jonathan, and we don't need a menu. Willie and I both want a nice, fat, juicy grilled rib-eye."

"Okay guys. How would you like them grilled?"

"I want mine medium rare Willie, how about you?"

"Medium rare is good for me too. Jonathan, have mine smothered in those sautéed onions and mushrooms you guys make."

"Damn that sounds good Willie. Do the same for me too Jonathan."

"That won't be a problem Droz. Dinner comes with a large crusty baked potato with a salted bottom. The vegetable tonight is fresh steamed broccoli. You can have the broccoli sautéed in butter and minced garlic if you like?"

"Definitely, Jonathan. That sounds delicious, right Willie?"

"I already know it is delicious Droz. But maybe we shouldn't be eating garlic before we meet the girls?"

I wave my hand at Willie replying, "I'll bet you these broads Johnny's bringing are all Italian. They probably stink from garlic already."

All three of us laugh and Jonathan leaves to put in our order. Billy and Georgie couldn't help over hearing my garlic comment and laugh along with us. Then Georgey asks, "You boys got condoms, right? If you don't have any condoms I got a few boxes in the office I can give you."

Before we could even mutter a word back, Billy takes a serious tone with Georgie saying, "Just wait one minute Georgie boy. I just bought those condoms. There's only one drug store around here and I'll look like a real fucking pervert if I have to run back over there. They're big boys, let them go get their own condoms."

Taken aback by what just came out of Billy's mouth, Georgie replies calmly, "You bought three boxes of a hundred Billy. Don't you think you look like a pervert already?"

Billy shrugs his shoulders. Then in a matter of fact tone replies, "What do you want from me Georgie. I got to have an ample supply. I got big hands and a big cock. Sometimes the fucking condoms break when I try to get them on."

Georgie shakes his head from side to side and says sarcastically, "Okay Hercules. Then why don't you let the ladies put them on for you?"

"Billy snidely snickers at Georgie before replying, "What do you think, I'm some kind of fucking dope? I know better than to trust a fucking broad. Women are devious fucking creatures. They have been known to put a little hole in the condom with their nails or their teeth. Next thing you know you're fucking trapped, and I aint getting trapped."

That seemed to convince Georgie and they both get up from the table. Before they walk away, Georgie points his finger at me and Willie saying, "Listen to Billy boys and always play it safe. Make sure you use a condom and make sure you put it on yourself. Oh yeah, and one more thing that Billy didn't cover. Don't believe girls when they say they're on the pill or that the doctor told them they can't get pregnant. It's the oldest trick in the book. Enjoy your evening fellas."

Mahoney puts a couple of fresh drinks down in front of us and gives us a look like we should listen. Willie and I look at each other in total disbelief over what we just heard. We couldn't believe the lecture, but most of all we couldn't believe an old guy like Billy was getting laid so much. After all, he had to be over forty. Jonathan brings out our meal and we both chow down like hungry hounds! After we're done eating, we go into the casino to see who's around. The first thing I notice is how many new faces are playing at the tables. Most of the men gambling look Italian, but some of their accents definitely weren't from New York. Billy is keeping an eye on all the action, so I walk up to him and ask quietly, "Billy, where are all of these new guys from?"

"Rocco got guys coming in now from New Orleans, Boston, Cleveland, Chicago, and even as far as Los Angeles. All of them are heavy gamblers. We got a good thing going here kid, so make sure you keep your fucking nose clean and don't bring any heat on us."

"I won't Billy."

It's a dream for me to own a club like this, so I can't fuck it up. If I do, Billy will probably kill me. Willie and I walk around listening to stories being told from all of the different wise guys. Every one of them has their own style of storytelling. We could have spent the entire night there just watching and listening, but pussy awaits us.

We get back to my house a little after eight. Johnny's Mercedes and two other cars are parked in the street. One is a nice Red Camaro and the other is a Yellow Mustang. Johnny's old school and knew to leave the driveway open for me. We get out of the car and there stands Johnny in all of his fucking glory. The ass master surrounded by six young vixens! Johnny walks up giving us both a hug and a kiss. Then he scowls and backs off quickly shouting, "Madone, how much fucking garlic you guys eat!"

Everyone starts laughing! "I told you so," Willie scolds me.

I put my thumb on the top of my first two fingers and wave them in the air like Italians like to do replying, "Ming Johnny! What a fucking meal we had! A couple of nice, fat, juicy ribeyes grilled medium rare, smothered in sautéed onions and mushrooms. With a nice, big side dish of fresh steamed broccoli loaded with garlic and butter."

Johnny with a look of yearning replies, "Now I'm fucking jealous. All I had was a fucking ham sandwich on white bread. They don't even have fucking Boars Head cold cuts down here. I got fucking agita from that cheap fucking ham. My uncle is working on getting Boars Head cold cuts down here and the sooner the fucking better."

Johnny reaches into his pocket and takes out a roll of breath mints. He hands me and Willie a bunch of them and says, "Come on boys. It's time to meet the girls."

The three of us swagger over to the girls sitting on the cars. Before Johnny introduces us one of the little hotties hops off a car and smiles. Then in her Brooklyn Italian accent says, "We already know who you are. Johnny told us all about you guys."

Willie raises his eyebrows and smiles back at her. Then in an inquisitive manner replies, "Oh really, and what did Johnny tell you about us?"

"You're Willie, and that's Droz. The both of you are gangsters just like Johnny."

The three of us grin from ear to ear with pride. Then another girl jumps off the car saying, "They still talk about you Droz at the High School. Did you really kick Mr. Backman in the nuts?"

"I sure did baby girl, and I'll do fucking worse if I see his faggot ass on the street. So I take it all you nice young ladies like gangsters?"

They all start giggling, so I ask, "How about we go inside my house and party a little?"

With that said, the girls line up at the door. Johnny and Willie pat me on the back. As I'm letting the girls in, the nosey neighbor lady is staring at us through her window. So I smile and wave at her. As I close the door behind me, I think to myself, "I need some landscaping!"

Inside the house, Johnny introduces the girls. "This one over here is Liz. Let's just leave out our last names, girls. We'll all be better off in the long run not using them. On the couch, we have Nicolle, Joanie, Annmarie, and Haley. Standing next to me is Stacy. Droz, is it okay if the girls help themselves at the bar while we get the hooch ready?"

"Absolutely Johnny, I'm sure the girls will find something they like. There's beer, Coca Cola's, and some orange juice in the fridge. You girls get high?"

Almost in unison, they all shout, "Yes!"

"That's a good thing because tonight ladies you're in for a special treat. Just give us a few minutes to roll it up. Willie, stay with the girls and make sure they all get their drinks. Johnny and I will go roll up the herb."

Willie nods with a smile. Johnny and I make a pit stop at the fridge for a beer and then head to my room. When we get there Johnny cockily says, "Stacy is Bennie the Bookie's fucking granddaughter. I know I can't get thirty grand of debauchery out of her ass, but I'm sure going to fucking try!"

"That's funny because she looks like a spoiled little Jap. She got a really pretty face Johnny. I wouldn't mind dropping a load all over it myself."

"By all means Droz, help yourself. The little Jap loves giving sloppy wet ones."

"That sounds like a beautiful thing Johnny. How about I mix the fucking Thai weed up in a joint with the pakalolo? What do you think?"

"I don't see why the fuck not. You mix great with great, you get greater."

We both laugh as we break up the two weeds and roll up a few joints. Meanwhile we can hear the girls all laughing out in the living room. This means Willie is being his personable, humorous self. Making girls laugh is always a key to getting pussy. We roll three bats. That will be more than enough to get all nine of us stoned. When Johnny and I get back to the living room, the girls seem right at home. I walk over to the stereo and throw on 'Hotel California' by the Eagles. I turn up the volume just loud enough so that we all could still hear each other speak. Then I hand a joint to Willie, one to Johnny, and I keep one. We light them up simultaneously and proceed to get everyone high. Between coughs, the girls are all talking about never smoking weed this good. Then Joanie asks me, "What kind of weed is this Droz? None of us have ever tasted anything like this before."

"You girls are smoking an exotic mix of Hawaiian weed called pakalolo, and Thai Sticks from Thailand," I say proudly.

"You get weed from Hawaii and Thailand?" Annmarie asks.

Looking straight into her pretty green eyes I reply, "Well if Johnny didn't tell you already, I was in the Navy and stationed at Pearl Harbor. We cruised most of the world and one of our stops was in Thailand. Let's just say I made some friends along the way."

Both girls smile wide eyed at me as the song 'Life in the Fast Lane' starts playing on the stereo, so now I smoothly ask, "If you two girls would like, I could show you some pictures of my voyages."

They give each other a quick look, and then both say sure. So we head to my bedroom. My dick gets hard as soon as I close the door behind us. Both girls sit timidly on my bed as I breakout my photo album. I sit down between them and start telling the stories behind the pictures. My wild and funny storytelling has both girls in stitches. When I get to the photos of the Hawaiian girls doing the Hula, the girls imitate them. Watching Annmarie and Joanie dancing together really turns me on. Both of these girls are overboard cute. Joanie has on tight jeans and a light blue tube top. She's about five foot six and weighs around 130 pounds. She has straight black hair and big dark eyes. Full blooded Italian for sure, with big boobs and a nice plump round ass to boot. Annmarie is shorter. I'd say she's about five foot three and weighs in around 110 pounds. She's got dirty blonde hair and beautiful green eyes. I know Annmarie has Italian blood in her, but like me, she might be a mixed breed. Annmarie has a perfect figure. She's wearing a pair of tiny little purple shorts and a black tube top. Her breasts are medium sized and she has a cute little bubble butt. It's time to make my move, so I stand up and smile. Then I take them by the hand and lead them into the bathroom. Before they can say a word, I drop my jeans and put on the shower. Both of them giggle, but follow my lead and take off their clothes too. We take turns soaping each other up, and it soon becomes obvious these girls like touching each other! So I ask coyly, "Have you two been together before?" They answer by tongue kissing with each other!

Then Joanie turns to me saying, "You have to keep this secret Droz. We both like guys, but since we moved down here all we run into are these fucking rednecks, and they're all fucking idiots, right Annmarie?"

"I hate the rednecks down here Droz. All of them are just pure fucking assholes!" Annmarie exclaims.

My cock is bobbing up and down listening to this. I look at the girls as the water runs down their beautiful naked bodies and sincerely reply, "I can vouch for that. These rednecks are worse than fucking idiots. Don't you girls worry one bit. Your secret is safe with me." Meanwhile, I'm thinking to myself, "Oh boy! I can't wait to tell Willie and Johnny!"

Joanie grabs me by the balls and playfully squeezes them before replying, "It better be Droz. You are the first person we shared this with. None of the other girls know and we don't want them thinking we're lezzies."

Annmarie now teasingly adds, "Neither one of us has had sex since we left our boyfriends almost a year ago back in Brooklyn. About a month ago, we got really horny talking about it and it just sort of happened. If you keep your mouth shut Droz we can probably have a lot of fun together."

"Of course I'll keep my mouth shut Annmarie," I reply earnestly while folding my hands like a priest.

Joanie believes me and let's go of my balls. I shut the shower and we dry each other off. When we walk back into the bedroom I find myself a bit confused on where to begin, so I let the girls take the lead. They both giggle at my hesitation and push me down on the bed. With innocent little smiles they begin licking and sucking my cock. Watching their pretty faces running their wet lips and tongues around my dick is like a dream come true! Joanie and Annmarie's mouths meet at the top of my cock. There they begin tongue kissing with each other with the head of my dick in the fucking middle! This drives me fucking wild! When it gets too intense, I pull Joanie away and onto my face. I hold her soft round ass in my hands and lap her pussy. I feel Annmarie rubbing the head of my dick on her wet pussy lips. I can't see her, but I can hear her moaning trying to fit my dick into her tight little pussy. As Annmarie slowly gets use to my size, Joanie is sliding her juicy snatch back and forth on my tongue. Annmarie lets out a gasp of pleasure when she can finally push herself down on my entire shaft. Her moaning gets louder and louder as she grinds herself on top of me. Joanie's breathing speeds up, so I suck her swollen clit into my mouth and swirl my tongue all around it. She explodes in orgasm all over my face! Joanie's climax really turns Annmarie on. I feel her pussy start contracting around my cock. Annmarie begins shaking uncontrollably on top of me. Then she creams all over my cock and balls! This sets me off like a fucking rocket and I cum deep inside her. I'm so fucking horny and excited by all of this that my dick stays fucking hard! So now I take turns fucking them both doggie while they eat each other out. Life is fucking good!

When I wake up the next morning, I have two beautiful young girls sleeping next to me. What a way to start the day! Everybody else must still be sleeping because the house is dead quiet. I get up to look around. Johnny and Willie didn't close the doors to their rooms, so I figured they were switching partners all night. The silence of the morning is broken by the phone ringing. It is only about a quarter to eight, so I figure it must be Rocco. I pick up the phone on the third ring and say hello. It's not Rocco; it's a girl screaming frantically in half Spanish and half English. Oh shit, it must be Willie's fucking girlfriend Mizar! Now she starts yelling in just English, "I know he's there Droz! You get him and put him on the phone right now!"

I think quickly, telling her he isn't here will just make matters worse, so in a calm, pleasant voice I reply, "Hi Mizar, I know we haven't met yet, but Willie has told me so many great things about you."

She cuts me off immediately yelling in her wild Cuban accent, "I don't want to hear any bullshit from you! Just go get William now!"

When I put down the phone, I can still hear Mizar yelling. I go into the bedroom where Willie is still asleep. I twist his big toe. He doesn't move, so I twist it harder. Willie wakes up and yells, "What the fuck Droz? What are you, some kind of fucking foot freak? Leave my fucking toes alone you fucking pervert!"

I smile and chuckle. Then I reply, "You better get up Willie and go answer the phone before Mizar jumps through it."

Willie rubs his eyes and shakes his head. Then he peels one of the girls off him and gets out of bed. Willie walks down the hallway mumbling in Spanish. I can still hear Mizar yelling through the phone. I personally think all of this is funny. Willie enters the kitchen and picks up the phone. Then in the sweetest voice he could most possibly muster, he starts speaking in Spanish to her. All that does is make her madder. I have to suppress my laughter. Willie smiles at me like he's enjoying it too as he holds the phone away from his ear. Every now and then, he will try to get a word in edge wise, but to no avail. Willie puts his hand over the receiver and says, "You have to understand Cuban women Droz. She needs to really get it all out before she'll hear anything I say to her."

"I think I'll put on a pot of coffee while she vents Willie," I nod my head replying.

"Good idea Droz."

Mizar takes a breath and Willie jumps in. It's like a serenade the way Willie talks so beautifully to Mizar in Spanish. I pour us both a cup of hot java and listen to Willie sweet talk his way out of trouble. Believe it or not, she calms down. It aint long before Willie has her giggling like a schoolgirl. After a few more minutes of chatting, Willie hangs up the phone with a kiss. He turns to me with his infectious smile and then takes a sip of coffee. Speaking with authority, Willie reiterates, "You have to understand Cuban women Droz. Mizar wasn't going to be happy no matter what I said to her if I didn't let her blow off all that steam first. Once she was done I started saying the things I knew she wanted to hear"

I take a sip of coffee before inquisitively asking, "And what were the things you told her that you knew she wanted to hear Willie?"

Willie smiles wide as he replies, "First I told her you and Johnny made a big problem out of a little one with our business. Then I say how it took me most of the night to fix it. By the time I was done, it was very late and I was too tired to drive home. When I awoke this morning, I felt like a lost puppy when I didn't have my baby next to me. Then I tell her I love her and I can't wait to see her. That's how you handle a Cuban woman Droz."

With that said, Johnny comes walking into the kitchen in his red silk boxers. He pours himself a cup of java. He puts two teaspoons of sugar in and stirs noisily. After Johnny takes a sip of coffee he turns to Willie and says, "You left out a very important part Willie."

"And what part is that Johnny my love?" Willie sarcastically replies.

"Where the Cuban woman cuts your fucking balls off when she sees the hickey on your neck."

Willie chokes and spits coffee all over the kitchen table! I take a closer look and now see the hickey myself. It is small, but it was fucking there! I now say to Willie, "Oh you're really fucked now Willie. There isn't enough sweet talking on earth to get your ass out of a hickey!"

Willie looks in the mirror over the sink. When he sees the damage, he cries out, "Ay, caramba! How did that happen?"

"Gee Willie? I don't know? Maybe it happened while you were sticking your dick in four girls last night?" Johnny sarcastically replies.

I hear the toilets flush, so I knew the girls were starting to get up. As Willie sits there holding his head in angst, I look at Johnny and ask, "What should we do about breakfast? I think

I got enough eggs and bacon, but I sure don't feel like cooking for the nine of us."

"There's an IHOP not far from here on Sample Road. Take the girls there. I can't go. My old man is expecting me to meet a guy with him. We're going to build him a new house on the beach. My uncle Rocco helped him get started in the trash hauling business up north. Now he's setting him up down here."

"Not a problem Johnny. Go to your meeting. Willie and I will take care of the girls. After that I'm heading down south with him to see his mom and dad."

The girls start piling into the kitchen half-naked and consoling Willie. Johnny now says, "While you're down in Miami have Willie fix you up with some designer clothes. You're going to need them when we hit the disco clubs. My family owns a piece of the two hottest clubs in Broward County. Make sure you hook him up Willie. We don't want Droz embarrassing us by looking like a fucking peasant."

"Don't worry Johnny. I'll make sure he gets the right clothes to wear," Willie replies as he feels up the girl on his lap.

Annmarie and Joanie now walk into the kitchen with Stacy. Stacy latches onto Johnny while Annmarie and Joanie latch onto me. Johnny now says, "Listen Stacy. Droz and Willie will take you girls to breakfast. I got a meeting with my father, so I can't go. Why don't you come help me find my clothes?" Johnny winks at us as he takes Stacy back into the bedroom for a quickie. Willie and I take the rest of the girls for a dip in the pool and a quickie of our own. The quickie turned into a fucking hour, so we hit the IHOP around ten. By 11:15, I exchange phone numbers with the girls and say our goodbyes. They understand Willie has a girlfriend, so none of them feel bad when he didn't give them his number. He took theirs instead. These girls are cool like Johnny said. They know the deal. If they want to hang around gangsters, they can't be a clinging fucking vine.

Back at the house, Willie and I smoke a nice fat joint of pakalolo as we compare notes from last night. I knew Willie wouldn't repeat what I tell him. As we are getting ready to leave the phone rings. This time it's Rocco. "How you doing kid, is everything alright?"

Sure Rocco, everything's great. Willie came by and Johnny brought over some girls. We all had an enjoyable evening together, if you know what I mean."

Rocco chuckles before replying, "Yeah, I think I can still remember what you mean. I'm glad to hear you're getting yourself acclimated to being home. You got anything planned today?"

"A matter of fact I do Rocco. I'm planning to follow Willie down to Miami and have lunch with his parents. I'm also going to pick up some new threads from Willie. Johnny wants me not to look like a peasant when he takes me out to the clubs."

"That's a good idea. After your night out, I want you tell me what you think of the clubs. I just got off the phone with Willie's dad. He's looking forward to seeing you. Look, I'll let you guys get going. I was just checking on you."

"Cool Rocco. Thanks for caring. Call me whenever you need me."

"Don't worry kid. I will. Have fun in Miami."

"I'm sure I will Rocco. Goodbye."

FUN IN MIAMI...

After hanging up the phone, I grab a few bones and lock up the house. Willie takes his car and I take mine. I follow him for about an hour before we get to his house. Willie's house looks like a Spanish hacienda. We both park along a large circular driveway. In the middle of the driveway sits a tropically landscaped island with a beautiful flowing fountain. I get out of the car saying, "Damn Willie. What a fucking nice place to live."

"Thank you Droz. You can always change your mind and come live with us."

"It's definitely tempting Willie," I smile replying.

The entire property is meticulously landscaped and maintained. We cross under a giant archway to get to the front entry. When Willie opens up the door, the aroma of home cooking starts my mouth watering! His mom is the first to greet us. Willie's mom is petite and curvy. She has long black hair and almond shaped dark eyes. Her skin is light tan and her smile will warm you on a cold day. Willie gives his momma a big hug and kiss saying, "Droz, this is my Momma Dominga."

Dominga looks at me solemnly saying, "I am so sorry for your great loss. I want you to know we are here for you."

As she hugs and kisses me I reply, "Thank you Dominga."

"Come boys. Poppa and Grandpa have been waiting for you."

I follow Willie and Dominga down a long hallway into a big bright kitchen. Large French doors look out over the property and a very large pool area. Willie's poppa and grandpa are sitting stoically at an old wooden coffee table. Willie's dad has a darker complexion than his mom. Very much like a Sicilian. He is stout in stature and very strongly built. Grandpa is much slimmer and taller. His complexion is dark tan too. Whatever age grandpa is, he looks lean and mean. They both stand up and Willie introduces them. "Droz, this is my Grandpa Fernando and my Poppa Luis."

"Pleased to meet you gentlemen," I reply as we exchange hugs and kisses.

"Michael, you should be very proud of your father and try to walk in his footsteps," Willie's grandpa says.

Willie's poppa looks at me teary-eyed saying, "I loved your father like a brother, Michael. There isn't a day that goes by I do not think of him. I know I asked my son to invite you to live here with us. My wife and I know we can never replace your parents, but we can give you a loving home to live in. Have you had time to consider it son?"

I'm breaking up inside watching this strong man who loved my father humbly ask me to live in his mansion. It takes all the courage I have to reply back, "Luis, Dominga. I have struggled very hard with this decision. Please understand that right now I want to live in my father's house. If the day comes I feel differently, I hope your gracious and generous offer will still stand."

"I respect your decision Michael, and of course my offer stands forever."

Grandpa adds, "My grandson tells me that the construction supplies are your idea. If it wasn't for you we would have never met Rocco. Rocco has become a very important part of our fight against that pig Fidel. For this, I must thank you."

"No thanks necessary Fernando, I'm just glad things are working out. In fact, I only played a very small part in this. After all, I wasn't even around. It was Johnny and Willie that made it all work."

Fernando and Luis look at each other smiling. Then Luis says, "That sounds just like your father, Michael. He always gave credit to the people around him for his own good deeds. Please sit down at the table and eat with us."

Willie sure didn't have to be asked twice. He about ran to his spot at the table. When we're all seated Willie says, "It's time for Momma's homemade pastelitos! Momma makes them all by hand Droz. Some are sweet with a homemade cream cheese. Some have guava and others have pineapple and coconut in them. The meat ones are filled with spicy meat and chicken. Momma also makes a homemade dipping sauce that's really spicy."

Momma keeps bringing out the pastelitos and we keep eating them. The dipping sauce is out of this world! After an hour of non-stop eating, Dominga breaks out the coffee. Willie says it's brewed in a very old coffee pot that has been handed down for generations. I never had Cuban Coffee before. After two small cups, I'm energized and hooked! I am thoroughly enjoying my Cuban experience! I sit around with Willie's family drinking coffee and listening to stories. When the phone rings Willie's momma gets up to answer it. Dominga quickly calls her husband over to the phone. Luis says a few words in Spanish and hangs up. Then he says, "I want you boys to come with me and Grandpa to the fishing docks."

"Poppa can we skip it? I had planned to take Droz to the warehouse. He needs clothes for when we go to the clubs."

Luis gives Willie a stern look replying, "There will be plenty of time for the warehouses later."

Willie always told me his old man was just like mine. He got away with one objection and didn't push his luck with another. He reluctantly replies, "Sure Poppa."

We all thank Dominga for a fabulous lunch and kiss her on the cheek before we leave. Willie's old man drives a brown Fleetwood Brougham. We both jump in the backseat and off we go. It's like sitting in a living room riding in the back of this car. As we float down the highway, Grandpa puts on a

Cuban radio station. The music isn't bad, but Grandpa's singing is. I try not to laugh, but it's pretty hard when Luis joins in. When we get closer to the docks, Fernando turns off the music. Luis pulls up to an open warehouse and parks. The outside air smells of wooden fishing boats and freshly caught fish. I see a bunch of men unloading fish from their boats. They are carrying them over to an area with giant sinks and large drains lining the floor. The fishermen nod their heads as they walk by. Some fish are so huge it takes two men to carry them. They throw the fish onto long tables where other men cut their heads off and clean them. Fish blood flows like a river off the cutting tables and is hosed down the drains.

We walk over to a large steel door where Luis knocks three times. The door opens up to a Twilight Zone of horrors! Inside the cold dimly lit room, I see six naked men bound and gagged to large heavy steel chairs. All of them are groaning in pain and bleeding from various parts of their bodies. Their faces are so swollen they don't even look human. One guy's eye is hanging from its socket, but it still seems to move following me eerily as I walk by. One of the henchmen begins speaking in Spanish to Willie's father and grandfather. After finishing their short conversation, Willie's grandpa turns to us saying, "Two of these men are brothers who worked for our cause. They were like family to us. We trusted them like family and they betrayed us. These other four men are Nicaraguan Contras working under the blessings of the CIA. With the help of the two brothers, they tried smuggling 4,000 kilos of cocaine through our port. The cocaine was destined for the streets of South Florida. They will suffer today and die for their crimes. When the men hear this, they struggle in their chairs. Willie's dad turns his attention to me and Willie. Staring at us with a blank expression, he calmly says, "I want you both to witness what happens to people who try smuggling narcotics through my port. I will spare no one. Not the child of my dearest friend, or even my own beloved son."

With those words a henchmen begins slowly cutting the throat of one of the men. Systematically now without emotion, the executioners slowly slit the throats of the other three. Huge puddles of blood work their way towards the drains. The two brothers watch in horror as the four men quiver and die. The henchmen turn the brother's chairs around so they face each other. Two henchmen stand behind each of the two brothers. One henchman forcibly holds the eyelids open while the other one slowly slits their throats. The last thing they see is each other's death. Willie and I look at each other for signs of weakness, but there aint any. His father and grandfather wanted to teach us a lesson today, and that lesson is simple. Mess with narcotics and this will be you. Grandpa says their bodies will be cut up into small pieces and used in chum buckets. Their heads will be burned along with the cocaine. On the ride home Grandpa puts everything into perspective for us.

"What you two young men witnessed is a necessary evil to defeat a greater one. As I speak thousands of innocent people are being killed in Cuba. Others will be thrown into prisons to be tortured for nothing more than speaking their minds. On April 17th, 1961, the American Government backstabbed 1,400 Cuban freedom fighters at the Bay of Pigs. The United States Government promised the Cuban invasion forces we would have air support. This air support turned out to be obsolete World War II B-26 bombers. The CIA painted them to look like Cuban Air Force planes. The bombers missed their targets and left Castro's Air Force intact. People very close to my heart died that day. Over twelve hundred freedom fighters were captured and thrown into prisons. Once in prison, they were tortured until they died. Those of us who were still alive and not captured escaped into the ocean. Think about this for a moment. America spends billions of dollars fighting the spread of communism all over the world. They send CIA agents and Special Forces troops overseas to support anti-communist groups. America fought a war very far away in Viet Nam to fight communism. Wouldn't it make sense then that the American

Government would have fought a war to stop a communist regime from taking power only ninety miles off its shores? Or are we to believe that an ill equipped dictator leading a group of untrained peasants was too formidable of a foe to stop? I don't think so. It only happened because the USA wanted it to happen. Now I will tell you why. Too many northerners are moving to South Florida every day. South Florida's population growth means more cities, schools, roads, more of just about everything. It's the tax dollars from tourism that pays for all of this. A free thriving capitalist Cuba would destroy South Florida's tourism industry. A free Cuba means lavish resorts and casinos only one hour from Miami. Gambling is illegal in Florida and the Bible wavers in North Florida will never vote in casino gambling. A free thriving capitalist Cuba would cause Florida to institute a state tax to survive economically. This made Cuba expendable."

When Grandpa finally takes a breath, I think to myself, "Grandpa sees how evil our government is too. He reminds me of a Cuban Rocco!" So now I say, "That was extremely informative Grandpa and I thank you for opening my eyes. This may be a stupid question, but who are the Contras, and how did your guys get mixed up with them?"

Luis jumps in. "That's not a stupid question Michael, and I will be glad to answer it for you. The Contras were created by Ronald Regan and the CIA. They are supposedly fighting the spread of Castro type communism and socialism in South and Central America. The Contras call themselves freedom fighters. What they really are is a bunch of filthy, greedy narcotics smugglers. They line their pockets with money made on other people's suffering. The CIA and certain high-ranking officers in the American Military protect the Contras drug smuggling efforts. The Contras are being allowed to smuggle cocaine freely into the United States and especially here into South Florida. They influence men like the two Cuban brothers who were working for me. Hopefully, their fate will serve as a deterrent to others.

The rest of the ride back to Willie's house went the same as the ride there. We got Cuban music playing on the radio with Luis and Fernando singing off key. When we get back to Willie's house we have another cup of Cuban coffee. After that, Willie and I head over to the warehouse to get my clothes. On the ride over Willie says, "Believe me Droz; I had no idea this was going to happen."

"Don't sweat it Willie. I could tell that you were just as shocked as me when that steel door opened. Your father and grandfather wanted to make a point, and they did. End of fucking story. Have you ever done blow Willie?"

Willie snickers before replying, "Of course I did. It's almost impossible not to in Miami. At first, I felt fucking fantastic Droz. Then like ten minutes later, I felt like I lost my fucking dog. The only way to get rid of that feeling was to do more blow. I hated that feeling, so I never did it again. Did you ever try it?"

"No, and I don't want to either."

Willie pulls his car up to the guard gate entering a warehouse compound. The guard recognizes Willie and opens the gate. He pulls around a corner and parks. When we get out of the car Willie says, "Poppa owns warehouses all over Miami. Him and Rocco bought land zoned for warehouses in Broward and Palm Beach County. Poppa says they are going to be building new warehouses soon. It's a good business Droz. Maybe we should find some land and build some warehouses too."

"Hell, if Rocco and your old man are doing it, we definitely should."

Willie unlocks the door to the warehouse and throws on the lights. I can't believe my eyes! I see rack after rack of men's and women's designer clothes. There's even a shoe department! Impressed, I turn to Willie excitedly saying, "Holy fucking shit Willie! I feel like I'm in a fucking department store!"

"My mother and her sisters go fucking nuts in here. They spend hours just trying things on. This warehouse is set up strictly for family members," Willie smiles proudly and replies.

He picks up a measuring tape and starts measuring my waist. Then he measures my inseam and my neck. I feel uncomfortable with Willie doing this so I say, "Willie I'll take the fucking clothes to a tailor."

"Bullshit Droz. I have relatives in Miami who are the best tailors in the world. I learned this as a boy working for them in the summer. Just relax. I'm almost done."

After finishing the measurements, Willie has me try on clothes. He uses chalk to mark where alterations are needed. I try on four different suits, eight pairs of slacks, and twelve shirts. Then Willie takes me over to the shoe department. He hands me a pair of dress socks and I step in that stupid foot-measuring device. Willie looks at the measurement and shakes his head. "Why the fuck are you shaking your head Willie?" I ask.

"You got fat ass feet Droz. You're a quadruple E. That really limits what shoes you can wear."

"I got a fat fucking cock too Willie, so the fuck what? I'll wear my fucking sneakers," I grumble replying.

"No you won't," Willie snaps back.

It takes Willie a half a fucking hour to find me a couple of pair of nice shoes that fit. He says all the alterations should be done in a day or two. Then the clothes will be delivered to my house. I pull out my wad saying, "I don't want to hear the word free come out of your fucking mouth Willie. What do I owe you?"

"How did you put it to me before Droz? Your money's no good here?"

"There's a big fucking difference between a few Thai Sticks and a fucking wardrobe."

Willie waves his finger at me saying, "I take care of you my way and you take care of me your way, comprende?"

I know I can't win here, so I reply, "Comprende."

We leave the warehouse and drive back to Willie's. Before we get in the house, Willie insists I stay for dinner. He doesn't have to twist my arm.

A Horse of a Different Color...

I get home around 11:30 PM and I'm stuffed from Dominga's cooking. Boy do I need a workout. I wobble into the garage and hit the old man's speed bag for a half hour. Then I do five sets of fifty pushups. Pops has a pull-up and dip station in the garage, so I do five sets of twelve. Tex and I would do pushups, pull-ups, and dips, out at sea on all the time. We called it getting prison strong because we figured that's where we're heading. After my workout in the garage I go swim laps in the pool. Pops always said swimming is the most complete exercise anyone can do. After I'm done, I smoke a nice fat joint of pakalolo and gaze up at the stars. Life is good.

I spend the next few days bumming around with Johnny going from jobsite to jobsite. Being Rocco's rat, I need to get close to Johnny's crew. It aint hard, they all get high and I have the world's best weed. Houses are popping up all over town and the Santori's have a piece of everything. All the construction supplies the builders buy are now coming from the Port of Miami. This means I'm getting richer and richer. Hanging out with Johnny everyday means eating Carina's Italian cooking every night. That's a great fringe benefit.

The doorbell wakes me the next morning around eight. I throw on my jeans and go peek through the blinds. I see two little, short Spanish guys and a white van in my driveway. These must be Willie's tailors with my clothes. I open the door and one guy starts talking in broken English. I think they want to be sure I'm Droz. I point to my chest saying, "I'm Droz, I'm Droz."

Once they're satisfied I'm Droz, they start unloading and asking, "Where I put, where I put?" I escort them to my room and they hang my clothes in the closet for me. What service. As the men are walking down the hallway, I shout, "Uno momento!" then reach into my front pocket and peel two C notes off my wad to tip them.

"No, no, no, Senor Droz," They simultaneously say.

"Yes, yes, yes, little Spanish guys." Then stuff a C note into each of their pockets. I quickly shuffle them out the door and close it behind them. I peek through the blinds watching them argue with each other in Spanish. I know Willie told them not to take any money from me. They eventually throw their hands in the air and leave. I go back to my room and marvel at my new wardrobe. Then I jump back in bed. As soon as I start nodding off, the fucking phone rings! I grab it on two rings. "Hello?"

"Good morning kid."

"Good morning Rocco. What's up?"

"I'll be by to pick you up at noon. There is someone very close to me that I want you to meet."

"Sure thing Rocco, I'll be ready."

"Good," Rocco hangs up the phone.

There goes another one of those short and sweet manly fucking phone conversations. I figure fuck going back to sleep. I might as well just get up and take a shower. I'm running low on a few things in the fridge, so after my shower I go to the store. By the time I get back, I still have an hour to kill. I go into the garage and grab my old man's fishing pole. It's rigged and ready with a purple worm for bass fishing. I head out back by the canal and start fishing. After only a few casts, I catch my first bass in Florida! It was a nice sized one too, It had to weigh at least 3 pounds! It wasn't long before I catch a few more of similar size. I throw them all back for prosperity. Feeling satisfied, I go back inside and get washed up. Sure enough Rocco is five minutes early again and I'm outside waiting.

When I get in the car Rocco says, "I heard you had a good time in Miami."

That little statement told me Rocco knew everything, so I reply sarcastically, "Dominga's cooking is out of this fucking world Rocco, but the dessert is something to die for, cut up Cuban a la mode. Next time you're at Willie's I suggest you to try some."

Rocco laughs saying, "You're alright kid. I'm glad you took it all in stride. I wanted you to see what happens to people who get caught dealing narcotics. This way you can't say you aint been warned when you find yourself strapped to a steel chair."

Rocco's right. After yesterday there are no excuses so I calmly reply, "It's cool Rocco. I got the message. On a more pleasant note, Fernando and Luis gave me a nice history lesson. You guys are sure on the same page about the government being corrupt and cooperating with drug dealers."

Rocco stares straight ahead at the road and nods his head before replying, "One day while Lucifer and God were playing chess, I'm sure Lucifer thought up governments. They all seem to be corrupt and evil. Today you are going to meet a man you can look up to. His name is Father Mcinerny."

"A priest," I reply shocked.

"He's a priest alright. He's truly one of a kind. We grew up together. We call him Father Mac. He needs help supplying marijuana to cancer patients. What he's doing is morally right, but still illegal. The people he's helping take highly addictive narcotics like oxycodone for their pain. Marijuana has proven to be much better. I hear you have a great pot connection in Hawaii and Thailand. Is that true?"

No use lying to Rocco. "Yes Rocco. It's true. I can get you guys some of the most potent weed in the world."

"That's what Father Mac said when I told him you were getting your pot from there. So, will you help?"

"I will definitely help the Father," I reply proudly.

"Good. He'll be happy to hear that. I have a house and a fishing boat on the Intracoastal Waterway in Boca. When the Father is in town, he likes to stay there and go fishing. We'll be there shortly."

"A pot dealing priest," I think to myself, "What could possibly be next!" Rocco pulls into a heavily landscaped circular driveway and parks his car. He pops the trunk and tells me to grab the freshly baked coffee cake he put there for the Father. Like my parents, Rocco never shows up empty handed. Even though it's Rocco's house, he walks up to the front door and rings the bell. Father Mac answers the door with a big Irish smile. Father Mac is a tall, nicely built man with salt and pepper hair. He's got high cheekbones and bright blue eyes. The Father has a glow about him. He's wearing a pair of loud colored tropical print shorts and no shirt. He must have been here for a while because he's sporting a nice tan. Not easy for a light skinned Irishmen to do.

Cheerfully in a strong Irish accent, he says, "Come in boys, come in! You're just in time for lunch! What are you holding there laddie? I bet it's my favorite coffee cake."

What an incredibly upbeat guy! So I smile wide and happily reply, "Yes it is Father. Rocco brought it for you."

The first thing I notice when I walk into Rocco's house is the view. You can look straight through the house and out the back patio doors to a very wide area of the Intracoastal. I see boats going by and a large pelican sitting on the piling of the boat dock. Docked out back is a big beautiful fishing boat. The boat is stunning from stem to stern.

"So, you're Georgie Droz's boy Michael," Father Mac asks.

"Yes I am Father," I proudly reply.

"Well let me tell you something Michael. Your dad is smiling down upon us while having a beer in Heaven with the rest of the firemen. Firemen are very special humans. They run fearlessly into burning buildings to save people while people are running out to save themselves. I know that's not much of a consolation son, but you're in good hands now. Rocco can't replace your father, but like your father, he's the salt of the earth."

I nod my head as Rocco puts his arm around me saying, "Why thanks for the vote of confidence Father. Not to change the subject, but is that corn beef and cabbage I smell?"

"It surely is Rocco! With boiled red potatoes and carrots! Just like me mother made for us when we were boys back in Brooklyn."

They both laugh together. Then Father Mac rubs me on top of the head saying, "I hope you brought your appetite Michael. I know old Rocco did, right Rocco?"

"You can bet on that Father."

"Aye, yes I could Rocco me boy, yes I could."

"I'm definitely hungry Father Mac. The last time I had corned beef and cabbage was on St. Patty's day with my father and the other firemen."

"Good, good, I hope you are thirsty too because I have an ice cold keg of Red Irish Ale that Rocco so graciously provided for me. Come on into the kitchen fellas."

When we get in the kitchen, I see a big pot on the stove. Father Mac walks over to it and picks up a meat fork. He takes the lid off the pot and stabs down pulling out a beautiful corned beef! He puts it on the butcher block and goes back into the pot for the cabbage, potatoes, and carrots. As Father Mac's putting them in a bowl he says, "Rocco me boy, get out some utensils, plates, and mugs."

Rocco does as the Father asks, and I help him set the table. After we're done, we go fill up three big beer mugs. By the time we get back to the kitchen, the food is on the table. After we all sit Father Mac says, "Boys, raise your mugs to the Lord and give Him thanks for what we're about to receive."

We raise our mugs and give thanks. Then we all take a big slug of Red Irish Ale. I never had this kind of beer before, so I comment, "This is a great tasting beer Father Mac."

"Aye, a fine Ale it is Michael. Now dig in me boy!" Before I can stick my fork in some corned beef, Rocco blurts out, "Father Mac, where's your homemade brown mustard?"

"May the Saints preserve us Rocco. I almost forgot."

Father Mac gets up and goes to the fridge. He comes back holding a strange looking jar and says, "Here you go boys, me very own homemade spicy brown mustard."

Rocco drops a healthy glob on his plate and passes me the jar. I take a glob too and pass the jar to the Father. I dab a little corned beef in it and try it. It's deliciously sweet and spicy!

Now after about an hour of eating, drinking, burping, and farting, Father asks me, "So Michael, Rocco says you can get very potent marijuana. Is that true son?"

I take a slug of beer and let out a manly belch before replying, "I sure can Father. How much do you need?"

"I'll take as much as you can get son."

I think for a moment before replying back. "I'm not exactly sure how much I can get at one time Father. I have very good connections in Hawaii and Thailand. I can set up a meeting with both of them if you like Father."

"Let's start with Hawaii first. That sounds the safest. How would you like to proceed Michael?"

"I think the best thing to do Father is set up a meeting for you in Hawaii with my good friend Keoni."

"You know this man Rocco?" Father Mac asks.

"Not personally Father, but Keoni comes from good stock like Michael here. His father's name is Keoki. He's a full-blooded Royal Hawaiian; in fact, the entire family is full-blooded Royal Hawaiian. They are loved and respected by their people. Michael has become like family to them. He's also banging Keoki's daughter, Princess Keona."

"What does that matter Rocco?" I frown and ask.

"Her father and brother weren't offended by this Michael?" Father Mac seriously asks.

"Sex is more open and free over there than it is here Father. The King doesn't want his son or daughter to marry a foreigner though. He wants to keep the Royal Hawaiian bloodline pure. King Keoki also has some very special powers."

Father Mac raises his head and stares right through me with his piercing blue eyes asking, "What type of powers son?"

"It's called Aumakua. King Keoki gets his powers from the land and his ancestors. I have seen him summon sharks and stingrays to do his bidding. He says they are his ancestors. It's rumored he can also control the tides and the weather on the Island too."

"Do you know these things to be true Rocco?" Father Mac asks.

Rocco sighs and takes a slug of beer before replying, "I haven't witnessed them myself Father, but I trust my sources. Droz is telling the truth."

Father Mac reflects for a moment before replying, "King Keoki isn't the only human capable of such things Michael. Rocco and I know firsthand, as you do, there are certain individuals possessing these gifts. I know a woman in Central America who has healed sicknesses, even cancer, with prayer. She will only help her local people and never leaves her village. In Africa, there was a medicine man who Rocco and I had both knew. He had incredible powers. Tell Michael the story Rocco."

Rocco let's out an even bigger sigh this time. He finishes off his beer and begrudgingly replies, "Alright Father, I'll tell the story. You go refill the beers."

"Gladly," Father Mac replies with a giant smile.

Rocco is already half lit from all the beers he drank, so I figure this ought to be good!

Using his heavy Italian Brooklyn accent, Rocco starts the story. "There was this small village in South Africa outside Botswana. The good Father and I were both there on a humanitarian mission."

"Tell the boy what you were really doing there Rocco," Father Mac brings our refills saying.

Annoyed, Rocco takes a slug of his beer before replying, "Geez Father can't you let the kid think I'm a fucking humanitarian?"

"Oh but you are Rocco, you are, just not always."

Rocco shakes his head and shrugs his shoulders. Then he takes a few slugs of beer and waits a few seconds before letting out a loud belch. Now he continues. "About thirty years ago Droz I got some wild information. It was from a Hassidic Jew in Brooklyn named Ezra about a lost diamond mine. It turns out these Hassidic Jews made good friends with native tribes working in diamond mines. My family gave Ezra's family over 100k to smuggle diamonds out of South Africa and back into Brooklyn for us. It turns out his deadbeat brother in-law Nathaniel disappears down there with our fucking money. The dirty bastard had a wife and six kids back in Brooklyn too."

"Maybe that's why Nathaniel didn't come back Rocco?" I interrupt sarcastically.

Father Mac and I both laugh. Rocco glares at me and continues. "After roughing him up a bit, Ezra tells my family about a lost tribe and a diamond mine. Not just any diamonds mine mind you, a diamond mine with diamonds the size of jumbo eggs. Ezra got this information about the lost tribe from the local natives where Father Mac was doing his mission work. Ezra gave me the name of two of those natives, Abazu and Mabula. He said these two guys could give me information about the whereabouts of Nathaniel. He told me that Nathaniel got information out of Abazu and Mabula about where the mine might be located. Nathaniel used our money to go off into the fucking jungle to find it, and that's the last they heard from him. Now my father tells me I have to go find this fucking prick."

"So what did you do Rocco?"

Rocco lifts up his beer mug and gulps it all down. He slaps his empty mug down hard on the table and replies gruffly, "What did I do? I got on a fucking plane you fucking idiot. Stop asking stupid fucking questions and get us another beer.

When you comeback keep your fucking mouth shut and just listen to the story."

"Priceless," I think to myself! Rocco is half drunk telling a story, and I'm busting his balls! I happily get up and get us a refill. When I sit back down Rocco continues.

"Okay, so when I get down there I hook up with Father Mac. He points me in the right direction to find Abazu and Mabula. These guys say they told Nathaniel everything they knew about where the mine might be located. In exchange, Nathaniel promised to hire them as guides and cut them in, but before he did that, he said he needed about a week or so to get his shit together. Abazu said they waited ten fucking days and then went looking for him. When they couldn't find him, they knew Nathaniel backstabbed them. So now I offer Abazu and Mabula the same fucking deal to find this son of a bitch."

"Did you find him Rocco?" I ask anxiously.

Rocco gets a shit eating grin on his face and chugs down his beer. Then he wipes the foam from his upper lip and replies, "Of course I fucking found him you numb nuts. It almost fucking killed me, but I fucking found him."

"He's right laddie. It did almost kill him. Rocco had me worried sick for a while, but as he always does son, he pulled through."

Rocco nods his head and smiles proudly before continuing. "Now listen to this fucking trek I go on. So here I fucking am with a machete in my hand chopping through this unforgiving fucking jungle. I could have sworn that at any minute I'd see fucking Tarzan swinging through the trees. The fucking bugs in this jungle are of prehistoric size. I'm telling you Droz, I must have gotten bitten at least once by every fucking insect God created. They must have loved my Italian blood because Mabula and Abazu didn't get bitten once. At the end of each day, you're exhausted. Then at nighttime, the jungle comes alive with predators. As you lay by the fire, you can see glowing eyes staring at you from the edge of the campsite. You take your fucking life in your hands every time you take a leak or dump. Then one night we hear fucking drums. 'Madone,' I say to myself, 'What the fuck is going on now?' I look over at my guides and both of them are cuddled up like two fucking faggots. They were scared fucking shitless mumbling back and forth to each other, so I ask them, 'What the fuck are you two guys mumbling about?'

"Shaking like a leaf Mabula replies, 'Cannibals.'

"'Cannibals, you got to be fucking kidding me Mabula? It's kind of late in the fucking game to be telling me there are cannibals out here. If you told me this before we left I would have brought a bigger fucking gun.'

"Abazu quickly shushes me and whispers, 'Please put out the fire Rocco and stay quiet.'

"I listen. Now the beat of the drums is getting louder and louder as they get closer to us. 'This can't be,' I think to myself, 'After all I fucking been through, I'm going out in a jungle bunnies' soup pot?' Then there's this horrible prolonged blood curdling fucking scream. It echoes through the jungle for at least a minute. I figure that can't be a good sign, but when I look at my guides they're fucking smiling! So I whisper, 'Is everything good?'

"'Everything is good now Rocco. They have found their meal.'

"'Well that's good news Abazu. Let's just hope they don't come looking for fucking dessert.' The three of us chuckle a bit. We couldn't start another fire, but at least we weren't somebodies fucking supper."

I blurt out, "Damn it Rocco! That's an incredible fucking story! It sounds like a fucking movie!"

"There weren't only cannibals in the jungle Michael. There were also headhunters. Would you boys like a refill?" Father Mac adds.

"Sure Father," We both reply.

Father Mac walks over to the tap and refills our mugs. After he comes back, he hands us our beers and Rocco continues.

"After two weeks of fucking hell working my way through this jungle, I finally find Nathaniel. I find this piece of shit digging all alone in a fucking cave. I walk up behind this cock-sucker and grab him by the neck. Then I start yelling at him, 'Where's my fucking money you Jew bastard!'

"Nathaniel breaks down into tears and babbles like a fuck-ing madman. I thought he lost his fucking mind. He looks like a fucking skeleton, but after what I been through trying to find this cocksucker, I don't show him any mercy. So now I get tough with him yelling, 'The money or the fucking diamonds, or I'll cut your fucking head off with this machete you cocksucker!' Nathaniel looks at me trying to speak, but he fucking can't. I figure it's been so long since he spoke to anyone, he may need a fucking minute.

"When this miserable son of a bitch finally gets a hold of his faculties, he yells at the top of his lungs, 'Please kill me! Please kill me! I beg you! I rather die than face the shame I have brought upon my family! I have been digging for months and have found nothing but my own despair! Have mercy on me and kill me please!'

"Now I'm really fucking mad yelling back, 'Don't you fuck-ing dare tell me you found nothing you worthless piece of shit!'

"Now he cries like a little fucking bitch, so I smack him around like one until he stops. Still fucking sniffling, he looks at me saying, 'According to everything I have learned this must be the cave, but I have found nothing. I am so ashamed for what I have done to my family. Please have mercy on me and kill me.'

"I'm so fucking distraught at this point I don't know what to fucking do, so I think real hard for a second. Then I say to my-self, 'Bull fucking shit! I aint killing this little fucking crybaby! That's letting him off easy.' So I tell the little Jew bastard, 'You know what Nathaniel? I changed my fucking mind, I aint going to kill you. I'm going to drag you out of this God forsaken jungle and bring you back to the village. Then I'm going to tie your boney Jew ass to a fucking tree and call your brother-in-law Ezra. I'm going to tell him to get on the next fucking plane and come out here to get you. Once you're back in Brooklyn, I'll let your own tribe fucking handle you. After the worry, pain, and suffering you put your family through, they will make you suffer more than I ever could. Your family owes my family a lot of fucking money, and you're going to help them pay it back.'"

Rocco drinks from his mug of beer. Now Father Mac says, "When I first seen Rocco come out of the jungle he had insect bites all over his body and his eyes were sunken into his head. He was so skinny and weak I thought he would surely die. There were no hospitals to bring him to, so I brought him to a couple native girls. They were known amongst the tribes to be healers. The native girls made Rocco special foods and herbal teas. They also made healing oils out of special plants and massaged them into his body. I knew he was better when I caught him dipping his wick into the girls."

I look at Rocco and start singing Jungle Boogie by Kool and the Gang teasing him.

Rocco laughs and drinks more beer. Then he says, "They're all pink on the inside kid."

Father Mac shakes his head and says, "Now let me tell you the part of the story we were getting too Michael.

"One morning before Rocco leaves a young woman comes running into the village holding a small child listlessly in her arms. She's screaming and crying uncontrollably. She frantically tells the other villagers her son accidentally drowned in the river while she was washing clothes. The old medicine man of the village took the boy from the mother's arms and laid him down under a big shady tree. The medicine man took a necklace from his neck and placed it around the neck of the drowned boy. Looking up at the sky, he began chanting in his native tongue. The medicine man then took the necklace from the boy's neck and placed it back onto his own. He whispered something to the mother and walked away. The mother called to her son. Miraculously the boy rose up and ran into to her open arms. Rocco and I both witnessed a miracle that morning, one thankfully of many. So, Michael, do you feel better that me and old Rocco here shared a little with you today?"

"Definitely, now how about some evil demon shit Father. You got any of those stories?" I reply like a wiseass.

Rocco shakes his head at me like he's embarrassed. Father Mac answers in a solemn tone, "Unfortunately son I have a lot of those stories. I get a new one every time I visit a drug rehabilitation clinic. The dirty devils pushing narcotics are turning people into demons every day. These demons then go around robbing, stealing, and killing for their master. They will perform unimaginable types of evil to feed their addiction. An addiction to a merciless master of evil that robs it's minions of their very soul."

Feeling like an idiot, I humbly reply, "I'm sorry for being such a wiseass Father Mac. That was a really stupid question."

Father Mac looks me in the eyes and rubs me on the head saying, "Aye, your apology is accepted Michael. So when will you be able to set up my meeting with Keoni?"

Wanting to make amends, I quickly reply back, "How about right now Father? It's still mid-morning over there and I'll bet Keoni is still sleeping."

"No better time than the present son," The Father says with a big smile.

I use Rocco's phone to dial Keoni. As I'm standing in the kitchen hoping Keoni answers, Rocco and Father Mac discuss something in the living room. After the seventh ring, I hear a pretty little voice with a Hawaiian accent say, "Keoni wants to know who dares call him this early."

"Tell the prince it's Droz," I reply grinning.

"Droz is the one who dares call you this early Keoni."

I hear Keoni laughing in the background. Then he says, "I knew it had to be a haole. Give me the phone."

I hear the phone drop as Keoni tries to grab it. He finally gets a handle on it and says, "I know you miss my sista Droz, but you cannot cry on my shoulder this early."

"How is Keona?" I quickly reply.

"She good sometimes and miserable others like all wahines. I know she miss you. You want me tell her you miss her too?"

"Definitely Keoni, but listen up. I met a priest. Not just any priest, but a really cool priest. He wants to come out to the Islands. Is that cool?"

Keoni hesitates for a moment and then replies, "I understand Droz. You give him my phone number and tell him to contact me when he is ready to travel. I will take very good care of him."

"Thanks Keoni. I hope to see all of you guys soon. Aloha."

"Aloha," Keoni says and we hang up.

I knew not to dilly dally too long on the phone in front of Rocco. He would take it as a sign of weakness like my Father. I write down Keoni's name and phone number. I proudly walk into the living room and hand it to Father Mac saying, "When you're ready to travel just give Keoni a call and he will take good care of you."

Rocco adds, "How about when you go out there Father you find us a nice fishing boat and a nicer place to dock it. A forty foot Bertram Sport Fisher would be nice like the one we got here. I want the house to be off the beaten path. I don't want any fucking tourists getting lost in my backyard. I'm sure Keoni and his family can lead us in the right direction, right Droz?"

"I'm sure they can Rocco."

"Good. When you find something you like Father just give me a call and I'll wire you the money."

Father Mac is ecstatic as he replies merrily, "Oh that's a great idea Rocco! A great idea indeed! We will have so much fun together!"

I think to myself, "How perfect is this!"

"Well thanks for the delicious lunch Father Mac. It's been another wonderful afternoon spent with my oldest and dearest friend."

"Aye, it was Rocco. I love you like me own brother and you know it. A fine young man Michael is. I only hope he lives up to his father's reputation."

Rocco looks at me and pats me on the back. Then he looks at Father Mac saying, "I think he will Father. If he knows what's good for him."

I give Rocco a hug replying, "I loved my father and I miss him dearly. I am humbled by all of the good men who loved and respected him. I am grateful that Rocco has taken me under his wing and I won't let him down."

Father Mac hugs me and then steps backward. He stares me in the eyes saying, "I get a good feeling from you son. Just follow your heart and trust your instincts. The rest will come easy."

"I told Michael when I first met him Father; he has the two things money can't buy and I can't teach, balls and instincts. If he listens to me and stays loyal there's no limit to where I can take him."

Father Mac laughs and turns to me saying, "Rocco's telling you the truth me boy, The God's honest truth. You listen to what Rocco tells you to do and stay loyal. If you do, there truly are no limits in this mortal world to what you can accomplish."

Feeling a bit invincible, I reply back with swagger, "How about a street kid like me becoming president. Is that possible Rocco?"

Father Mac and Rocco both laugh. "Why the fuck would you ever want to be president Droz?" Rocco seriously asks.

"Well, because it's the top job aint it?" I sheepishly reply.

"The president is nothing but a puppet. What you want to be is the puppeteer," Father Mac smiles at Rocco and Rocco smiles back at.

"It's time to go Droz. Say goodbye to the good Father."

"Thank you Father Mac for a great lunch and an even greater time," I hug the father and say.

"I enjoyed your company too Michael. Now I'm looking forward to meeting your friends in Hawaii. Goodbye son, and may God travel with you both."

With that said, Father Mac blesses us and we leave. As we're pulling out of the driveway I say, "That is the coolest priest on the planet Rocco."

"Not only the coolest Droz, but also the toughest."

"No shit? So the priest can fight?" I reply surprised.

Rocco chuckles and says, "Fight aint the word Droz. Father Mac's a one man wrecking crew. Listen to this fucking story. About twenty-five years ago on a hot summer's night in Brooklyn, all of us wise guys are outside my old man's social club drinking and playing cards. That night three wise guys from a crew up in the Bronx were hanging out with us. Everybody's having a good fucking time shooting the shit, drinking, and gambling. A pretty, young girl from the neighborhood comes walking down the block past us. Instead of doing the right thing and respecting our neighborhood, the wise guys from the Bronx start hitting on her. One of the guys decides to pat her on the ass as she walks by. That raises a few eyebrows, but wasn't enough to cause a problem. After all, we're all having a good time drinking and playing cards. The young girl ignored him, which was a good thing, but he got up and followed her, which was a bad thing. Now this fucking gavone from the Bronx goes too fucking far. He sticks his hand up her fucking dress and feels her up."

I interrupt now emphatically saying, "Now that's fucked up Rocco. I can understand letting him get by with a little pat on her ass, but reaching under her dress for some fucking pie? I don't fucking think so. Wise guy or not Rocco, this guy deserves a fucking beating."

"He sure did kid, and he fucking got one too. From the fucking girl! She starts beating the shit out of him with her fucking purse! I don't know what she had in that fucking thing, but it did some major fucking damage! He starts yelling like a little bitch, 'My eye, my eye, I think she blinded me!' Everybody's fucking laughing except his two fucking friends. They run over and push the poor young girl into the gutter. When she starts crying they fucking spit on her, so now we all go after them.

Out of fucking nowhere, Father Mac appears. He's on these guys like stink on shit. Biff, bam, boom! He's pounding away on them like a fucking jackhammer!

"We move in to help the Father and he yells, 'Stay back fellas, these dirty pedophiles are all mine!'

"Everybody listens to Father Mac because we know once he gets going you better stay out of his fucking way. Father Mac bloodies them up good, but they aint giving up, so they get down and dirty with the Father. One of the cocksuckers gets behind Father Mac and holds his arms while another guy takes of his belt. He wraps the belt around his right hand and starts punching Father Mac in the mouth. Blood splatters all over Father Macs face."

Absolutely appalled Rocco let this happen, I rudely interrupt saying, "How could you stand there and let that happen to your best friend Rocco? Never mind that even. How could you let that happen to a priest? You'll burn in hell for that one Rocco."

Rocco laughs and waves his hand at me saying, "You want me to stop here? Because it gets even worse for the poor Father."

"Of course I don't want you to stop, but I'm telling you now Rocco, this better end well or I think I might hate you."

Rocco waves his hand at me again as he continues. "Now the third guy takes off one of his leather boots and smashes Father Mac repeatedly across the head with it. This opens up a big ugly gash in the middle of his forehead. Blood pours out of it like a fucking waterfall. His nice white priest shirt turns bloody red. Father Mac back head butts the guy holding him from behind and stomps his foot. This loosens the guy's grip, so he breaks free from the hold. Father Mac wobbles backwards going down to one knee. The three guys hesitate for a minute thinking he's finished, but they didn't know him like we did. Father Mac looks down at his priest shirt and sees it's ruined. With blood streaming down his face, Father Mac looks at the three men saying, "My beloved mother gave me this priest shirt. She scrubbed floors to buy it for me, and you boys ruined it. You'll all pay for that."

"With those words, Father Mac stands up and pulls out a blackjack. The three men charge Father Mac and he starts cutting them down. You can hear their skulls cracking with every blow. Blood is flying everywhere, and this time it aint Father Mac's. Father Mac proceeds to beat each one of these cocksuckers to death. What a fucking mess he made of these guys. We get the bodies out of there and hose down the sidewalk before the cops come. Then we take Father Mac to a doctor friend and get him stitched up."

Rocco's story lasts all the way to my front door. Before I get out of the car I say, "Rocco I can't even begin to tell you how much I loved hearing your stories, and how much I loved meeting Father Mac."

"I'm glad Michael. You need a sense of family in your life. I want you to feel that you can reach out to me or the Father anytime."

Hearing those words come out of Rocco's mouth makes me feel loved, so I reach over for a hug.

"Who's that lady staring at us with her hand over her mouth and shaking her head?" Rocco asks.

"Oh shit Rocco. That's the nosey neighbor lady. She saw me and Willie hug. Then she ran to her husband screaming that Georgie Droz's son is a homo. So now you're a homo too."

Rocco shrugs his shoulders saying, "Some people are really fucked up that way. They think if a man shows affection to another man he's a homo. In any event, you need some privacy landscaping. I'll tell my brother. He knows a guy who owns a nursery."

"Thanks Rocco. You read my mind. You and Father Mac don't worry; I will live up to all of your expectations."

As I am walking to my front door Rocco rolls down his window saying, "Always remember this kid. It's more important to live up to your own expectations than to someone else's."

With those words, Rocco rolls up his window and leaves.

EYES WIDE OPEN...

In the coming weeks my kickbacks from Johnny's crew grow larger and larger. I start picking up the tabs for all of Johnny's guys at my club. My prestige amongst everyone is growing by the day. I call Keoni and tell him to start sending me five pounds a month as soon as possible. My pakalolo arrived airmail that week. Now I'm supplying Johnny's crew with the best weed in the world. It turns out Carmine's a huge fucking pothead. We become good friends, so I set him up dealing weed for me. He's real happy about it. He makes some extra cash and smokes for free. Carmine helps cement my relationship with the rest of Johnny's crew. It isn't long before Johnny's crew likes me more than they like him. As a result, Johnny's resentment towards me grows. Soon Johnny's finding reasons not to bring me around his guys anymore, so I go see them on my own, which leads to even more resentment.

Annmarie and Joanie are my steady girls. They're beautiful, young, clean, and freaks in the sack. I fulfill my sexual desires with them daily. Johnny and Willie have been real busy working for their fathers, so going to the clubs is put off for a while. Tomorrow though is Friday, and we are finally going. Rocco called and is picking me up Friday at noon to meet someone new. I'm excited and looking forward to it. I invited the girls over tonight for a barbecue. We really do enjoy each other's company. The kinky sex is just icing on the cake. I cook the girl's breakfast in the morning and then shuffle them out the door before Rocco arrives.

As usual, Rocco is five minutes early and as usual I am outside waiting for him. I get in the car and give him a kiss on the cheek then ask, "Where are we heading today Rocco?"

"Ft. Lauderdale kid, my cousin Frankie got a beautiful house on the Intracoastal there. You need a legitimate job Droz to show how you pay your bills. You will be getting what we call a no show job as a consultant from the Navy. Frankie's not your boss and you will not answer to him. You only work for me. Frankie runs a company for me called Future Visions. It is the most important company I own. Future Visions invests in cutting edge technologies. We make investments in companies throughout the world. We even invest directly with foreign governments. Right now, anything and everything to do with computers is huge. We made a major bet on new software coming out that will make using a computer easy for everyone. Pretty soon, everyone will own a computer and Future Visions will have a piece of everything involved. You must keep all of this to yourself. Johnny and everyone else thinks Future Visions is a front, or shell company. Future Visions is our future. I already told Frankie all about you. I told him I'm taking you under my wing.

It intrigued me hearing Rocco is behind this and I want in. We pull down a street lined with absolutely gorgeous mansions. The masts of very large sailboats poke out above some of the roof tops. We pull up to a big house with large windows. I can see straight through the front of the house to the Intracoastal. We pull up the driveway, and a woman is standing at the end of it. She's waving and calling out Rocco's name.

"Who's that?" I ask.

"That's Frankie's wife Phyllis. His third wife I might add," Rocco chuckles and replies.

Phyllis is a short, bubbly woman. She has bleached blonde hair, big blue eyes, and humongous fucking tits. I mean they're like fucking watermelons. Phyllis is wearing a multi colored sequence blouse and black pants. She's also wearing way too much makeup. If you get too close, her false eyelashes could take out an eye. You can open a pawnshop with all the fucking jewelry she's wearing. I guess you can call her attractive if you like that kind of broad, but she aint my type.

"When I pop the trunk get the pastries," Rocco says.

"No problem," I reply.

We get out of the car and while I'm getting the pastries, Rocco gets assaulted by Phyllis. She's hugging and kissing him like he just came home from a war. I wish I had a camera because her lipstick is smeared all over his face. After Phyllis is done, she looks at Rocco saying, "Oh I did it again, didn't I Rocco? Give me your hanky and I'll wipe my lipstick off your face."

Rocco heroically puts forth a fake smile and pulls out his hanky. Then Phyllis does the rest. I walk over with the pastry box, and Rocco takes it from me with a smile saying, "This is Michael, Phyllis. He's the young man I was telling you and Frankie about. Michael, this is Phyllis, my Cousin Frankie's wife."

Before I can even speak, Phyllis blurts out, "Michael, you have no idea how many nice things I have heard about you! I am so pleased to meet you!"

"Why thank you Phyllis. I am Pleased to meet you too," I extend my hand replying.

Phyllis got a look in her eyes like a fat kid in a bakery. She pushes my hand aside saying, "We're all family here Michael. Handshakes are for strangers."

Oh shit, here she fucking comes! All puckered up with her arms wide open! I close my eyes so they don't get poked out and brace myself for the worst! She smashes herself against me smothering me with kisses. I bounce off her boobs like I'm bouncing on a trampoline. It's a good thing too because her perfume would have suffocated me. When the assault's over, she uses Rocco's hanky to clean me up too. Then she escorts us to the front door. Frankie's house looks like a fucking palace. Future Visions is paying big dividends for Frankie. No expense has been spared decorating this place. I look towards the patio area and see the kind of statues you see in a movie about Ancient Rome. Some of them are spewing water out into the massive pool.

Phyllis now says, "Frankie's in his study. You know the way Rocco. I'm going outside to check on the caterers. It's a beautiful day, so I decided we should have lunch on the patio. Is that alright with you?"

"Sounds great Phyllis, after all, it's another beautiful day in paradise!" Rocco smiles graciously replying.

"You always say that Rocco, and you're always so right too!"

"By the way Phyllis, what are we having for lunch?" Rocco asks hungrily.

Overjoyed Rocco asked, Phyllis replies jubilantly, "The caterers set up an ocean feast for you Rocco featuring Jumbo Stone Crab Claws, Maine Lobster, and grilled Swordfish. We didn't forget your favorite either, Key West Jumbo Pink Shrimp!"

"That sounds absolutely fabulous Phyllis. Have you ever had Key West Jumbo Pink Shrimp Droz?"

"I can't say that I have Rocco."

"Then you're in for a treat Droz. Key West Jumbo Pink Shrimp are the best in the world."

"Sounds great Rocco, I can't wait to try them."

Phyllis leaves us, and I follow Rocco down the marble tiled hallway. Along the way I can't help noticing the family pictures hanging on the walls. The kind of pictures you take at Christmas, birthdays, picnics, and vacations. Rocco notices me gawking and points to one picture in particular saying, "That's a picture of my son Bobby and Frankie's son Joey. They were best friends. In fact, they were inseparable. Look at how happy they both looked together."

Frankie's son Joey is a good-looking kid. He has long, straight, black hair and dark eyes. Joey has a muscular build and a big, warm smile. Bobby is a good-looking kid too. He has long, light, brown hair and brown eyes. Bobby also has a warm smile. Rocco was right. They did look happy together. Rocco gets a little teary eyed so I give him a big hug. It's really cool seeing a tough guy like Rocco get emotional. It makes me respect him even more. I can't help feeling the both of us are filling a void in each other's lives. When we get close to Frankie's study, we hear him talking on the phone. Rocco just opens up the door to his office and walks in. This startles Frankie, and he hastily says goodbye to whomever he was speaking with.

"Rocco, it's good to see you!" exclaims Frankie.

Frankie is an average looking guy in every way. If you were riding on a bus, you wouldn't even notice him. He dresses conservatively like a banker. Frankie has short, black, thinning hair and dark eyes. He gets up from his chair to give Rocco a hug and a kiss. Then looks at me saying, "Hello Michael. You have my sincerest condolences son. I didn't know your father and mother personally, but I have heard a lot of good things about them."

"I appreciate that Frankie, and thank you for inviting me to your beautiful home."

"You're welcome young man, and I'm glad you like it. So Michael, I hear I am employing you as a consultant. Is that correct?"

Rocco interrupts Frankie, "Future Visions is employing Droz as a consultant Frankie, but he only works and reports to me."

"That's right. You told me you were grooming Droz. May I ask what for Rocco?" Frankie frowns replying.

"I don't know yet Frankie. The kid comes from good stock. I'm sure I'll find something, as long as he keeps his nose clean."

Frankie gives me a stern look now saying, "There's a lot of temptation down here in South Florida to get involved with the wrong people Droz. Right now, you're involved with the right people. I'm sure Rocco has lectured you on this already. We can ill afford having anyone working for us getting caught up in the narcotics racket, right Rocco?"

"Oh don't worry Frankie. The kid's been warned."

"Rocco knows I've been lucky with my son Joey. I want to keep it that way, so I sent him over to Europe to study."

Hearing Joey's name brings a smile to Rocco's face, so he replies, "I'm glad you brought Joey up Frankie. How is the boy? He used to send me a letter every now and then, but I haven't received one in a while."

Frankie waves his hand saying, "Don't feel bad Rocco. The only time I hear from Joey anymore is when he runs out of money."

"He's probably found himself a girlfriend to spend it on," Rocco laughs replying.

"You're probably right Rocco. As long as he stays out of trouble and studies, I'm happy. So what kind of compensation is Future Visions giving Droz?"

"I figure I'll give him a salary and benefits package totaling around eighty thousand. That should look good for Uncle Sam."

"Whatever you say Rocco," Frankie raises his eyebrows replying.

"Now tell Droz what we got going on here Frankie."

"Sure Rocco. Right now, it's all about computers Droz and everything to do with them. Hardware, software, microprocessors, you name it; there's money to be made in it. The next big money maker will be cell phones and towers. Remember Rocco when I tried giving you that mobile phone?"

Rocco gets a really sour look on his face as he replies, "Yeah I remember. I told you to stick it up your ass. You remember that?"

Frankie frowns again before replying. "Yeah I remember, and now we're losing ground Rocco. I really wish you would reconsider and invest the capital I have been asking for."

Annoyed, Rocco replies, "I don't see any future in them Frankie. Why would any rational human being want to be bothered by a phone ringing wherever they go? The last thing I want when I'm out is to be tracked down by anyone. The phone should be left at home where it belongs. Maybe I could see doctors using one, but I can't see business big wigs wanting one. What big shot wants to be bothered when they're playing golf, or out fishing on their boat? I would fire a cocksucker if they disturbed me out on my boat!"

Frankie shakes his head replying, "I think you're wrong Rocco. You may not like to be bothered, but other people may want to be. The type of phone you carry may define who you are to the public. Mobile phones have already become a symbol of status and wealth."

Rocco gets even more annoyed now and waves his finger at Frankie replying, "There you go again Frankie. You're always thinking of wealth and social status. I might be more interested in mobile phones if I knew that one day everyone would be able to afford one."

Frankie keeps trying. "Well eventually Rocco different model phones will be manufactured for people from all walks of life. These new phones are going to need plenty of towers for transporting and receiving their signals. New satellites will also be needed to relay the traffic around the world. Future Visions can secure strategic points of presence mobile phone companies will need. There will also someday be retail outlets for sales and service creating a new source of skilled jobs."

Rocco looks extremely frustrated now. He turns to me asking, "What do your instincts tell you about this kid?"

Thrilled Rocco's asking my opinion, I quickly reply. "My instincts tell me for guys like you and my father no fucking way, but for other people, fuck yeah. Especially fucking broads Rocco, they can't get off the fucking phone as it is. You'll make a billion dollars just by selling phones to fucking woman alone. Plus all the nagging bitches will make their husbands and boyfriends carry one so they can keep tabs on them. Parents will buy their teenagers one so they can keep track of them. No more excuses for not calling home like I couldn't find a pay phone or I didn't have any change."

Rocco puts his hands on both sides of his head and yells, "Holy fucking shit Droz! What a fucking nightmare of a world you just described to me!"

Rocco now looks at Frankie saying, "You know what Frankie. This kid made fucking sense. You got my blessings. Go full force into this mobile phone business. Leave no stone unturned."

Frankie cracks a big smile and pats me on the back happily saying, "I see now why Rocco likes you so much Droz. You got vision kid, Future Visions. You may just bring Rocco out of the fucking Dark Ages."

Rocco glares at Frankie saying, "Enough of your fucking gloating Frankie, I'm hungry. Get out the kid's paperwork."

Frankie quickly wipes the smile off his face and opens the top draw of his desk. He pulls out my employment papers saying, "Print your name and address where indicated. Then sign the bottom and my secretary will do the rest. Here's my card. If you don't get a check in the mail about every two weeks, call me and I'll straighten it out."

I quickly do what Frankie says and hand him back his paperwork. I look at his card and his last name is Pastori. I put the card in my back pocket and tell Frankie thanks.

Rocco claps his hands and says, "Let's go eat."

The view of the main Intracoastal from Frankie's backyard is simply awesome. The tables are elegantly set. Some are adorned with flowers and fruit baskets. Others are stacked with seafood sitting atop mountains of crushed ice. Two formally dressed waiters are holding wine bottles for Frankie's perusal. Frankie looks at the labels and nods his head. Rocco is seated at the head of the table and I'm seated to his right. Frankie and Phyllis sit directly across from us. As the waiters pour wine we all get up and help ourselves to King Neptune's Buffet. The formal lunch meeting with Frankie is a stark contrast to the informal meetings and home cooking of the previous two. There isn't any story telling at this meeting, just some chitchat.

"Hey kid, how do you I like the shrimp?" Rocco asks.

I have mouth full of them when he asks, so I take a second to swallow before replying, "Fantastic Rocco, Key West Jumbo Pink Shrimp are the best."

Rocco smiles and proposes a toast. "To great food and great family to eat it with, Salud!"

Right after coffee and pastries Rocco graciously excuses himself. We thank our hosts and head for the door. In the car Rocco asks, "What did you think of the meeting?"

"I'm very excited about Future Visions Rocco. If computers and cell phones are just a part of it, I can't wait to learn about the rest. If Frankie didn't need you, he would drop you like a bad habit Rocco. And you don't particularly like him or his wife either."

"Hmm, it's that easy to spot?" Rocco raises his eyebrows asking.

"Yup"

Rocco nods his head saying, "Good boy Droz. Frankie and I grew up together, but we're two different people. I respect him as businessman heading Future Visions, but I don't respect him as a man."

"And why's that?" I inquisitively ask.

Rocco sighs and then replies, "He's ruled by money and shallow woman Droz. Frankie's first wife's name was Camille. She may not have been pretty, but she was a strong woman of high moral fiber. She gave Frankie his son Joey. He cheated on her all the time. Frankie said she was frigid. There's no so such thing as a frigid woman Michael, only clumsy men. Frankie must be one of them. When Camille couldn't take the embarrassment of Frankie's philandering anymore, she divorced him. After the divorce, she moved back to Italy with Joey. Joey didn't like growing up poor in Italy when he could live rich in America, so it wasn't long before he came back to live with his father. This left Camille alone and brokenhearted. In under a year she withered away and died of a broken heart. Frankie and Joey didn't even attend her funeral."

Stunned by the story, I ask, "Rocco, if you really don't respect Frankie, why the fuck you keep him in charge of Future Visions?"

Rocco stares straight ahead at the road for a few seconds before replying, "For one reason Droz. Frankie's good at it. I got no complaints about his performance and he aint a fucking rat. Sometimes you need to put your personal feelings aside for business."

"When you change your mind Rocco, I want his fucking job."

"I admire your ambition Droz," Rocco replies smiling.

Now I change the subject. "Rocco, Willie and I are thinking about investing some of our money in real estate like you and his father did. Do you have any suggestions?"

Rocco waves his head from side to side to side before replying, "There's a city right next to Coral Springs named Parkland. Pretty soon there will be a big change in the zoning there. It's a sure thing, if you know what I mean. I got my brother already in on it. It needs to be kept quiet, so don't tell anyone. Not even Johnny or Willie. Just tell Willie you got a sure thing for him."

"Sounds perfect Rocco, how much dough you need?" I nod my head and ask.

"You need to buy the five acre tracts. Parkland is designed for people who have money and want room to breathe. It's a great place for you and Teresa Sue to settle down in. Teresa Sue can have her horses there."

"That's nice Rocco, but who says I'm settling down?" I cockily reply.

Rocco frowns and changes the subject. "I want you to come by for Sunday dinner at two o'clock. You can tell me what you found out at the clubs. If you want in on the land, bring me a hundred large for two five-acre tracts. You'll triple your money overnight after the new zoning is passed."

"I'm in Rocco. If Willie aint down, I'll keep them both." Then I chuckle asking, "So, I guess you cook?"

"You'll find out Sunday you're not the only one that can make sauce and meatballs," Rocco sneers.

"I hope so Rocco because the last thing I need is fucking agita," I reply sarcastically with my hand on my belly.

Rocco gives me a playful little smack on the back of the head saying, "You give me agita without fucking eating."

We both laugh as Rocco pulls into my driveway. I give him a kiss on the cheek and leave. When I get in the house it's almost 4 PM. I say to myself, "It's a good time for a workout and a swim. Then I'll take a little nap, so I'm nice and refreshed for tonight." When I wake up it's almost 7 PM. That gives me about two hours before Willie and Johnny come over. I put a steak on the barbecue, crack open a beer, and relax. It feels good to be by myself. Before my steak is ready, I put together a nice little salad for myself. I use some Romaine Lettuce, half a sliced cucumber, and a cut up beefsteak tomato. Then I toss it all in some vinegar and olive oil. After I'm done eating, I clean up and go roll a bunch of joints for this evening. Next comes the hard fucking part. I have to get fucking dressed. Wearing fancy clothes just aint me. Before I can get too upset about how faggy I look the doorbell rings. It's almost nine, so I know it's Willie and Johnny. They're dressed to the fucking hilt and look fantastic.

"My tailors did well. Your clothes fit great Droz," Willie says in an upbeat tone.

"If I didn't know it was you, I wouldn't know it was you. You look terrific Droz," Johnny happily adds.

"I think I look like a fag Johnny," I sigh and reply.

Willie winks at me as Johnny says, "You said it first."

We all start laughing and shoving each other around until Johnny says, "Alright, alright already, let's get out of here before we wrinkle our clothes. We'll take your car Droz. I want the valet guys and the bouncers to recognize you and your car."

"That's cool Johnny. Let me grab the joints I rolled and we're out the door."

I put a few joints in my sock and the rest in the ashtray. "Where are we heading Johnny?" I ask.

"Our first stop is Eruption in Fort Lauderdale. They start cranking as soon as the doors open. We'll hang out there for a few hours and then head over to Blue Diamonds. Light up a joint Droz, and let's get this party started!"

I light up a doobie while Johnny gives me directions. As I pass the joint back to Willie he asks, "You dance Droz?"

I give a cocky laugh before replying, "I love to dance Willie. I get my rhythm from my mother. When she was only 16, she performed with one of the big bands. When I was in the Navy, we visited some ports where the local girls didn't speak a lick of fucking English. I found out quick that dancing is a universal language. I dance like I fuck, and the chicks caught on quickly."

Willie passes the jay to Johnny saying, "That's good. I'm glad you don't dance like a lot of Italians do. When they get drunk they all copy John Travolta in Saturday Night Fever.

We all laugh as Johnny imitates some of the hand moves from the movie. When we get to Eruption, cars are lined up onto the highway waiting to get in. "Wow! What a fucking line!" I exclaim.

Johnny points to his chest saying, "Johnny Santori doesn't wait in fucking lines. Go around these fucking cars to the exit lane and pull in like you own the fucking place."

I gladly listen and drive into the out exit. As soon as I do, two gorillas in suits step in front of my car. Both men holler at me to turn around. Willie and Johnny laugh. Then Johnny says, "They don't recognize the car Willie. Just put it in park Droz and we'll get out." Using his heavy Brooklyn Italian accent Johnny barks, "I come here with my cugines and you two fucking jamokes embarrass me?"

"I'm sorry Mr. Santori. I didn't recognize the car," The bigger guy apologizes. The other guy humbly apologizes too as Johnny puts his arm around me saying, "Well from now on you better fucking recognize it. And you better fucking recognize this guy too. This is Droz. You treat him with the same fucking respect you treat me and Willie, capisce?"

"Capisce Mr. Santori, it will never happen again."

"You better fucking capisce, or you'll go back to being day laborers. Now go park the fucking car. One more thing, not one fucking joint better be missing from that fucking ashtray."

I feel bad for these guys, so I pull out my wad and peel a couple of C notes off for them saying, "You guys can take a joint for yourselves. Be careful though. You aint never smoked shit like this before."

Both monsters thank me for my generosity. Then they give me the traditional hug and kiss. After they pull away Johnny says, "You're a fucking softy Droz. My uncle's clubs are so fucking hot people would kill for their jobs. Those two lamb chops are each pulling down over two grand a week running security and valet."

We strut over to the front of the club where there's a line stretched around the building waiting to get in. The guys park my Lincoln right up front next to a beautiful green Ferrari. The bouncers at the entrance nod their heads and part like the Red Sea when they see Johnny. The people's faces waiting in line watching us are priceless. You feel the pounding of the music before you even get through the door. Inside, Johnny is bombarded by people acknowledging his presence. I recognize some faces from his crew, but most of them are new to me. Eruption is a real glitzy place with dazzling lights hitting you from every direction. The décor is extremely fancy. It's not my type of place at all. Everyone is dressed to impress, so I feel really good about my clothes. This place is full of hot chicks at the bar and on the dance floor. The music is so fucking loud you have to shout to speak. Johnny and Willie lead me up a flight of stairs to a private roped off area. Willie says, "We only sit in the VIP room." I'm glad because it's quieter, so we can at least carry on a conversation. The bouncer recognizes Johnny and Willie right away. He greets them with a smile and unhooks the velvet rope to let us in. The VIP Room is very nicely furnished.

It has the look and feel of a plush living room. Every seat has a bird's eye view of the dance floor. A really hot cocktail waitress recognizes Johnny and leads us to a reserved table. She kisses us all saying, "Great to see you again Johnny, you too Willie, whose your friend?"

"This is Droz, Cindy. If he comes here by himself make sure you treat him the same way you treat me."

Cindy looks at me flirtatiously saying, "My pleasure Johnny, what can I get you guys?"

"Bacardi and Coke for me Cindy," Willie says.

"Top shelf Martini for me," Johnny adds.

"Bring me a bottle of Bud, Cindy."

As Cindy walks off to get our drinks, Johnny gives me a dirty look and sarcastically says, "I suppose you're going to drink your beer out of the bottle too?"

"Of course I am Johnny. We're in a fucking bar right? You never know what's going to happen in a fucking bar Johnny. The bottle may come in handy."

Willie and Johnny shake their heads looking at each other like, "How embarrassing." I fake smile at them shrugging my shoulders. Then look back like, "I don't give a shit what you think."

Glancing around the room, I notice a bunch of Spanish guys entertaining a group of ladies. They have champagne buckets lined up all around their tables. All of them are wearing fancy clothes and expensive jewelry. There are two different groups of them. Even though they are seated near each other, they're not partying together. In fact, they look like they are purposely ignoring each other. Both groups of Spanish guys are laying out lines of coke for the girls to snort. The girls take turns shoving as much blow up their noses as they can. I turn to Johnny and Willie asking, "You can't smoke weed in these fancy fucking clubs, but you can snort coke?"

The waitress interrupts us briefly to set down our drinks. Johnny tells her to start running a tab. Now I tell Johnny and Willie, "Back in Hawaii it's just the fucking opposite. In Hawaii you're allowed to smoke and deal weed in the clubs, but never blow. If you get caught using coke, you would get a fucking beating from the Mokes. Then after the Mokes got done sweeping up the floor with you, you get barred from the clubs. If you got caught dealing the shit in or around the clubs you would end up face down in a pineapple field."

Johnny replies sarcastically, "Yeah well, you aint in fucking Kansas anymore Droz, and the last time I looked you aint wearing ruby slippers either. You're in South Florida now, so you better get fucking used to it. Cocaine is dealt, used, and abused down here in. You and my uncle may hate that fact, but there's nothing neither one of you can do about it. It's a fucking epidemic without a cure. If you don't like what you see here wait until we go over to Blue Diamonds. It's way fucking worse there."

Willie chimes in, "Same at the big clubs down in Miami. Johnny and I just ignore it. Let all the assholes ruin their lives. Let them sell their souls to the devil."

"It's not my fucking business what they do anyway Droz. As long as they're not bothering me or my family I don't bother them," Johnny adds.

Willie continues. "The Spanish guys you see here in this club are mostly Colombians and Peruvians. They form drug cartels named after their hometowns. Most of them will either end up killing each other or go to prison."

Just as Willie finishes his sentence, I see Pauley and Tommy Palermo sit down with one of the groups of Spanish guys. The Spanish guy at the head of the table seems very happy to see them. They exchange some pleasantries and then leave together. I kick Johnny under the table and say, "You turn a blind eye to that too?"

"What are you kicking me for Droz? You're going to dirty my pants you cocksucker. I turn a blind eye to fucking what?"

I motion my eyes to Paulie and Tommy Palermo leaving with the Spanish guy. Johnny looks at them and looks back at me saying, "I see Pauley and Tommy Palermo leaving with Antonio, so what?"

"So you know the Spanish guy, Johnny?"

Willie chimes in, "Everyone knows Antonio, Droz. He runs the biggest Colombian drug cartel down here. The cops don't even fuck with him."

"Aren't you worried Johnny that your guys may be dealing blow with Antonio?" I raise my eyebrows asking.

Johnny gets pissed off now replying, "I don't care what my fucking guys do when they aint working. I fucking told you Droz. I mind my own fucking business and I suggest you do the fucking same."

"Well you should fucking care Johnny. Your boys hanging around with Antonio can bring heat down on you, your old man, and your uncle. If cocaine gets connected to the construction business we all fucking lose."

Johnny is visibly upset now. He taps himself on his head a few times saying, "I keep fucking forgetting, you've been hanging around with my uncle. I bet he's been brainwashing your ass about how narcotics will ruin us all. Tell me the fucking truth Droz. Did he also tell you that was the only true part of the Godfather movie too?"

I was set back a bit by Johnny's reply, so I hesitate for a moment before confidently saying, "You're right Johnny. He did, and I fucking believe him too. So fucking what?"

Johnny takes a deep breath and says, "I told you once already Droz and I'll tell you fucking again. I mind my own fucking business. I don't give a rat's ass what these other guys are doing. Not Tommy, not Pauley, not Antonio, or anyone else for that matter. I'm not a fucking cop and I aint no motherfucking rat. I would bet my life that neither one of you are a fucking cop or a rat. My father tells me that Uncle Rocco preaches this shit to him all the fucking time. What you don't understand yet Droz is that my Uncle Rocco is always trying to fucking save the world. Don't get me wrong, that's not a bad thing, but it's not me or my father's thing, capisce?"

Not wanting Johnny or Willie to get suspicious, I back off replying, "I capisce Johnny."

"Good. Right now, the three of us are pulling down a phenomenal amount of cash. Let's forget about this bullshit and enjoy our success."

I nod my head agreeing, and then Willie says, "Johnny's right Droz, let's forget this bullshit and have a goodtime tonight."

Willie calls the waitress over and orders another round of drinks. Then like a bolt of fucking lightning, it hits me! I'm a fucking rat! I get a vision in my head of a big, filthy, ugly rat with yellow teeth gnawing on a piece of cheese. My old man always said, "The only thing worse than a coward is a squealer." Those words now echo in my head. I start panicking inside. I think of Shayne and how he tried to keep narcotics out of his neighborhood. I think of Father Mac and his story about the demons in the rehab. It helps a bit, but the bottom-line is I'm Rocco's rat.

I turn to Johnny saying, "You're absolutely right Johnny. Why should I give a fuck about who's buying and selling that shit? It's not my job to save the world either."

"I'm glad we got through to you. I thought we were going have to drop you like a bad date," Johnny says smiling.

"Bad date? What the fuck do you mean bad date? I would be the best piece of ass either one of you ever had!" I indignantly reply.

We all bust out laughing and high five each other. Our boisterous behavior catches Antonio's attention as he's returning to his table with Pauley and Tommy. Antonio says something to them and they both glance over at me. They say something back to Antonio and sit back down with him. Antonio says something loudly in Spanish to his men making them all look towards us and laugh. Johnny and Willie are oblivious. Johnny's busy with Willie pointing to a group of girls downstairs. Johnny says he knows them from Brooklyn and suggests we go sit with them. I down the rest of my beer and motion to the waitress for another. I tell the guys I need to take a piss first.

"That fucking beer goes right through you, don't it Droz?" Johnny says laughing.

Willie now adds, "It's a good thing you thought of it up here in the VIP Room. The bathrooms are really nice up here. The bathrooms downstairs are a crowded mess. We'll meet you downstairs at the table where those chicks are."

Johnny and Willie head downstairs. About a minute later, Cindy hands me my beer and I go hit the john. Willie's right. This really is a nice bathroom, and it's empty too. I walk over to the urinal to take a whiz and hear someone come in the door. A guy steps up to the urinal next to me, and it's fucking Antonio. Antonio's a slim man and looks to be in good shape. He's about my height with dark eyes and darker hair. He has a few battle scars around his forehead and chin. He looks like he grew up in a rough neighborhood. His skin tone's darker than Willie's, and I'd say he's about ten years older. Antonio starts taking a piss. Then in a strong Spanish accent, he says, "So I hear you're Johnny's boss."

I stand there quietly and finish taking my piss. When I'm done, I grab my beer from on top of the urinal and kick the handle to flush it. Then I calmly reply, "Were partners."

Antonio finishes his piss and then pulls the urinal handle to flush. He now says with a smile, "I unfortunately cannot kick that high, or I would have done the same as you. Who knows who's been touching these things?"

I start to laugh as I head towards the sink to wash my hands. Antonio follows right behind me. Then I reply, "Kicking the handles to flush toilets in public bathrooms is a habit I got in since I was a kid."

We both wash our hands and grab a paper towel to dry them. Antonio now says, "It's a very good habit to get into. I think I will buy some looser fitting pants before I try it."

We both chuckle. Then Antonio looks me in the eye and extends his hand saying, "My name is Antonio."

I shake his hand firmly while staring him in the eye replying, "Pleased to meet you Antonio, my name is Droz."

"In case you don't know it Droz, Johnny's crew thinks you're his boss. Maybe it's because they have grown to like you so much and want you to be their boss. Or maybe it's because you supply them with such good weed."

"Everybody loves the weed man Antonio," I reply smiling.

Antonio laughs and says, "I love the weed man too Droz, especially when he gets better weed than me. You wouldn't happen to have some of that good weed with you, would you?"

"Of course I do Antonio," I slyly reply. Then grab a joint from my sock and hand it to Antonio.

"Thank you Droz," He replies while taking a lighter from his pocket to light it.

"Is that cool to do here?" I ask.

"If I want it to be it is."

"I like that answer, but do be careful with your first hit."

"Oh I already found out the hard way when Pauley brought me some. I know better now. Maybe you would like to try something strong from my country." Antonio reaches into his pocket and takes out a lunch baggie full of blow. He hands it to me saying, "This is uncut cocaine from Colombia. Help yourself Droz. If you like, it you can keep it. Just throw me a few ounces of this weed when you can."

I hold the baggie in my hand and it feels to be at least an ounce. The coke looks like shiny little fish scales. I hand it back to Antonio saying, "No thanks. I'm a weed man Antonio."

Antonio laughs and takes another hit off the joint. He passes the joint to me saying, "Me too Droz, but you can give it to the girls. They'll suck your dick for it."

I laugh and grab my crotch saying, "The only thing I have to give a chick to suck my dick, Antonio, is my dick."

Antonio laughs really hard and says, "You're a cocky fuck Droz. I like that."

"Yeah, well, it comes natural to me Antonio. I better get back downstairs before they think something happened to me. Smoke the jay and I'll check you later."

"Thank you Droz, but I think I will finish the rest later. I am really stoned from what I have already smoked."

As we walk out of the bathroom, two of Antonio's men are standing right by the door. Antonio wanted to speak to me alone and undisturbed. It's pretty obvious he's running this club and not the Santori's. Before I go downstairs Antonio says, "Droz, it's been a pleasure getting high with you. If it's at all possible, I would love to become a customer of yours. Paulie and Tommy can only get me small amounts from their friend you are supplying."

"I can sell you a few ounces Antonio. I'll work it out with Pauley or Tommy."

"I'll look forward to it, thank you Droz."

Making my way downstairs I see Pauley and Tommy smiling. This is a good thing because now they will trust me even more seeing me make friends with Antonio. When Willie sees me he shouts, "Damn Droz! What took you so long? Did your number one turn into a number two?"

Everyone laughs at my expense including the girls. I go along with the joke smiling while Johnny turns to Willie saying, "Don't forget Willie. Droz was in the Navy. Maybe he met an old shipmate in the bathroom and they started reminiscing about all the nights they spent out at sea together."

Everyone laughs again. Then one of the girls loudly asks me in her Brooklyn accent, "Were you really fooling around with a guy in the VIP bathroom?" Before I can answer the bitch, three waitresses come over with Champaign glasses. Right behind them are four waitresses wheeling Champaign buckets with eight bottles of Dom Perignon in them.

"Hold on baby dolls, we didn't order these," Johnny says.

A waitress points upstairs saying, "They are compliments of Antonio." The girls at the table are fucking ecstatic. I can tell by the way they're acting getting Champaign from Antonio raised their status. So now I ask the wisecracking bitch, "When was the last time a guy bought you eight bottles of Dom Perignon for a blowjob?"

Everyone belly laughs while she turns ten shades of red. I look up at Antonio and nod my head. Willie gives me a strange look as Johnny whispers in my ear, "What the fuck's that all about?"

"I'll explain later Johnny."

Just as I say that one of my favorite songs, Heart of Glass by Blondie, hits the speakers. I look around the table, grab the hottest chick sitting there, and head to the dance floor. Willie and Johnny follow suit. The music kept getting better, and the girls are great dancers, so we keep dancing. When the songs start sucking, we go back to the table and drink Champaign. Pretty soon, Johnny suggests we leave Eruption and head to Blue Diamonds.

"What about the chicks?" I whisper to Johnny.

"Don't worry Droz. They'll be plenty more at Blue Diamonds."

To be polite I invited the girls anyway, but they said they were staying put. The Champaign wasn't nearly finished, so I figured the material bitches want to keep looking like they're rich. Just for the hell of it I got the phone number of the girl I danced with. We settle up our tab with the waitress and leave. Outside the club, the staff jumps like soldiers to get my car. I give the valet guy a Ben Franklin and we drive off. Quickly Johnny asks, "Why did Antonio buy us Champaign Droz?"

I take a joint from my sock and light it up before replying, "This is why Johnny. Tommy and Pauley have been getting Antonio high with the dope I sell Carmine. Antonio followed me into the bathroom and asked me for some, so I lit up a joint with him."

I hand the joint to Willie while Johnny angrily replies, "So my guys got big fucking mouths. I'll take care of that."

"It's cool Johnny. I'm not mad. It's hard not to share good weed, and I sincerely doubt Antonio is a rat. In fact, he tried giving me a fucking sandwich bag full of blow for getting him high. I turned him down of course."

We hear the roar of an engine pulling up alongside us. It's that green Ferrari I saw parked out in front of the club. "It's Antonio. Man, I love that fucking car," Johnny says with envy.

Antonio yells out his window, "Droz, I'm so fucking high from that joint!" As he yells something else in Spanish, I quickly memorize the license plate, BHS263. Antonio punches it and pulls away like we're standing still!

"He's fucking showing off. He knows how I love that fucking car," Johnny blurts out.

"What did he say in Spanish Willie?" I ask.

Willie replies by saying the same fucking thing to me back again in Spanish. Johnny laughs as Willie hands him the joint. I now bark at Willie, "You fucking douche bag! You know what the fuck I mean! In English you prick, in English!"

Willie keeps laughing enjoying the moment. Then he finally replies, "Antonio says you are the man!"

I can tell by Johnny's face he didn't like hearing that. I just added another thing he could be jealous of me for. We stay pretty quiet after that and finish the joint. When we get to Blue Diamonds, it's even more crowded than Eruption! I know the deal now, so I pull up into the exit lane. Johnny rolls down the window and hollers, "Joey, hey Joey!" Joey sees Johnny and waves us over to a spot right next to Antonio's Ferrari. We get out of the car reeking of weed. Joey in his strong Brooklyn accent asks, "Yo fucking Johnny, where you been man? What's up Willie?" Joey exchanges a hug and a kiss with Johnny. Then he does the same with Willie.

Johnny's demeanor with Joey is very friendly as he replies, "My old man got me slaving for him. Joey, I want you to meet a good friend of mine, Droz. I want you take care of him just like you take care of me when he comes here. Droz, this is my good friend Joey. He's in charge here. We hung out together back in Brooklyn."

I exchange the traditional Italian hug and kiss on the cheek with Joey. Joey now says, "I smell something really fucking special here Johnny boy. Am I right, or am I fucking right?"

We all laugh as Johnny replies, "I found this new fucking cologne Joey. It's called fragrance of pakalolo."

Joey puts his two fingers over his thumb like Italians like to do when they express themselves. Then he waves them in the air replying, "So where's mine?"

Johnny gives me a look and I nod my head okay, so he says, "In the ashtray Joey, take a joint for yourself, but be careful smoking this shit. You could lose a fucking lung."

"Sounds very fucking promising," Joey replies smiling.

I hand Joey the keys and we swagger over to the entrance of the club. The line getting into Blue Diamonds is worse than Eruption. The doorman immediately recognizes Johnny and opens the door for us. This place isn't as fancy as Eruption, but a helluva lot livelier. Everyone seems to be having a great time here. The music isn't as loud as Eruption either, so you can hear yourself speak. Johnny turns to me with a grin saying, "Since you're not being such a fucking prude anymore Droz, take a look at this."

"Oh no Johnny, don't push it," Willie says.

I get an attitude face replying, "Push fucking what Willie?"

Johnny walks over to the men's bathroom door and opens it. I look inside and there's pure fucking hedonism going on in there! Everybody is stuffing their noses with blow! By the stalls, there are two chicks on their knees giving fucking blowjobs, and a line of guys waiting to go next. Up against the wall, I see a cute little girl with her pink lace panties around her ankles being plowed from behind.

"Does anybody just go in there to use the bathroom?" I sarcastically ask.

Willie and Johnny laugh and close the door. They lead me upstairs to another roped off VIP room. Johnny again gets the royal treatment from the cocktail waitresses and the bouncers. The sexy little waitress escorts us right over to a reserved table. This VIP room is less elegant than Eruptions, but still plush. Antonio and his crew are already in there. I look around the room recognizing two more of Johnny's crew, Michael and

Joseph Rannelli. The Rannelli brothers are hanging out with the other group of Spanish guys from Eruption. It seems like the movers and shakers all leave Eruption to go over to Blue Diamonds at the same time. Antonio walks over to our table with four glasses and a bottle of Dom Perignon. He smiles politely asking, "You gentlemen mind if I join you?"

"Of course not," Johnny cheerfully replies.

Antonio sits down and pours us all a glass of Champaign. Then he nods to his men and they take seats close to our table. After Antonio sits with us, the other Spanish guys leave with the Rannelli brothers. Antonio seeing this snickers and says loudly, "Ah, they left! The air in here smells better already! I can't stand fucking Peruvians!" Antonio's entire crew breaks out laughing. "Why do your guys deal with them fucking Peruvians Johnny?"

Johnny shrugs his shoulders and takes a belt of Champaign. He puts down his glass and replies, "What do want from me Antonio? Maybe they can't stand fucking Colombians."

The four of us laugh and then Antonio says, "That's funny because most of the Italians I know love Colombians."

"Why are you asking me this shit Antonio? You know I mind my own fucking business when it comes to this shit."

Antonio downs his Champaign and motions for the waitress to bring more before saying, "Let me ask you guys something. Are all three of you making so much fucking money with your fathers that you won't even consider going into business with my family?"

Willie answers first. "You know my father's and grandfather's reputation Antonio. I will never disgrace my familia. We have too much at stake trying to free our people from that pig Castro."

Antonio smiles as the waitress pops open another bottle of Champaign. She refills our glasses as Antonio sarcastically replies, "Ahh yes, the privileged Cubano People. Cubans get special treatment from the American Government, and Colombians get a kick in the ass back to Colombia. I grew up very poor in Colombia Willie. Many nights my mother cried because there was no food or medicine for us. Cubans always like to talk about how bad Castro is. Our small villages in Colombia are terrorized by armed bandits all the time. They steal our food, steal our livestock, and rape our women. Cocaine money buys us the guns to kill the rapists and murderers terrorizing our villages. Cocaine money buys us power in our government and national businesses. Exporting cocaine to America has bought many poor Colombians the American Dream that so many Cubans like yourself Willie has already achieved."

Willie downs his Champaign. Then in a rare serious tone from him, he replies, "I'm very happy for your familia Antonio, and the Colombian people. Just keep your business away from our ports."

Antonio snidely chuckles and his men grumble. Drinking more Champaign, Antonio turns his attention to Johnny asking, "How about you Johnny? What's your excuse for not doing business with me?"

"My old man doesn't want the Santori family dealing this shit, so I honor him."

Antonio laughs at Johnny saying, "Who are you kidding Johnny? Your crew is dealing cocaine right under your fucking nose. You may honor your father by not dealing it yourself, but what do you say to your father when he asks you about the others?"

Johnny grins and downs his glass of Champaign. He fills it back up again before replying, "Rats have no honor Antonio and I aint a fucking rat. Nobody in my family respects a fucking rat." Hearing Johnny say that gets me all agitated inside. Johnny continues. "My father and I both know that trying to tell a wise guy not to deal blow or heroin is like trying to tell a fat kid to stay out of the fucking refrigerator. My guys are taking their lives in their hands by dealing with you Antonio. If they get caught, you'll never see them again."

Antonio nods his head reflecting for a moment before saying, "It is very admirable of you Johnny to be so loyal to your father. I also find it very admirable you are not willing to rat on your friends. I too hate rats. My men hate rats. I'm sure all four of us can agree that we all hate fucking rats."

Ironically I add, "The worst thing about a fucking rat is you usually don't know who he is until it's too fucking late."

Everybody nods and takes a drink of their Champaign. Now Antonio asks me, "How about you Droz? You can make a lot of money dealing with me."

I shrug my shoulders and nonchalantly reply, "Weed and gambling is my thing Antonio. My father and mother were recently killed in a car accident. My father left me his social club and his house. I don't plan on living any larger than that."

Antonio looks at me sadly saying, "I am very sorry to hear that Droz. Just so you know, there is a place for you with me if you so choose."

"Thank you Antonio."

After Antonio gets everything off his chest, things lighten up. His men now join in with us drinking and having a good time. They are a pretty decent bunch of guys. Four very hot young Spanish chicks walk over to our table. The four of them are wearing tight little skirts and skimpy little tops. Antonio has a short conversation with them in Spanish and then says, "Droz, these girls don't speak any English, but they like to have a good time. You got me high at Eruption; let me show you how I can return a favor. Let's take my girls out to your car and get them high."

Willie and Johnny crack a huge smile hearing this, so I smile replying, "That sounds good to me Antonio."

"Just give me a second Droz to get a cup of lemon and lime slices from the bar," Antonio says.

"What do we need the lemon and lime slices for?" I reply with a puzzled look.

"The girls will get cotton mouth from the weed Droz. The lemon and lime slices will remedy that," Antonio winks replying.

Johnny, Willie, and I smile simultaneously. Then we pat Antonio on the back for having such great foresight. When we get downstairs, Johnny tells the bouncer to have Joey bring my Lincoln around back. We take the girls out the back entrance and wait for Joey. Joey pulls up stoned as a motherfucker. He's grinning from ear to ear seeing the girls. As he's walking away, he assures us no one will bother us. I go into my ashtray and pull out three joints to pass around. I give one to Antonio, one to Johnny, and one to Willie to light. The girls seem so happy to be getting high with us. They're talking and giggling a mile a minute with each other. We blow the girls shotguns to get them really fucking stoned. After they have enough weed, Antonio passes around the cup with lemon and lime slices. We all take one. While talking to the girls in Spanish, Antonio opens all four doors to my Lincoln. The girls giggle some more and then each one of them takes a seat inside the car. Two girls sit in the front seat and two girls in the back. Antonio reaches into his pocket and takes out a sack of coke. Then he goes into his back pocket and whips out a pearl handled switchblade. He pops it open and hands both to the girls. While they're snorting away, the four of us position ourselves in front of each one of the girls. We bullshit for a few minutes letting the girls get all tooted up. After Antonio takes his knife and blow back, he unzips his trousers and we follow his lead. The girls know exactly what to do. They go full fucking throttle sucking on our cocks! A slurp here and a moan there, we're all in heaven. The four of us give each other a blow by blow description. Each girl has their own technique for sucking cock, and they're all fucking great at it, so we decide to switch around and enjoy their variety of cock sucking. Johnny likes the ball sucker and ball squeezer. Willie likes the girl with the talented tongue. Antonio and I like the two girls who suck cock using spit soaked hands. The lemon and lime slices are a fantastic idea!

I look at Antonio saying, "Way to return a favor Antonio. You got more weed coming your way buddy."

Antonio laughs saying, "Make sure you guys don't get off because this is just the beginning." Antonio speaks Spanish to the girls. This triggers Willie to say, "Oh yeah baby; now we're going to get some coochie."

The girls take off their clothes and wave their asses in the air giggling! Johnny now says, "Okay men. No short dicking these girls. The first guy to cum pays everybody a fucking C note, agreed?"

We all grin like horny Chinamen agreeing. Then we drop our pants and go to work on them coochie's! The girl I'm fucking has a nice, soft, round booty perfect for spanking. I start squeezing her fine ass and giving her a few playful spanks. This little Latin sweetie starts moaning and getting wetter, so I spank the little hottie harder. This catches on quick, and now everyone is spanking their girls! Man this is a hot scene! I look up at the stars and say to myself, "Life is good!" Now of course we compare notes again, but this time on how each girl's coochie feels, how wet it is, and how she's fucking using it. The temptation is just too fucking great, so we start playing musical pussies. With our pants down around our ankles we two-step around the car with our flagpoles bobbing in the breeze! The sex gets even hotter now because the girls are enjoying the variety as much as we are! Johnny cries out in the heat of passion, "Oh no honey, please no, not fucking that! I can't handle that! I'll lose the fucking bet!"

Johnny's girl is grabbing his cock and pleading with him passionately in Spanish. Willie's eyes light up hearing her. Antonio says, "Ahh, you got Conchita really hot Johnny. Now she's trying to stick your dick in her ass, right? Do it Johnny. Fuck Conchita hard in her ass."

Hearing that, Johnny's eyes turn crazy wild. He violently pushes his hips forward and both of them let out a loud moan of pleasure. They start thrusting back and forth fucking like animals. Johnny is fucking her ass so hard my car is shaking! He lets out a major howl as Conchita is desperately yelling, "No, no, no, no!"

It's too late. Johnny drops his load leaving poor Conchita begging for more. As Johnny fades away, the three of us know what we have to do. We come to Conchita's rescue and take turns lustfully fucking her tight little asshole. Conchita has orgasm after fucking orgasm as we all bust a nut in her ass. Nobody pulls out a fudgesicle and Johnny happily pays up, so it's all good. Antonio gives the girls the bag of blow and they go to town on it like they did our cocks. Antonio's right, coke makes chicks horny and wild. Well, at least these chicks. After we get dressed, Johnny turns to Antonio saying, "You sure know how to train your fucking women Antonio."

Antonio just smiles and pats Johnny on the back. Willie and Antonio exchange a few words in Spanish that end in a hug. I hand Antonio a couple of more joints saying, "I'll make sure you get more pakalolo Antonio."

"Thank you Droz. I'm sure you will," Antonio hugs me and replies. Then Antonio turns his attention to all of us saying, "It's been a pleasure gentleman. I have some business to attend to now, but I should be back before you leave the club."

We all say cool. After thanking the girls, I lock up my car and we walk back inside the club. All we can talk about is how fucking hot that scene was. We all agree we want another dose of those sexy, little Latin chicks. When we get back upstairs to the VIP room there are four guys sitting at our table with cocktails in their hands. I can tell by Johnny's face he isn't happy to see them. Spotting Johnny, one of them yells, "Johnny boy, I bet you're surprised to see me!"

"When did you get out Nicky?" Johnny replies without emotion.

Nicky is a decent looking guy in his early thirties. He dresses nice, but not flashy. He stands about six feet tall and weighs around a hundred eighty pounds. Nicky's lean and muscular, his hair is black, and his eyes are dark. Nicky also has a really sinister fucking smile. He looks pretty tough to me.

Upset with Johnny's lack of enthusiasm, Nicky replies back gruffly, "Well don't look so fucking happy Johnny. Now introduce me to your friends."

"Sure Nicky. These are my two best friends down here, Droz and Willie," Johnny quickly replies.

Nicky gives us the traditional kiss and hug saying, "Any friend of my cousin Johnny is a friend of mine. Let me introduce you to my boys. This here's Vinnie, Sally, and Joey. Johnny knows them," We all nod to each other.

Vinnie is a tall, skinny guy. He's dressed casually and definitely not the most handsome guy in the room. Vinnie has long, straight, black hair that he keeps tied back neatly in a ponytail. He is wearing dark sunglasses, so I can't see his eyes. He's got a tattoo of the Grim Reaper on his neck. Sally has brown, wavy hair and brown eyes. Sally is built really strong and is about my height. He seems to have the demeanor of a gladiator. He's better looking and better dressed than Vinnie, but still no lady killer. Joey is a big, heavy set, jolly kind of guy. He's got dark hair and dark eyes. Joey is also a good-looking guy; he dresses nice, but is way overweight.

"How did you know I would be here Nicky?" Johnny asks.

"I didn't. When I saw Joey, he told me. He also told me that you, Antonio, and your friends were having a little party with some girls, so we figured we'll have a drink at your table and wait for you to get finished."

"You know Antonio, Nicky?" Johnny asks surprised.

"Not yet, but I will shortly. Charlie Wings set up a meeting for me here with him."

"So I guess this means you're going back into business."

"It's more like I'm taking over business Johnny," Nicky replies with his sinister smile.

Johnny looks over the balcony and see's Antonio. He calls Nicky over saying, "See that guy talking to Pauley Leone and Tommy Palermo? That's Antonio."

Seeing Pauley and Tommy talking to Antonio, Nicky asks, "What's your crew kicking back to you Johnny?"

"Nothing Nicky, I don't get involved. You know how my old man feels about this shit. I'm making enough fucking dough from our construction business anyway."

Nicky gives Johnny a hard look replying, "Good for you cousin, but I aint making a fucking dime from your construction business, and neither are my boys. Come on fellas, let's go wet our beaks."

With that said, Nicky nods to his crew and they head downstairs. Johnny shakes his head from side to side saying, "That's my mother's sister's kid. He could have had any job he wanted with my father, but he chose to deal narcotics instead. My guys don't know it yet, but hard times are coming, and they're coming fast."

"They deserve what they get Johnny," Willie adds.

Johnny nods his head in agreement as we watch Nicky and his crew approach Antonio. Johnny puts his arms around both of us saying, "Let's just forget about Nicky and have a good time."

We spend the rest of the night drinking, dancing, and hitting on chicks. None are as hot as the Latin chicks, so we cut them loose before we leave. My car is still parked out back, so we head out the back door of the club. Outside we see the Rannelli brothers on their knees with their hands tied behind their backs. They're bleeding from their heads and faces. Sally and Vinnie are holding guns to their heads while Nicky berates them. Pauley and Tommy Palermo are also there standing next to Joey.

Nicky's heavy Brooklyn Italian accent echoes off the walls, "If you deal with those fucking Peruvians again I'll cut your fucking hearts out with a dull knife. From now on, you buy from Antonio and kickback thirty percent of your fucking profits to me. Just like Tommy and Pauley."

Tommy and Pauley look afraid, but the Rannelli brothers are crying like bitches. These fucking guys are not cut out for this business. If I were them, I would agree with Nicky and then kill him later. Me, Johnny, and Willie watch and keep our mouths shut. Nicky smiles when he sees us and asks Johnny, "Did you know your guys were such fucking pussies? I didn't even have to lay a finger on Tommy and Pauley. They knew what the fuck was up as soon as they fucking seen me. These two fucking jadrools actually had the balls to talk back to me. They told me they were protected. Imagine that?"

Nicky, Sally, and Vinnie laugh as they sadistically work them over again. Tommy and Pauley turn away as the Rannelli brothers cry out in pain from the beating. Nicky mocks their suffering and then asks, "So what are you two fucking pussies going to do from now on?"

Gasping for air, Michael replies first, "Whatever you want Nicky."

Joey spits out a mouthful of blood and then replies, "Deal with Antonio and kick back thirty percent to you Nicky."

Nicky turns around pointing his gun at Tommy and Pauley asking, "What are you two fucking pussies going to do?"

In unison Tommy and Pauley reply, "Kick back thirty percent to you Nicky."

"That's music to my ears boys," Nicky says with a sadistic smile.

Out of nowhere, a yellow Camaro screeches around the corner slamming the breaks! Two Spanish guys jump out firing small machine guns right at Nicky's crew! Everybody takes cover! Nicky and his boys start shooting back from behind their car. Me, Johnny, and Willie are crouched down behind my car. Tommy, Pauley, and the Rannelli brothers hide behind the dumpster. Bullets fly everywhere, but luckily not at us. As the gun battle rages, a white pickup truck pulls in behind the Camaro. Two more Spanish guys stand up in the bed of the truck with pump shotguns. These two guys start pumping away at the other two Spanish guys! The shotgun blasts are deafening! Then there's silence. My ears are ringing like church bells. The Spanish guys from the Camaro are lying in a pool of blood. One of them is still squirming on the ground moaning in pain. Nicky walks up and puts two slugs in his head. The doors of the pickup truck open and there's Antonio! Surprisingly, no one has come out of the club. Either the music is too fucking loud, or they're just too scared. Antonio is standing over the two dead bodies with a shit eating grin talking to Nicky, "Your car doesn't look so good Nicky."

Nicky looks at his Lincoln riddled with bullets replying, "Yeah well, better the car than us Antonio. Thanks for helping out."

"It was my pleasure Nicky. I hate fucking Peruvians. One of these Peruvian scum seen you take the Rannelli brothers out the back door. When they saw what you were doing to their mules they decided to take you guys out. I have men all over the clubs watching these Peruvian pieces of shit. Luckily for you Nicky, one of them caught on to what was happening. From now on, you must be very careful. The Peruvians have you as a marked man for interfering in their business."

Nicky shrugs his shoulders and puts his gun back in his waistband replying, "It goes with the fucking turf Antonio, and thanks again for helping. You won't regret it. Charlie Wings will increase your business tenfold. I'm just leaning on these punks for pocket change until our deal gets rolling."

"I understand Nicky. Everyone must eat."

Willie pats me on the back now saying, "Welcome to South Florida, Droz. You shared a little bit of the good and the bad tonight."

"That's for sure," Johnny adds.

"Yeah, we got lucky twice tonight. Either those machine guns sucked, or their aim sucked," I say smiling.

As soon as those words leave my mouth, we hear a loud thud. It's Nicky's friend Joey hitting the ground. Nicky and his crew kneel over Joey's body checking him out. Joey has small bullet holes all over his abdomen. Nicky gives him mouth to mouth, but to no avail. Joey's dead. Sally and Vinnie do the sign of the cross. Everyone follows suit.

Nicky jumps up yelling, "Son of a fucking bitch! Joey never said a fucking word! Not a fucking whimper came out of his mouth! The car's in Joey's name. The car's shot up and Joey's shot up. We'll leave him right here next to the car."

Antonio turns to his men saying something in Spanish. One of them immediately runs around to the front of the club. Antonio tells Nicky, "My man will be right back with another car for you. We should all get going."

"Are those girls still here at the club Antonio? I can't get Conchita off my mind," Johnny asks.

Before Antonio can answer, Nicky jumps in laughing, "That's my fucking cousin for you Antonio. Bullets flying everywhere, dead bodies on the ground, and all he can fucking think about is pussy."

We all laugh as Antonio replies, "It's ass this time Nicky. Johnny fell in love with Conchita's ass."

Everybody busts out laughing even harder now as a blue Cadillac pulls around back. Antonio's man gets out of the car and leaves it running. The sound of sirens in the distance is our cue to get the fuck out of here fast. Nicky thanks Antonio and jumps in the Caddy with his boys. As Antonio jumps back in his truck he shouts, "Don't worry Johnny. There will be another time. Meantime, I will tell Conchita you want to marry her!"

Johnny's face turns pale hearing that! Before he could yell something back, both of our vehicles peel out in different directions. On the ride home, we smoke another doobie and rag Johnny about having to learn Spanish. We don't even discuss what happened at the club. When we get back to my house we all kiss and a hug. Then we do the sign of the cross thanking God for coming home in one piece. Johnny says he has work to do in the morning, so he hops in his Mercedes and goes home. That's good because now I can tell Willie about the real estate deal. Willie's in. After he leaves, I work out and start thinking about what I will report to Rocco at Sunday dinner. I know right off the bat the Rannelli brothers, Paulie, and Tommy Palermo, are dead men. It's just a matter of how, when, and where. I got Antonio's plate number plastered in my head for Ariella. After my workout, I take a hot shower and hit the rack around 3 AM.

I get up around ten and make myself bacon and eggs. After breakfast, I relax by the pool until I hear a knock at the door. Begrudgingly, I get up from my cozy lounge chair and go inside to peek out the window. Shit, it's Nicky and his fucking crew. A million thoughts run through my head, and none are good. Are they here to whack me because of what I witnessed last night? Are they here to hideout? Are the police following them? I know the worst thing I can do is act afraid, so I open the door smiling and say, "What's up boys?"

There's an awkward moment of silence before Nicky calmly says, "I know it's kind of fucking early Droz, and I hate showing up unannounced, but there's something really important I need to discuss with you. Do you mind if we come in?"

My head is buzzing with all kinds of scenarios, but I'm determined not to act afraid. I won't say anything stupid either like, "Is everything alright Nicky? Is this about last night?" So I calmly reply back, "Sure Nicky. Come on in. You guys want a cup of coffee or something harder?"

"We already had our coffee and breakfast, but an eye opener would be nice, right fellas?" Nicky replies.

Vinnie and Sally nod their heads smiling, so Nicky asks, "You got any good scotch Droz?"

"Sure do Nicky. My old man always kept good scotch in the house. I'll crack open a bottle of Oban. You guys want it straight up, or on the rocks?"

Almost simultaneously, they all reply, "Straight."

"Cool. Take a seat while I grab a bottle and some glasses from the bar."

Everyone looks relaxed sitting around the coffee table. When I bring the bottle and the glasses over I ask, "You guys like to smoke weed?"

"Definitely," Sally replies.

"We heard about your Hawaiian weed Droz. They say you get it straight from Hawaii," Vinnie adds.

"Johnny told us. He said you got some Thai Stick too. We aint seen them since we were in Vietnam together," Nicky says.

I give Nicky a sly smile. Then looking in his eyes I bluntly reply, "I guess Johnny told you where I live too, right Nicky?"

Nicky snickers and pours everyone a drink before coolly replying back, "Johnny's my cousin Droz. Do you really think he would lie to me?"

"Of course not Nicky, why would I ever think that?" I reply sarcastically.

Nicky laughs and takes a gulp of Oban. Now he says, "I heard you followed the old school rules. I know Johnny broke one Droz, but do me a favor. Let him slide."

I take a slug of my Oban and then look Nicky in the eye saying, "Cousin or no cousin Nicky, that's between me and him. I'll be right back with some hooch."

Vinnie and Sally let out a brief chuckle as I walk back to my bedroom. I grab a bag of pakalolo, some Thai Sticks, and my papers. I return to the living room and take a seat as Nicky tops off our drinks.

"I smelled that weed as soon as you walked in the room Droz," Vinnie says.

The three of them smile as I break up some buds and a Thai Stick. I figure I'll roll up a nice fat bat of each and get these guys really fucked up. All of them start inspecting the buds and the Thai Sticks. Nicky runs the Thai Stick under his nose like a fine cigar and hands it to Sally. Sally does the same and then hands it to Vinnie. They all look at each other and nod their heads. "I never thought I would see that shit again," Nicky says.

I take a sip of scotch before I lick the papers. I hand Nicky the pakalolo joint and light the Thai Stick joint. I don't warn Nicky, so he takes in a big pull. His cheeks pop out valiantly trying to hold in the smoke. When he can't hold it down any longer, he exhales coughing his fucking brains out. Sally barks at him in his heavy Brooklyn accent, "Pass the fucking joint Nicky before you fucking die over there." Nicky passes the joint to Sally and I pass mine to Vinnie. Vinnie and Sally play it smart after seeing what had happened to Nicky. They enjoy the weed by taking in a few small hits at a time. I can see in their eyes they're savoring each one. I love when people know how to appreciate and enjoy good weed. I get the joint back and take in a big draw. The three of them watch me in silence waiting for me to cough, but to their amazement, I don't. After all, I did have a lot of practice in the Navy. When you're getting high on the ship, you have to hold your hits in until there's no smoke left. If you coughed it out all over the place, you'd get everybody pinched because of the smell. After smoking and drinking for a while, we're all feeling pretty fucking good, so I ask, "So what's so fucking important Nicky?"

"I fucking forgot," Nicky replies like a burnout.

We all laugh and then Nicky gets dead serious saying, "I know about the deal you made with Willie and Johnny before you went in the Navy. I also know all of Johnny's crew down here kickbacks to you because of it. A deal the almighty Rocco Santori himself is presiding over making a shit load of money on. I know it's a sweet deal for you too Droz, so you aint hurting for dough. Not to mention the social club your old man left you. You can rest assured whatever Rocco Santori is paying you is a fraction of what he's making. He can also cut you out of the deal anytime he fucking wants. Since your parents were killed, word has it Rocco's treating you like a son. You hang out with him, and he even gave you the coveted fucking no show job. It's the kind of stuff fairy tales are made of, but too bad Rocco aint about fucking fairy tales Droz. He aint about happy fucking endings either. He's only about Rocco and partners like you disappearing. When you deal with Rocco your eyes better be wide fucking open."

Taking a confrontational tone, I interrupt Nicky saying, "You come over my house talking a lot of fucking shit Nicky, but where's your fucking proof? And furthermore, why the fuck should you care what happens to me?"

The three of them are taken back by my aggressiveness. Nicky slowly nods his head up and down. He refills our glasses finishing the bottle of Oban. Nicky takes a slug of his scotch and then aggressively replies, "There's no fucking proof tough guy because when Rocco's done with a fucking partner he just disappears. Either you believe me, or you fucking don't. I only care because right now you're in a position to fucking help me, and I'm in a position to provide you with insurance against Rocco."

I take a moment to let what Nicky said sink in. I take a sip of my scotch before replying, "Okay Nicky. Speak your fucking piece."

Nicky takes a sip of his drink and says, "I'm here to offer you a deal Droz. A deal that will make you enough fucking money in one year to be independent of Rocco forever. To get out from under his heavy fucking thumb and never look back."

I interrupt Nicky saying, "It doesn't matter how much fucking money I make Nicky. I'm a dead man if I cross Rocco."

Nicky takes the edge off his voice replying, "You think I don't know that Droz? We all fear that. That's why I need you to pull the wool over his fucking eyes while I move narcotics through Florida. Rocco got you planted right in the middle of his crown jewel here in South Florida. He's only being nice to you so you snitch about narcotics for him. I know you don't want to be his fucking rat, right?

"I aint nobody's fucking rat," I indignantly reply.

"Of course you're not Droz, so when he asks you whose dealing narcotics you use your fugazzi father son relationship with him to lie. Instead of Rocco playing you, you play him instead. If you can do that for one year, we'll all be home free for the rest of our fucking lives. I'm talking tens of millions of dollars Droz in a short period of time. Antonio likes you, and I already told my boss Charley Wings about you too. Charlie Wings has a plan to leverage our heroin suppliers from Turkey and Afghanistan with our new Colombian cocaine suppliers down here. We have distribution channels in place through our existing mafia members and connected guys. The demand for coke is on the rise and everybody wants in. The niggers we supply in the northern cities are turning blow into something they call crack, and it's sweeping the fucking nation. Heroin has taken a backseat in the ghetto to crack cocaine. Rocco will surely kill anyone who brings that shit around him or near any of his interests."

Intrigued, I ask, "So Rocco will still kill someone himself?"

They all laugh and lift their glasses in a toast. They take a sip of scotch and then Nicky replies to me like he's talking to a kid brother, "For being so street smart you're pretty fucking naïve Droz. Either that or you really bought into Rocco's fathering bullshit. Drill this into your fucking head and remember where you heard it first. Rocco is a stone cold fucking killer, and he's only getting better with age. You probably thought your old man and Billy were fucking altar boys too?"

"Watch it Nicky," I reply sharply.

"No offense Droz, but there's a lot of things you just don't fucking know."

"So smarten me up?" I reply angrily.

Nicky looks at his boys and then replies back with a big shit eating grin on his face, "Like who killed your boy Shayne?"

"How the fuck do you know about that Nicky?" I reply shocked.

"Let's just say I know," He coyly replies.

"I was fucking there Nicky. It was old man Rose's crew that took out Shayne."

"It was old man Rose's crew that beat him down Droz. You knew Shayne wasn't dead when they dragged him out of that room. It was Billy and your father that finished the job."

I sit back quietly and try not to look too fucking stunned. I think to myself, "Until I find out how Nicky knows about this I can't call him a liar. What if he's also telling me the truth about Rocco? What if Rocco is only using me and when he's done I do disappear?" Nicky's got me all fucking twisted. My instincts tell me to play along for now and on Sunday confront Rocco."

"How and when do I get paid Nicky?" I bluntly ask.

"You get paid after every successful shipment we make. The first load of a 1,000 Kilos will be on the first of the month. Your end is 500 dollars a kilo. That's a cool five hundred grand Droz for practically doing nothing."

"Who the fuck are you kidding Nicky? If I were practically doing nothing, you wouldn't be paying me so fucking much. You mentioned heroin too, so what's my fucking cut on that?"

"The heroin deal isn't finalized yet. When Charlie Wings gets down here, we'll figure it out. Nicky extends his hand saying, "So do we have a deal, or not?"

"Before I shake your hand Nicky, you need to know I have a partner. He's coming out of the Navy next week. I will take care of him out of my end."

Nicky looks at his boys and they nod their heads. "A friend of yours Droz is a friend of ours. Just remember you are responsible for him, capisce?" Nicky answers.

"Not a problem Nicky, I capisce"

We shake hands and then Nicky says, "Johnny said we'd be wasting our time coming over here. He said you would be too pig headed to make a deal. Antonio told me you were smart. He said everyone in Johnny's crew thinks you're his boss now."

All three of them start laughing, so I reply, "I'm not Johnny's boss. We're partners Nicky."

"Yeah, yeah, whatever you say Droz, but his boys think different. You need to stop being so fucking modest. You got more power and respect than you think. Otherwise I wouldn't even be talking to you."

With that said we all exchange hugs and kisses. "Can you sell us some of that weed Droz?" Vinnie politely asks.

"Sure, what do you guys need for your heads?"

"Antonio busted my balls about getting him weed too Droz, so sell us a pound for the same price you sell Carmine. Also, how many of them Thai Sticks can we get?" Nicky asks.

"I'll sell you a pound of Pakalolo, but I can only give you a few Thai Sticks for now. I need to find out how much it will cost me to ship them to Florida versus shipping them to Hawaii. When I get that established I'll be able to give you a price for hundreds at a time."

Nicky's eyes light up replying, "Sounds good to me Droz."

I go back to my room and grab a pound out of my closet. I also count out ten Thai Sticks. I charge Carmine $2,100 for a pound of pakalolo. The weed's so fucking good, I bet they think I pay $2,000 and I'm only making a hundred bucks on them. Nobody cares if you make a C note on a pound of weed, but little do they know. Carmine's been selling the pakalolo for two hundred an ounce, and they beg him for more. I go into the kitchen and get a garbage bag to put it in. Then I walk over to Nicky saying, "$2,100 for the pound Nicky, and here's some Thai Sticks until I get more."

Nicky takes the bag from me and nods to Vinnie. Vinnie pulls out his wad and counts me out twenty-one Bennies. I say thank you and we all hug again. After they leave, I feel mentally drained, so I take a nap.

After I wake up I can't stop thinking about everything Nicky told me. Nicky's influence over Johnny is greater than my own. Johnny told Nicky everything about my relationship with Rocco. He told Nicky how strongly I am against narcotics. This means Johnny put my life at risk with Nicky if he didn't get the right answers from me at our meeting. Nicky probably wouldn't have tried to whack me right there at my house, but he most definitely would have tried to kill me at some time in the near future. There's just way too much money at stake not to. Granted, I know it's smarter for Nicky to strike a deal with me than to whack me because of my relationship with Rocco, but I couldn't help wondering if Johnny was in on maybe whacking me too. Would Johnny even be the one to set me up? Another thought pops in my head, maybe Johnny objected to Nicky whacking me and might have warned me? Hmm, let's see. Right from the start, I felt Johnny's resentment and jealousy of my relationship with his uncle Rocco. His resentment grew greater when I started getting closer to his crew and selling them pakalolo. Antonio and Nicky have both mentioned to me behind Johnny's back his guys say I'm his boss. No matter how much money Johnny makes, his gambling habit left him broke. With me out of the way, Johnny and Willie would split my share. That means more money for Johnny. For these reasons alone, I can't trust Johnny any longer. As far as Nicky's character is concerned, I figure he's capable of deceiving anyone. Nicky obviously knows more about Rocco's past than I do. For that reason, my instincts tell me at least some of what Nicky told me about Rocco's past is true. How much is true I don't know for sure, but on Sunday, I will try to find out. The thing bothering me the most is what Nicky knew about Shayne's death. It's not so much the thought of Billy and my old man killing Shayne, but how in the fuck did Nicky know about it? Johnny couldn't have told Nicky because I never told him the story. Even if Rocco knew the entire story, I sincerely doubt that Rocco would openly discuss the details of a murder with the likes of Nicky. If I confront Billy, the first thing Billy will want to know is who told me. Nicky is the only one that can tell me who told him, and I will have to get a lot closer to Nicky to find out.

I take a shower, get dressed, and head to the club. It's Saturday night and the parking lot is fucking jammed. I find a spot around back and park my Lincoln. I start walking around to the front of the club and notice Jason the waiter having a smoke. "Hey Jason, what's up man?"

"Hi Droz, just having a smoke on my break, you want one?" He smiles replying.

As he pulls out the red box of Marlboro's from the front pocket of his shirt I wave my hand replying, "No thanks Jason. I have enough vices already."

Jason laughs and puts his cigarettes back in his pocket. Then he asks, "If want to go in through the kitchen just go through this door behind me."

"Cool, thanks Jason."

Jason nods as I enter the door. In the kitchen, the smell of garlic and clams hits me like a wave on the North Shore of Hawaii. Georgie sees me and shouts, "Mikey boy, it's good to see you kid! I was just going to order dinner for myself. We just got in a load of fresh littlenecks. As you can see, they're chopping them up to make linguini and white clam sauce. Do want to join me?"

"My mouth started watering as soon as I walked in the door Georgie."

"Terrific. How about having some clams on the half shell with me too?"

"You don't have to ask me twice Georgie. I love littlenecks."

"That's great Mikey. Go on up front to the bar and order us a couple of drafts. I'll be out there in a little bit."

"Okay Georgie."

Up front, the club is buzzing. All kinds of wise guys are shooting craps and playing black jack. The roulette wheel is packed. I wave hi to everyone and everyone gives me a big welcome. Damn, I love this fucking place! My old man sure knew how to live! I see Billy making his rounds keeping a sharp eye on everything. He waves to me and gives me a big smile. There's no fucking way I'm confronting him about Shayne's death. Mahoney is tending bar again. I walk up to the bar and cheerfully say, "Hey Mahoney, how's it going buddy?"

"Real busy Mikey, how are things going for you? I bet you're knocking these Florida girls dead," Mahoney smiles replying.

"I'm doing good Mahoney, really good in fact, thank you. As far as the girls go, me, Johnny, and Willie took turns banging four little Latin cuties last night," I brag with a smile.

Mahoney takes a step back and gives up a big Irish grin before replying, "Geez, you guys are like a pack of dogs. Bang them while you can Droz because it's all over once you get married. When you get married you're dead, but you just don't know it yet. What can I get you kid?"

I think to myself, "Geez marriage sounds horrible! No wonder my old man was out every night!"

"Two drafts Mahoney. One for me, and one for Georgie. He'll be up here in a minute."

"Coming right up kid"

Mahoney serves up the beers and here comes Georgie carrying a large tray of littlenecks. Georgie puts the tray on top of the bar and sits down on a stool. He points to the tray saying, "Be careful with the cocktail sauce Mikey. I mixed it up myself with some freshly ground horseradish."

"That's fine with me Georgie. My best friend in the Navy is from Texas. He got me used to hot foods. In fact, he will be here next week."

"You bring him to the club Mikey and we'll make him feel right at home."

"I will Georgie."

The clams are fresh and tender. It doesn't take long before we finish off the whole tray. With a little bit of help from Mahoney of course!

All of a sudden, I catch a big woof of garlic. I look over my shoulder and here comes Jason carrying out the linguini and clam sauce! Me and Georgie sit at the bar and eat like fucking kings! It's so easy to see why my father loved his life so much. The linguini and white clam sauce are to die for! The dinner plates at the club are huge, but that doesn't stop me from finishing it all. I even sop up all the juice with some garlic bread. Georgie watches this saying, "Just like your father."

I spend the next four hours listening to firemen stories with my father's friends. Life is good! After a while, I say my goodbyes and head to my car. I have a big day ahead of me with Rocco, so I want to spend some time alone gathering my thoughts. The beach at night will be the perfect place to do it. When I get there, it's empty. I take off my sneakers and socks. Then I light up a joint and start walking. The star filled sky and the sounds of the ocean bring back memories of the nights I spent out at sea. The first thoughts creeping into my mind are of my father. I knew he wouldn't want me involved in any of this shit. He always tried his hardest to keep me away from it. Pops would say, "Michael, why can't you just be a good boy? You are always looking for trouble. Always trying to prove to the world what a tough guy you are. If you keep this up, trouble is going to find you."

My father was right. Trouble did find me. Now I have to deal with it without him around to help. I think about how Rocco fills the void left in my heart after my father's death. Rocco may like me, but I'm not his son, and he surely isn't my father. This doesn't mean we can't have a very close relationship. Rocco can be my mentor into his way of life. I surely have the skills and talent to become his protégé. Every powerful man wants to mentor someone to follow in their footsteps. This kind of relationship between Rocco and I makes sense, so I decide to trust him. Let's face it, if Rocco wants to fuck me over there aint shit I can do about it anyway. Tomorrow at Sunday dinner, I'll confide in him. I will tell Rocco everything Nicky told me. I'll rat him out and every other son of bitch involved with narcotics, so I might as well admit it to myself. I'm Rocco's fucking rat. I can't let it bother me anymore. I finish the joint and walk back to my car.

By the time I get home, I feel very comfortable with my decision. I put the key in the door and then turn around to look at the beautiful car Rocco had given me. I start thinking about how many times I wished I could work for a guy like Rocco Santori. Then right before I fall asleep, I remember an old saying my father used to tell me. "Be careful what you wish for."

THE PLAN...

I wake up Sunday morning knowing after today there will be no turning back. I work out and swim a few laps before eating breakfast. I'll only have a bowl of cereal to make sure I have a good appetite for later. I entertain myself while I'm eating visioning Rocco making meatballs. It's pretty funny thinking of him in that way. After breakfast, I go into my floor safe and count out a hundred grand. I place it in the briefcase Rocco gave me. Before I go to Rocco's, I need to stop at the bakery to pick up some fresh Italian bread and coffee cake. I grab my briefcase and head for the door when the phone rings. I think about not answering it, but it could be Rocco. I pick up the phone and it's Johnny.

"Droz, you don't know how happy I am you and my cousin worked things out. I was fucking worried you and Nicky would butt heads," Johnny enthusiastically says.

"Why should you be worried Johnny, you think I'm fucking scared of him?" I reply toughly.

"Calm down Droz, calm down. No one thinks you're scared of anybody even though maybe you should be."

"Really Johnny, I don't fucking think so," I angrily reply.

"Geez Droz. You're such a fucking hothead. Nobody can say anything to you without you wanting to fight. I'm just glad you both are going to be friends. You would have put me in a bad position if you and my cousin were to become enemies, capisce?"

"Yeah Johnny, I capisce," I reluctantly reply.

"Just one more thing Droz, be a man of your word. If Rocco asks you anything, we can count on you, right?"

Now I lose my cool replying, "I dare you to fucking ask me that to my face you cocksucker!"

"Believe me Droz, I didn't want to ask you that, but I'm being fucking pressured. If you know what I mean," Johnny replies nervously.

I knew what Johnny meant. I still think he's a scumbag and don't trust him, but I knew what he meant. Nicky's holding Johnny responsible for my actions. I'll bet Nicky's standing there next to him. Johnny probably got a smack in the head for saying he's being pressured, so I calm down and reply accordingly. "I know what you mean Johnny. Don't worry, your cousin made sense about a lot of things. I got everything worked out in my head. I'll talk to you guys when I get back." I hang up the phone and take a deep breath. Then I grab my briefcase and head to the bakery. The name of the bakery is Marie's. It is owned by one of Rocco's friends from Brooklyn. When I walk in the bakery, I smell fresh baked sfogliatelle! They were my father's favorite! I ask Marie for a loaf of Italian bread and a dozen sfogliatelle. I pay and leave with a smile. I can feel through the bag that they're still a little hot. In the car, I snatch one out of the bag and take a crispy bite. The warm, sweet cheese filling pleasures my taste buds. It takes all my self-control to only eat one more. I pull up to the guardhouse at Rocco's condo, and the guard raises the gate like I live there. I park the car, grab what I need, and head to the elevator. When I get off the elevator, the entire floor smells like Italian cooking. I knock on the door and hear Rocco singing to an Enrico Caruso record. This is fucking priceless. Rocco's obviously lost in his own little world. I have to keep knocking until the fucking song was over. Rocco opens the door with an apron on and a glass of wine in his hand. "Come on in kid," he says smiling.

"Thank you Rocco. You can smell your cooking all the way down the hallway. It smells pretty damn good too. I'll reserve comment on the singing."

Rocco sneers as he sips his wine. "What are you carrying?" he asks politely.

"I picked up a loaf of Italian bread and some fresh baked sfogliatelle from Marie's. They just came out of the oven, so of course I couldn't fucking help but eat a few. They're really fucking delicious Rocco."

Rocco takes another sip of wine. Then he smiles wide replying, "Marie makes the best sfogliatelle in all of New York. That was really very thoughtful of you kid. Just leave the briefcase by the couch and bring the baked goods over to the table."

I listen to Rocco as he takes off his apron asking, "How about having a little vino with me out on the terrace?"

"Sure Rocco," I reply happily.

Even though I was here before, I still can't help being awed by the view. Rocco shows me a bottle with no label saying, "Wait until you taste this Michael. This wine is made special for me in Brooklyn."

Rocco pours me a glass. I try to look like I know what I'm doing by swirling it around and smelling it before taking a sip. I'm shocked how good it is. I reply amazed, "Rocco, this wine is fantastic! They make this for you back in Brooklyn?"

"Yup, I know an old Italian guy who makes a few barrels of this every year in his basement. There's nothing like it," Rocco replies proudly.

"You're right Rocco. I've never tasted wine this good before."

Rocco and I sit back sipping wine looking out over the ocean. Breaking the silence, Rocco asks, "How was your night at the clubs?"

I sway my head back and forth and take another sip of wine before replying, "I don't know if I should tell you before or after dinner."

"So it's that bad?" Rocco laughs replying.

"In all seriousness, it's pretty fucking bad Rocco."

Rocco leans over grabbing a newspaper off his table. The headlines read, "Drug Turf Wars Heat up between South Florida Drug Cartels and New York Mafia. Two Peruvian Cartel Members were Gunned Down along with Reputed New York Brooklyn Mobster Joey 'Jumbo' Conniglio behind the Blue Diamonds Club Friday Night. Police Are Investigating, but Say They Have no Witnesses."

I raise my eyebrows saying, "That's just the beginning of your worries Rocco. Cocaine is used and dealt openly in both clubs."

Rocco refills our glasses with his special vino replying, "That doesn't surprise me Michael. I'm sure every popular club in South Florida has a drug problem."

"You're probably right Rocco, but if that didn't surprise you maybe this will. Friday night at Blue Diamonds, I met Johnny's cousin Nicky. Johnny says Nicky just got out of prison. Nicky brought three guys with him to the club. He introduced them as Vinnie, Sally, and the recently departed Joey Conniglio. Nicky came to the club to meet a guy named Antonio. A lot of people seemed to know Antonio is the head of a Columbian drug cartel here in South Florida. He drives a beautiful green Ferrari Rocco. I got his plate number for Ariella."

Rocco takes a sip of wine and asks, "Does the car impress you Droz?"

I shrug my shoulders, take a sip of wine, and reply, "No, not really, but it sure is a nice fucking car. Anyway, a guy named Charlie Wings made the connection for Nicky with Antonio."

Rocco smiles when I mention the name Charlie Wings, so I figure he knows him, or at least knows of him. I continue. "I found out Michael and Joey Rannelli were already dealing for the Peruvians. Tommy and Pauley Palermo were dealing for the Colombian guy Antonio."

"Did my godson know about this?" Rocco asks inquisitively.

Looking Rocco square in the eyes, I reply, "Yes."

Rocco looks disappointed, but not surprised. He now says, "You're doing good Droz. Keep talking."

"When we leave the club we see Nicky and his crew beating the shit out of the Rannelli brothers. They got them on their knees with guns to their heads. Nicky told the Rannelli's they can't deal with the Peruvians anymore. They can only deal with Antonio. I guess Nicky struck a deal with Antonio, so fuck the Peruvians. It didn't take long to figure out the Peruvians and the Colombians hate each other."

Rocco interrupts saying, "Sadly that reminds me of a lot of my own people. How can we achieve world peace when people from the same country can't even get along? Sorry kid. I'm getting on my soapbox. Please continue."

"No problem Rocco. I like hearing your thoughts. That's how I learn from you."

"Why thank you Michael," Rocco replies humbly.

"Next, Nicky tells all four of Johnny's guys from here on out they'll be kicking back thirty percent of their drug profits to him. The little fucking pussy faggots cried like bitches Rocco. They'd a sucked Nicky's dick if he asked them too."

Rocco laughs and then takes a sip of his wine before saying, "What would you have done in that position?"

I take a slug of wine and reply like a tough guy, "First off Rocco, I wouldn't be in that fucking position. But if I was, I can damn sure promise you I wouldn't be crying like a little fucking bitch. Tex and I would have given Nicky some ear candy to get him off us. Then later on when the time was right we would have wacked him and his whole fucking crew."

Rocco laughs saying, "Nice strategy Droz. It's good to know you're not going to cry when someone puts a gun to your head."

Rocco seems to be having a good time listening to me, so I continue my story with more zeal. "All of a sudden, out of fucking nowhere Rocco, a Camaro races around the corner. Two guys jump out of the car with small machine guns and start spraying fucking bullets everywhere. We all duck for cover while Nicky and his boys start firing back with handguns. Then a small pickup truck pulls in real fast to the melee. Two guys pop up out of the bed with pump shotguns. These guys make short fucking work out of the guys with the little machine guns. I learned right then there's nothing like a fucking shotgun when it comes to killing. Then to my surprise, guess who pops out of the pickup truck Rocco?"

"Richard Nixon? They blamed that poor man for everything. He was really a good president," Rocco seriously replies.

I give Rocco a side eyes look and then continue. "It's fucking Antonio, Rocco, coming to Nicky's rescue! So evidently, the Peruvians found out Nicky and his crew was muscling in on their two dealers. One of the Peruvians was still convulsing around on the ground. Nicky just walked right up to him all casual like and put two bullets in his fucking head. It was a real fucking bloodbath. Everyone was feeling pretty fucking good they came out unscathed until the fat man hits the ground."

Rocco is unfazed by the story. He picks up his glass of wine and slowly sips it. Then he puts down his glass saying, "The fact that the Peruvians and the Colombians hate each other will work to our advantage. The headlines in the newspaper linking the mafia to the cartels in a drug war will work especially well for us. Before I come up with a plan, is there anything else I should know?"

I down the rest of my wine before replying, "Unfortunately, Rocco there is."

Rocco pats me on the knee and says, "Okay, let me stir my sauce first. Would you like some more vino?"

"Some more wine would be good. Thank you Rocco."

Rocco refills our wine glasses and then journeys into the kitchen to stir his sauce. This gives me a moment to look out over the ocean and gather my thoughts. How Rocco reacts to the next part of my story will tell me whether I can trust him or not. When it came to Johnny's cousin Nicky, I found out real quick where I stood. Let's see where I stand with Rocco when it comes to his godson.

Rocco returns to the balcony and sits down beside me. He sips his wine as he looks out over the turquoise shaded ocean.

Rocco takes a deep breath and then says, "I love the smell of the ocean. Do you ever miss being out at sea Droz?"

"I sure do Rocco. I will always miss being out at sea, especially at night. Staring up at the stars with a cool wind in my face is part of my soul. I will never miss the Navy though."

"That's understandable Droz. Most of the people who stay in the military do so because they can't make a living at home. Some small towns in America can't offer a decent future for young people. For them, the military is a good choice. Now Michael, what else is it that you have to tell me?"

"Saturday morning Nicky and his boys paid me an uninvited visit. Johnny not only told Nicky where I lived, but he also told him about how close you and I have become."

I could tell by the look on Rocco's face this upset him. Rocco takes a gulp of wine and then bluntly asks, "What does that tell you?"

"It tells me Nicky owns Johnny and we can't trust him."

"Correct. When Johnny told Nicky about our relationship, he gave Nicky an edge over the both of us. So the purpose of Nicky's visit was to get you to betray me, right?"

"You hit the nail right on the head Rocco."

"How does Nicky want you to go about this betrayal?"

"Nicky wants me to take advantage of our close relationship by lying when you ask me who is dealing drugs. He thinks you're too busy to check it out yourself and you'll believe me."

Taking another gulp of wine Rocco shakes his head replying, "Johnny must have really convinced Nicky we're that close. It's a simple enough plan. It would work in the short run. But if we're so close why should you betray me?"

"Well first off Rocco, Nicky tried convincing me I couldn't trust you."

"Well that's fucking original."

"He also said you fuck all your partners and then they disappear."

"Really? Did Nicky give you the names of any of these partners?" Rocco laughs asking.

"No. Nicky said everybody's too afraid of you to even talk about it," I shake my head replying.

"Let's see how Nicky's logic plays out Droz. He says everyone is too afraid to talk about my fucked over missing partners. Yet Nicky isn't afraid to tell you all of this behind my back? Doesn't that sound a little fishy to you?"

"Of course it does, but that's not all Rocco. Nicky says I need a backup plan where I can make a lot of money, so I don't need you anymore."

Rocco stands up with his glass of wine in his hand saying, "I'll bet you Nicky told Johnny something along those same lines. The way Johnny loses money gambling the millionaire pitch will work perfectly on him."

"You know about Johnny's gambling problem Rocco?" I ask surprised.

Rocco looks at me like I'm an idiot asking, "How much money does my nephew owe you?"

Surprised again, I reply, "Thirty grand, and how did you know I lent him money?"

"I didn't. It was just an educated guess. My brother complains about Johnny's gambling habit all the time. Now tell me what Nicky offered you."

"Nicky offered me five hundred dollars on every kilo he ships out of South Florida. Charlie Wings and Nicky will also be supplying the cartels down here with heroin. I'll get a piece of that too."

Again, the name Charlie Wings brings a smile to Rocco's face. Now he says, "Good old Charlie Wings. Did you ever see that movie with Gene Hackman called the French Connection?"

"Did you ever pick your feet in Poughkeepsie?" My father took me to see that movie. I fucking loved it."

Rocco chuckles at my answer and then says, "Remember the guy who got away at the end of the movie?"

"You mean the French guy?"

"Yeah, Charlie Wings is the French guy, but he aint French, he's Italian. When this guy disappears, even Ariella can't find him. I can't tell you how happy I am to hear his name again. I believe Charlie Wings can tell me who in my family supplied the heroin that killed my son. I'm hungry, how about you?"

"Sure Rocco. I'm hungry."

"Good, let's go inside and I'll get the water boiling for the raviolis. I made three kinds from scratch: cheese, meat, and spinach. You'll love them."

"Oh man that sounds too good to be true Rocco. But before we eat, there's just one more thing I need to get off my chest."

Rocco puts his arm on top of my shoulder like a father saying, "By all means son. You can't enjoy your dinner if something's bothering you."

"This part really did bother me Rocco, so I hope you can give me some answers. Nicky told me that my father and Billy killed Shayne for old man Rose back in Yonkers. I would like to know if it's true, and who told Nicky."

Rocco puts his hand to his chin and pauses for a moment. He then looks me in the eyes replying, "All I know about Shayne's death is that old man Rose had him killed because he thought Shayne sold his son heroin. I never ask the particulars and you shouldn't either. Old man Rose is the only one who could tell you if your old man and Billy killed Shayne. Even if you found old man Rose, he wouldn't tell you anyway."

"How do you think Nicky knows Rocco?"

"Old man Rose might have told his son Howie to scare him. If he told his son Howie, there's no telling who a junkie might have told. There's the danger of dealing with junkies. It doesn't matter if they're friends or family. They'll run their mouth for a fix. I'll tell you what kid, before this is over with Nicky; I'll get him to talk. Okay?"

"Cool Rocco," I reply with a big smile.

Rocco rubs me on the head asking, "You ready for my raviolis now?"

"I sure am Rocco," I hungrily reply.

"Would it be okay if I play a little music with dinner?"

"Sure Rocco, as long as you don't start singing again," I reply smiling.

Rocco gets a hurt look on his face while asking somberly, "You don't like my singing?"

I could tell Rocco needs a little positive reinforcement here, so I cheerfully reply, "Sure I liked your singing Rocco. I was just teasing you."

Rocco smiles and struts over to his stereo. He pulls a very old looking album out of his collection and admires it for a second. Very gently like he's handling a newborn baby, Rocco slides the record from its sleeve. He carefully puts it on his old phonograph saying, "I have some very rare Enrico Caruso Albums. Wait until you hear this."

Rocco adjusts the volume so we can easily still speak to each other. As the record starts playing, he drifts into bliss. Rocco floats into the kitchen on a cloud of euphoria and turns up the stove under the pot of water. He turns to me merrily saying, "It won't be long before the water boils. I had it simmering the entire time we were out on the terrace."

Rocco was right. It didn't take long for the water to boil, and in go the raviolis. Fresh homemade Raviolis only take a few minutes to boil. When they're done, Rocco gently pours them into a colander waiting in the sink. He throws some sauce onto a platter and gently pours the raviolis over it. Then he puts a little more sauce on top and grates some fresh parmesan cheese over them. Next, Rocco takes his meatballs and pork hocks out of the gravy. He puts them into a separate bowl and grates a little cheese on top. Now he brings everything over to the table. Now he goes back to the fridge and pulls out another bowl containing a fresh salad. As he is pouring his homemade Italian dressing over the salad, he says, "Pour us both some more wine, and I'll cut up the Italian bread."

"Sure Rocco."

When everything's on the table, we bow our heads and say grace. Then we dig in. The cheese raviolis melt in my mouth. The meat raviolis have a little spicy kick to them, which I loved.

The spinach raviolis are full of garlic with a touch of cheese. The sauce and meatballs are almost as good as my own, and that's saying something. There are only two of us, but Rocco cooked for six. Taking a breath, Rocco looks up from his plate and politely asks, "Well Droz? How do you like my cooking?"

I take a few seconds to swallow what's in my mouth before replying, "The food, the music, the wine, and the host are all fantastic."

This brings a big smile to Rocco's face. It takes us awhile, but we manage to almost finish everything on the table. Rocco looks at what's left saying, "Perfect. There's just enough left over for a midnight snack. You got any room for a sfogliatelle and some black coffee?"

"Of course Rocco," I burp replying.

"Good. I thought you would."

We both clear the table and then Rocco makes the coffee. He neatly aligns the sfogliatelle in a circle on a fancy silver platter. When the coffee is ready, Rocco goes over to his bar and picks up a very old liquor bottle. Walking back to the table he says, "There's nothing like a little anisette after dinner with your coffee."

"I can get used to this treatment pretty fast Rocco," I smile replying.

Rocco laughs and pours the coffee leaving enough room at the top for the anisette. We both grab a sfogliatelle and sit back enjoying our after dinner treat. After a few sfogliatelle and a couple of cups of coffee, Rocco suggests we take a walk on the beach to digest. We go down to the beach and start walking north along the shoreline. It's a gorgeous afternoon. There's a wonderful breeze coming off the surf. The sky's deep blue with big puffy clouds floating across it. I keep quiet as we walk, and within minutes, Rocco starts to speak. "I thought of a plan Michael. I want you to know, if I was your father I wouldn't ask you to do this."

"Funny you should say that Rocco because I thought about that last night. I accept you as my mentor into a world I always wished I could be in. I'm prepared to do whatever it takes to walk in your footsteps."

Rocco stops dead in his tracks and faces me. He stares deeply into my eyes trying to read my soul as he asks, "Are you sure Michael? I mean really sure because once you do these things for me there will be no turning back."

I stare back into Rocco's eyes with fervor replying, "I'm sure Rocco. This is what I have wanted my entire life."

Rocco stares intensely into my eyes for a few seconds more. Then he slowly nods his head while cracking a sinister smile. I guess he saw what he wanted to see. We both start walking, and Rocco starts talking, "So here's what I want you to do Michael. Tomorrow morning you'll meet with Ariella. I want you to give her Antonio's plate number. She will find out everything we need to know about these Colombians. From what I understand, you do not have much experience with handguns. Tomorrow Ariella will give you a crash course. When does your friend Tex get here?"

"I pick him up at Fort Lauderdale Airport this Friday at seven."

"Perfect. You don't think he'll mind hitting the ground running do you? I don't want to put things into motion and at the last minute you tell me he got cold feet."

"Tex aint got cold feet about nothing Rocco. He's as solid as they come."

Rocco nods his head continuing. "Here's the plan kid. I'll tell my brother on Friday morning I'm paying out bonuses to the men this week. I do this from time to time, so it won't seem unusual. I put the cash in a bag along with a list of how I want it to be paid out. I'll tell my brother I will meet him a little later than usual. Say around seven when Tex's plane gets in. If his plane is late, you call my brother's house looking for Johnny and I'll modify the plan on the fly."

"Okay Rocco."

Rocco nods his head again continuing. "My brother and I always insist the bonuses are handed out by Johnny as soon as he gets them. My godson hates to do this on Friday's so he tries to make it as easy as possible. Coral Springs is west of everything, so what Johnny does is have everyone who lives east meet at someone's house who lives west. Tommy and Pauley Palermo live together in a condo by Ft. Lauderdale Beach. Michael and Joey Rannelli live in a house together on a half an acre out in Davie. Everyone else lives in either Coral Springs or right next to it. Johnny will make sure that the Palermo brothers meet him at the Rannelli's in Davie. Is this all sinking in Droz, or am I moving too fast for you?"

"Come on Rocco. Give me a fucking break. Just keep talking," I frown replying.

"I know. You're a fucking genius. How can I forget your military test scores? You know I keep a copy of them if you ever want one," Rocco replies with half a smile.

"You keep a copy of my military test scores?"

"Definitely, so when you do something stupid I can remind you of how smart you're supposed to be."

"Just continue Rocco," I shake my head saying.

"My pleasure kid. The Palermo's will show up at the Rannelli's eager to get their bonuses around seven thirty. They know if they aint there when Johnny shows up they aint getting it until Monday. Johnny has strict instructions to pay them individually because everybody usually gets a different amount. That's my way of telling the guys if they're doing a good job or not. When two guys are working side by side and one guy gets a grand while another one gets fifty bucks, it sends a message. We had a couple of incidents in the past where money left behind for one guy ended up in the wrong pocket, so now Johnny has to hand it all out individually. If all goes well at the airport, you and Tex should arrive at the Rannelli's before eight. I will make sure Johnny gets a late start, so you will have more than enough time to complete your job. The guys all know you pretty good by now and they know how close you are to Johnny, so when you knock on the door there's a very good chance they'll think you're there to pay them their bonuses. They may even think since you're in with Nicky, you might be there to buy some blow. At any rate, I really don't think they will be alarmed by your presence. I want this to look like the Peruvians whacked them, so you're going to have to chop off their heads. Peruvians have been known to send a message by chopping off the heads of their enemies."

Rocco pauses for a second to gauge my reaction. I'm stunned, but I play it off, so he continues. "The Colombians do a thing to their victims called a Colombian neck tie."

"What's a Colombian neck tie?" I ask inquisitively.

"A Colombian neck tie is when they slit the throat of their victim and pull their tongue out through the slit they made in their throat."

"This is all pretty fucking gruesome Rocco. In fact, it sounds like a gruesome horror flick."

Rocco gives me a blank stare saying, "Real life murders can be way worse than any movie you will ever see. I'm sensing a little apprehension here Droz. Are you up for this or what?"

Rocco just challenged me, so I reply back with some anger, "Of course I'm fucking up to it Rocco, but you can't blame me if I'm a little bit shocked by all this. You just asked me to kill four guys by chopping off their fucking heads."

Rocco sighs in angst replying, "No, no Droz. You don't chop off their fucking heads while their still alive. You shoot them first. You make sure they're dead, and then you chop off their fucking heads, capisce?"

I stand there nodding my head while visualizing what Rocco just said. Then I reply, "You're absolutely right Rocco. Chasing them around trying to chop off their heads could be difficult. It'll be a lot easier after we shoot them, I definitely capisce."

"Okay, after you pick up Tex from the airport you'll drop your car off at Ariella's. Make sure you bring a change of clothes and leave them in your car. Tex will have his luggage, so he'll already have his clothes with him when you get him. Ariella will have another car at her house waiting for you to do the job with. She'll arm you guys with two Smith and Wesson 45's.

They're loud, but powerful. Even if someone hears the shots, they won't pay it any mind out there. It's not unusual to hear gunshots in Davie. This will be your first hit, but the two of you have to try not to be nervous. The element of surprise is on your side and that's almighty. To make this as easy and as quick as possible, you want all four of them to be in the same room. Make some small talk first to get them to relax. Try to get them all to sit down on a couch or at a table together. Before you go in the house, you and Tex have some kind of pre-arranged signal worked out. Then when the moment is right, the both of you pull out your guns and start blasting. After you shoot them all a couple of times, make sure they're dead. Another round or two in the head always does the trick. After that one of you calmly walk back out to the car and go in the trunk. The house is on a half an acre with a private driveway, so no one will see you. In the trunk will be two machetes, two pairs of gloves, and a kilo of coke. Go back in the house, put on the gloves, and chop off their heads. It's going to be messy, but try to stay as clean as possible. When you're done, drop the kilo of coke in the middle of the mess. Then leave the house and make sure you leave the front door unlocked. Put your guns, your gloves, and the machetes, back into the trunk. Then calmly drive away. If by the unfortunate chance you are caught in the process, or arrested after the fact, don't say a fucking word. Not even you're fucking names. You have nothing to worry about Droz when it comes to our criminal justice system. Just stay calm and remember help is on the way. When you get back to Ariella's you'll be able to both clean up and change your clothes. She'll take care of the rest. Do you have any questions?"

"No matter what goes down Rocco, you'll get me and Tex out of jail right?"

"You have my word you and Tex will never do time for any-thing I ask you to do."

"I believe you Rocco. So what happens next?"

"Johnny will be arriving shortly after you guys have left. He'll knock on the door and get no answer. He'll try the door and then go inside. When my nephew sees all the blood and the four headless bodies, he'll go find Nicky. After he tells Nicky what he seen, Nicky will go see Antonio. Nicky will tell Antonio his dealers got their heads chopped off. Antonio will immediately assume they were executed by Peruvian cartel members. Payback will be planned by Nicky and Antonio."

"You thought all this up during dinner Rocco?"

"To tell you the truth, I actually didn't start making up the plan until right after dinner. Dinner was so fucking good it took up all of my concentration just to eat it."

"To come to think of it Rocco, dinner was so fucking good my mind wasn't thinking of anything else either."

Rocco smiles and pats me on the back saying, "I hope we share many more meals together Michael."

The both of us joke around a little more on the beach and then walk back to the condo. When we get upstairs Rocco makes another pot of coffee, and we both eat a couple of more sfogliatelle. After that, we sit out on the terrace talking about the future and enjoying the ocean breeze. Rocco says he had both titles for the land drawn up in my name. That way I would have no problems if Willie decided to back out of the deal. After that, Rocco says he has a long day tomorrow and wants to retire early. I take the hint and thank him once again for the great meal. As I'm heading to the door, Rocco asks, "Hey kid, are you forgetting something?"

I think quickly to myself and reply, "No."

"You're forgetting your briefcase. You need it to put your titles in."

The briefcase is still sitting by the couch where I left it, so I ask, "Where do you want me to dump all the dough Rocco?"

"Keep the dough and the land," Rocco waves his hand replying.

I'm stunned by Rocco's continued generosity. I try saying something, but Rocco immediately cuts me off saying, "Not one word kid. Put the titles in the briefcase with the money and be careful on your way home."

I give Rocco a big hug and kiss. Then he looks me in the eye saying, "You can't buy loyalty, but you can surely reward it."

I'm on cloud nine when I leave. It's not so much about the land and the money, but more about Rocco returning my loyalty with his own. When Rocco didn't take sides with Johnny, my instincts told me I could trust him. Now that I trust him, I will carry out his plan.

Here We Go...

I'm still stuffed when I get home, so I roll up a nice fatty to help me digest. After taking a few pokes, I put my money and titles to the property in a floor safe. Once I feel a nice buzz coming on I go into the garage and work off Rocco's raviolis. After an intense workout, I take a leisurely swim under the stars. It's a beautiful starry night, and I'm feeling blessed to have Rocco as my mentor. After about an hour of mind drifting out by the pool, I go inside and take a really hot shower. That relaxes me for a good night's sleep.

The sound of the phone ringing wakes me from a deep slumber. I peek at the clock, and it's only 6 AM. Reluctantly, I pick up the phone and it's Rocco.

"Good morning kid," Rocco says in a wide-awake and cheery voice.

"Good morning Rocco," I reply to the best of my ability.

"I hope you slept well because Ariella wants you at her house by seven thirty."

I peek at the clock again before replying, "I'll be there."

"Good, and don't keep her waiting. Her time is very valuable, literally. Also, Father Mac will be flying out to see your friend in Hawaii today. I hope they don't treat him too nice."

"Why would say that Rocco?" I ask surprised.

"I say that because he won't want to come back," Rocco chuckles

"Well just so you know Rocco they probably will. So be prepared."

Rocco laughs and then says, "Ariella will let me know how things go. Good luck and don't be late."

"I won't Rocco."

We both hang up and I get up. I go into the kitchen and put on a pot of coffee. While it's brewing, I start my breakfast. There's nothing better in the morning than the sound and smell of bacon cooking. After my bacon is done I crack open my eggs and let them drop right into the bacon grease. That's how my old man taught me to cook them. I make some toast and flip my eggs over for a few seconds. When I finish eating, I clean up my mess and head out the door. There is a little bit of traffic from people going to work and school, but I still manage to arrive ten minutes early. Ariella and Katrina are already outside waiting for me. They're both dressed in faded fatigues that cling perfectly to their bodies.

I get out of the car with a big smile saying, "Good morning ladies."

"Good start Droz. You got here early," Ariella replies.

"Good morning Droz. I just made fresh squeezed orange juice from the oranges in our grove. Would you like some?" Katrina asks smiling.

"Sure Katrina. That would be great," I cheerfully reply.

As Katrina walks back towards the house, I can't help but stare at her perfect ass. Ariella notices me staring and says, "I don't blame you for staring at Katrina's ass Droz. After all it is quite inviting," She says teasingly.

"You can say that again Ariella," I reply while getting a last glimpse before she walks into the house.

"Rocco said things are moving along quickly Michael, so if we concentrate too much on Katrina's ass instead of your mission we will both fail."

"I'm sorry for staring Ariella, but both of you girls are very beautiful."

Ariella smiles at me and then condescendingly replies, "That's okay Droz. You are a young man, so it's perfectly un-understandable we entice your thoughts. The fact you cannot have us makes the fantasy even more desirable to you. Right now you need to put your hormones to rest and concentrate on your mission."

"Gee Ariella, you sure know how to take the wind out of a guy's sails," I sigh.

Ariella smiles as Katrina brings out a glass of OJ. I take a gulp and then say, "Wow Ariella, this orange juice is super sweet and tasty. Can I buy some oranges from you?"

"Not a problem Droz. When we're done I'll give you a sack of oranges and a hand juicer to take home with you."

"Thank you Ariella. How much I owe you?" I reply reaching in my pocket.

"You owe me your undivided attention from here on out. No more distractions. Is that a deal?"

"It's a deal Ariella."

"Good. Now let's get started."

Katrina and Ariella both start walking towards a big concrete building sitting on their property, so now I have two gorgeous asses to look at. When we get to the entrance of the building, Ariella opens up the door to a super cool gun range. Ariella turns to me saying, "Today I want to familiarize you with how to use a handgun and a pump shotgun under various conditions. Rocco told me that you liked shotguns, so I want to make sure you are able to use one properly. Follow me and keep quiet unless I ask you a question."

I smile at Katrina as we both follow Ariella over to a counter. On top of the counter, there are three pistols and three pump shotguns. Ariella now says, "This is the type of pistol you and Tex will be using Friday night. It is a 45 caliber Smith and Wesson. I will supply you and Tex with two extra clips. Amateurs make the mistake of not carrying an extra clip with them. The bullets you will be using are flat-nosed full metal jacket. Hollow points are used mainly for law enforcement and not assassinations. Law enforcement requires a hollow point bullet because the rounds will not travel through walls, or out of the bodies of their targets. Hollow points do carry considerably more knock down power than a full metal jacket, but aren't as lethal. How do the majority of people die from gunshot wounds Droz?"

"I guess they die from the damage caused by the bullet hitting their internal organs, right?"

"Wrong. Most victims of gunshot wounds simply bleed to death. A flat nose full metal jacket round will not only cause severe damage to a victim's internal organs, but it can also create two holes in the body to bleed out from. Law enforcement's goal isn't to kill. It is to control and apprehend. To accomplish their goal, law enforcement uses a hollow pointed round to knock their suspect down and reduce any collateral damage. Our goal is to kill our targets. Unlike law enforcement, you want your bullets to travel through your target. In a gunfight, often times a person will try to shield their body with the body of another. If a trained assassin is forced to fight in the open, they will fight from a sideways position. This gives your adversary as little a target as possible. Hollow points will not penetrate through an arm or shoulder into the body cavity, but a flat nose full metal jacket will. In a real life and death situation, you want your ammo to be penetrating right through its striking point. If you hit a main artery, death could occur in less than five minutes. If your bullet misses a main organ or artery, but leaves two holes, your target will generally bleed out in twenty minutes or less. Do you have any questions?"

"Not really, but I sure did learn a lot."

"Good. Now let's learn how to properly fire the weapon. You must grip the handle of an automatic firmly to avoid jamming. Limp wristed shooters tend to jam automatics. Holding the weapon with two hands should avoid that problem altogether."

Katrina brings over three pairs of earmuffs. Before we put them on Ariella says, "Observe Katrina and I as we both shoot at the stationary targets in front of us. You first chamber a round by firmly pulling back the slide and letting it go quickly."

In unison, Katrina and Ariella chamber a round. Then they take aim and fire off several shots. The 45's have kick, but the girls hold them steady. They both place their shots perfectly.

Ariella turns to me saying, "It's your turn Droz."

I give the girls a cocky smile while chambering a round. I take steady aim at my target and fire off three shots like they did. All three shots are perfect. Both girls look at each other nodding their heads smiling. Ariella tells me to fire off the rest of my clip. I follow her instructions and create what she says is a perfect spread.

Katrina looks at Ariella saying, "Droz has some natural ability."

"I was born with all kinds of natural abilities," I wink replying.

"Modesty obviously isn't one of them," Ariella adds.

Katrina laughs and Ariella quickly gets serious saying, "Okay Droz, now let's see what you can do with moving targets. I want you to observe us first and then it will be your turn to try."

Katrina and Ariella enter the middle of the firing range. Ariella pulls a remote control from her pocket and hits a button. The entire shooting range comes to life. Bad guy dummies and dummies of innocent looking people start popping up from various places. Ariella and Katrina work the moving targets like a well-oiled machine. I watch both of their movements closely as they pivot flawlessly through the course. They crouch and turn sideways protecting each other's backs while striking only the enemy targets with their shots. When they're done, Ariella says it's my turn. After watching them, I'm more than anxious. As I enter into the middle of the firing range, Ariella hits the button on her remote putting everything into motion. I go fucking gangbusters on this place! On the fun scale, this is a fucking ten! When I'm finished, Ariella says I did an excellent job. She says my footwork and body position is nearly perfect. Ariella tells me to load up two clips for a final test. She warns me the next phase of the test includes a lot of distractions. Ariella says this will show her how I might perform under adverse conditions. She hits a different button on her remote, and immediately everything on the range goes bonkers! Multi-color lights and beacons start blinking all over the range. Loud sirens and sounds of explosions are all around me. Strobe lights circle the room accompanied by smoke screens. It freaks me out at first, but I quickly get my bearings. I finish one clip and pop in another. This is an incredibly fun experience! When I'm done, in a congratulatory tone Ariella says, "Very good Droz, in fact it was surprisingly good. There were a few civilian casualties, but it's your first time on the course. Rocco will be very pleased."

Next, I learn how to use a pump shotgun and a snub-nosed 38 caliber properly. The 38 caliber will be a back-up weapon. When we're done on the range, I reach into my pocket and give Ariella Antonio's license plate number. I asked her to find out everything about him. Ariella says she will have an intelligence report on Antonio within forty-eight hours. Katrina excuses herself by saying she'll be right back with my oranges and juicer. After Katrina leaves, Ariella bluntly asks, "Are you mentally prepared to take the lives of these four men?"

"I am Ariella, but I'm a little worried about my soul. You know, for committing murder? The Ten Commandments say 'Thou Shall Not Kill?' The first guy I killed back in Yonkers was in self-defense. The guys overseas me and Tex killed were also in self-defense. These four guys never did anything to me. They're just drug dealers."

Ariella doesn't even hesitate answering. "The Christian interpretation of the commandment 'Thou Shall Not Kill' is wrong. The Ten Commandments were written in ancient Hebrew and the true translation is 'Thou Shall Not Commit Murder.' All narcotics dealers should be considered terrorists and killed like the dogs they are. As we speak Michael, the narcotics they sell are ruining lives, destroying families, and killing people across the planet. Think of yourself as a shepherd protecting your sheep from the wolves. Killing them is not murder Michael. It is justice being served."

This makes sense to me, so I nod my head up and down before replying, "You're right Ariella. For their own monetary gain these guys are preying on the lives and the souls of others."

"Absolutely Michael, a conventional terrorist will use a gun or bomb. A narcotics dealer uses a drug. A gun or bomb is a more merciful death than a lifetime of addiction."

"That's for sure Ariella."

Ariella supplies me with me two Winchester 12 gauge pump shotguns, two Smith & Wesson 45 caliber semi-automatic handguns, and two Smith & Wesson snub-nosed 38 calibers plus a shit load of ammo. She says the weapons are untraceable.

"You think all of this will fit in my trunk?" I ask.

"It's a Lincoln Droz. In our business we like to call it a four body trunk."

I laugh out loud replying excitedly, "You two chicks are right out of a fucking James Bond movie. Knock down drag out gorgeous and both professional killers! Of course you know this is an incredible fucking turn on for me."

They look at each other smiling coyly. Katrina says, "I bet you would love to play James Bond with us right now, wouldn't you Droz?"

"You know it Katrina, and I'll assure both of you girls you won't regret it," I cockily reply.

Katrina looks at Ariella, and Ariella nods her head in approval. Ariella starts walking towards the house and Katrina holds out her hand to me. I take Katrina's hand and she flips me over her shoulder like a sack of potatoes! As the dust clears from around me, I see both of them laughing at me! Ariella looks at Katrina saying, "I can't believe he really fell for that."

Now they laugh even harder at the pun Ariella made. I can't believe they fucking planned this. Ariella reaches her hand down to help me up, and I politely say, "No thanks."

I get up dusting myself off, while Katrina asks, "Are you mad Droz?"

"Mad no. Disappointed yes, but I should have known better," I calmly reply with a fake smile.

"The both of us just love to play with men's egos. Especially with a man who has an ego as big as yours Droz," Ariella boasts.

"A little humbleness and humility can go a long way with a woman. You ought to try it sometime," Katrina adds.

"Gee thanks Katrina. I'll try to keep that in mind," I sarcastically reply.

They both give me a big hug for being such a good sport. I feel like a schoolboy who had just been schooled. The girls help me load everything into my trunk. Katrina puts a sack of oranges and a juicer on top of the arsenal. I then promptly take my guns, my ammo, and my bruised ego home with me. As I drive off, I watch the both of them in my rearview mirror smiling and waving goodbye. "What a pair," I think to myself.

By the time I get home, it's almost 11 AM. I take a look across the street and see the nosy neighbor lady's car is gone. I pop open my trunk and methodically unload my new arsenal. I put everything neatly into one of the spare bedrooms. I take one of the forty fives out of the box to carry. I put the gun in my waistband and look at myself in the mirror. My tee shirt covered the gat just fine. I begin sitting down and getting up with it under my shirt. Then I practice reaching for my 45. There's a knock at the door. When I peek through the window, I see an old black man wearing overalls and a bright white tee shirt. I also see a large black truck with a trailer parked in front of my house. The truck and trailer are loaded with landscaping. I open my front door, and I'm greeted with a big smile. In a heavy southern accent, the old man says, "Good morning sir. Are you Mr. Droz?"

"Yes I am sir," I reply with a smile and an extended hand.

The old man reaches out with his calloused hand and shakes mine firmly while saying, "Well that's good, that's good. I've been paid sir to landscape your property. Would it be okay if I get my men started?"

"That would be fine sir. Just knock on the door if you need anything."

"Yes sir I will," He replies smiling. The old man turns around and walks towards his truck. His demeanor does a 360 as he starts barking out orders to his men.

I go back to my mirror and continue practicing my quick draw for about another hour before taking a nap. When I awake, the landscapers are gone. I go outside and walk around my house and it looks like a jungle! The new landscaping is absolutely stunning! The old black man and his crew did a fantastic job! I need to thank everyone involved.

I spend the next few days going by the jobsites cracking jokes and getting high with Johnny's crew. At night, I either go to my club or stay home fucking my girls. Rocco comes by my house early Friday morning. He wants to talk and check out the landscaping. I meet him in the driveway and as soon as he gets out of his car, he asks, "How do you like your new landscaping?"

"It's beautiful Rocco. Thank you. I already thanked Johnny and his father but I missed thanking the old black man."

"You'll get a chance. Let's go inside."

We exchange a hug and kiss then walk inside my house. "Can I get you anything Rocco? A cup of coffee, some fresh squeezed OJ?"

Rocco smiles and waves his hand as he's sitting down saying, "I'm good Droz. I just ate breakfast. Thank you. Ariella told me you did fantastic on the range. She also said you were a good sport when Katrina threw you on your back."

"You would have loved to see that one Rocco," I reply smiling.

"I did see it. It was fucking hilarious. I had to watch it at least five or six times. Ariella has hidden security cameras all over the place," Rocco replies laughing and smiling.

I shake my head back and forth in disbelief. Then Rocco says, "She also gave me the information on our Columbian friend Antonio. Between him and his family members, they own twenty five companies. Fourteen are located in South Florida.

Eight of those fourteen are importing and exporting companies operating out of guess where."

I think for second and then reply, "The port of Miami?"

"You got it Droz. They also own restaurants, clothing stores, and even a credit union. Lots of money is being moved between here and Columbia where they presently own three banks."

"Antonio's family owns three banks in Columbia?"

"Yup, they are pretty big operators."

"Have you told Willie's old man yet?"

"No. Not yet. There's no telling who in his family might be playing along with Antonio. Until I can find out who they are, I don't want to go off halfcocked. For all he knows his own son may be involved."

"Willie and I have talked about this shit Rocco. I don't think he's involved."

"I hope he's not involved Droz, but until I have all of the information I need we'll keep our cards close to our chests. In the meantime, you just play a dead hand about the whole thing. So, are you mentally and physically prepared for tomorrow night?"

"Yes I am Rocco," I reply confidently.

"Good. Then nothing more needs to be said. I got a lot going on today, so I need to hit the road. You tell Ariella how things went and she will know how to inform me, capisce?"

"I capisce Rocco."

With that said, we hug and kiss once again. As Rocco pulls out of my driveway, I feel slightly frightened by what lies ahead.

THE INVINCIBLE DUO...

I sit watching the clock Friday like a schoolboy waiting for dismissal. I can't believe how fucking slow the time is moving. My mind is racing at a mile a minute while the hands on the clock move only a minute a mile. I roll up a few joints for later, and then go smoke one out on the patio. Outside in the yard the birds are chirping away. The sky is deep blue with big puffy white clouds floating across it. As Rocco would say, "It's another beautiful day in paradise." What the Rannelli and Palermo brothers don't know is it's their last. I take a few hits off the joint while pondering the thought of Tex and me killing them. The thought doesn't bother me in the least. All I really care about is what clothes I should wear because of how messy it might be. I have plenty of old jeans and tee shirts to choose from. I also have an old pair of sneakers left over from high school sitting in my closet. The same pair I wore when I killed Jose. I'll wear them for good luck. I grab Tex an old pair of flip-flops and the biggest tee shirt I can find. I know none of my jeans will fit him, that's for sure. He's on his own there. Joanie and Annmarie will be hanging out with their friends until around midnight. After that, they'll head over to my place to spend the weekend. I already told the girls all about Tex and showed them pictures. Tex is a cool, good-looking dude, so I know they will like him. When six o'clock finally arrives, I call the airport making sure Tex's plane is on time. It is, so I grab everything I need and head out the door. The closer I get to the airport the more excited I get about being reunited with Tex. There's no doubt in my mind Tex will help me whack these guys. He's my partner in crime, and I will compensate him accordingly.

When I pull up to the Delta terminal, I don't see him yet. The road around the inside of the airport is nothing but a big circle. It takes about five minutes to drive all the way around again. When I turn the corner for the Delta terminal, I see Tex! He's standing on the curb with his duffle bag thrown over his shoulder. I park at the curb and get out. Dropping his duffle bag when he sees me, he picks me up in a bear hug hollering, "Droz, I bet you thought you got rid of the old cowboy!"

Shaking me like a rag doll, I holler back, "I can't breathe you fucking ogre! Let me down!"

Tex lets me down. Grinning like a troll, he pats me on the head saying, "Sorry Droz. I forgot what a fragile little flower you are. I guess civilian life has softened you up even more."

"I aint soft you cocksucker; you're just a fucking beast. I missed you too, but I aint about to kill you over it. Throw your duffle bag in the trunk and let's get out of here. "

Driving away, I fire up a joint and start some small talk. "Well Tex how was your flight?" I ask passing him the joint.

Tex takes the joint from my fingers and sniffs the smoke coming off the head. Then he takes in a big hit and passes the joint back to me saying, "It was real good Droz. I made time with a couple of the stewardesses and gave them your phone number. They said they would give me a call when they had a layover back here in Ft. Lauderdale."

I take a nice big toke off the joint and pass it back to Tex. I hold it down for a while. Exhaling, I reply, "That's great Tex. What did they look like?"

"Well one of them is a blonde with big old knockers. Every time she bent over to serve someone, her big titties hit them in the face. She had nice long legs too, but a bit light in the ass for your taste Droz, so I'll fuck her."

I nod my head while Tex pauses a second to take another hit off the joint. Then he continues. "Now the other one is kind of short like you. She has long dark hair and a bubble butt. I thought to myself, this one has you written all over her. The blonde is 26 years old and the brunette is 27. Both girls are from big cities up north, but they loved the big cowboy. You know Droz? I told those girls all about how I ride bulls, and I even showed them my scars."

I give Tex a side eyes look as he passes me back the joint. Then I reply sarcastically, "No? You don't say Tex. I would have never guessed you would have been that open with them."

Tex chuckles then says, "I got all the money we made in my duffle bag and a bunch of weed too. I brought back 500 Thai Sticks and a pound of pakalolo. I gave Grandma some money, but I had to be careful. I couldn't give her too much or she would be suspicious and not take it."

"How did grandma feel about moving down here Tex?"

"Let's just put it this way Droz. Grandma doesn't have a hell of a lot of faith in me. She wished I just reenlisted in the Navy instead of running off to Florida. Grandma says all I'll do now is drink beer with my buddy and chase girls in bikinis. She says she better keep her place because it won't be long before I'll have to move back in with her."

We have a good laugh and then I reply, "Money is going to be the least of our problems Tex."

Tex gives me a shifty grin replying, "I knew it wouldn't take you long Droz to figure out how to make money here on the outside."

"No it didn't Tex. In fact, it kind of found me. In a very short period of time, I've become like a son to a man named Rocco Santori. This guy, Rocco, is a bigtime mafia godfather Tex. I made more than a half a million dollars off his construction business already. He also gave me a high paying job I don't even show up for. He gave me these wheels I'm driving too."

Tex stares ahead at the road silently for a moment before replying, "I figured this car was your daddy's. So we got a shit load of money?"

"Yup, and it keeps coming in Tex as long as we stay loyal to Rocco. And do what he says of course."

Tex ponders again for a second before asking, "Why did this big shot pick you?"

"I thought the exact same thing Tex. This guy knew almost everything about me before I even met him. He even knew what we did to those punks in the Philippine's." I snicker replying.

Tex looks at me dumbfounded saying, "Are you sure you can trust this guy?"

"I'm absolutely sure as long as we do what he says and stay loyal. Rocco said I got the two things money can't buy and he can't teach, balls and instincts."

"You do at that Droz. You do at that," Tex says shaking his head laughing.

"Yeah I do Tex. So tonight, I need you to help me kill four coke dealers and cut off their heads. I'll give you fifty grand. Is that cool?"

"Why do we have to cut off their heads?" Tex asks scratching his head.

"We need to start a war between two drug cartels. The rival drug dealers to the Colombians are the Peruvians. The way the Peruvians whack people to send a message is to cut off their heads."

"I've heard about these drug cartels back in Texas, Droz. They're some pretty bad hombres."

"Well the guys we're whacking tonight are Italians working for the cartels. The guy we're working for is a hundred times more powerful than the cartels. We don't even have to worry about the law Tex. If we ever get pinched for anything, we just keep our mouths shut and Rocco will make sure we never do any prison time."

"You know this is hard to believe Droz. If anyone else tried telling me this story I would tell them to stick it you know where."

"I appreciate the vote of confidence Tex. You won't regret it," I say graciously.

I turn down Ariella's long driveway. "Are we here?" Tex asks.

"Right now we're going to meet two ladies who are part of Rocco's inner circle. The both of them served in Israeli Special Forces. The older of the two, Ariella, used to be in charge of the whole fucking bunch of them. Rocco planned the job, and the girls will be supplying us with what we need to get it done."

"Damn Droz. I feel like we're in one of those movies they make out there in Hollywood," Tex rubs his hands together replying.

"No fucking shit Tex. The funny thing is my instincts are telling me the movie will only get better and better as we go along."

As I pull up the driveway, I see another Lincoln parked near Ariella's house. I pull up next to it and park. The car looks almost the same as my car. Ariella and Katrina are dressed in their fatigues standing outside on the porch. Tex takes a look at the two girls, chuckles, and says, "Droz, do you really expect me to believe the two girls standing on that there porch are Special Forces?"

"They're dressed for the part aint they?"

Tex laughs and replies, "Let me tell you something Droz. Those two sugar babies look ripe and ready for fucking, not killing. These chicks are just way too hot to be killers. Did you bang them yet?"

"No."

"Please tell me you at least banged one of them?"

"I said no Tex. Now keep quiet and get out of the car before they think something's wrong." I reply annoyed.

We both exit the car and I leave it unlocked with the keys in the ignition. Ariella and Katrina smile at us as we step up on the porch. "So this is your friend Tex?" Ariella asks.

Tex holds out his hand and with his cowboy charm replies, "Yes ma'am. Whom do I have the pleasure of speaking with this evening?"

Ariella graciously extends her hand to meet Tex's replying back sweetly, "I'm Ariella and this is Katrina." Tex kisses Ariella's hand. Then Katrina extends her hand out and Tex kisses it too. I roll my eyes in embarrassment, but to my surprise, the girls eat it up!

"What a gentlemen your friend is Droz," Katrina comments.

"He sure is Katrina," I reply sarcastically.

Tex looks at me like I should stop being so jealous. Ariella hands me a set of car keys and asks us to follow them. As we're walking behind the girls, Tex uses his hands to size up their butts. He nods his head to me pointing at Katrina like that one is his. We get to the car, and Ariella tells me to open up the trunk and check off my gear. I open up the trunk, and inside there's a large black gym bag. I unzip the bag and see two 45-caliber semi-automatics with two extra clips. I count two machetes, two sets of gloves, and a sealed bag containing a kilo of coke. I nod to Tex to come look. Tex looks in the bag and grabs a machete. He twirls it around in his hands like he's been using it his entire life saying, "This sure is a nice machete. I need to change my clothes Droz before I go chopping off heads. I got my good boots on and my favorite pair of jeans. I've chopped the head off a cow or two, and I can tell you it's messy."

"I'm way ahead of you Tex," I smile replying. I go get Tex the flip-flops and old tee shirt I brought for him.

I hand them to Tex and he asks, "What about my jeans Droz? I got to change my jeans. These are my favorite pair. I rode Old Lucas in these jeans. They got sentimental value."

Ariella and Katrina both try to cover their smiles, but couldn't help letting out a giggle.

"Lucas almost killed you Tex. Those jeans are bad luck. You should be glad to get rid of them," I sigh loudly replying.

Tex now looks like a little boy who just was told there aint no Santa Claus. He replies back to me like one too, "Oh no Droz, that's where you're wrong. These old jeans are good luck."

Now he turns his attention to the girls. Using the same tone he says, "Its true ladies, Old Lucas may have almost killed me a couple of times, but he didn't. Old Lucas hurt a lot of cowboys real bad, but I'm the only cowboy to stay on his back for eight seconds. Both me and Lucas will always be remembered back home in Texas." Then Tex turns back to me saying, "I got an old pair of cutoffs on the top of my duffle bag I was going to use for swimming. Just give me a minute Droz and I'll change."

"We aint got a minute Tex," I reply gruffly.

"Don't worry Tex. You have time to change," Ariella looks at her watch saying.

"How can you be so insensitive to your friend Droz? Obviously the jeans have a very special meaning to him," Katrina scolds.

I take a deep breath and roll my eyes again. Tex sticks his tongue out at me and goes into the trunk for his duffle bag. After he gets out his cutoffs, he looks at the girls with a boyish grin saying, "Since we're running a little short on time ladies I hope you don't mind if I change my clothes in front you."

"Oh we won't mind Tex," Katrina quickly replies with a flirtatious smile.

"Katrina and I were both in the Israeli military Tex. Men and women serve together in our country. You go right ahead and change. It won't bother us at all," Ariella adds.

"It's nothing we surely haven't seen before Tex, but if you feel uncomfortable we can both turn around until you're done," Katrina giggles.

"Who me, feel uncomfortable? It would be my pleasure to change clothes in the presence of two such beautiful women."

With my hand on my hip, I sarcastically mimic Tex, "It would be my pleasure to change my clothes in the presence of two such beautiful women."

Tex gives me a dirty look and then turns to the girls saying, "I must warn you ladies. I'm not wearing any under garments."

I blow up now shouting, "Would you just cut the fucking bullshit and change your fucking clothes before I throw up!"

Katrina and Ariella are giggling like schoolgirls watching our antics. Maybe I should have told Tex about them being lesbians before we got here. All of a sudden, Katrina and Ariella notice Tex's scars, so Katrina asks, "My God Tex, did Lucas the bull do that?"

"Yes ma'am. He sure did. We're running a little short on time, and old Droz here is running short on patience, so I'll tell you all about it when we get back. I promise."

Tex is finally done changing his clothes, so we get in the car and leave. As soon as I pull away, Tex turns to me and states confidently, "I'm going to fuck Katrina."

"Oh you think so, do you?" I reply sarcastically.

"Definitely Droz, I'm going to fuck her," Tex replies cockily with a grin.

"Don't think that little cheese ball routine you laid on them back there and a little strip show is going to get you laid buddy," I meanly reply.

"You sound like you're jealous Droz," Tex chuckles

"Jealous! For your information Tex they're both fucking lesbians and therefore unfuckable! You hear me, unfuckable!" I angrily reply.

Tex starts laughing at me now. This pisses me off even more, so I ask tempestuously, "What's so fucking funny?"

Tex puts his hand over his heart dramatically replying, "Shall I dare say? The Droz is letting a little thing like the girls being lesbians stop him from fucking them?"

"A little thing like being lesbians you say!" I blow my top replying.

Tex looks down his nose at me raising his eyebrows and calmly says, "Well I'll be damned Droz. I think civilian life really has weakened you."

I calm myself down a bit before replying, "Weakened me Tex? Just tell me what you're refusing to understand here? Once and for all, get this through your thick fucking head. They are lesbians!"

I can tell Tex is thoroughly enjoying getting me so upset. He waves his hand up and down slowly as to calm me before replying, "Take a deep breath Droz and then answer this question for me. Say the both of us have been out at sea for a couple of weeks with no pussy. We drop anchor and go on liberty. In town, we meet two really hot chicks like Katrina and Ariella. We both get along with them like we just did, or at least I did. When we ask them to go home, they confess to us they're lesbians. Would the both of us take that for a no and walk away? Or would we find a way to get us some pussy?"

"Well yes. I mean no. Oh hell Tex, I don't know what the fuck I mean anymore. All I know is me and you aint getting any pussy from neither one of them."

"I'm sorry you feel that way Droz, but I'm getting laid."

"So you really fucking think so, do you Tex?"

"I don't think so Droz. I know so."

"Okay Mr. Fucking Irresistible how about putting your money where your mouth is. I'll bet you a hundred dollars you can't fuck Katrina. I lost a hundred dollars to Rocco when he bet me I couldn't even go out with Ariella. Before I made that bet I didn't have the luxury you got of knowing she's a lesbian."

"Did you try Droz?"

"Well no. I saw her kiss Katrina and backed off."

"So you didn't even try?" Tex replies shocked.

"No. I didn't. They even made a fool out of me the other day by letting me think I might get some pussy," I sheepishly reply.

Tex's eyes light up as he excitedly says, "Really, I can't wait to hear that story Droz."

"It wasn't funny Tex. I was flirting with them by saying how they remind me of the girls in James Bond movies. They both smiled somewhat flirtatiously at me, so I thought I was getting somewhere. That's when Katrina asks me, 'I bet you would love to play James Bond with the both of us right now. Wouldn't you Droz?' So I figure I'm in, right?'"

"Then what happened?" Tex asks anxiously.

"Katrina smiled at Ariella and Ariella nodded her head as if to say okay. Then Ariella started walking back to the house and Katrina extended her hand to me like 'come on, let's go.' I reached out for her hand and the bitch flipped me over her shoulder onto the ground."

Tex laughed so fucking hard tears shot out of his eyes like bullets! I shove him saying, "I hope you bust a gut you cock-sucker. It's not funny."

When Tex catches his breath he says, "Oh you're right Droz, it's not funny. It's hilarious! I'd a given anything to be there to see that one."

I picture it all in my mind again and it was funny. I smile at Tex replying, "Come to think of it Tex, it was hilarious. A fuck-ing cloud of dust came up around me like fucking Pigpen in a Charlie Brown cartoon. I looked up and both girls are looking down at me laughing their fucking asses off. So there, I bared my shame. After all of that you still want to bet me?"

"Of course I still want to bet you. It's your fault you didn't get laid," Tex confidently replies.

"What do you mean it's my fault?"

"You were just too damn cocky for these girls, so they de-cided to take you down a peg or two."

"Take me down a peg or two!" I indignantly reply.

"Well hell yeah Droz. You thought you were James Bond!" Tex exclaims.

Tex's riles me again, so I yell, "That's it Tex! Put up or shut up!"

"Oh I'll put up Droz. Just don't cry when I slip the old sa-lami to Katrina."

"Believe me Tex; I will cry real fucking tears if you slip it to Katrina."

We're both laughing as I pull up the Rannelli's long drive-way. Two cars are parked there so I feel pretty sure the four of them are in the house. As I park the car Tex asks, "What kind of guys are we dealing with here Droz?"

"They're fucking pussies compared to us Tex."

Tex snickers as I pop the trunk. When we exit the car, I see the drapes move, so I know we've been spotted. I turn to Tex saying, "These chumps know me, so they won't be spooked. Rocco says the job will be easier if we can get them all to relax. You know, like get them to sit down next to each other at a couch or a table."

"How about I just kick down the door and we both put a few bullets in their heads."

"Cool down big guy. I got an easier way. They think I'm partners with their boss and friends with their supplier. They also know I got a friend getting out of the military. I'll knock on the door and tell them you smuggled a kilo back to the states. Since they're all coke dealers, I'm sure they have a scale. I'll tell them you'll give them half an ounce for letting us use their scale."

"That's my boy Droz. Good thinking. Let's do it," Tex replies with a big smile.

We put our pistols in our waistband and the extra clip in our pockets. I grab the gym bag out of the trunk, and we walk towards the door. I like the idea of not having to go back out to the car, less risk that way. I knock on the door and Joey Rannelli looks out the window. He smiles and then opens up the door. In a surprised but happy tone he says, "Droz, what's up man? I was expecting Johnny."

"Yeah Joey, I know. I'm supposed to meet Johnny here. I guess I'm a little fucking early. This is my buddy Tex from the Navy. If it's cool, we got a little business to discuss with you." I wave the gym bag at Joey.

He gets the hint replying, "Well sure Droz. That's definitely cool. Come on in. Tommy and Pauley are here too. My brother's in the bathroom."

Inside the house I introduce Tex. "Guys, this is my buddy Tex from the Navy."

Tex shakes everybody's hand. Then Tommy asks, "So I guess you're from Texas Tex?"

"Sure am. Born and raised."

I hear the toilet flush. Michael walks out of the bathroom and steps into the living room. Michael must have overheard the conversation from the john, so he chimes in with his heavy Brooklyn accent, "Damn, I guess everything really is fucking bigger in Texas! Tex is as big as Joey fucking Jumbo, but in a good way, if you know what I mean." They all laugh while Tex plays right along.

"So what's in the gym bag?" Joey asks.

"My buddy here smuggled a kilo of coke back to the states, so we're wondering if we could use your scale to break it up."

"I'll give you boys half an ounce of toot for your trouble," Tex adds.

The four of them look at each other and then Michael replies, "Come on Droz, your buddy doesn't have to pay a tax to use our fucking scale."

"Thanks Michael, but Tex feels better if he gives you the half ounce." Tex nods his head agreeing.

Michael shrugs his shoulders replying, "Sure. I understand. Come on in the dining room while I go get the Triple Beam. That's where we usually bag up our blow. You guys need any fucking baggies?"

"Sure, if it won't be any trouble," Tex replies.

"No trouble at all Tex. I got a whole fucking menagerie of different sized baggies you can choose from."

Tommy, Pauley, and Joey all sit down at the dining room table. Michael walks down the hallway to another room to get the scale and baggies. Tex and I casually walk over to the table. I put the gym bag on the floor just out of everyone's view and unzip it. Michael returns with a Triple Beam scale and a bunch of different sized baggies. I carefully take the kilo out of the bag and put it on the table. I pull out my buck-folding knife and cut it open. Everyone's eyes widen as the blow sparkles under the light of the chandelier. The flakes of cocaine reminded me of fish scales reflecting in the sun.

"That's some rude looking shit you got there Tex. How much you want for the kilo?" Pauley asks.

"I'm just going to sell enough to get my money back and party with the rest. But thanks for the offer Pauley."

"Can you get anymore Tex?" Michael asks.

"I wish I could, but it was a one shot deal."

Joey takes out a razor blade and starts chopping up some lines. Everyone looks as comfortable as can be, so I give Tex a nod. Then we both pull out our guns and start shooting. Just like Rocco said, all of them are caught completely off guard. My first shot hit Michael Rannelli in the left side of his jaw. The bullet exploded right through the other side of his face taking what looked like his tongue with it. Without hesitation, I turn to Pauley and plant my next shot in the middle of his forehead. The bullet blows out the back of his skull along with a nice fat chunk of his brains. Pauley jerks back in his chair and falls forward listlessly onto the table. Michael Rannelli is still alive. The bottom of his face is hanging from a thread and spewing blood. He's choking and gagging on what's left of his tongue. It's a hideous fucking sight. I pull the trigger and put Michael Rannelli out of his misery. I look over at Tommy and Joey lying dead on the floor. Tex put them both away with bullets to the head. Seeing this I say, "Nice shooting cowboy."

Tex grins and pretends he's blowing smoke away from his barrel. We start laughing. In a happy upbeat mood Tex says, "Alright Droz, let's hurry up and get this job over with so I can go fuck Katrina." Tex gets the two machetes out of the gym bag and hands me one saying, "Watch and learn city boy. One clean shot. That's all it takes."

Tex straightens out Tommy's dead body on the table. With his empty hand, he grabs the hair on top of Tommy's head and stretches out his neck. Tex takes one giant swoop with the machete and boom! Off pops Tommy's head! A river of blood pours out of his body covering the dining room floor. Tex pushes Tommy's headless body off the table and helps me put Michael's up there. Now it's my turn. I grab the hair on top of Michael's head and stretch out his neck. I take a mighty swipe and boom! I totally miss my mark and the machete gets stuck in the meat of his back! Laughing at me Tex says, "Sorry ass city boy."

"Give me a fucking break Tex. It's my first fucking time. So I over compensated a little because I was afraid of hitting my hand. It's better to be safe than fucking sorry, right?"

Shaking his head Tex bemoans, "Excuses, excuses, stop your yapping and help me get the other bodies on the table. I'll finish the job or we'll be here all damn night."

"Be my guest tough guy," I cheerfully reply.

The smell of all the blood starts becoming nauseating to me. After Tex is done chopping off their heads, I put our guns, the extra clips, and the machetes back into the gym bag. We never used the gloves. Our clothes look like we were rolling in red paint. We glance around the room at what we have just done. Tex and I nod to each other like mission accomplished. I make sure the front door is unlocked for Johnny. I can't help but chuckle inside thinking about the look on Johnny's face when he opens up that door. I pop open the trunk, drop the gym bag in, and we calmly leave the scene. I spark up a joint take a nice big hit and pass it to Tex. Before I knew it, I'm turning down Ariella's driveway. Ariella and Katrina are outside on the porch talking to another man. He's a short fat guy with thick gray hair smoking a cigar. He looks Italian. I park the car in the same spot I had driven it away from. We both get out of the car reeking of weed and walk up to the porch. The three of them stand there silently eye fucking us from head to toe. Then they look at each other and nod. I guess being covered in blood is our testimonial. Ariella now asks, "Were there any problems gentlemen?"

"Not a one Ariella," I reply confidently.

"Good. Now take off all your clothes and put them in the trunk of the car you used for the job." Tex and I look at each other like, "okay." Then we walk over to the car and do as she says. After throwing everything into the trunk, Ariella asks me to throw her the car keys. She catches them and then hands them to the old guy smoking the cigar. Without a word being said, the old guy gets into the car and drives away. Ariella turns to Katrina saying, "Go get two bars of soap, two towels, a bottle of shampoo, and the fingernail brush."

So here we are basking in the moonlight butt naked in Ariella's yard. It's a gorgeous night and the stars are shining bright. Tex now enthusiastically says, "When Katrina gets back Ariella, I'll tell you both all about how I got my scars."

"We are looking forward to it Tex," Ariella smiles warmly replying.

I'm in a good mood now, so I smile too. Katrina comes back outside saying, "Okay gentlemen; walk over to where the hose is located."

Katrina tosses us both a bar of soap and walks over to the hose. She turns it on and starts spraying us down from head to toe. As the water and soapsuds are flying, Tex starts telling his story. No matter how many times Tex tells this story he never loses his enthusiasm for the dramatic. By the look on the girls' faces, they love every minute of it. When we're both squeaky clean, Katrina walks over and hands us our towels. After we get our clothes on Ariella shouts out, "Come on in the house boys and have a drink. I have some homemade prickly pear cactus wine from Israel. If you have any more of what I smelled when you got out of the car, bring it in with you."

Tex and I are thrilled they smoke weed! Ariella's home is sparkling clean and the smells of a home cooked meal still lingered. Candles bathed the room in a soft glow. Ariella pours wine into our glasses saying, "I propose a toast gentleman, to the success of your first mission!"

All four of us touch our glasses towards heaven and then drink heartily from them. Tex and I both compliment Ariella on the fruity sweet taste of her homemade prickly pear cactus wine. I light up a joint and pass it to her first. Watching them smoke I knew right away they weren't rookies. Both of them handled the pakalolo well. Soon the mixture of homemade wine and Hawaiian herb has us all telling stories. Half way through a story, Ariella stops and says, "This Hawaiian weed is really good Droz. You will have to sell us some."

"Not a problem Ariella, but we don't want your money. We'll just give you some before we go. In fact, we also have some Thai Sticks in Tex's duffle bag. We'll be happy to leave you girls a few of those too."

Their faces light up with happy smiles thanking us. Ariella then gives us a bottle of wine to take home. We all continue having a great time trading stories, getting high, and sipping wine. Out of nowhere in a sweet little girl voice Katrina asks Tex, "Would you like to be alone with me Tex?" I am in the middle of sipping my wine when she says that and choke it right back into my glass!

"There's nothing in this world I would love better Katrina," Tex replies with his cowboy charm.

Katrina smiles and stands up. She extends her hand to Tex just like she did me. "The bigger they are the harder they fall," I think to myself. She's going to flip him! Flip him my fucking ass, she takes his hand and leads the big cowboy down the hallway! As Tex turns to walk into Katrina's bedroom, he gives me the biggest fucking shit eating grin I ever seen! It shined so fucking bright you could have read a book by it on a pitch-black night. I give Ariella a perplexed look asking, "I thought you two were fucking lesbians?"

"It's complicated Droz," Ariella sighs replying.

"Complicated? What's complicated about your girlfriend getting fucked by my best friend?"

"We share an open relationship. Katrina has this wild fantasy about fucking a real cowboy. Then low and behold, here comes Tex. I knew this would happen if Tex turned out to be as nice of a man as he did. She'll fulfill her little fantasy with Tex and move on."

"Well I just lost another hundred dollars Ariella. I bet Tex the same bet Rocco bet me," I reply sadly.

"Poor boy, it's not the hundred dollars that has you looking so blue Michael. It's the fact your best friend is fucking Katrina and you aren't," Ariella replies condescendingly.

I put my elbows on my knees and my hands on the sides of my head. Then I face the floor shaking my head before replying, "Alright Ariella, I'll admit it. You're absolutely right, so don't rub it in. But you can't tell me that you're not at least a little bit upset about this?"

"On the contrary Michael, I love Katrina. I only hope Tex lives up to her expectations and he doesn't disappoint her. Do you mean to tell me you're not happy Tex is getting what he wants?"

I look up from my lair of despair replying, "I'll be happy for him later Ariella, but right now I'm too damn competitive to be fucking happy. Not to worry, Katrina won't be disappointed. Tex can lay pipe with the best of them."

"You make it sound so romantic Droz," Ariella replies looking down her nose.

Her eyes quickly widen as we hear the bed start banging against the wall. Within seconds, moans of pleasure emanate down the hallway. I look teasingly at Ariella saying, "They sound like they're having a really great time Ariella. Shouldn't we be doing the same?"

Ariella ignores me by picking up a Soldier of Fortune Magazine and casually thumbing through it. The bed bangs harder and faster against the wall while Katrina wildly screams, "No! No! Not yet Tex! Please don't cum yet!"

"Don't you worry little darling, I'll keep pumping you as long as you want me to," Tex proudly boasts.

Now that makes Ariella put down her magazine. Thinking I see an opening, I stand directly in front of her boldly displaying the bodacious bulge in my jeans saying, "Look how bad I want you Ariella. My dick's so hard it hurts."

Ariella briefly smiles and then quickly retreats back behind her magazine saying, "If you're trying to get me to feel sorry for you Droz, forget it. I don't give sympathy fucks."

Trying to look like a lost puppy I grab my manhood replying, "Okay, so how about a sympathy blowjob?"

Ariella falls off her chair with laughter. When she regains control of herself she says, "Droz, if I'm not inclined to give you a sympathy fuck where I would at least be pleasured, why in the world would you ever think I would even consider giving you a sympathy blowjob? If things don't work out with Rocco you should seriously consider comedy."

After Ariella shoots me down Katrina goes on a lustful rampage. "Oh Tex, you're making me so fucking hot! Keep fucking me baby! Keep fucking me! Don't stop! I'm ready to gush all over you! Cum with me baby! Cum with me! Shoot your hot load deep inside me cowboy!"

"You want it, you got it Katrina! I've been holding back a big load for you baby girl!"

Tex is banging Katrina so fucking hard now that the pictures fall off the wall in the living room! He lets out a fucking lions roar sending Katrina into fucking overdrive! I look at Ariella asking, "Pretty fucking theatrical, isn't she?"

"Actually this is pretty mild for her," Ariella proudly replies.

I raise my eyebrows wondering to myself, "How fucking wild are these two together?"

Tex and Katrina walk out of the bedroom drenched in sweat. Ariella and I both clap at their performance. They take a bow and head to the shower where they go at it again. I can't take hearing it anymore, so I walk out to the car and grab some weed out of Tex's duffle bag. When I come back inside, they were thankfully finished. Katrina is snuggled up tight next to Ariella. We drink some more wine and smoke a Thai Stick joint. After getting really stoned, I give the girls ten Thai Sticks and a handful of pakalolo. As dense as the Hawaiian weed is that's probably two ounces. The girls are more than thankful, and we're more than happy to give it to them. We thank the girls for the wine and their hospitality. On the way out the door, Katrina gives Tex a big juicy kiss. When we get in the car, I reach into my pocket and pull out a C note for Tex. He takes it with a big smile saying, "As soon as we got into the bedroom Katrina told me fucking a real cowboy was a fantasy of hers."

"Yeah I know. Ariella told me."

When we hit the main road, I ask Tex, "So big guy. How was the pussy? It sure sounded good."

"Katrina is almost perfect in every way Droz. Nice firm little titties with thimble sized nipples and a succulent little bald peach. I turned her around doggy style and made her poke that cute little butt of hers in the air. Then I buried my face right in it. That got her really hot Droz. The juices from her peach dripped down my chin. Then I turned her back around and she returns the favor. I'll be damned Droz if this little lesbian wasn't a natural born cocksucker. After she sucked my dick purple, I turned her little ass back around and plowed her doggie style for a while. Her pussy was so tight and wet it made those sexy little squishy sounds while I was banging her. She got on top and rode me until she got tired then I finished her off missionary. Let me tell you something Droz, that was some piece of ass I had right there boy! Oh by the way, did anything happen between you and Ariella?"

"Oh yeah Tex, a lot happened. I begged for pussy and she read a Soldier of Fortune magazine," I depressingly reply.

Tex slaps his knee laughing and says, "You know I can't feel sorry for you with all the pussy you get."

"I know Tex. I don't need anybody to feel sorry for me. I'm doing a good enough job myself."

"You know what I think Droz?"

"What's that Tex?"

"Katrina is the younger of the two. I'll bet Ariella taught her everything she knows. Lesbians like to put on them strap on dildo's and go to town on each other. I'll bet you Ariella could fuck circles around Katrina. Boy, I bet you wish you could have found out."

Now Tex is busting my balls, so I look at him with a cunning little grin replying, "You know what I wish Tex?"

"What's that Droz?"

"I wish Ariella snuck into the bedroom, put on her strap on, then worked your cowboy ass over the way you did her girlfriend. That's what I wish Tex."

"You would have really let that happen to your old Navy buddy Droz?" Tex replies solemnly.

"Gladly, and who the fuck are you kidding Tex? You would have loved it! How's that old saying go again? 'Only steers and queers come from Texas.'"

Tex punches me in the arm as we both start laughing together. While smoking another joint, I tell Tex all about Annemarie and Joanie. After I'm done telling him everything I've been doing with them he says, "You see Droz. How can anyone ever feel sorry for you when it comes to pussy?" I just grin.

As we pull into my driveway Tex says, "Well I'll be darned Droz. Your daddy sure left you a nice house. You couldn't even see it from the road with all of that landscaping."

"Thanks Tex. The landscaping Rocco just put in for me. I got this nosy ass neighbor lady across the street."

"Well that problem's gone. It sure is beautiful the way they made it so private for you."

We get out of the car, and I take Tex for a stroll around the property. As we're walking around he says, "I can't believe this is all yours Droz. You can live here for the rest of your life."

I walk over to the mailbox to check for mail replying, "It's ours Tex. We can live here for the rest of our lives."

This gets Tex all emotional, so he picks me up and gives me a big hug. When he puts me back down, there she is walking her dog. The nosy neighbor lady! She stands there staring at us in her bathrobe and bedroom slippers. Tex says, "Watch this Droz."

He casually strolls over to her and her little dog starts barking at him. Tex picks up the little doggie and starts petting it. The nosey neighbor lady stands there in shock watching her little dog lick Tex's hand. Tex extends his other hand politely saying, "Howdy ma'am, my name is Tex. I'm your new neighbor."

The woman reaches her hand out to shake Tex's and he kisses it. Now she gets all flustered and flirtatiously replies, "Pleased to meet you Tex, my name is Mildred. You can call me Millie. My, my, what a gentlemen you are. So, I guess you aren't gay like your friend over there, are you?"

"Why no ma'am, my friend's not really gay either. He's just a little confused right now. We were in the military together. Poor feller accidentally got himself caught in a bombing test field and got shell shocked."

Mildred puts her hand over her heart replying, "Really? You don't say Tex. What a shame. I knew his parents. They were very nice people. Tragedy just seems to hover over some families."

"Yes it sure does ma'am. Right now, he doesn't even remember he had parents. Which is a good thing, considering."

"Oh why yes Tex, considering," Mildred says while putting her hand on Tex's arm.

"The doctors say he needs help with his daily activities. Being he's a good buddy of mine, I volunteered to help him."

"That is so admirable of you Tex. I'm sure you will be rewarded. If it ever gets too stressful for you, we can chat about it over coffee. Just so you know my husband plays golf on Mondays, Wednesdays, and Fridays."

Tex gives her a big smile and puts her little doggie down saying, "Well I just might do that Millie."

Mildred giggles like a schoolgirl and two steps happily back into her house. I almost die! Tex walks over saying, "See Droz, she's not so bad. She's just lonely and needs a good humping. Her husband probably ignores her."

"Gee, I wonder why? Please don't tell me you're going to fuck that old broad."

Tex wavers back and forth. He looks across the street and then back at me before replying, "Maybe."

337

I roll my eyes as Tex takes his duffle bag out of the trunk and follows me inside. I turn on the lights and show Tex the rest of the house. "Droz, your mom sure knew how to decorate. This place is beautiful."

"Why thank you Tex. My mom always had an eye for decorating, especially around the holidays."

I show Tex his room. When he sees he has his own bathroom in it he says, "Well I'll be Droz. Now I feel like the captain of the ship."

"Me too," I reply.

The doorbell starts ringing and I can hear the girls giggling through the door. I let Tex answer it. Tex greets them with a big Texas smile saying, "Well come on in little ladies."

The girls both look at each other giggling. Then Annmarie says, "You just have to be Tex."

"That I am. And who might you two pretty girls be?"

"I'm Annemarie and this is my best friend Joanie."

"Didn't Droz tell you we were coming over?" Joanie asks coyly.

"Well I believe he did mention something to me about two young ladies coming over. But what he failed to enlighten me on is just how beautiful you girls are." Joanie and Annmarie are smiling from ear to ear eating up every bit of Tex's charm. When they see me, they rush over giving me hugs and kisses.

Tex sees this and like a little lost boy asks, "What about me? Don't I get hugs and kisses?"

"Of course you do!" Joanie exclaims.

Both girls rush over to Tex and share their affection with him too. Joanie puts her hands on her hips saying, "Why can't the guys in New York be gentlemen like you Tex?"

"I often ask myself that same question Joanie. I guess it's their upbringing," Tex says.

Both girls put their arms under Tex's. Then we all head out onto the patio to smoke some weed. I put on the landscaping lights and the pool lights. Tex compliments me on how beautiful it all looks. It's another gorgeous night in South Florida. The stars are shining bright, and a cool breeze caresses us from the west. Everything went as planned tonight. Best of all, Tex and I are reunited!

We enjoy the rest of the evening getting high and fucking pretty girls just like we used too.

THE FALLOUT...

After a night of hedonistic frolicking, we all sleep in until around ten. The phone not ringing and no knocks at the door pleasantly surprise me. Tex and the girls take a nude morning swim while I cook breakfast. The sun is shining bright, and the sky is beautifully adorned with big puffy white clouds. As Rocco would say, "It's another beautiful day in paradise." I feel surprisingly good considering what Tex and I did last night. The bacon and eggs are almost ready, so I call everyone inside. The girls' wet nipples stand at attention in the cool morning breeze. The three of them wrap their towels around themselves and rush to the table.

"Boy that smells good," Tex says with a hungry smile.

"It sure does!" Annmarie gleefully exclaims.

"We would have gladly helped you cook breakfast Droz," Joanie politely adds.

"Thank you Joanie, but it's my pleasure," I humbly reply.

Everyone gives me compliments on how delicious breakfast is and that makes me happy. After breakfast while the girls are cleaning up, Annmarie says, "We told our girlfriends we would meet them at Pompano Beach today. You guys are invited if you want to come along."

"Johnny will be there," Joanie adds.

"Won't that be interesting?" I think to myself. I ask, "How do you know Johnny's going to be there Joanie?"

"Stacy and Johnny got a motel room right on the beach last night."

"How romantic," Annemarie excitedly adds.

"They have barbecues on Pompano Beach. You know how you love to cook Droz. We can make a day of it and then spend the night with you guys again," Joanie flirtatiously suggests.

Tex gives me a look to let me know he's down, so I reply, "Sure, why not. Let's all go to the beach and have some fun in the sun."

Both girls jump in the air yelling, "Great!" Then Annmarie says, "Our towels, sun tan lotion, and bikinis are in the car. We'll go get them."

While the girls go out to the car, we head to our rooms. I roll up a bunch of joints and Tex makes a pair of swim trunks out of a pair of old jeans. Then I give Tex the lowdown on Johnny and how he plays into all of this. My parents had bought everything for entertainment, so I grab two large coolers and a fancy set of barbecue tools out of the garage. By the door, Annmarie and Joanie are in their bikinis wagging their tales eager to leave. They look so hot in their bikinis I have to force myself out the door without fucking them. We stop at the Publix by the beach to pick up what we need for the barbecue. I ask the girls how many of their friends will be there. Joanie says six counting Johnny. All of us grab a cart and start shopping. I make the meat manager grind up a large cross rib roast for chop meat. Once people eat a hamburger made from cross rib roast they're spoiled for life. Hebrew National hot dogs are great for grilling, so I grab six packages of them. The girls go to the deli to get cheese and salads. I figure I'll grill steaks for dinner. My father taught me how to pick out meat, so I had the meat manager show me a bunch of whole New York Strips. I found one with a big eye and tiny speckles of fat running through it. I tell him to cut the steaks an inch and a half. Tex goes over to produce to pick out the sweet corn and baking potatoes. I tell the girls to get plenty of paper plates, plastic silverware, paper towels, aluminum foil, salt, pepper, and condiments. I pick up the pickles, sauerkraut and buns. I need another two carts for the charcoal, lighter fluid, ice, and beer. We check out at a hefty sum, but just like my old man, I'm glad to pay it. We load up the Lincoln and drive the last couple of miles to the beach. The girls spot their girlfriends, and I spot Johnny. You can't miss him wearing that fat Gucci link gold chain around his neck. There's road construction cones placed in a parking spot right in front of the biggest Tiki Hut. Johnny walks over to the cones smiling. He kicks them aside and waves me in.

"I guess that's Johnny," Tex asks.

"You got it Tex, the prince of the city," I reply.

I park the car and we all get out. The girls run down to the shoreline joining their friends. Johnny looks at Tex and me saying, "When I go to the beach or an event I always put a couple of construction cones in the trunk in case I need them."

I walk over to Johnny with open arms. We exchange our traditional hugs and kisses. "So, you knew I was coming?" I ask smiling.

"Of course I did. Once the girls spilled the beans I'd be here I knew my best friend Droz would join me," Johnny replies cockily.

"Johnny, this is my friend Tex from the Navy. Tex, this is Johnny."

They both shake hands and hug. "I heard a lot of good things about you Tex," Johnny says smiling.

"Old Droz here spoke highly of you too Johnny," Tex smiles replying

"I got a car full of food and drinks that needs to be unloaded Johnny."

"Cool. We'll show these fucking rednecks what a barbecue's all about. Excuse me Tex, I didn't mean any offense. I'm sure Droz told you about these fucking rednecks. They hate our New York fucking guts. I can't say we care too much for them either, right Droz?"

"Not one fucking bit Johnny," I strongly reply.

Tex laughs patting Johnny on the back saying, "No offense taken Johnny; Droz knows I aint no damn redneck anyway. Didn't he tell you? I'm a cowboy."

Johnny smiles snapping his fingers replying, "That's right. That's right. I remember now. Droz told me. You ride fucking bulls! That must be some fucking rush Tex!"

"Hell yeah it is Johnny. There's nothing like climbing on the back of 2,700 pounds of pissed off and trying to hold on," Tex proudly replies.

"For me it would be fucking scary. But looking at the size of you Tex, I'm sure you aint afraid of nothing."

"Well Johnny, outside of getting hitched to a bitch or being on Grandma's bad side, I can't rightly say that I am."

We all laugh and then Johnny says, "I get a real fucking kick out of that accent Tex."

"What accent?" Tex replies looking confused.

The three of us burst out laughing again. Now I tell them we need to get everything out of the car and set up. Johnny quickly says, "Whoa, whoa, what the fuck we got the girls here for? We need to go get high." Johnny whistles and then yells, "Yo girls your presence is requested here!"

They stop their yapping with each other and march up to the Tiki Hut. I figure Joanie and Annemarie told their friends about Tex already, so I let them introduce him. Tex gets big hugs and kisses from all of them. Tex eats it up. After everyone's done getting acquainted, Johnny tells the girls to set up everything for the barbecue. The girls gladly oblige and start on it right away. Tex quietly says to me and Johnny, "These little ladies sure look like they would make some great wives."

Johnny gently pulls Tex aside saying, "Don't let their little act fool you Tex. Believe me when I tell you this, they're all dying to get married, but things change drastically after you say I do. The Italian girls will still listen to you, but make you fucking miserable while they're doing it. Then before you have sex, they'll bring up awful things you don't want to talk about like how bad your mother treats them. The Jewish girls are even worse. Once they're married, they'll make you miserable and expect you to listen to them. After marriage, sex becomes a chore for a Jew broad. They bitch and complain the entire time they're doing it." With a stunned and frightened look on his face, Tex just nods his head. After Johnny gave Tex a little lesson on the girls, I go back to the car and get us a joint for the walk. I grab another two bones for the girls, so they could get high while they set everything up for the barbecue. As the three of us walk to the shoreline together, Tex and I keep quiet. Without even having to tell each other, we knew to let Johnny talk first. Johnny's demeanor isn't showing any signs he saw the massacre we left for him last night. I light up the joint take a nice big hit and pass it to Johnny. I feel the warm surf gently rolling over my feet as the first buzz of the day slowly passes through my body. The first high is always the best high. Johnny takes a few hits before passing the bone on to Tex. Starting to feel a buzz, Johnny speaks, "I know you told Nicky Tex will be involved with everything we do, so I will speak freely in front of him."

I nod my head agreeing and Johnny continues.

"After dinner last night Rocco and my old man had me go pay out bonuses to all the men. They make me do this from time to time and always on a fucking Friday. When I get to Joey and Michael Rannelli's house out in Davie I found them fucking butchered along with Tommy and Pauley Palermo."

"Butchered? What the fuck do you mean by butchered Johnny?" I reply confused.

Johnny shakes his head as in disbelief of what he's about to say. "All four of them Droz had their heads chopped off."

Tex and I start laughing. Then I shove Johnny replying, "What's this, some kind of fucking joke Johnny?"

"I wish it was a fucking joke. It was like walking into a fucking nightmare, but I was awake. The inside of the house was covered in fucking blood, and they were all headless."

Tex and I immediately change our body language from joking to serious, "What did you do?" I ask Johnny.

"Well first off, I got fucking scared. I thought the crazy fucking bastards that did it might still be in the fucking house. When I realized they weren't, I tip toed in for a better look. I was careful not to leave any footprints or fingerprints on anything. The last thing I fucking needed was to be linked to this shit."

Johnny is visibly shaken recalling all of this. He takes the joint from me and finishes it off before continuing. "There was blow all over their fucking dining room table along with their scale. It was pretty obvious they were involved in a drug deal that went horribly fucking bad, so I carefully back tracked my ass out of there and went to go find Nicky."

"Did you find him?" I ask.

"Yeah I found him. He was at his place. I told him everything I just seen."

"What did Nicky say?"

Johnny chuckles replying, "What did he say? Nicky just starts fucking laughing. When he's done laughing he says, 'Fuck them pussies. They let some jerk offs come into their own fucking house and kill them. As far as I'm concerned they got what they fucking deserved.'

"Then I say to Nicky the guys that did this Nicky are some really sick fucks. What kind of fucking nut chops off somebody's head? Doesn't that fucking worry you a little?

"Nicky laughs again saying, 'Worried? Why the fuck should I worry? Motherfuckers need to be worried about me Johnny. I'll guarantee you it was those fucking Peruvians from the club. They're trying to scare me after what happened to their fucking guys.'

"So now I ask him, 'If you're right Nicky, what are you going to do about it?'

"With a real shit eating grin on his face he says, 'What am I going to do about it? Well the first fucking thing that I'm going to do is eat the fucking chink food I sent Vinnie and Sally to go get. Then when we're finished pigging out, we'll go visit Antonio. I'll give him the fucking bad news, and we'll both plan our next moves together. In the meantime, you just be a good fucking boy and go tell your old man.'

"After that, I give Nicky a hug and leave. Nicky aint afraid of these guys Droz."

Tex shakes his head now saying, "Damn Johnny, your cousin Nicky sounds like a pretty rough hombre. That gruesome story didn't faze him one bit."

I knew what Tex was doing with that comment. He wants Johnny to feel his cousin Nicky is a bad ass and he's impressed by him.

"My cousin Nicky is feared all over New York Tex. You're going to be glad that you're hooked up with him."

I reinforce Tex saying, "I met Nicky and let's just put it this way Tex. It's better to be with him than against him."

That puts a big smile on Johnny's face. I can easily tell Johnny believes we're sold on his cousin. The ruse was on.

So now I ask, "How did your old man react when you told him Johnny?"

"Well it wasn't fucking pretty Droz. At first, he got really fucking sad. Then he gets really fucking angry yelling at me, 'You better not be involved in any of this shit Johnny! If I find out you're dealing blow with these idiots I'll kill you myself! You understand? I'll kill you myself!' While he's fucking yelling, his spit flew over me. He just finished his coffee too, so it was fucking horrible. I needed a real shower after the shower he gave me. When I told him say it but don't spray it, he went fucking ballistic on me. He grabs me by the shirt ripping it and starts banging me up against the wall. Now my mother walks in the door after having coffee with the neighbor. She yells at the old man to stop. 'Stop?' he says, 'Wait until I tell you what he told me.' My old man tells her the whole fucking story. My mother starts balling like a fucking baby. Then she goes into the kitchen and comes out swinging with her fucking broom. I duck a couple of times, but she finally connects and breaks it over my fucking head. Here, feel the fucking bump."

Tex and I feel the bump. Then Johnny continues his highly animated and entertaining story.

"When they're both done abusing me they tell me they love me. Then they start hugging and kissing me with that fowl fucking coffee breath. Now my father gives me the old fucking story. You know, the one where your old man tells you how it'll kill your mother if anything bad happens to you?"

"Of course I fucking know. If I heard it once, I heard it a thousand fucking times Johnny," I wave my hand saying.

Johnny nods his head continuing. "Then I tell my old man he ruined my new Ralph Laurent shirt, so he goes in his pocket and hands me a fucking C note. Then he puts on his shoes and leaves. He probably went to see my uncle. It's going to be a heartbreaking scene when all the moms get together for the wake. There probably won't be an open coffin, but who the fuck knows. We need to keep all of this between ourselves."

"Don't worry Johnny. Tex and I didn't hear a fucking thing."

Johnny smiles giving me a hug and we trek back to the Tiki Hut. The girls did a fantastic job setting everything up for the barbecue. The Tiki Hut has two big barbecue grills. I pour the coals into the grills and start the fire. Tex, Johnny, and the girls all go down to the shore for a swim. As I'm getting my game plan together for the cooking, I ponder on how well everything is going. Rocco knew exactly how it would all play out. I crack open a beer and take a slug while looking out over the gorgeous aquamarine colored ocean. The girls are having a ball taking turns diving off of Tex's shoulders. After they hit the water, Johnny swims up under their legs and picks them up. I hadn't forgiven Johnny for betraying me, but I'm happy Johnny and Tex are getting along. The coals are starting to get white, so I put the hotdogs on. You don't want the fire to be too hot for the dogs or they'll burst. When the hotdogs are ready, I put on the burgers. The smells of the barbecue start spreading across the beach. "Hotdogs are ready!" I bark out.

Everyone piles out of the water and charges the Tiki Hut. I make everyone form a chow line like in the military. As I'm passing out the dogs, I take burger orders. "Would you like your burger rare, medium, or well done?"

They all appreciate the VIP treatment, and I love giving it to them. Without a care in the world, we all sit around the Tiki Hut stuffing ourselves and drinking beer. Tex of course tells the rest of the girls and Johnny how he got his scars. After we eat, I break out a few more joints. Then Tex and I tell a few sailor stories together. The girls listen with wide-open eyes as we tell them about the ghost ship we seen. The old ship eerily crossed our bow late one night in the middle of the South Pacific. Ghosts of ancient sailors stood stoically on deck staring at us as we passed by. We all seen it, but it never registered on radar. That's how we knew it was a ghost ship. Then I tell everyone about the super colossal waves and forty-degree rolls I steered the ship through in the Tasman Sea. The waves were so brutal they broke the screw of our ship. We went dead in the water until another ship could reach us and tow us into Sydney Harbor. When the joints are finished and the stories ended, we all go for a swim. After a while, Johnny, Tex, and I left the girls for the cool shade of the Tiki Hut for an afternoon snooze. After an hour or two, we're rudely awakened by the girls throwing buckets of seawater on our heads. They all run away screaming for their lives as we chase them into the water! After about an hour of water games, I head back up to the Tiki Hut. I need to get my coals ready for the steaks. I yell for Annemarie and Joanie to come help out. I need them to prepare the corn on the cob and the potatoes. When the coals get white hot, I put the steaks on the grill. Then I yell for everybody to come back to the Tiki Hut. I take everyone's orders on how they want their steak grilled. Tex says grace before dinner. It's a feast to behold and a day to remember for all of us. After dinner, us guys drink a few beers and relax while the girls clean up the mess. When we're ready to go the sky is purple and crimson. As we're packing up the car, a big four-wheeler truck pulls up to the beach blasting Sweet Home Alabama by Lynyrd Skynyrd. A bunch of foul looking rednecks jump out of the back of the truck and open the tailgate. I count six. They have a keg of beer on the bed of the truck and are two sheets to the wind already. When they notice the girls in bikinis, they start hooting and hollering catcalls at them.

"Fucking rednecks," Johnny exclaims loudly.

In true Brooklyn form, the girls start throwing these guys the bird and telling them to go fuck themselves. That throws fuel on the fire. The rednecks start exposing themselves and yelling at the girls to come suck their dicks. One of the redneck's yells, "Listen to these dirty mouthed bitches boys! They're nothing but a bunch of New York gutter sluts!"

"They probably even fuck niggers!" Another guy yells.

The rest of them start laughing. Now another redneck hollers, "You got to use two rubbers when you fuck these whores in case one of them breaks! Hell, their cunts might be so damn foul they burn right through the rubbers!"

All the rednecks are belly laughing and refilling their beers. Feeling thoroughly and totally humiliated, the girls all turn around and stare at us with their hands on their hips. This is a clear message that if we wanted a good piece of ass tonight we better defend their honor. We would still get laid if we didn't, but the pussy will be a helluva lot better if we kick the shit out of these rednecks. We're outnumbered 6-3, but I got Tex with me, so they're outnumbered.

Johnny has steam coming out of both his ears. His Sicilian temper is in overdrive. He turns to Tex saying, "See Tex? See what I fucking mean? This is the kind of fucking bullshit we deal with down here. Our girls have to put up with this ignorant shit all the fucking time." Like a Kamikaze, Johnny runs at the rednecks and wails away at whoever's in reach. Of course, he starts getting his ass kicked, but he's used to it, so he knows how to cover up well. The girls are screaming at the top of their lungs for me and Tex to go help.

Tex turns to me smiling and calmly says, "Johnny sure is a feisty little feller."

"That he is Tex. When I first seen him he was getting his ass kicked by rednecks. Every time they knocked him down, he kept getting back up just like now."

We quickly bolt into action to save Johnny before he gets hurt. Tex peels two guys off Johnny and throws them to the side. The biggest redneck see's Tex and charges him. Tex catches Sasquatch with a vicious right knocking him cold. I hear his head crack open on the sidewalk as he hits the pavement. I start getting a few good licks in on the guy in front of me when I get tackled from behind. When we're on the ground, I wrestle my way on top of him. I get my hands around his throat and start banging his head on the concrete. Another redneck jumps on my back gouging my eyes. I hear the crash of glass and feel the splash of cold beer. The guy lets go. When I turn around, I see Johnny with a broken beer bottle in his hand. Blood is squirting out of the top of this rednecks head like a fucking lawn sprinkler. The guy I had on the ground tries to get up and we both stomp him until he gives. That leaves three more and they're all on Tex trying to bring him to the ground. Johnny tries to run and help, but I stop him saying, "Just watch my boy Tex fight, Johnny."

Tex is covering up keeping his balance until he sees an opening. When he does, he picks one of them up and body slams him savagely into the ground. You could hear the air come right out of his body. He lied there motionless. Tex pushes one of the rednecks towards me and then grabs the other one. Tex holds his arms behind his back while Johnny works him over. I'm now going toe to toe with a guy who can really fight! I see why Tex pushed him my way. This guy's quick with his hands and feet. Tex prefers brawling with big guys. I manage to block everything he's throwing at me, but he manages to block everything I throw at him! I decide to let him think I'm afraid of him, so I back away. He charges me and I kick him in the nuts. The redneck drops his hands grabbing his family jewels. Now he's at my mercy. I let loose with a sharp combination of punches leaving him dazed and confused. Battered and bloodied, he staggers up the sidewalk towards Tex. Tex crushes him with a right hand to the face. His listless body crashes face first onto the ground. A pool of blood spreads out all around his head. The brawl is over almost as fast as it started. The girls are cheering and clapping for us. In the distance, we hear the sound of police sirens. This is our cue to jump into our cars and head back home. The three of us are big heroes to the girls for defending their honor. When we get back to my house, we receive a heroic fucking from all of them. Life is good!

I awake the next morning around 8 AM. I share my morning woody with Annemarie because out of all of the girls I like her the best. She's got a gorgeous little pussy and is a natural at using it. It's perfect for lapping, and I love lapping her. As I lick her pussy, Annmarie moves her hips in rhythm up and down with my tongue. The hotter she gets, the harder she grinds her pussy against my mouth. Now I suck her swollen clit into my mouth and swirl my tongue all around it. Annmarie's body starts quivering and shaking, exploding all over my face! Drenched in her juices, I hear those immortal words every man yearns to hear. "Fuck me." Annmarie spreads eagle for me and I plunge my big cock deep inside her tight wet pussy. We both moan loudly with pleasure! Our bodies move in unison as we passionately fuck each other to orgasm. Sweating from head to toe and smiling from ear to ear, we softly kiss. Then we grab a couple of towels and head out to the pool. It was another beautiful day in paradise! As we're enjoying the pool, we couldn't help gazing into each other's eyes. I pull Annmarie close, and she melts in my arms. Our relationship is definitely changing. The phone begins to ring. Reluctantly, I leave Annmarie's arms and go answer it.

"Hello?"

"Is my son there with you?"

It's Johnny's father, and I knew not to lie to him. "Yeah Angelo, he's here, but he's still sleeping."

"Get him up and get both your asses over here in fifteen minutes," He orders.

Before I can get a word in edgewise, Angelo hangs up the phone. Shit's about to hit the fan. I wake up Tex first to tell him what's going on. Then I go wake up Johnny. I grab him by his big toe saying, "Your old man just called. He sounds really fucking pissed. He says we got fifteen minutes to get over to your house."

Johnny still in his sleepy stupor replies confused, "Fifteen minutes? Fifteen minutes?"

"Yeah Johnny, we got fifteen fucking minutes. So get the fuck up before he comes over here."

Johnny's sleeping between two girls. He pushes them aside, and they don't even wakeup. He jumps up, grabs his clothes, and heads to the bathroom. I tell Tex to have the girls clean up the house and I'll be back as soon as possible. I get dressed and hurry Johnny out the door. Johnny speeds off first in his Mercedes, and I follow close behind him. We get to his house, and Rocco's Lincoln is parked in the driveway. We both park and get out of our cars. Johnny walks over to me saying, "Looks like you're going to have to earn that cut Nicky's giving you."

A silent nod is my reply.

When we get inside the house, Johnny's mother is waiting for us in the hallway. Before Johnny can say good morning, she starts beating the shit out of him with a large wooden spoon. Carina's yelling and swinging at the same time. "Your father and Uncle Rocco are in the kitchen eating breakfast! Both of you get in there right now and make sure you listen to everything they have to say!"

Now Carina starts whacking me with the wooden spoon yelling, "Your poor mother Michael! She can't even rest in peace! She has to look down from heaven and worry that her son is going to get his head chopped off!"

When Carina's satisfied with the beating she gave us she starts crying uncontrollably. Johnny chuckles saying, "Isn't it nice to be loved Droz?"

Oh, that little comment fires Carina up again! Now she starts a whole new tirade yelling, "You think this is funny Johnny?

You think all of this is funny? Do you know what I was doing last night?"

"Sleeping?" Johnny answers like a smartass.

Now she goes absolutely berserk on Johnny. Carina whacks him with the wooden spoon so fucking hard the head flies off leaving a sharp end. Fearing I could be mortally wounded, I don't dare laugh. This gives me flashbacks of my mother. One Sunday morning when she's frying meatballs, I start busting her balls about something. She's already pissed because my old man stayed out all night drinking and slept at the firehouse. My mother turns to me yelling, "Listen you little son of a bitch! I'm sweating over a hot fucking stove, so the last thing I need is your fucking bullshit! If you know what's good for you, you'll just shut the fuck up right now!"

Of course, I didn't listen and continue busting her balls. My mother turns her head around like the girl in the fucking Exorcist movie. Pointing the fork at me she's using to turn the meatballs, she screams out, "I warned you!" and then throws the fork right at my face. Good thing I was quick enough to lift my arm and block it because it stuck right in. I still have the scar.

Carina, continuing her harangue, now tells Johnny, "While you were out last night carousing around with your friends, I was up all night with those poor boys' mothers. Your father and I had to go get Father Tomalini out of his sick bed at the Rectory to calm them down." As Carina starts crying again, Angelo comes walking down the hallway wiping his chin with a napkin asking, "Are you finished with them yet Carina?"

Carina clears the tears from her eyes sternly replying, "Well yes Angelo, but don't you hurt them, and if you're going hit them don't hit them in the head. You know what happened to your Uncle Stevie from his father always hitting him in the head."

Angelo looks at Carina like he heard this from her a thousand fucking times, so he replies accordingly. "Carina, how many times do I have to tell you? My Uncle Stevie was born retarded.

His father didn't believe the doctors and kept hitting him in the back of the head because he thought he was stubborn."

And I thought my family had problems, I think to myself.

Carina kindly asks us now if we would like some breakfast. We reply yes. She then hugs and kisses us both before we walk down the long hallway into the kitchen. In the kitchen, Rocco is sitting at the head of the table calmly sipping his coffee and reading the newspaper. The headlines read, "Drug War Massacre Four Headless Bodies Found in Davie Home!"

As soon as we sit down, Rocco says to Johnny, "So Johnny, it's good to see that the brutal murders of the Rannelli and Palermo brothers didn't interfere with your weekend."

Johnny looks down at the table and stays silent.

"How would you boys like your eggs?" Carina gleefully asks.

"Scrambled," Johnny replies.

"Scrambled is good for me too Carina. Thank you."

"I suppose you knew nothing about their narcotics dealing Johnny?" Rocco sarcastically asks.

"I swear to you Uncle Rocco, not a clue. If I did I would have told my dad," Johnny replies with a saintly look.

"You boys want sausage or bacon with your eggs?" Carina asks politely.

"Both," Johnny answers.

"Same here Carina. I'll have both too."

Rocco chuckles to himself. Then he nods his head smiling before saying, "It's good to see none of this is upsetting either one of your appetites."

We both stay silent.

"I think it's wonderful they still have their appetites Rocco. If you ask me, it shows they aren't involved. Would you boys like an English muffin or toast?" Carina asks.

"Give me two English muffins Ma," Johnny answers.

"Would you also like two Michael?"

'Sure Carina. I would love two."

"You may be able to shit your dear mother over there cooking your breakfast, but don't try and shit me Johnny. I know better," Rocco sternly says.

Angelo interrupts Rocco amicably saying. "We both know that Johnny has his faults Rocco. He's lazy at times and gambles way too much for his own good, but being a rat surely isn't one of them."

Carina serves us our breakfasts. As we dig in, Rocco amicably replies back to his brother, "I agree with you Angelo, but in this case being a rat might have saved those boys lives. Never mind the pain and suffering they're parents are experiencing as we speak. Our people being involved with narcotics threaten our very existence."

"I agree 100% Rocco," Angelo concedes. He turns to Johnny now saying, "If you hear about any of our guys dealing or using narcotics you have to tell us son. You're not being a rat. You're protecting your family."

Between bites, Johnny looks at his old man nonchalantly replying, "I'm just as shocked as you are by all of this. If I had known anything about what was going on, I would have stopped them myself."

Everyone is silent for a moment; Carina walks over to the table with the coffee pot and fills everyone's cup. Rocco drops a teaspoon of sugar into his coffee and stirs. He takes a sip and then asks Johnny, "What about your good for nothing cousin Nicky? Is he involved with these boys dealing drugs? I heard he got out of jail and is down here with his crew."

Carina does the sign of the cross and then pleads with Johnny, "Please Johnny. Tell us if Nicky has been trying to influence you to do bad things."

"I saw Nicky at the club Mom. He told me he gave up that life because he doesn't want to go back to prison."

Hearing that, Carina does an about face. "Nicky is good at heart Angelo. You know he's had a tough life. He was always being influenced by bad people."

Rocco and Angelo both give Carina a look like, "You got to be fucking kidding me right?" Then Angelo scratches his head replying, "Nicky was the bad influence Carina."

Carina puts her hands on her hips and firmly replies back, "What if it's true Angelo, and Nicky wants to straighten out his life? Can't you find it in your heart to at least give him a job? He is part of the family you know."

Angelo looks like he's been down this road with Carina before, so he turns to Johnny saying, "If Nicky wants a legitimate job tell him to come see me."

Carina all excited hugs and kisses Angelo sweetly saying, "Thank you honey, I knew you would do this for me. I'm sure you won't regret it."

"I'm doing it because I love you Carina, but I already know I'll regret it," Angelo replies with a halfhearted smile.

Rocco finishes his coffee. Then he reaches across the table putting his hand on top of mine. He stares into my eyes saying, "Michael, I'm going to ask you this question one time and one time only. I want you to tell me the truth, no matter who it may implicate." Rocco briefly stares at Johnny and then back at me before he continues. "If you tell me the truth Michael, I will protect you and all of your interests here in South Florida. If I find out that you have lied to me today, you will forfeit everything. Including your club, capisce?"

"I capisce Rocco."

"I hope so for your sake son that you do. Now tell me. Does Johnny, you, or Nicky know anything about the Rannelli and the Palermo brothers drug dealing?"

Johnny squirms in his seat. Carina holds her hand over heart while Angelo just stares down at the table expecting the worst. I stare into Rocco's eyes replying, "It's just like Johnny said Rocco. Neither one of us had a clue they were dealing drugs. If we did, we would have stopped them ourselves. I met Nicky at the club too. All he wants to do is go straight and stay out of jail."

You can feel the tension ease in the room. Carina breathes a big sigh of relief. Angelo quickly picks up his head joyfully saying, "You see Rocco; the boys didn't know a thing. You had yourself all worked up for nothing."

"I sure hope you're right Angelo. I have way too much on my plate to be worrying myself sick about this. What I've decided to do is call in some favors from the feds. I will have them look into the boy's deaths. Hopefully, they will have the local police arrest somebody. In the meantime we will do all we can for the families of these poor boys. Their horrible deaths should serve as a lesson to you two."

Johnny and I nod our heads silently in agreement. Carina puts on a fresh pot of coffee and breaks out the sfogliatelle she was hiding. The conversation quickly becomes lighthearted. When the timing is right, Johnny and I slip out the door.

We get back to my house, and the girls are gone. Tex is catching some rays by the pool. Johnny looks at me now and says, "I knew you wouldn't rat Droz. Nicky had his doubts about you because he didn't know you like I did. I knew you were true blue. Just keep pulling the wool over my uncle's eyes and we'll all be rich."

Johnny opens up his arms for a hug. When I hug him I feel guilty about being Rocco's rat, but I also feel special. Before we go out on the patio I ask Johnny, "Where does Willie fit into all of this?"

"He doesn't. Willie purposely stays oblivious to everything that's going on Droz. All he cares about is getting high and pussy."

I'm thrilled Willie isn't involved. Well, at least he's not involved on this end with Nicky and Johnny. There's still a question of whether Willie is involved with Antonio and the traitors that work for his father. Johnny and I walk out onto the patio and disturb Tex's solitude. "Time to rollover cowboy; it looks like you're getting too cooked on one side."

"Ah hell, I knew that would happen. I got too darn comfortable and nodded off," He grumbles.

"What happened to the girls Tex?" Johnny asks.

They said they had to go home and go to church with their families. Except for your girl Stacy, Johnny; she said she don't do church. She told me she's Jewish. She said she goes to Temple on Saturdays."

Johnny laughs. Then seriously asks, "Let me ask you guys something. Out of all the girls we were fucking last night, doesn't Stacy give the best fucking head?"

Tex jumps in first. "I'll give you this Johnny. The little lady sure does show a lot of enthusiasm when she's got a stiff dick in her mouth. She milked me like a cow. When she was done she even licked her fingers like she was at a Texas Barbecue."

"I'll tell you what Johnny. Out of all the girls, Stacy definitely enjoys sucking cock the most. Last night she was moaning and groaning while she blew me. When I shot my load down her throat, I could have sworn she had a fucking orgasm. I mean she actually shuddered. It was an incredible fucking turn on. You're a lucky man Johnny."

You know Droz; I think you're fucking right. I think Stacey does have a fucking orgasm when she sucks cock. Her fucking pussy is always lathered up after I bust a nut in her mouth."

After Johnny says that, we hear car doors slamming in the driveway. I motion to Johnny to go take a peek out front. When Johnny leaves, I smile and nod my head at Tex. This lets him know everything went our way at Johnny's house.

"Droz go unlock the door! It's my cousin Nicky!" Johnny shouts.

"Enough of lounging around cowboy, it's time to go to work."

Tex laughs and pats me on the back. I go unlock the door and there's Nicky smiling with his arm around Johnny. He's got Vinnie and Sally with him. I step aside and invite everybody into the living room. Tex is standing in the background, so I call him over and introduce him. "Boys, this is my buddy Tex from the Navy I was telling you about. Tex, this is Johnny's cousin Nicky and his two friends Sally and Vinnie."

Everybody exchanges hugs and handshakes. Then I ask, "You guys feel like getting high?"

"Fucking "A" we do," Nicky replies first in his Italian Brooklyn accent.

"That weed almost fucking killed me last time," Vinnie happily says.

"You should have seen him when he left here Droz. He was so fucked up he had to take a fucking nap," Sally sarcastically adds.

Everyone laughs and then Nicky asks me, "You still got that fucking Oban Droz?"

"Sure do Nicky. Why don't you guys help yourselves to the bar while I go break out some buds."

They walk over to the bar and I go to my room. I take my time hoping they get better acquainted with Tex, and they did. It didn't take Tex but a minute to start talking about the Navy and riding bulls. By the time I get back to the living room, Johnny is boasting to Nicky about the fight with the rednecks. Johnny gives Tex and me our due praise while also blowing his own horn. Then Johnny goes right into bragging about how he knew all along that I would lie to his uncle.

"Droz showed big fucking balls Nicky lying to Uncle Rocco the way he did. The greedy old prick threatened to take everything he had if he lied."

Nicky pats himself on the back now saying, "So there it is Droz. Didn't I fucking tell you Rocco would find a way to fuck you? After he takes everything you got, you'll fucking disappear just like everyone else."

"That's the way our business works Droz. Eat or be eaten," Sally adds.

"You did the right thing Droz. You won't regret it. Soon you'll be making enough money to forget all about Rocco," Vinnie puts his arm around me saying.

I give off modest body language while Tex sits quietly. Johnny now continues to brag about me.

"You should have seen him Nicky. Droz didn't flinch an inch when Uncle Rocco asked him," Johnny rudely mocks Rocco now as he repeats what he said to me, 'I'm going to ask you this question just one time and one time only. Does Johnny, you, or Nicky, know anything about the Rannelli and the Palermo brothers drug dealing?"'

We all bust out laughing at Johnny's insulting imitation of Rocco. Johnny continues now in his normal tone, "Without hesitation Nicky, Droz looks the old bastard in the eyes and lied right along with me. He backed up every fucking word I said."

"So the asshole knows I'm here? Some motherfucker must have ratted on me," Nicky says with a smile.

"I guess so Nicky because he straight out asked me about you," Johnny starts mocking Rocco again. "'What about your good for nothing cousin Nicky, is he involved with these boys dealing drugs?"'

After Johnny says that, Nicky gets really fucking indignant. He violently points to his chest saying, "I'm good for nothing? He's the cocksucker who's good for nothing. He sits on his fucking throne telling all the old bosses what they can and can't do. Meanwhile he lines his fucking pockets down here on their families sweat. They told me they aint fucking happy. Rocco aint sharing like he used to. I told them I got a fucking solution, right boys?" Nicky turns to his boys and the three of them all high five each other. Then Nicky points at us saying, "You guys stay fucking loyal and do what the fuck I tell you to do. When I'm done setting things up for Charlie, I'll give you fucking Florida. Of course you'll have to kickback, but it will be yours to fucking run."

Johnny gets all excited like a fat kid in a bakery blurting out, "You see Droz! You fell into a good thing here with me and my cousin! Instead of getting fucked over by my Uncle Rocco, the three of us will have Florida all to our fucking selves!"

"What about your old man Johnny? Won't he try and stop us?" I seriously ask.

Johnny waves his hand at me quickly replying, "Don't get me wrong Droz, my father loves his brother, but he would love nothing better than to get out from under his apron strings. Once my old man sees the amount of money we'll be making, he'll forget all about his loyalty to his brother."

"What about men like Frankie Pastori Johnny? Are they going to go along too, or are we going to have to fight them?"

Nicky, Sally and Vinnie laugh like they knew something we didn't. Then Nicky says, "You won't have to worry about Frankie Pastori. Frankie and Charlie Wings are old friends. Remember, the things I say in this room stay in this fucking room, capisce?"

Each of us in our own way shows Nicky we understood exactly where he's coming from. I can't wait to rat to Rocco how Charlie Wings and Frankie Pastori are old friends and what Johnny said about his father! Plus, Nicky seems to have feared giving up this information. This must mean that Nicky's afraid of Charlie Wings and/or Frankie Pastori.

While Nicky and Johnny start talking, I roll up a few joints. Everyone has finished their drinks and is heading to the bar for another. When they sit back down I hand a joint to Nicky to light and I light one. It didn't take long before everybody gets nice and toasty.

"Nicky, what happened when you told Antonio?" Johnny asks.

Nicky takes a sip of Oban and then a hit off a joint. He struggles to hold it down and then lets out the smoke before replying. "It turns out Antonio had some fucking trouble of his own that night. It looks like these Peruvian pricks were pretty fucking busy. They torched the inside of a mansion he's renovating on Palm Island. They also torched his car and one of his fucking restaurants."

"Not his beautiful Ferrari!" Johnny shouts in pain.

"Yeah, they torched his fucking Ferrari," Nicky chuckles.

As soon as I heard this, I knew Rocco and Ariella were behind it.

"What's Antonio going to do?" Johnny asks.

"Antonio is one pissed off Colombian. He took this very fucking personal. Antonio says his family trains paramilitary hit squads back in Colombia. He told me before this weekend's over the families of the Peruvian cartel leaders will all be dead."

Now I see a perfect opportunity to get closer to a guy like Nicky. Taking a rough tough tone I bark at him, "I hope this don't fucking delay anything Nicky. I risked everything I fucking got and my fucking life by lying to Rocco. I don't want to hear any fucking bullshit about waiting for this fucking shipment. I did my fucking part. Now I want to get paid."

Johnny jumps to Nicky's defense saying, "Droz, you shouldn't be talking to my cousin like that."

Now I go off on Johnny. "You better mind your own fucking business Johnny, or I'll fuck you up right here in front of your cousin!"

Johnny quickly crawls back into his shell. The look on his face tells me he wishes he never said anything. Nicky, Vinnie, and Sally all start laughing their fucking asses off! Tex follows their lead and starts laughing too!

Nicky high fives his crew and proudly states, "You see boys? I told you there was something about this prick I liked."

"Fucking "A" Nicky. Droz is a greedy cold hearted fuck just like us!" Vinnie exclaims.

Sally chimes in while he's still laughing, "You got to fucking love this guy Nicky. Four guys just got their fucking heads chopped off. Another guy got all his favorite things torched. A bunch of Peruvian families are going to get butchered over the fucking weekend. And all this greedy cocksucker cares about is, 'Where's my fucking money?'"

We all bust out laughing together, except for Johnny of course. He just sits there on the couch licking his wounds. Johnny knew he wasn't a match for me on his own. He was wholeheartedly expecting Nicky to back him up and he didn't. Nicky now pats me on the back saying, "Droz I can't help but like your style. It mirrors my own. What you just said to me is almost the same exact fucking thing I said to Antonio. I told him that under no fucking circumstances could I accept any fucking delays. Antonio fucking respected me for that, just like I fucking respect you."

Nicky and I slap five. My instincts were right on, and my balls got me closer to Nicky.

Nicky continues. "This is the way business should be fucking conducted. No fucking Jew lawyers, just a man's word and his fucking handshake. Our first shipment will arrive at the Port of Miami Thursday night. If all goes well on my end, I can expect a shipment every week. You will be paid accordingly Droz."

I nod my head and then Nicky adds, "I want you to know I had you checked out Droz. There are three things about your reputation everybody fucking agrees on. First is you got big fucking balls and don't back down for nothing. You showed me that just a minute ago. It took a set of fucking grapefruits to talk to my cousin like that in front of me. Second you aint a fucking rat. Everybody in this room knows how important that is. Third is you're a man of your fucking word. You can be trusted to do what you say you're going to do. Those are all important fucking qualities. After losing Joey Jumbo, the three of us agreed we needed to replace him. After you checked out we decided to invite you to join our crew."

I look over at Johnny and see he's totally fucking devastated. I look Nicky in the eye replying, "I don't do anything without my buddy Tex."

Nicky looks at his crew and they nod their heads. Nicky looks back at me replying, "As long as you understand you're responsible for his actions and you pay him out of your end, capisce?"

I nod my head agreeing. Now I ask, "What's my cut Nicky?"

"Joey's cut. Since it's my crew, I get 40%. Vinnie, Sally, and you get 20%."

Johnny looking like a lost puppy meekly asks, "I thought you were going give me Joey's cut Nicky?"

Nicky puts on a consoling face replying, "I was Johnny, but I changed my mind. I have a much safer position for you. It will make you a ton of fucking dough with a lot less risk."

"What kind of position Nicky? Being your fucking water boy?" Johnny snaps back.

Nicky quickly changes from nice to mean angrily replying, "Don't be a fucking wiseass Johnny. You'll do whatever the fuck I tell you to do and like it."

Johnny bows his head. Nicky sees his feelings are really hurt, so he goes back to being nice and says, "Listen Johnny, there's a lot at stake here. I thought about it really fucking hard before I made up my mind. It's just too fucking risky for you to be on the frontlines with me. Let me ask you a question. What would happen if you got busted with me?"

Johnny tries to speak, but Nicky stops him cold saying, "Your old man and prick face uncle Rocco will whack me and my crew. If they spare you, you'll be in fucking jail smelling jerry curl juice for the next fifteen or twenty years."

Johnny bows his head again apologetically replying, "I'm sorry for being such a wiseass Nicky. I see your fucking point." With a smile Johnny now says, "I don't want you guys dead and I hate the fucking smell of jerry curl. So what do you want me to do Nicky?"

Nicky smiles saying, "I want you to work on recruiting new distributors for me Johnny. There are plenty of capable fucking people in our circle of friends who want in on the coke business. If we don't start recruiting them, someone else will. Our people's loyalty lies where the money is being made."

Johnny nods his head okay and Nicky fills everyone's glass with Oban. Then he proposes a toast, "To our success!" After the toast Nicky says, "We're out of here boys. We got some loose ends to tie up. Sally, give Droz the directions to the house." Sally goes into his back pocket and hands me a piece of paper.

"Thursday night I want you and Tex to be at our house by 9 PM. Make sure you two come strapped," Nicky orders.

"That won't be a problem Nicky," I reply with a grin.

Before they leave we all exchange hugs and kisses. Johnny may have convinced Nicky he was happy with his new role, but I knew he wasn't. First his godfather, then his crew, and now his cousin have all chosen me over him. Johnny hates me more than ever and would love to see me dead.

THE DOUBLE LIFE...

When we're alone, Tex pats me on the back saying, "Nicky really aint such a bad guy Droz; he's just in the wrong business."

"That's funny Tex. I was just thinking the same thing."

"I like Nicky a whole lot better than I like Johnny. Your buddy Johnny was pretty quick to take sides against you with his cousin."

"Johnny can't make it on his own Tex. so he needs to ride on the back of someone else."

Just as I finish my sentence, the phone rings. I pick it up, and it's Rocco. "Hey kid. Good job this morning."

"Thank you Rocco," I reply proudly.

"I want you and Tex to meet me at the house in Boca in an hour."

"No problem Rocco."

Rocco immediately hangs up and Tex says, "Boy Droz, that was a quick phone call."

I chuckle before replying, "Yeah, they all are Tex. Rocco's just like my old man that way. Neither one of them use the phone for chitchat. They say what the fuck they have to say and hang up. Anyway, Rocco wants us to meet him in an hour at his house up in Boca. I'm really glad he called because I got a lot to rat about."

"I know this must be eating you up inside," Tex says.

I take a deep breath and raise my eyebrows before replying, "Of course it is Tex. I struggle with it all the time. But I swore my loyalty to Rocco, so I'll live or die with the consequences."

Tex nods his head. Then he says, "I'm anxious to meet this guy Rocco. He sounds like somebody right out of a movie."

"He is Tex. I know he's responsible for putting that match to Antonio's lifestyle. I gave Ariella his license plate number. When she found out everything about him, she reported it back to Rocco. He's the one who planned what happened next."

Tex nods his head replying, "Ariella, Katrina, and Rocco sure are something else Droz. I'm really glad you sided with them. Try not to let being a rat bother you too much. Just remember I got your back no matter what. You keep following your instincts, and I'll keep following you."

Tex's comments make me feel better, but it doesn't take away the shame I'm feeling. I give Tex a big hug and thank him for being my friend. Then we leave to go meet Rocco.

I take the scenic route all the way up to Boca. I want Tex to see millionaires' mile. His eyes open up wide as he stares at the giant yachts docked on the Intracoastal. I tell him he's looking at the rich people's front yard and their backyard is the ocean.

When we pull up to Rocco's house there's a large black pick-up truck parked next to his Lincoln. When we got out of the car, Tex can't help but admire the truck. It's a brand new GMC Sierra. Tex says GMC trucks are built for real men. Before we get to the front door, Rocco comes walking out. He walks up to Tex smiling while extending his hand saying, "Pleased to meet you Tex. I'm Rocco."

Tex smiles back shaking Rocco's hand replying, "It is a pleasure to meet you too Rocco."

"I couldn't help but see you admiring the truck Tex. You like it?" Rocco asks.

"Hell, you don't like a truck like that Rocco. You love it! Back in my hometown, a man could work his ass off his whole life and still never afford a truck like that."

"Well as far as I'm concerned Tex, you've already earned it. You'll find the title in the glove box. All you have to do is sign it and the truck is yours. Enjoy it in good health." Rocco hands Tex the keys.

Tex's jaw drops down into the driveway. The big cowboy stands there speechless staring at his new truck. Rocco pats Tex on the back breaking him out of his trance saying, "Come on inside boys. We got a lot to talk about."

Inside Rocco motions us to follow him out through the back patio doors. We all sit down outside by the dock. A beautiful breeze is coming off the Intracoastal. I'm happy to see Rocco's boat docked out back so Tex could see it.

"I just made some sun tea. Would you boys like some?" Rocco cheerfully asks.

"Sure," We both reply.

"What's sun tea Rocco?" I ask politely.

"Take a look by the other patio door Droz."

I look over and see a large glass jar with tea bags in it basking in the sun. Rocco now says, "I'm going to give you that jar before you leave so you can make it too. You just fill the jar up with spring water and put a bunch of tea bags in it. Then you let it sit out in the Florida sun for half a day and it's done. Of course, you add sugar and lemon to taste. I prefer to use honey. I get my honey from the Indians. They have a fruit stand at the corner of 441 and Hillsboro Blvd."

Rocco gets a serious look on his face pointing to us saying, "Listen to me when I tell you this. Make sure you use bottled spring water. The tap water down here can kill you. Boy how I miss New York water. It's ice cold and crystal clear! Not like the shit that comes out of the tap down here. It's always fucking lukewarm, and there are little pieces of who knows what floating around in it. Hold a glass of it up to the sun one day and you'll know what I'm talking about."

When Rocco finishes his little speech, he goes back inside the house. Tex leans over to me quietly saying, "Rocco sure does take his water seriously. That was some little lecture he gave there."

"If you think that was a lecture wait until you do something that pisses him off," I quietly reply back.

Tex nods his head as Rocco walks back outside on the patio carrying a silver tray. On top of it, there are three tall glasses and a large crystal pitcher of tea. Rocco gracefully takes the pitcher and glasses off the tray. He pours us a glass and then one for himself. Rocco sits down in his chair and waits for us to taste our tea before drinking any of his own. Tex and I pick up our glasses and take a big gulp. "Wow Rocco. This is delicious," I say first.

Tex downs his entire glass and lets out a big ahh. Then he looks at Rocco saying, "I can't believe it, but this here iced tea is better than my grandma's. May I have another sir?"

Tex's compliment puts a big smile on Rocco's face. He happily gives Tex a refill. Rocco proudly now sips his tea before speaking. "While you boys were busy Friday night, my people were busy too."

I quickly interrupt, "We know Rocco. Nicky and his crew came by this morning. He told us everything. As soon as I heard what happened to Antonio's stuff I knew it was you."

"Yeah well, I felt that I needed to escalate things. I didn't want what happened out in Davie to be an isolated incident. My people left enough evidence behind for Antonio to find so there wouldn't be any doubt who to retaliate against."

"Well whatever your guys did Rocco, it worked like a fucking charm. Antonio told Nicky he's sending military trained hit squads to kill the Peruvian cartel leaders' families."

Without any sign of emotion, Rocco replies, "Perfect. So what else did Nicky have to say?"

I take another gulp of sun tea before replying, "Nicky said he had somebody check up on my reputation back in Yonkers. Evidently he liked what he heard."

"What's not to like for a guy like Nicky. You were a fucking hoodlum, right?" Rocco spiritedly says taking another sip of tea.

Tex laughs while I give them both a sarcastic look and continue. "Nicky likes me so much now, he's asked me to join his crew Rocco. He offered me Joey Jumbo's cut of twenty percent."

Rocco perks up in his chair looking absolutely thrilled with this little bit of news. "You agreed right?" He asks anxiously.

"Yeah I fucking agreed. You should have seen Johnny's face Rocco when Nicky offered me that. He looked like his fucking world dropped right out from under him. He complained like a little bitch too, but it didn't work. Johnny really fucking hates me Rocco."

Rocco takes another sip of tea and then shakes his head before replying back, "It appears that my Godson isn't cut out for much in this world. Please continue Droz."

I told Nicky I don't do anything without Tex. As long as I vouch for Tex's actions and pay him out of my end, they're all cool with it. The first shipment is coming in Thursday night at the Port of Miami. I even asked Johnny about Willie, Rocco. Johnny said Willie is oblivious to all of this shit and I believe him."

"I will find out a lot more about who's involved with Antonio and who isn't at the Port Thursday night. I want you guys to know your vehicles have a military tracking device installed in them. This makes life easier for me and Ariella. Do me a fucking favor and don't try to look for these fucking things. Just forget about them. In the future as you earn my trust, more will be revealed to you."

I'm more than a little curious about being tracked, but I blow it off and ask, "What do you want us to do now Rocco?"

"Be part of Nicky's crew and become drug dealers. The both of you are street wise enough to handle the role. You can rest assured I'm always one step behind you. The two of you truly have nothing to worry about. If you get pinched dealing drugs, my promise to protect you still stands. As long you're working under my blessings, no jail will hold you."

"I believe you Rocco, but I do have some more to tell you."

"Sure kid. Shoot."

"Nicky said all you do is sit on your fucking throne and tell the old bosses what to do, and you line your pockets on the sweat of their families. Nicky said they aint fucking happy about it either Rocco. They say you aint sharing like you used to. Nicky told them he's got a solution. I think he's recruiting them to sell his drugs Rocco. After he makes them a ton of money they'll try whacking you."

Rocco finishes his sun tea and refills all our glasses. He sits back in his chair smiling for a moment before replying, "I got to hand it to him. Nicky is an ambitious cocksucker. He's not the sharpest pencil in the box, but he's ambitious. Too much ambition and not enough brains is a very bad combination."

"So you're not worried Rocco?"

"If I worried every time somebody wanted to whack me Droz, I'd be dead already. Guys like Nicky always end up fucking themselves."

"What about the old bosses Rocco?"

Rocco chuckles before replying, "The old bosses can gripe all they want, but I pull the fucking strings. Nicky needs to worry about them a lot more than I do. As soon as the old bosses learn how to go around Nicky in the drug business, he'll disappear. So, you got any more good news for me?"

"In fact I do Rocco. I asked Johnny what his father and Frankie Pastori would do when Nicky moved against you. Johnny said they would gladly take the money from Nicky's drug dealing over you. He also said his father would love to get out from under your apron strings." I stay quiet waiting for a reaction. Rocco slowly picks up his tea and takes another sip. When he puts down his glass, he smiles at me saying, "Now tell me something I don't know."

"I'll try. Nicky seemed a little scared when he told me this one Rocco. He said Charlie Wings and Frankie Pastori are old friends. He made it even sound like they're working together."

This news makes Rocco's face crinkle. He looks fucking pissed now. Slowly he picks up his glass of tea taking another sip. Then he stares silently down into his glass for a moment before replying, "We all grew up together in the same neighborhood as kids. I always thought Charlie and Frankie parted ways many years ago. If they are indeed working together, that would be something I didn't know."

Rocco now sits back in his chair and reflects for a moment. Takes another sip of tea and then says, "Now you understand, Droz, why I needed someone from outside my family to find out what's going on in it. I'm too close to everyone that lies to me. The both of you just do what Nicky says. I believe Nicky will lead me to the person who imported the heroin that killed my son Bobby. For this, I will be forever grateful. Anyway, I've had enough of this depressing shit for one day. It's another beautiful day in paradise boys, so why don't we go and enjoy it. How about I take the two of you out on the boat and we do a little fishing?"

Rocco didn't have to ask twice. We're both dying to get back out on the water. Rocco grabs his little captain's hat and we all jump on board. Tex and I where boatswains' mates, so we take care of the lines. Rocco starts up the boat, and off we go!

Rocco shows us how to get his fishing boat from the Intracoastal to the ocean. The path isn't hard to remember, and it takes less than ten minutes to hit open water. Rocco teaches us everything we need to know about the Bertram. His boat is loaded with all the bells and whistles! Pretty soon, the fish finder finds fish. We bait our poles with live Pilchards from the bait well. The three of us cast out into different directions, and soon all three of us were catching fish! Tex hooks the first one; Rocco is next, and then finally me. We all catch Dolphin Fish. Boy did they put up a fight! Rocco says Dolphin Fish are great for eating. They're all white meat with hardly any bones.

Pretty soon, we're throwing them back because we had more than enough for dinner. After taking turns cruising around for a while, we head back to port. After we dock, Rocco bakes some potatoes and grills the fish. What a treat and what an end to another perfect day! We help Rocco clean up after dinner and head for home. Tex is grinning from ear to ear passing me a few times showing off the Sierra's powerful engine. When we get home, we're both exhausted. We head straight for the shower and right into bed for a good night's sleep.

The next morning Tex and I work out in the garage. We follow our workout by swimming laps in the pool. After that, we work on our full body tan. Soon after, our stomachs are growling, so I make us both some bacon and eggs. Boy life is good!

After breakfast, I break out our arsenal. Tex loves the guns! The 45 fits his hand like a glove, but the pump shotguns are his favorite. Tex says both of the shotguns will fit easily behind the seats of his truck and we should carry them for now on. Tex's new truck will be put into action Thursday night.

When dinnertime rolls around, I take Tex to my club. He can't believe his eyes when he sees the casino. I introduce him to Georgie and Billy. Tex and Billy stand eye to eye and hit it off right away. Billy loves hearing Tex's stories about the Navy and riding bulls back home in Texas. Billy loves the bull riding stories so much he tells Tex he would love to try it. For dinner, we have fresh baked meatloaf and garlic mashed potatoes drowned in mushroom gravy. Also, a side of steamed green beans smothered in garlic and butter. We wash it all down with ice-cold drafts served in frosty mugs. After dinner, Billy personally shows Tex the rest of the club while Georgie asks me to follow him to his office. When we get inside, he closes the door behind him. "Take a seat Michael," Georgie says in a curt tone as he sits down in his big leather chair. Georgie's face and demeanor are all business. This is something totally new to me. I've never seen Georgie act this way before. He has always been a very jubilee and cheery man around me. I sit there and keep quiet while he opens up the safe. Georgie reaches inside and pulls out a few ledgers. Then he reaches for a pair of half glasses old guys use to read with. They are sitting on his desk next to his New York Giants ashtray. Georgie has been a die-hard Giants fan since he was a kid growing up in Yonkers. He used to tell me stories about all the games he froze his ass off watching at the Polo Grounds. Georgie looks over the top of his old man glasses saying, "It's time for the two of us to go over this month's receipts."

I sit quietly and listen as he rattles off a bunch of numbers to me. I nod my head in agreement whenever I think it's appropriate to do so. I aint paying attention because I know screwing me is like screwing my father. Billy and Georgie loved my father, so I figure that aint happening. What concerned me is Georgie's sudden change of attitude. After explaining the monthly totals to me Georgie puts the ledgers back in the safe and grabs some large stacks of cash. As he's counting out my monthly take, he starts talking about the deaths of the four brothers. Now I know what the fucking attitude is all about! He's fucking worried!

Georgie hands me 57k and says, "I know this aint nearly as much as you could be making running drugs from here to New York, but at least it's an honest living. What these other kids got themselves caught up in you better never be. If you decide to go down that road Michael, Billy and I will turn our backs on you. You will be cut out of the profits and barred from the club."

I look Georgie straight in the eye and lie. "I swear to you Georgie. I aint got nothing to do with that shit."

After a few more words of fatherly advice, Georgie puts my money in a brown paper bag and hands it to me. I think to myself, "This is chicken feed compared to what I will be making with Nicky."

When I find Tex, he's still hanging out with Billy. They're sitting at the bar with the rest of my old man's crew drinking beer and swapping stories. I gladly join in. We have a blast drinking and bull shitting half the night with the men.

When we get back to the house, I dump the bag of money on top of the coffee table. Tex looks at me saying, "Damn Droz. What did you do, rob your own club?"

"No you big dummy. When you were touring the club with Billy, Georgie gave me my monthly cut. He also gave me a little fucking speech about the four dead brothers. He told me if he found out I was selling coke they would cut me out completely."

"What he doesn't know won't hurt him, right Droz?" Tex grins replying.

"I guess not Tex. Even if he did find out, Rocco will make things right for me with Georgie and Billy.

I count out ten grand for me and ten grand for Tex. This will replenish our pockets for walking around money. The rest goes into an empty floor safe along with the money from the sale of our Thai Sticks. Every dime that goes into this safe we split 50-50.

We hang out with Annmarie and Joanie the next few days relaxing on the beach and night fishing. We catch Red Snappers and Yellowtail Snappers using live shrimp. I cook them right on the beach using two little hibachis. When Thursday night comes around, Tex and I are primed and ready. We tuck our forty fives into our waistbands and put our pump shotguns behind our seats. We feel uncomfortable with the 38's on our ankles, so we leave them home. On the way to Nicky's house we throw 'Let it Bleed' by The Rolling Stones into the cassette player. Then we light up a fat pakalolo joint mixed with Thai Stick and get stoned to the bone.

When we get to Nicky's house, he and his crew are outside waiting for us. As fate would have it, Midnight Rambler hits the speakers as we pull up. The three of them get big smiles on their faces when they hear it. Sally shouts out, "Alright, fucking mood music!"

We pass the boys a joint and let the song play out. When it's over Nicky says, "Nice fucking truck Tex."

"A cowboy without a truck Nicky is like a New Yorker without a wisecrack," Tex smiles replying. Everyone loves Tex's humor.

"You guys fucking strapped?" Nicky asks. Tex and I both pick up our shirts showing Nicky. Nicky nods saying, "That's a good thing. Alright boys, let's get going. You two follow us."

Nicky and his crew get into a midnight blue Mustang. When Nicky starts up the engine, you know this aint no ordinary fucking Mustang. Tex and I jump back into the truck and follow Nicky. When we reach the entrance to the Port of Miami, the guard at the gate recognizes Nicky. They exchange a smile and a few words. Then the guard let's all pass through. We make two rights and then a left. Then drive for a little while until we arrive at a loading dock. I see big cranes stacking large containers on top of each other. It's nighttime, but there's lots of people working on the docks. It looks like a lot of Willie's dad's people have been compromised by Antonio's drug money. I count nine cars and three trucks parked by a large warehouse. As we get closer, I spot Antonio laughing away with a group of Spanish guys. We park our vehicles near Antonio and his men. I wait for Nicky to get out of his car first and then we follow. The five of us swagger right up to Antonio and his boys. When Antonio sees Nicky, he starts smiling from ear to ear saying, "Nicky, you were right my friend. You convinced fucking Droz. Good to see you again Droz. Thanks for the weed my friend. I hope all is well with you."

We hug and then I reply, "My pleasure Antonio, it's good to see you again too. I hope all is well with you also."

Antonio shrugs his shoulders frowning. Then he sighs before saying, "I'm sure Nicky told you about what happened to my car, my restaurant, and my house."

With a sad look, I sympathetically reply, "That's a fucking shame Antonio. Some people just have no fucking respect. You work so hard to accumulate a few nice things in life and then boom. Some jerk offs come along and fuck it all up for you."

With a very sincere look, Antonio says, "I couldn't have put that any more perfectly Droz. That's exactly how I feel. My car was one of a fucking kind. The house I can rebuild, but having to live for a while without my favorite place to eat is simply unbearable."

"Can't you get your chef's to cook for you somewhere else Antonio?" Nicky asks.

In a frustrated tone Antonio replies, "Yes Nicky. I can have the food prepared at my other house, but it's just not the same fucking thing. I created an ambience in my restaurant that made me feel like I was home in Colombia. I personally handpicked all the décor and plants. Everything is original and some of it was irreplaceable. I ate there almost every night."

"It sounds like they knew where to hurt you buddy," Nicky adds.

"You can rest assured these cocksuckers and their families will regret the day they were born." Antonio replies with vengeance in his eyes.

Antonio looks like he needs a hug, so we all gave him one. Then I introduce Tex. "Antonio, this is my friend Tex." Antonio and Tex shake hands without exchanging words.

"You got my money Nicky?" Antonio asks.

Nicky nods to Vinnie, and Vinnie walks back over to the Mustang. He pops open the trunk and takes out a large suitcase. He labors with it back over to Nicky.

"Truck loaded Antonio?" Nicky now asks.

"Yes it is Nicky. 1000 kilos of pure Colombian cocaine for 1.5 million as agreed upon. The keys are in the ignition."

Nicky smiles and puts the suitcase next to Antonio. Antonio says something in Spanish to one of his men. The man immediately takes the suitcase over to one of the warehouses. "This won't take long Nicky. I have money counters set up here. Your boys can check the cargo while you wait." Nicky waves his hand at Antonio while saying, "No need Antonio. Your reputation speaks for itself."

"I appreciate that Nicky," Antonio humbly replies.

Antonio starts barking out orders in Spanish to his men. His men jump on forklifts and start loading more cargo into the back of the truck camouflaging the drugs.

"As soon as Charlie can arrange security he'll be down here to finalize the other half of our deal," Nicky tells Antonio.

"That's music to my ears Nicky. Combining my family's cocaine business with Charlie's CIA connections and heroin trade will skyrocket our profits. You are going to be a very wealthy man Nicky."

"That's the plan Antonio," Nicky replies smiling.

One of Antonio's soldiers emerges from the building. He walks over to Antonio mumbling something in Spanish. Then he hands Antonio a wad of money. Antonio laughs and hands the wad over to Nicky saying, "You fucking guys are over by $5,400! You really need to invest in some new money counting machines Nicky. One of my companies sells them worldwide."

"Wow, thank you Antonio. Maybe I should."

Antonio reaches into his back pocket for his wallet. He takes out a business card and hands it to Nicky saying, "Just tell Manuel I referred you. He will ship them anywhere you like."

Nicky looks at the card and places it in his back pocket. Then he nods his head saying, "Antonio, you're more honest than any legal businessman I ever dealt with."

"Without honesty Nicky, there can be no friendship," Antonio replies as they both hug.

Nicky now tells Vinnie to get going. Vinnie gives us all a goodbye hug and kiss. Then he hops into the truck and drives off into the night. Antonio hands Nicky a set of keys saying, "Benitez and most of his men left here with another thousand kilos about a half hour ago."

"Good. They should be at their warehouse by now breaking up their shit," Nicky replies.

"He left a few of his men and his second in command behind to unload their portion of my marijuana shipment. It should be arriving by freighter at about eleven. With me and my men being here at the docks helping them unload, they won't suspect us."

"Maybe they will blame it on one of their own?" Nicky says.

"Let's hope so Nicky. I estimate I'm losing over thirty million dollars a month in retail drug sales in South Florida to these fucking Cubans. I hate these cocksuckers. I would love to do this myself, but I cannot take the chance of starting another war. Battling with these Peruvian dogs is costing me enough of my time and money already. I really appreciate what you're doing for me tonight Nicky."

"It aint like I'm doing it for fucking free Antonio," Nicky winks replying.

Antonio laughs patting Nicky on the back saying, "Stolen water is sweet my friend. They already paid me for the thousand kilos anyway, so I'm happy."

Antonio and Nicky both nod their heads in agreement. Then they hug and kiss. Nicky now turns to me and Tex. "The two of you get into your truck and follow me. When I wave my hand out my window, you shut your fucking lights. Then carefully pull up close behind me. I'll tell you the rest of the plan when we get there."

Tex and I nod our heads okay. Then we head for the truck. Antonio wishes us all good luck and then immediately goes back to barking out orders to his men. It's obvious Antonio's night and our night are just beginning.

Tex and I didn't say a word to each other as we follow Nicky's Mustang. The both of us knew once we joined Nicky's crew anything could happen. Tex puts the Stones tape back into the cassette player and rewinds it. Gimme Shelter starts playing over the speakers as I reach down into my sock and pull out a joint. I spark it up taking in a big hit. I pass it carefully over to Tex and he gives me a big smile. We are both being careful to not drop any ashes or burn any holes in his new truck's interior. We're heading south and then west of the turnpike. We follow Nicky to a small, secluded warehousing area just off the main road. There are no streetlights, so it's very dark. Nicky waves his hand out the window. Tex immediately cuts his lights and follows close behind. Nicky slows to a crawl and Tex follows suit. Nicky comes to a stop on a grass median. Tex snuggles up close behind him. A concrete wall separates the warehouses from the road. Nicky and Sally emerge from the car carrying pump shotguns. Nicky motions us to get out. We get out of the truck and pull out our own pump shotguns from behind our seats. The both of us stuff our pockets with doubled 00-buck shells. When we walk over to them, Nicky has his thumb over the bottoms of his first two fingers. He's waving them up and down like Italians like to do. Then he softly says, "Ming, you fucking believe this shit Sally? They're armed like fucking pros."

"I don't know Nicky, but something tells me they aint fucking virgins. Maybe we were worried for nothing," Sally quietly replies back.

Nicky nods his head and then he opens his trunk pulling out four black cylinder shaped devices. They kind of looked like hand grenades. Nicky hands one of the black devices to Sally and pockets the other three.

Nicky goes into his pocket and takes out two small packages. He hands them to me and Tex saying, "Take these earplugs. I learned over in Nam to use cheap ones. This way you can still hear what you need to hear during the battle. When we hop this fucking wall, the warehouse is about a hundred yards away. There's an office located in the front part of the warehouse and open warehouse space in the back. That's where the truck will be parked."

Nicky takes the keys Antonio gave him out of his pocket. All the keys have identification tags on them. Like the ones you see when you get your car fixed at a dealership. Nicky carefully checks them over and then hands one to Sally.

Nicky continues. "These guys own the entire fucking property. They sit at the top of their food chain down here in Miami, so they are feeling pretty fucking safe and comfortable right now. That's going to work well for us. Droz and I will take the front door. Sally, you and Tex take the back. We'll make our approach from the back. Sally, I want you to count to sixty before you gain entry and throw in your flash bang. That'll give me and Droz enough time to get into position up front to do the same. We're outnumbered boys, but we have the element of surprise. Tex, Droz, be careful of crossfire. We go in alive. We come out alive. Sally and I will go over the wall first. You guys hand the weapons over the wall to us and then climb over yourselves. Let's move."

Nicky and Sally hop over the wall. Then we pass the shotguns over to them. After we hop the wall, Sally hands us our shotguns. Nicky tells us to lock and load. The four of us move quickly and quietly up to the back of Benitez's warehouse. Once Sally and Tex are in position we leave for ours. When we arrive at the front of the building, Nicky gives me the key to the front door. I hear women's laughter. In my head, I'm also counting and my heart is pounding. I'm down to fifteen seconds. Nicky nods to me to unlock the door as he pulls the pin on his flash bang. I open the door, and Nicky quickly throws it in. Somebody begins yelling in Spanish and then BOOM! BOOM! Both of the flash bangs go off as planned! Nicky bolts inside blasting away, and I'm right behind him! Some men are clearly stunned, but others are reaching for their weapons. A man turns to shoot me, but I fire first hitting him in the chest. The twelve-gauge shotgun blast knocks him right out of his fucking shoes! Another man grabs his assault rifle, and I shoot him in the shoulder. I quickly pump in another round and fire again. This time I hit him in the stomach. Blood and guts splatter all over everything. I look over to where Nicky is and he already downed three men. I see a woman crying and crawling on the floor over to one of the men. Nicky walks up behind her and blows her head right off her fucking shoulders! Fragments of skull matted with her hair decorate the floor. Two guys get up from being stunned by the flash bangs and start running to the back of the warehouse. I nail one in the back and Nicky nails the other guy in the back. We walk up to them chambering another round. Both men are squirming on the floor pleading in Spanish. Nicky winks at me chuckling, then both of us blow their faces off. You can't even tell they're humans anymore. What's left of their heads looks like the undersides of mushrooms. As we're reloading, we hear automatic gunfire and shotgun blasts coming from the back. Cautiously, Nicky takes the lead and I follow. At the back of the warehouse, we take cover behind some stacked up cargo. From our cover we see Tex and Sally pinned down behind the truck by automatic gunfire. We count four remaining men and a woman. They also have taken cover behind cargo. The five of them are laying down heavy automatic gunfire on Tex and Sally. Nicky pulls his remaining two flash bangs out of his pockets and hands me one. On the count of three, we pull the pin and toss them over the cargo they're firing from. BOOM, BOOM! Before they can recover, the four of us move in pumping out shells. Chunks of flesh, some big, some small, fly off their bodies. When the smoke clears, they all look like chop meat.

Nicky barks out, "Pull out your earplugs and reload! If you're out of shells, use your sidearm! Be on your fucking toes! It aint over until we make sure everyone's fucking dead!"

After I pull out my earplugs, I hear the cries of pain and agony echoing through the warehouse. The guy I shot in the shoulder and stomach is still alive. His entrails are oozing through his fingers from the large hole in his stomach. He seems to be praying in Spanish. I put him out of his misery by blowing his head off. I look over by Nicky and see a man crawling along the ground. He's begging Nicky in English for his life. He says he has a wife and four kids. Nicky sticks the barrel of his shotgun into his mouth saying, "You should have thought about that, Pedro, before you became a fucking drug dealer." Then Boom! After hearing a few more shotgun blasts from Tex and Sally, a ghostly silence blankets the warehouse. The same type of haunting silence I remember after killing the four brothers. When we make our way back up to the front office we find kilos of cocaine piled on a table. There's also a large safe loaded with cash conveniently left opened. Nicky empties the garbage bags from the trash cans and we help him throw all of the money into them. He then tells us to pick up the loose kilos and bring them back to the truck. I speak up saying, "Nicky, we should leave a kilo behind so the cops treat this like another drug related massacre."

"I think Droz has been watching too many fucking police shows," Nicky says smiling.

We all laugh and then Nicky says, "Good idea though. We'll leave a little fucking money too. Let the fucking cops have a payday instead of an investigation." Everyone laughs again. Nicky hands Sally the rest of the keys Antonio gave him saying, "You need to get going Sally. I'll see you back at the house after you're done."

Sally nods to Nicky and then turns to me and Tex saying, "You fucking guys came up aces tonight."

"Sally's right. You guys did come up like aces," Nicky adds.

We both humbly nod and toss the trash bags full of cash over our shoulders leaving as silently as we came. On the ride back, we find ourselves saying nothing but good things about Nicky and Sally.

It takes about an hour to get back to Nicky's house, so Tex and I are really stoned when we get there. Neither one of us feel a bit of remorse for killing the coke dealers. We carry the trash bags full of money inside and Nicky turns on the lights. I take a look around and find myself pleasantly surprised by how clean Nicky's place is. I even smell sauce simmering on the stove.

Nicky says, "I got my cash counting machines in the other room. When we're done counting, I got a pot of sauce and meatballs ready in the kitchen. I hope you boys are hungry."

"We're always hungry Nicky," Tex quickly replies.

"That's good because I got a fridge full of homemade ravioli. There's an Italian guy from my old neighborhood living here in Hollywood. He opened up a little Italian market and he makes them fresh daily. I always like to eat a big meal after a job."

I now suggest to Nicky, "Maybe we ought to get some of those cash counting machines from Antonio's guy Nicky? Remember how you overpaid him? Good thing Antonio and his men were honest and gave it back to you."

"You should mean good thing for them. I overpaid his Columbian ass on fucking purpose. That's how I fucking test people." Nicky snidely snickers.

Tex and I nod our heads. Then Tex says, "Learn something new every day."

When the machines are done counting the total cash take is $987,700.00. My end came out to $197,540 and that's exactly what Nicky gives me.

Nicky calls us into the kitchen and says, "Check these bad boys out. These are what I call fucking raviolis!"

"Oh yeah Nicky, they look fucking delicious!" I comment.

"I don't know a whole lot about raviolis Nicky, but they sure are plump little darlings," Tex adds with his Texas drawl.

"How many do you think you can eat Tex?" Nicky asks.

Tex looks at the open box saying, "I only see twelve in that there box Nicky, so I figure two or three boxes anyway."

"Madone," Nicky replies.

Nicky pulls out a giant pot. I remember my dad used one like it for crabs and lobsters. He looks at us saying, "I think this ought to fucking do. Sally should be here shortly, so I better get the water boiling."

As Nicky's filling the pot up with water, I light up a joint. While we're passing it around, Nicky says, "Vinnie will get paid five grand a Kilo in New York because we delivered. We get forty five hundred a kilo on the heist we made tonight because it gets picked up. You got a lot of money coming your way Droz."

"When will I get it?" I quickly reply.

"If all goes right, Vinnie should be back in about five days. The other thousand kilos is going to our guys in Cleveland. They will call me as soon as their truck hits Florida."

Nicky just paid me close 200k tonight. I don't have to trust him, but I don't have any cause not to either. The 57k Georgie handed me truly is chicken feed. I hear the water start boiling just as Sally walks through the front door. We all give him a big welcome. "I don't know what smells better. Droz's weed or Nicky's fucking meatballs," Sally says as he grabs the joint from Tex.

"Everything go okay Sally?" Nicky asks.

Sally pulls down a big hit and struggles holding it down. As he starts coughing it out he nods his head yes. Nicky smiles and tosses in the raviolis. As they boil, everybody helps set up for dinner. Sally gets a few loafs of fresh Italian bread out of the pantry while Tex and I set the table. Nicky takes the monster pot of raviolis off the stove and pours them into two giant colanders. He lets them drain for a minute while he gets out a couple of platters. Nicky lays a bed of sauce on the platters and gently pours the raviolis on top. As Nicky's puts a little more sauce on top of the raviolis, he barks to Sally, "Sally, get out the block of Pecorino Romano and grate it over the raviolis."

While Sally is doing that, Nicky puts his meatballs into a large bowl and pours some sauce over them. A meal fit for kings! Two large platters of homemade cheese raviolis, a big bowl of homemade meatballs, and two long loafs of hard crust Italian bread! We all sit down ready to dig in, and then Nicky shouts, "Son of a bitch, I forgot the fucking wine!" Nicky jumps up and goes back to where I guess his room is. He comes back with a gallon bottle of wine with no label on it. He hands it to Sally and gets four wine glasses out of the kitchen. He gives us all a glass and Sally pours the wine. Long-faced now, Nicky says, "I'm losing my fucking marbles Sally. I almost forgot old man Petrizzi's wine."

Sally nonchalantly shrugs his shoulders replying, "It's the fucking weed Nicky. It makes us all a little stunod."

Nicky nods his head and proposes a toast, "To the four of us and a job well done, alla salute!"

We all touch our glasses together and then take a gulp of the old man's wine. It's fantastic! I must admit Nicky's cooking is fucking good. Not as good as mine, but as good as Rocco's. Rocco's homemade raviolis are better than Nicky's friends though. Old man Petrizzi's wine is a draw. We all eat like fucking pigs and drink like fish until everything's finished. After dinner, we smoke another fatty and talk about our future. On the way home in the truck we both agree we really like Nicky and love the lifestyle.

CHANGE OF HEART...

When we get home, I dump the money Nicky gave me into our floor safe. Then we both take a badly needed hot shower. When we're done we crack open a couple of cold ones and head out on the patio to smoke a bone. It's a beautiful, clear, starry night in South Florida. A cool, gentle breeze refreshes us from the west. Sparking up a doobie under the stars brings back fond memories for me and Tex. As sailors, we spent many a night together out at sea getting high under the stars. It wasn't long before we both grew weary. After a few more beers, we headed inside for the comfort of our racks and much needed sleep.

Unfortunately, morning comes early when we're suddenly awakened by a loud persistent knocking at the front door. I peek at my clock, and it's barely after seven. I hear Tex stomping down the hallway towards the door. I tell him to peek out the window to see who it is before he opens it. "It's Johnny!" Tex hollers.

Johnny keeps knocking as I begrudgingly get out of bed yelling, "I hear you already you cocksucker! Just give us a fucking minute!"

Tex and I throw on a pair of jeans and head down the hallway. When I open the door, Johnny looks at us with a big smile cheerfully asking, "Did I wake you guys?"

"Go fuck yourself you cocksucker," I reply like a grumpy old man.

Still standing in the doorway with a shit eating grin Johnny, elatedly says, "I got your money Droz! I wanted to pay you back before I fucking lose it again. First race at Calder starts at 1 PM and I plan on being there."

"Well then. Come on in Johnny," I now happily reply.

Johnny chuckles as he walks into the house talking away. "My old man had a bunch of closings yesterday and he paid me. I would have come by and paid you fucking sooner, but I knew you would be busy with my cousin. The sooner I came by and paid you the better. God forbid I had a bad fucking day at the track and lost it all before I got a chance to pay you. That would have been a fucking disaster."

I put my arm around Johnny saying, "That would have been a disaster Johnny. Now that you got us both up, I might as well make breakfast. Are you hungry?

"A matter of fact I am Droz. Thank you."

I walk into the kitchen and put on some coffee. Then I start getting everything together to make breakfast. Tex excuses himself to take a swim before he eats. Johnny throws three wads wrapped in rubber bands on the kitchen table saying, "Here's your thirty grand Droz. You can count it if you like."

"No need Johnny. Thank you for paying me back."

"It's my pleasure Droz."

Johnny sits at the table and starts idly whistling. I give him a funny look and he stops. I turn around to cook and he starts up again. After a few more minutes of his whistling, I turn around gruffly asking, "What the fucks up with the fucking whistling Johnny? It's getting on my nerves here."

"Well aren't you going tell me Droz?"

"Tell you fucking what Johnny? To stop fucking whistling while I'm making breakfast?"

"No. Aren't you going to tell me how things went last night with my cousin?"

I should have fucking known. After being passed over by Nicky, it's fucking killing him not knowing what happened last night.

I give Johnny a snide snicker before calmly replying, "Everything went just fine Johnny. If you want to know anymore you'll have to ask your cousin."

Looking hurt, Johnny sadly replies, "I knew you would say that Droz."

"Then why the fuck did you ask?" I reply sarcastically.

"I don't know Droz. I feel like fucking shit being cut out at the last minute. This was supposed to be my fucking deal with my cousin, and now it's fucking yours. Put yourself in my shoes and tell me how you fucking feel."

Now Johnny's trying to make me feel guilty. Believe me, I know firsthand how good Italians are at laying on the guilt trip. My mother excelled at it. She'd always say shit to me and my father like, "Good, go out tonight in the fucking downpour. See if I fucking care if you end up dead in a car accident. Why should I care anyway? You don't care about me while I sit at home worrying myself sick at night. My heart skips a beat every fucking time I hear a siren or the phone rings."

Then Mom would put her hand over her heart saying, "I swear to you one night I'll croak from a fucking heart attack. You'll come home and find me stiff as a fucking board lying dead on the kitchen floor, but don't worry about me. Just go out and have a good fucking time with your drunken buddies."

With that thought in mind, I give Johnny some of his own medicine. "Johnny, I would probably feel like shit too if I was you, but you know this aint any of my doing. If it were up to me, I would have included you in everything, but as you well know, it isn't up to me. It's up to your cousin Nicky, so I suggest you complain to him about it."

The coffee's ready. I pour us both a cup and one for Tex. The kitchen's built with a pass through window to the patio. This makes serving food and beverages to your guests by the pool easy. I open the sliding glass window and tell Tex to come get his coffee.

Tex dries off and comes inside the kitchen to join us. I'm hoping he can keep Johnny busy with small talk while I finish cooking breakfast.

"Is eggs over easy and bacon good for you guys, or what?"

"Sure," They both happily reply.

It only takes a minute before Johnny starts teaching Tex about horse betting. Tex seems really interested too. When the bacon and eggs are almost ready I make the toast. I plate it all and put it on the table.

"Nothing like a hearty breakfast to start your day," Tex says merrily.

"Even better when someone else cooks it for you, right Tex?" Johnny adds smiling.

"We used to have breakfast cooked for us every day in the Navy Johnny, right Tex?" I comment between bites.

"You got that right Droz. Eggs, bacon, biscuits, sausage gravy, flapjacks, you name it. We ate like kings."

When we're done with breakfast, Tex and Johnny clean up the kitchen while I go roll a joint. I bag up a few ounces too. I wanted to give one to Willie when I see him. This means I have to give one to Johnny too or he'll suspect something. I walk back out to the kitchen handing Johnny the bag. He looks at me saying, "You read my mind Droz. I was going to ask you if I could buy some pakalolo from you. What do I owe you?"

"As long as I got weed you got weed," I reply smiling.

Johnny feels loved, so he gives me a hug and a kiss. Then the three of us walk out on the patio to get high. As we're passing the joint around, Johnny becomes emotional saying, "Droz you're absolutely right about everything you told me before breakfast. It's my prick face fucking cousin Nicky and not you who cut me out of the deal. I'm sorry for taking it out on you. You've always been a good friend to me, and I'm fucking sorry for not being a good friend back."

I'm totally shocked at Johnny's change of heart, but keep silent as I pass the joint back to him. He takes a few hits and passes it to Tex. Now Johnny's demeanor goes from apologetic to all business saying, "I've been planning something I want to share with guys. You need to swear not to tell anybody except Willie of course."

"Our lips are sealed Johnny," I reply.

"I knew that, but I had to ask anyway. After Nicky fucking insulted me by brushing me off I decided to go on my own."

"It wasn't really a brush off Johnny. Nicky did offer you another position," I reply pragmatically.

My seemingly innocent comment makes Johnny's Sicilian blood boil. His face turns sour like he bit a lemon. He begins shaking and struggling to form words. Then he explodes into a totally animated unholy fucking tirade! Using every part of his body, he yells, "Come on Droz! You fucking know it and I fucking know it! My scumbag cousin had the fucking balls to offer me! Me! Johnny Santori a fucking lackey job! Tell me if that aint a fucking bunch of fucking bullshit! Nicky telling me what to fucking do! I should be telling him what to do! That cocksucker treated me like fucking Fredo in the Godfather! I'm telling you right fucking now I aint no fucking Fredo!"

Johnny looks like he's going to bust a vain, so I say, "Calm down Johnny. Calm down. Take a few hits off the joint. Nobody thinks you're fucking Fredo."

Tex is trying not to laugh. Johnny calms a smidgen as he hits the joint. Then nervously starts nodding his head up and down like a chicken saying, "You know what? You know fucking what Droz?"

"What's that Johnny?"

"I just made up my fucking mind. I aint doing another fucking thing for that cocksucker! I should have never helped him with you! It's one of the biggest fucking regrets of my life! He gave me that old fucking story about how blood is thicker than fucking water bullshit. Like a fucking jamoke, I fell for it!

You're more my family than Nicky has ever fucking been! I'm a sucker for being influenced by him!"

There's an awkward moment of silence staring at each other. Then all of a sudden, we all burst out laughing! After all, Johnny put on quite a performance!

Calm and upbeat now, Johnny continues. "You know what Droz?"

"What's that Johnny?"

"My cousin Nicky fucking me over is the best fucking thing that has ever happened to me."

"And why's that?"

Johnny's enthusiasm heats up again. "I'll tell you fucking why because it pissed me off. It pissed me off so fucking much I thought of a job on my own. No fucking Nicky, no old man, no fucking Uncle Rocco, and not even you or Willie. It's a once in a lifetime heist, and I thought of it all by myself. It's a big fucking score too Droz. All fucking cash, and the cash can't be traced. No fucking guards or alarms to get around, and best of all, no fucking cops coming after me. Not a fucking one; just easy fucking money boys."

Johnny's quiet for a second. Then his demeanor changes from upbeat to downbeat saying, "I'll have to disappear for a while though until things get smoothed out for me."

"Disappear Johnny? Disappear where?" I inquisitively ask.

Johnny shrugs his shoulders shaking his head like he aint got a clue.

"What about your mother Johnny? She'll be at home worrying herself sick about you."

"No need to worry about that Droz. I'll call her after I pull the job."

"Speaking of jobs, you're going to leave your old man hanging too?"

"He's got plenty of fucking ass kissers just waiting in line to take my fucking job. The only thing I'm worried about is where to disappear too."

"That's a good question Johnny. Where are you going to disappear too? With your old man and Uncle Rocco looking for you, it won't be easy."

Johnny lets out a big sigh replying, "Tell me about it, but maybe you guys can help me. The both of you been to a lot of different countries together right?"

Tex and I nod in agreement. Now Johnny gets hopeful saying, "I'm sure you guys have some fucking friends in the world you can trust. You know. The kinds of people that can maybe help me hide out for a while."

Scratching my head I reply, "Well I guess we do Johnny."

"We might be able to help you out Johnny, but you'll need a passport to get there," Tex now comments.

"Tex is right Johnny. We were in the military when we traveled to these places, and military personnel don't need a fucking passport."

"I'm way ahead of you. I already got a passport for me and my girl," Johnny winks replying.

"You got a girl Johnny?" I ask surprisingly.

"Yeah, my girlfriend Stacy. I'm going to marry her."

"Stacy! You fucking piece of shit Johnny! You're going to rob Bennie the Bookie!"

Johnny glows with pride saying, "Stacy and I have it all planned out. I figured the old Jew was sitting on a fucking fortune. Being as big of a fucking bookie as Bennie is, his cash needs to be handy, so I was betting he kept it stashed somewhere in his fucking house. Bennie has accumulated a shitload of players down here from my old man and Uncle Rocco. All of these fucking guys from Brooklyn are cashing in bigtime building houses here in Coral Springs. These fucking idiots have been losing a fortune to Bennie. They're all degenerate fucking gamblers."

I can't resist being a smartass asking, "Aren't you one of those degenerate fucking gamblers Johnny?"

"Go fuck yourself Droz."

"My dick is big Johnny, but it aint that fucking big," I sarcastically reply.

"Are you implying you would if you could Droz?" Tex asks seriously.

I turn to Tex with my hand on my hip replying, "Go fuck yourself Tex."

Johnny and Tex laugh. Then Tex asks, "Droz, do you practice that little gay pose in the mirror, or does it just come natural to you?"

The three of us crack up together and then Johnny continues. "So I tell Stacy if she helps me rip off her grandfather I will marry her. Before I could even take another breath, the little cunt agreed. Then she started hugging and kissing me. Being the opportunist that I am, I take full advantage of the situation by sticking my cock in her mouth." Johnny places his hand over his heart saying, "There's nothing better than a heartfelt pipe drainer from a girl that loves you."

Tex putting his hand over his heart sarcastically adds, "Your sentimental soul brings tears to my eyes Johnny."

Johnny takes a bow while replying back graciously, "Why thank you Tex, I appreciate you noticing that."

Now Johnny continues. "So after Stacy gets done creaming in her panties swallowing my load, I ask her to go see her grandfather. I tell her to hang around him until she finds out the combination to his safe, and guess what?"

"She gave her grandfather a blowjob and got the combination?" I reply like a wiseass.

Johnny shakes his head looking at Tex asking, "Out at sea, how did you guys not throw him overboard?"

"He was our pakalolo connection," Tex seriously replies.

Johnny nods his head continuing. "In less than twenty four hours without giving her grandfather a blowjob, the sneaky little bitch had the combination."

"Boy, I just can't wait to have grandkids!" Tex slaps his knee exclaiming, and the three of us crack up again.

Johnny continues. "So now I start thinking to myself I need to be sure the dough's really there and she's got the right combo. So I ask Stacy to go back to her grandfather's and do a little reconnaissance mission. I tell her to open the safe and make fucking sure there's a bunch of money in there. When nobody's home, Stacy goes back over there and opens up the safe. Inside she sees stacks of cash, so she starts fucking counting."

"What a girl," I interrupt saying.

"You better believe it Droz."

"So how much dough is in there?" Tex asks anxiously.

Johnny swaggers back and forth before saying, "She stopped counting at 1.6 million, and she says there's probably double that."

Tex and I nod our heads loving Johnny's plan. Then I ask, "How long you think it will take before things get smoothed out?"

Johnny waves his head back and forth. Then he scratches it before replying, "That'll depend on how much they miss their fucking granddaughter. If I knock the bitch up it'll be less than a year."

"Johnny, you know you're not fucking kosher."

Johnny gets animated again replying, "Not fucking kosher you say? Hell, I aint even fucking circumcised!" Johnny pulls down his pants and proudly shows us his hooded shame. Johnny pulls his foreskin back and forth as we laugh our asses off at his antics.

With my hands folded like a priest, I wave them up and down asking, "Johnny, you know how these old Jews feel about not marrying another fucking Jew. What happens if Bennie the Bookie just writes her off?"

Tex interrupts in a riled tone asking, "What in the heck does being a Jew got to do with it Droz? We're talking about the old man's granddaughter here! Maybe even a grandchild!"

Johnny and I laugh because Tex doesn't know Jews, but our laughter gets him even more upset. I try to calm him down saying, "We're not laughing at you big guy, so don't get upset. Just give me a minute to try to explain. If one Jew doesn't marry another Jew they tear off a piece of their clothing and act like you're fucking dead."

Tex shakes his head in disbelief over what he just heard. Then he looks at us saying, "Where I come from, kin is kin no matter who you marry."

"What if they marry a nigger?" Johnny asks.

"Hell, they can get by with a nigger Johnny, but not a New Yorker."

We all have a good laugh over that one!

"So tell me Johnny. What if Bennie does disown Stacy for marrying an uncircumcised prick like you? Never mind the fact she helped you rob his ass. Then what are you going to do?"

"That just aint going to happen Droz, and I'll tell you why. Stacy's mother's name is Sarah. Sarah is Bennie the Bookie's daughter and Stacy is Sarah's only child. It turns out Stacy's mother became a causality of her parent's Jewish matchmaking. They fixed her up with an up and coming Jewish Wall Street banker named Bruce Goldstein. When Bruce became a big shot on Wall Street, he started frequenting high-end Manhattan brothels. One night the whorehouse he's in gets fucking raided. Bruce aint connected in any way to the mob. That's the way Bennie wanted it. So when the place gets raided Bruce is arrested with the rest of the fucking johns and hookers. The cops haul his ass out of the brothel handcuffed to a black hooker. Adding insult to injury, Bruce is dressed in women's lingerie and heels. In other words, he's a cross dressing pervert nigger fucker. Picture that scene in your fucking heads."

That's just too fucking much, so we laugh our fucking asses off! After we calm down Johnny continues. "Just when you think things couldn't possibly get any worse for Bruce, they do. There are two news reporters waiting outside the brothel snapping pictures of the raid. Sure as shit the story lands in the morning papers. Later that year the story becomes part of an investigative reporter's undercover work on high priced johns and their hookers. Needless to say, Bruce's indiscretion not only cost him his fucking job, but his marriage too. After their divorce, Bruce's reputation is ruined and no one will hire him. That means he can't pay his six figure alimony and child support. When Sarah threatens to have him thrown in jail, he kills himself. Can you see where all of this leading?"

"Ah yeah, but it seems a little cloudy to where it's ending."

"When I'm finished it'll be clear as a fucking bell. So now, Stacy's mother constantly blames her parents for fucking up her life. You and I both know Droz how the fucking Jews lay on a guilt trip."

"Of course I do Johnny. They lay it on just like the fucking Italians."

"Funny you should notice that. Anyway, it goes without saying Bennie and his wife feel really fucking guilty about it. After all, they did set her up with the cross dressing pervert nigger fucker. I mean really. How much worse can it fucking get?"

"They could have set her up with a Sicilian?" I reply sarcastically.

Johnny gives me a dirty look and the middle finger before continuing. "Stacy says her grandparents still pay for her mother's therapy. Stacy says her mother tells everybody if it weren't for her, she would have killed herself a longtime ago. Old Bennie's caught between a rock and a hard place."

Tex pats Johnny on the back saying, "It sounds like you got yourself a perfect situation here Johnny. Stacy's mom will want her daughter to be able to come back home as soon as possible."

"I don't want it to be too soon big guy. I need to get a few months' vacation out of this caper. My old man has been fucking slave driving me for over a year now."

"I get your drift Johnny, but you know what?"

"What's that Tex?"

"My guess is if Stacy is happily married and pregnant her mom will make her parents treat that cash you both stole like a wedding gift."

"That's exactly what I'm thinking Tex!" Johnny exclaims as we all high five.

"When you plan on doing the job Johnny?" I ask.

"Well it's all kind of up to you guys now. I'll need a place to lay low while the shit hits the fan here in Coral Springs. Bennie the Bookie owns racehorses and he's racing them tomorrow at Calder. He always takes his wife with him to the track. So truthfully, tomorrow's a perfect fucking day to pull the heist. Is that too short of a notice for you guys to set something up?"

"You know Droz, most of the people we know are either too bad or too nice for Stacy and Johnny," Tex says rubbing his chin.

I scratch my head thinking for a moment before replying, "You're right Tex. He's going to be married, so the Philippines are definitely fucking out."

"That's for damn sure," Tex chuckles

"With all that money in his pocket, Johnny would end up getting himself killed in Olongapo City anyway Tex," I add as Johnny rolls his eyes.

"Australia really aint such a good place for Johnny either," Tex adds.

"You're right about that Tex. All of the fucking guys we know down under are desperados."

"You can sure say that again Droz. Those old boys we hooked up with outside of Esperance are some pretty rough hombres," Tex replies with a sly grin.

"Yeah they were Tex. We both slept with one eye open after that heist," I reply chuckling.

"Well I hate to say it Droz, but the safest place for Johnny and Stacy is under Keoni's watch in Hawaii."

Johnny's face lights up like a Christmas tree. Thrilled to the gills he shouts, "I was hoping you guys would say that! You bragged how tight you fucking are with the Hawaiians Droz. You have to agree with Tex. Hawaii's the safest place for me and Stacy to hide out in."

Irritated by this revelation, I reply gruffly, "Cool your fucking jets Johnny. I'm not sure if I agree with Tex or not."

Johnny raises both hands saying, "I'm cool Droz, I'm cool, but just so you know, when I mentioned Hawaii to Stacy she fell in love with the idea. She even had a dream about a Hawaiian wedding."

"Oh she did, did she?" I raise my eyebrows replying while Tex laughs.

"She really did Droz. Also, Hawaii's only a short flight away from Santa Anita Race Track. I mean really. Here I am pulling a big fucking job, and I can't even show my face in Vegas. Between the fucking cameras and Uncle Rocco's people, I would be spotted in an hour. If that aint a fucking sin I don't know what is."

"The sin would be you showing up in Vegas with the fucking money. You'll lose it all and a fucking marker before Rocco's people even get to you!"

"You really know how to hurt a guy," Johnny frowns replying.

"Not a problem Johnny. So really Tex, Hawaii?"

"Well Droz, there are four islands Keoni can keep moving them around on, so they should be pretty safe doing that for a while."

"I'm not worried about Keoni keeping them safe Tex. I'm worried about what happens if Johnny fucks up and pisses him off."

Tex nods his head and then says to Johnny, "If we hide you out in Hawaii, Johnny, we need to get something straight."

"No problem Tex. Just tell me what to do."

"That's good Johnny because your life and our reputation will depend on it. You must never disrespect Keoni, his family, or his culture."

"On my mother's eyes, I'll be on my best behavior," Johnny sincerely replies.

"Forget about your mother's eyes Johnny. If you don't listen to our warning, you'll become fertilizer in a pineapple field. You got that?" I toughly add.

"Yeah Droz, I got it. Are you sure tomorrow isn't too short of a notice?"

"There's only one way to find out. I know Keoni's direct number at the club. With the time difference he should still be there."

Before I start dialing the phone, Johnny grabs my arm saying, "From the bottom of my heart I appreciate this favor you two are doing for me. I don't want anybody to be offended, but I'm paying everyone a cut."

"Do you want a cut Tex?" I ask.

"I'm not fucking asking Droz," Johnny sternly interrupts.

"Okay big shot. What kind of cut are we talking about?" I reply.

"A cool hundred grand a piece. I'll drop yours off before I leave."

"Once you give me my cut Johnny, it's mine and I can do what I want with it right?"

"It's your fucking cut Droz. You can do whatever the fuck you want with it. You can stick it up your ass in pennies for all I fucking care. I just want to know I gave it to you."

"Fine, I want you to give my cut to Keoni."

"I want to give my cut to Keoni too Johnny," Tex adds.

Looking perplexed, Johnny paces back and forth for a moment before saying, "This guy Keoni must really mean a whole fucking lot to you two."

"We love Keoni like a brother Johnny."

"That's all well and good fellas, but I'm not just giving you guys a fucking cut for hiding me out. After absconding with Bennie the Bookie's cash shit will hit the fucking fan back here. My old man and Uncle Rocco are going put the fucking screws to the both of you. You guys know that right?"

Unfazed by Johnny's little speech Tex and I casually nod our heads. Then

Tex puts his arm around Johnny saying, "Thanks for the warning Johnny, but me and old Droz here have had the screws put to us before."

"Tex is right Johnny. In countries where they torture you, lock you up, and throw away the fucking key. Tex and I know how to keep on the same page no matter how much pressure is put on us."

Johnny nods his head and hugs us both.

"Let me call Keoni before he decides to leave."

I dial the phone. One ring, two rings, three rings, four rings, five rings, six rings. Finally, a girl answers in a sexy island voice, "Hello?" It's Keona!

"I love you princess."

There's silence on the other end. Then Keona starts yelling, "You full of shit haole boy like all mainlanders! If you still love me why is this the first time you call?"

"Whoa, whoa Keona, Keoni told me you're like engaged or something. I didn't want to mess anything up. If you missed me, why didn't you call me?"

Keona is silent again. Now in a much calmer voice replies, "I tell fadda I not happy, so no more marriage talk. I don't call you because you don't call me. So, you miss me Michael?"

"Terribly, it's almost unbearable at times Keona."

Tex and Johnny roll their eyes. I hear Keoni in the background laugh saying, "Droz finally call you Keona? I told you he love you."

"If you love me and miss so terribly Michael, why don't you come back to see me?" Keona asks coyly.

"It might be sooner than you think Keona. I have a proposition for Keoni."

Now in a pissed off tone Keona replies, "I'm sure you do. Now I know why you called. Keoni come talk to your haole friend. I don't want to talk to him anymore."

Keoni's laughing as he picks up the phone saying, "Me sista mad at you haole boy, that means she still loves you."

"I do not!" I hear Keona yell.

Keoni laughs as I reply, "I love her too Keoni. I miss her really bad sometimes. So no more getting married shit, huh?"

"I told you she would make whole family miserable. Your friend, the priest, loves living here Hawaiian style. My madda and fadda love him. They want him to stay. They make special place for him in the main house. So I guess he stay?"

"Who knows Keoni? Did he find a house and a boat yet?"

"Not sure. He and fadda keep tight lips."

"Look Keoni, I have a business proposition for you. A close friend and his girl want to disappear on your island for a while. It needs to be kept secret if you know what I mean."

"I know what you mean haole."

"They will hand you 300k upon arrival and will be beholden to you."

"Is money all for me, or do I have to use some of it for their living expenses?"

"It's all yours Keoni. They'll pay their own expenses. They will also pay you for a Hawaiian style wedding. You need to be very discreet about it."

"Understood, no priest friend then?"

"No. Keep them hidden and safe for me somewhere within your realm."

"If they listen to me I will guarantee you their safety. If they don't I will guarantee you nothing."

"Understood, I knew I could count on you."

Johnny is doing cartwheels as Keoni continues, "You know braddah; this means you have to do the same for me one day. Maybe who I send you doesn't have money like your friend, but will still need your help."

"I look forward to the day I can repay your kindness Keoni. I'm going to give my friend Johnny your phone number. When he arrives on your island, he'll call you. He should be arriving with his girl by early Sunday morning. It all depends on what flights are available."

"Not a problem Droz. I will have it covered."

"Okay Keoni. Call me if any problems arise. If not, I'll be in touch. Tell Keona I love her."

We both hang up the phone, and I turn to Johnny saying, "You're in Johnny."

Johnny flies into orbit! He gives us both hugs and kisses shouting, "I love you guys! I love you guys! Stacy will be on cloud fucking nine tonight! Let's go to the track and celebrate! The entire day is on me!"

Tex and I look at each other replying, "Sure."

TAKING A RIDE...

As we head back to our rooms to get ready the doorbell rings. Johnny peeks out the window and depressingly says, "It's fucking Nicky."

I raise my eyebrows to Tex and go open the door. I invite Nicky inside and he says, "Perfect fucking timing, I can kill two birds with one stone here. I needed to speak to the both of you mugs."

"What's up Nicky? Can I get you some coffee or something?"

"Not now Droz, we need to take a ride. I got a message from Charlie Wings. We have to pick up a shipment at a small airport just south of here off of Commercial Boulevard."

Nicky goes into his pocket and hands Johnny a large wad of cash. He gives Johnny a pinch on the cheek saying, "Didn't I tell you I would take care of you?"

"What's this for Nicky?" Johnny asks shocked.

"It's for you, and all you have to do is entertain the Rossetti brothers for me this weekend. I'm way too busy right now to spend time fucking entertaining."

"Lucky me," Johnny says half-heartedly.

Nicky quickly senses Johnny's displeasure. He stares him in the eyes asking, "Why the fuck you looking at me like I just ran over your fucking dog Johnny? I just handed you a load of fucking cash to go out and party."

"Don't get me wrong Nicky. I really do fucking appreciate it, but I already have something special planned with my girl. She's been really looking forward to it too. If I break it off now it'll cause me some major fucking heartache."

Nicky laughs and playfully shoves Johnny saying, "Get the fuck out of here Johnny. You're busting my balls, right?"

"I'm not busting your balls Nicky. I'm fucking serious."

Nicky's body language immediately turns aggressive and he gets nose to nose with Johnny. He sticks his finger in Johnny's face saying, "Just break the fucking date, or I'll break your fucking head, capisce?"

"Capisce," Johnny replies submissively.

Nicky turns to me and Tex and continues voicing his displeasure with Johnny. "Are you guy's hearing this fucking bullshit? Here I am trying to do this little fucking pansy a solid and he spits in my fucking face."

Tex and I play right along with Nicky. "I can't believe it either Nicky," Tex answers shaking his head.

"That's some fucked up shit if I've ever heard it Nicky. If I wasn't standing here listening to it coming out of Johnny's mouth, I never would have believed it," I disappointingly add.

Nicky turns to Johnny. "You see you ungrateful piece of shit? Both of your fucking friends can't believe what there fucking hearing coming out of your fucked up mouth."

When Nicky turns his back to me, I wink at Johnny. This lets him know to just play along with his cousin.

"Where's Sally?" I ask Nicky.

"He's fucking taking care of what we heisted last night. You want to get fucking paid don't you?" Nicky rudely replies.

"Calm down Nicky. Don't cop a fucking attitude with me because you're fucking pissed at your cousin here."

Nicky checks himself and turns his anger back on Johnny. He puts his finger in his face again saying, "You got anything else you want to fucking tell me?"

Johnny bows his head again. Then he looks at Nicky passively replying, "I don't know what got into me Nicky. I wasn't thinking. I'll break the date."

Nicky stares stone faced at Johnny for a moment. Then he breaks a smile saying, "Good boy Johnny."

They hug and kiss. As they're hugging, Johnny winks back at me. Nicky goes into his pocket taking out a lunch baggie full of blow. He hands it to Johnny saying, "Give this to the Rossetti brothers. Tell them to see me if they want more. The Rossetti brothers are staying at the Yankee Clipper on the beach in Ft. Lauderdale. Give them a call at the hotel tonight around 9 PM. Show them both a good fucking time. I know their ugly, but get them both fucking laid. Make sure they go back to Brooklyn with great memories of Florida."

"Okay Nicky. That won't be a problem," Johnny replies in an upbeat manner. Johnny now says, "Look guys, I know you got things to do, so I'll just split. I'll take care of the Rossetti brothers for you Nicky. Don't you worry; they'll have a fucking ball down here."

Nicky stares Johnny down one more time and nods his head. We all give Johnny a goodbye hug and kiss as he walks out the door.

After Johnny leaves, Nicky turns to me asking, "What the fuck's wrong with my cousin? I thought he would be fucking thrilled to get a wad of cash from me. It's not like the little fucking prick could earn on his own you know. If he wasn't a fucking Santori he'd be shoveling cement like the rest of the fucking grease balls down here from New York."

I smile patting Nicky on the shoulder replying, "It's nothing to worry about Nicky. He'll be alright. I really don't think breaking the plans with his girl is what upset him."

"Well that's a fucking relief Droz. With all of the other shortfalls my cousin has I would hate to fucking think that he's pussy whipped too. If it wasn't the bitch that upset him, what the fuck was it?"

"I really think Johnny was looking forward to the three of us going to the ponies today."

Nicky slaps himself on the forehead shouting in horror, "The fucking ponies! Don't tell me he's on his way to the fucking racetrack!"

"Yeah he is Nicky," I reply with a shit eating grin.

Nicky holds his head with both hands like he's in great pain. After a moment, he raises his head cracking a halfhearted smile. Then he begrudgingly says, "Ah, what the fuck, it's only fucking money. There's even the off fucking chance he might win. The first thing you worry about when you hand a guy a wad of cash and a bag of blow is that he'll do the blow. Then he'll use all the cash to buy more. Not Johnny boy. He'll gamble away all of the fucking money and sell the blow, so he can keep chasing what he lost."

Tex and I laugh. Then Tex replies, "Well at least you're mentally prepared for the worst Nicky."

Nicky laughs patting Tex on the back saying, "We need to get going boys."

"Just give us a minute Nicky and we'll be ready."

Tex and I quickly get our asses in gear. We go back to our rooms and arm ourselves. I quickly roll up a few joints and head out the door with Nicky. As I'm locking up the house, Nicky asks, "You mind if I drive the Lincoln Droz?"

"No, I don't mind. Just don't fuck with my mirrors and my seat. It took me for fucking ever to get them the way I wanted."

Nicky laughs waving his hand saying, "Don't worry about it. I understand where you're coming from with that. Guys get shot over that kind of shit back in Brooklyn."

Nicky pops the locks and I jump in the shotgun seat. Tex spreads himself out in the back. As Nicky pulls out of the driveway, Tex says, "This is pretty comfortable back here Droz. A man of my size can get used to driving around like this."

"Don't get any fucking ideas Tex. There aint no fucking way I'm chauffeuring you around."

Tex rubs my head saying, "Don't worry Droz; I don't want you to be my chauffeur. But you know what?"

"What's that Tex?"

"You sure would look cute in one them there little chauffeuring outfits. You know the kind with those cute little hats. Wouldn't he Nicky?"

"That's funny Tex. I think you're fucking right. He would look cute in a little fucking chauffeur's outfit."

The both of them have a good laugh while I take it all in stride.

"This is a nice fucking ride Rocco gave you Droz. I guess he really does like you."

"He would like me a whole lot fucking less if I didn't make him money."

Nicky smiles nodding his head replying, "You better never fucking forget it. When we get to this little airport, I want you guys to keep quiet. Let the guy I'm meeting do all the fucking talking."

We reply, "Sure."

Then I turn on some tunes and go into my sock for a bone. I go to light it up and Nicky stops me saying, "Put it away Droz, we're almost there already."

Nicky soon pulls into an unmanned gate entering a small commercial airport. He parks my car next to a large black Cadillac with tinted windows. There's a diplomat shield and license plate on the back of the car. Parked next to the Cadillac is a large white van. The side of the van reads "Middle East Imports Inc." A bearded dark skinned man is perched in the driver's seat. Sitting next to him is another dark skinned man with a beard. A white man steps out of the driver's side door of the Cadillac. This guy is well dressed and well groomed. He's wearing a black jacket and black pants with a white shirt. He opens the backseat door of the Cadillac, and out pops a man dressed just like a sheik. When this guy sees Nicky, he shouts, "Allah Akbar."

Nicky smiles and waves back while saying to us, "Allah Akbar, it means 'God is Great' in Arabic."

"We know what it means Nicky. We were in Bahrain and Karachi," Tex replies.

"These guys love Charlie Wings. He makes money for all of these Arab cocksuckers. They're always kissing his ass. I'll tell you guys all about it later. Let's get out of the car before Hakim thinks something's wrong."

We get out of the car and Hakim walks up to Nicky hugging him. I couldn't help noticing the fancy fucking Rolex he's wearing. I'm almost blinded by all the diamonds on it sparkling in the sunlight.

"It's been a long time Nicky," Hakim says.

"Too long Hakim."

"Where have you been Nicky? I was worried about you."

"I had to go away for a while Hakim, but I'm back working with Charlie now."

"It brings me great joy knowing you're back working with Charlie. He's truly blessed doing Allah's work. My driver will open the van for your two workers. We will walk and talk as they unload the shipment for you."

Nicky pops open the trunk while Hakim's bodyguard opens the van. In the back of the van, I see stacks of burlap bags. They look to be about a foot long and a half-foot wide. Nicky tells us to put them all into the trunk. As Tex and I unload the van, we smell the pungent odor of hashish. The two of us smuggled it out of Karachi, so we knew what it smelt like. We had seen blocks of hashish the size of dining room tables. One Pakistani man rolled a chunk of hashish the size of a truck tire right up to the fantail for us. We traded cartons of Marlboro and American fuck books for it. Karachi is one of the poorest and dirtiest places on the planet. The burlap bags have a logo with two words burnt onto them, "Free Afghanistan." The burlap packages smelling like hashish have small blue X's around the logo. While I'm loading the trunk, I ask Tex, "Did you fucking notice that shit Tex?"

"Notice what Droz?"

"That fucking rag head wouldn't even acknowledge our fucking presence. The fucking prick just called us Nicky's workers. He's got some fucking balls."

"What's the matter Droz? You don't remember how they treated us when we were in Bahrain?"

"Yeah I do Tex; they treated us like fucking dog shit. They locked up all of the fucking women in their houses so we couldn't defile them. The crew was pissed, so we all got drunk and tore the fucking place down."

"Yeah we did Droz. The Captain had to get us all out of there before they started hanging us." Tex is laughing as he's remembering the riot we caused. He now slaps his knee saying, "Remember how the captain told the authorities in Bahrain he would be back in the morning to pay for all of the damages the crew did?"

Picturing it all in my head again, I start laughing too replying, "Yeah sure he was. Wild Bill pulled up anchor and split in the middle of the fucking night under darkened ship! What I wouldn't have given to see their faces in the morning when they saw our ship gone!"

We laugh really loud and high five each other. This draws Hakim and Nicky's attention. Nicky gives us a dirty look, but we can give a shit a less. We just keep carrying on as we load the trunk.

"Old Hakim over there is probably from one of them Royal Families," Tex says.

"It sure looks that way Tex. But what the fuck is he doing in Florida dealing drugs?"

"Who knows Droz, but I'll tell you this. With that diplomatic license plate no one can touch him."

"That's for fucking sure Tex. Hakim has his own get out of jail free card there."

When we finish loading the trunk, I whistle for Nicky. Seeing we're done, they hug and Hakim says something in parting making Nicky laugh. Hakim then barks out something in

Arabic to the driver of the van. He immediately starts up the engine pulling away. Hakim's bodyguard opens the backdoor of the Cadillac and Hakim gets in. Nicky's still laughing, so I ask, "What's so funny Nicky?"

Smiling as he's waving goodbye to Hakim, Nicky replies, "Hakim's wondering when I'm going to train you guys to act proper."

"So what did you tell him?"

"I told him you guys aint trainable." After a good laugh, Nicky invites us to lunch. We get into the car taking a short ride to a Char Hut. Before we get out of the car I ask, "Some of them burlap bags I loaded into the trunk has hashish in them Nicky."

With big grin Nicky replies, "The hashish is a gift from Charlie Wings. I told him about your Hawaiian dope and how you guys like to burn. I've had this shit before. It'll break your fucking lungs if you aint careful. The rest of them burlap bags are kilos of uncut heroin. They're for Antonio to put to work on the streets of Miami."

Tex pats Nicky on the shoulder saying, "That's cool of Charlie about the hash Nicky. We both know how good it is. When we were in Karachi most everyone on the ship smuggled some onboard."

Nicky nods his head and then I ask him, "Tell me something Nicky. What the fuck's up with that "Free Afghanistan" logo on the fucking bags?"

Nicky snidely snickers before replying, "That's Charlie Wing's idea to promote the fucking business. He likes to put a little patriotism into his drug dealing. When he was on the lam from the "French Connection" bust, his CIA friends hid him out in fucking Afghanistan. They wanted him to set up shop there. Afghanistan was quickly becoming the next hot spot for the spread of Soviet communism. The place is dirt fucking poor and is loosely ruled by a bunch of Muslim warlords who hate each other. According to the CIA, this is a perfect recipe for a Soviet invasion and it turns out they're right. When Charlie

Wings first got there, he used CIA money to make friends with the warlords. This was no easy task because some of these tribes hated each other for fucking centuries. Charlie Wings is the king of persuasion. He convinces all of these motherfuckers to work together."

"How did he do that?" Tex asks.

"Charlie gave them what he calls the millionaire pitch. He convinces the warlords that if they work together instead of against each other, they can bring in ten times more profit from their poppy fields. As long as the money keeps rolling in the way it is now, they'll keep the fucking peace. Money and greed overcome a lot of fucking differences, so with the blessings of the American government, and under the protection of the CIA, they all began prospering as international drug dealers."

"Why the fuck does Charlie Wings have the protection of the CIA, and the blessings of our fucking government to deal drugs?" I ask.

"One word says it all Droz, and that word is communism."

"Communism?" I reply.

"Well the spread of it anyway. Our government and all of the rich fucking cocksuckers backing them will do anything to stop the spread of communism. Communism would mean losing their fucking money and power. They would eat their fucking children before that happens. Not all wars are sanctioned by our fucking government Droz. If they aint fucking sanctioned then there aint no fucking taxpayer money to run them. That's when they turn to guys like Charlie Wings. This aint the first fucking time they did it either. Charlie Wings told me he began smuggling heroin under the CIA's protection in the sixties. Back then, he said it was to support anti- Communist Chinese Nationalists near the Sino-Burmese border. Charlie even recruited some fucking native tribe called the Hmong to help them in Laos, so he's had a lot of experience dealing with these kinds of people. Charlie Wings was an instrumental fucking part of forming the infamous "Golden Triangle." Now with the help of our government and the CIA, Charlie has formed the

"Golden Crescent." Smuggling drugs and fighting communism in Afghanistan just like he fucking did in Southeast Asia. Right now Charlie's drug smuggling helps finance a bunch of Afghan freedom fighters called the Mujahedeen, thus the logo "Free Afghanistan." Charlie says these guys are ruthless religious zealots from all over the fucking Arab world. They're fighting what they call a jihad. That means a holy war. These fucking fanatics are led by a filthy rich Saudi Prince. This fucking prince turned his back on his mega wealthy lifestyle to lead this jihad. Charlie doesn't trust this guy or his Mujahedeen fighters."

"Why doesn't he trust them?" Tex asks.

"I'll tell you why he don't fucking trust them Tex. This fucking guy left the life of a fucking prince to go live in the mountains with a bunch of fucking fanatics. Instead of being fanned by beautiful women getting his dick sucked, he sleeps on cold fucking rocks and eats crickets. Charlie says you just can't trust a guy like that, and I fucking agree."

"He sounds really dedicated," Tex says.

"He's either that or fucking crazy," I add.

"He's probably a combination of fucking both. Right now he's got Soviet attack helicopters chasing him and his boys all over the fucking mountains. Not to mention the fucking missiles the Russians are firing at his ass. Would you fucking guys trust a nut like that?"

"No fucking way," I reply.

"When the time is right, this guy will turn on everybody that isn't like him," Tex warily adds.

"Those are my sentiments exactly Tex. That's why we all have to line our fucking pockets as fast as we can. Enough of fucking politics, let's go eat."

I think to myself, "Rocco is so fucking right about our government being the biggest drug dealer in the world. I remember him saying the government uses drug money to finance illegal wars. It looks like Charlie, Nicky, and Rocco can all agree on something."

It's just before noon, so there isn't much of a line waiting to order. Tex orders three large burgers, three large orders of fries, and two large cokes.

"Why two cokes?" Nicky jokingly asks.

"You're right Nicky. I made a mistake. Sir, make that three cokes please."

Nicky and I laugh. We only order one large burger, one large order of fries, and one large coke a piece. They grill your burgers to order. If they taste as good as they smell we'll all be happy. It didn't take long for everything to be ready. Nicky pays the tab and we all sit down to eat. There are only three of us, but because of the size of Tex's food order, we need the largest table in the room! After taking a few bites, we all agree this place makes a tasty burger.

Chewing away with his mouth full of food Tex says, "I hope my grandma's still getting along alright back home. I love my grandma. She took good care of me when no one else would. She's getting pretty old now and can't work nearly as hard as she used too. Her social security checks barely pay for her medicine, never mind her normal bills. Now that I made a bunch of money I'm looking forward to bringing her down here with me."

"So why don't you?" I ask.

"Well Grandma's kind of hardheaded Droz and very religious too. She taught me the Bible from cover to cover. She belted me over the head with it a few times too, so I'll have to convince her I'm making the dough on the up and up, or she won't come."

"That shouldn't be a problem Tex. We can tell her we started building houses together. I'll get Johnny's family to back us up on it."

Tex nods his head agreeing as he grabs a napkin and wipes ketchup off his face. He grabs one of his cokes and washes down the burger he just finished. He takes a giant bite off another one and with his mouth full says, "You know Droz; I think that idea will work on old granny."

Nicky chimes in, "You're a lucky man Tex. You still got your grandmother around to love. My grandmother took care of me too when no one else would. She gave me the only love I had growing up."

"I know how that goes. Is your grandmother still alive?" Tex asks with his mouth still full.

"No. She died of leukemia when I was only thirteen," Nicky solemnly replies.

"Is your grandpa still alive?" I ask Nicky.

"No. He's dead too. My grandpa was one of them old time Mafiosos. A "Mustache Pete" is what they called them. Grandpa got killed in a street fight before I was even born. My grandmother raised three kids on her own. Grandma had two boys and one girl. The girl became a schoolteacher and the two boys became gangsters like their old man. One died in prison and the other disappeared. Which in our profession means you got whacked. Grandma tried her best to save me from the same fucking fate. You guys might not believe this, but I was a pretty good kid before my grandmother died. I got good grades and was hardly ever in trouble. After her death things quickly went downhill."

"What was up with your parents Nicky?" I ask.

Nicky wipes his mouth with his napkin and takes a gulp of his coke before replying, "Less than a fucking year after my grandmother died my old man went to fucking prison. The judge gave him fifteen years for trafficking heroin. Three fucking months into his sentence, my old man took a shiv in the back. He died the next day. My mom was told by the prison officials Pops was killed by a fucking junkie. Two days later, she gets another call from the prison. A prison official told her the junkie who killed my father was found dead hanging in his cell. They said it was suicide. Right after that, I quit going to school. Soon I became known as the worst kid in the fucking neighborhood. Pretty soon, my reputation for violence became noticed. One of the mob bosses has one of his soldiers ask me to do a hit. I did a great job, so one hit led to another. Once I earned the boss's trust, he told me what really happened to my father. The fucking junkie who killed my father was hired by a mob boss in the Bronx. His name will go unsaid. My old man grew up in the Bronx and moved to Brooklyn after he met my mother, so this made sense to me. My old man didn't shit where he ate, so he operated out of the Bronx. My father was serving fifteen years for trafficking heroin for this mob boss. The boss got worried my old man might snitch on him to get his sentence reduced. Prison walls can do many things to a man, but my old man wasn't a fucking snitch. Everybody on the street who knew my father said he was a stand-up guy. He took his sentence like a fucking man, but the mob boss didn't want to leave anything to chance, so he has my old man killed. He covered his tracks by paying off two prison guards. They hung the junkie in his cell making it look like a fucking suicide. Later I was recruited by another up and coming gangster named Frankie Pastori."

"Is that the Future Visions Frankie Pastori Nicky?" I quickly ask.

Nicky gives me a blank stare and then continues. "Frankie knew I wanted revenge for my father's death, and it fit right into his plans. Frankie wanted to expand his heroin business into the Bronx. The mob boss who killed my father was in his fucking way, so Frankie gives me the hit. On an ice cold Sunday morning in late January, I hid outside this prick's house. Every morning rain or shine, this mob boss went outside to retrieve his morning paper. His driveway was lined on both sides with giant fucking oak trees. That morning I was hiding behind one of them. When he bends over to pick up his newspaper, I sneak up behind him and shoot him in the head. Then I stick the gun down his fucking throat and blow the back of his skull out. Ming, what a fucking mess I made in that driveway. My two childhood friends, Sally and Vinnie, were waiting in the wings to pick me up. Making that hit for Frankie made him his first million. Frankie walks some tightrope in life between his world and Rocco's."

"What about your mom?" Tex asks.

"My mother died of an overdose on her next fucking birthday. Enough of the fucking history lessons, let's go drop off this shipment.

"Where are we heading Nicky?" I ask.

"We're heading to one of Antonio's safe houses in Miami Lakes."

Before we get in the car, Tex and I give Nicky a hug. Nicky smiles and hugs us back. I didn't think a guy like Nicky was capable of opening up like that. I'm starting too really like Nicky, but I still have to tell Rocco what he said about Frankie Pastori. Is this where Rocco's son Bobby got the dope from? Did Frankie's son steal it from his father and give it to Bobby? I doubt Frankie sold it to him. Maybe Nicky sold it to them both? Lots of questions still need to be answered. All I know is I want Frankie's fucking job!

As we pull out of the parking lot, I spark up a doobie and Nicky starts talking again. "Tonight you guys will be going with me to the port. I got my mob connections from New York meeting me there to pick up a shipment. Antonio aint going to be there, but his men will still offload and load for us."

"Where's Antonio?" I ask Nicky passing him the joint.

"Antonio had to fly back to Colombia for his sister's wedding. His family is very religious and they expect him to attend all of the pre-ceremony bullshit. Antonio says if he doesn't go to church with his mother every fucking day she won't cook for him."

We all laugh and Tex says, "Home cooked vittles are worth an hour in church in my book."

"If you say so Tex," Nicky replies passing the doobie back to him.

"It's probably better Antonio and your mob guys don't meet anyway Nicky."

Nicky raises an eyebrow giving me a queer look before asking, "You think I'm fucking scared of being back doored?"

"I don't think you're fucking scared Nicky, but isn't it just better your guys and Antonio never meet?"

"Look Droz. I know you've been around the block a few fucking times, but you're still a little wet behind the ears," Nicky smugly replies.

"Yeah, how's that Nicky?" I ask defiantly as Tex hands me back the joint.

"Do you want to learn something here asshole, or do you want to play tough guy with me," Nicky arrogantly says.

Curious, I ease off the attitude and pass Nicky the joint replying, "I know I can't know everything Nicky, so tell me what I'm missing here."

Tex snickers, and I quickly turn around giving him a dirty look. He laughs, and Nicky starts his lecture. "Correct me if I'm wrong here, but neither one of you has experience doing narcotics deals of this size, right?"

We nod our heads like boy scouts listening to their scoutmaster confirming we haven't.

"It's always best to know right off if somebody's going to try and circumvent you. If you try to hide your connections like most assholes do, they'll know you're afraid of them. A whiff of fear at this level and you're finished. When you're dealing in narcotics deals of this size, you're dealing with the worst type of cutthroat motherfuckers on the planet. No matter how civil and polite some of them may seem up front, it's all a fucking façade. This most definitely includes our host Antonio."

"How about you Nicky, don't you fall into that category too?" I boldly ask.

"Especially fucking me. So should you and Tex if you want to survive."

Nicky turns down a couple of side streets entering an older upscale neighborhood. The streets are lined with mature trees giving each house its own little slice of privacy. It's a perfect place for a safe house. Nicky slows down and stops in front of a very nice house. The entire house is painted white with a tan barrel tiled roof. It has a beautifully landscaped circular driveway with a blue Eldorado parked in the middle. There's also a large mango tree growing on the right side of the house.

Nicky backs my Lincoln into the driveway by the garage door. We all get out making our way to a big foyer area with a small fountain. The front door is etched glass. When Nicky rings the doorbell, it plays a pretty melody. A really hot Spanish chick wearing a bikini and large gold-hooped earrings answers the door. When our eyes meet, I know we have chemistry. She politely invites us inside, and I watch her sexy ass wiggle down the hallway. The house smells like a Spanish restaurant. The inside is elegantly decorated in a tropical style. There's lots of plants and bamboo furniture arranged around the house. Spanish music is playing on the stereo in the living room where you can see out the back patio doors. The pool area is designed like an island paradise and has a waterfall flowing into it. They even have two large white cockatoos roaming around by the pool. Two Spanish men come out of the kitchen wiping their hands and face with a napkin. One of the guys is a grey haired stocky man, and the other one looks like a younger version of him. The older man knows Nicky and introduces the younger guy as his son Miguel. That explains the similarities. Miguel introduces the hot chick as his girlfriend Maria. I thought to myself, "No wonder this chick is flirting with me, her boyfriend is a toad!" Nicky now introduces me and Tex to the father Jose. We all exchange handshakes and are invited to join them for lunch. Nicky politely declines saying we just ate lunch before we came. Jose nods his head and tells Miguel to go open the garage door. Nicky hands me the keys to my car and tells me to go back the car in. The garage is clean as a whistle and empty, so it's obvious what it's being used for. Miguel opens the garage door and I back in my car. After closing the garage door, Nicky and Jose walk in. Nicky tells me to pop the trunk. Nicky grabs a burlap sack out of the trunk and we all head back inside the house. There's one large couch and two lazy boys in the living room. Nicky sits on the couch with Jose, Miguel, and Maria. Tex and I plop our asses on the lazy boys. Nicky asks Jose for a knife to cut open the package. Jose says something in Spanish to Miguel who quickly gets up and heads to the kitchen.

Miguel returns with a kitchen knife handing it to Nicky. Nicky cuts open the burlap and hands Jose the knife. He licks it clean pausing for a moment before smiling. Jose nods his head to his son Miguel. Miguel immediately gets up and goes into another room. This makes me edgy, but when I look at Nicky, he's cool as a cucumber. Miguel returns with a suitcase handing it to Nicky. Nicky put the suitcase on the table and thumbs through the cash. When he's satisfied, he nods to Jose. Happy the business side of the visit is over, Jose asks, "May I get you gentlemen something to drink? Maria just made fresh squeezed orange juice."

We all say, "Sure."

I would have said sure even if I didn't want any juice just to see Maria walk into the kitchen. A happily smiling Maria gets her gorgeous body off the couch to get our juice. This Spanish girl has an incredibly hot ass and knows how to work it. I have visions of working it too. While Maria's in the kitchen Nicky asks, "What kind of stereo is that Jose?"

"It's a Nakamichi, Nicky," Jose proudly replies.

"It sounds fantastic Jose. I think I need to get one."

"Nakamichi makes a great stereo Nicky. You won't be disappointed. We all love listening to Colombian music. It makes us feel at home."

"I'm sure it does Jose."

Maria returns to the room wheeling a cart with a large crystal pitcher of juice and glasses. Marie gives us all a glass and pours our juice. She pours mine last dropping a small piece of paper in my lap. Then she makes eye contact and smiles. Oh yeah! She just gave me her fucking phone number! Then slowly she walks back over to the couch teasing me with her hot ass. When she sits down next to her boyfriend, she's still smiling at me. This makes Miguel mad. If looks could kill, I would be dead already. I look back at him like, "too bad pal, your bitch wants me." Everyone drinks some juice and compliments Maria on how good it is.

"I can't get over how great that stereo sounds José. I really want to buy one. Do you mind if I play with it a little?" Nicky asks.

"Not at all Nicky, play with it all you want. You won't break it. It's matched so perfectly to the speakers it's impossible to blow them."

Nicky walks over to the stereo and cranks up the volume. Quick as a flash Nicky pulls his pistol shooting Jose and Miguel in the head. Jose convulses as Miguel's spews blood and brains all over Maria's lap. The wall behind her is painted in blood. Maria's beyond hysterical. Nicky grabs her by the hair and jams his pistol right through her fucking teeth. He pulls the trigger twice blowing the back of her head right the fuck out. Pieces of her skull and a few of her teeth drip bloodily down the wall behind her. The first thought crossing my mind is there goes a mighty fine piece of ass. Nicky casually walks back over to the stereo and lowers the volume. He turns around with a giant shit eating grin on his blood splattered face saying, "What did I teach you guys? When you're dealing in narcotics deals of this fucking size, you're dealing with the worst type of cutthroat motherfuckers on the planet. And I'm the worst cutthroat motherfucker of them all!"

Tex and I are stunned at what just happened, but we managed to high five Nicky anyway. I now ask, "What the fuck do we do now Nicky? You just whacked Antonio's guys. Not to mention a really fine piece of ass I wanted to fuck."

"What do we do now? What are you, fucking stupid Droz? We take the fucking dope and the money you asshole. There's a million fucking dollars in that suitcase and two hundred grand of it is yours. As far as the fucking broad goes, everyone in the room knew you wanted to fuck her, especially her boyfriend."

"Fuck him Nicky. She was way out of his league. It was obvious the bitch wanted me too. She even snuck me her fucking phone number. If you had fucking waited I would have fucked her in the fucking bathroom, or least got a fucking blowjob."

Nicky nonchalantly shakes his head back and forth before saying, "Looking at her now, a blowjob is definitely out of the question Droz, but you can fuck her while she's still warm. If you time it just right the pussy will get tighter and tighter as she stiffens up."

I look at Maria and almost barf while Tex laughs. "You know Nicky; you're one sick fuck if you think I'm going to do that."

Nicky and Tex laugh so fucking hard they almost cry.

"What about Antonio Nicky? What happens when he finds out?" I blurt out.

"Boy Droz, you worry like a bitch. Is he always this way Tex?"

"No, not really. He's just pissed he didn't get to screw Maria before you blew her brains out."

I quickly nod my head frowning. Nicky smiles at me as he goes into his back pocket and pulls out a small flag. He walks over to the coffee table and picks up the kitchen knife used to cut open the heroin. Nicky takes the knife and plants it through the flag right into Jose's chest releasing a gasp of air from his body. He wipes off his prints with his shirt and proudly says, "That's a Peruvian fucking flag. Antonio will think it's retaliation for what he did to their families back in Peru."

"Are you sure Nicky?" I cautiously ask.

Nicky shrugs his shoulders calmly saying, "No, but who gives a shit anyway. Prove I fucking did it. Better yet, why would I fucking do it? I got everything to lose and nothing to gain as far as Antonio's concerned. The best fucking crimes to commit are the ones people think you wouldn't be stupid enough to commit. Do I have to teach you two fucking rookies everything?"

I could tell Tex took offense to that last statement, and he says bluntly, "It would have been nice if you told us two rookies what you were planning here Nicky."

Nicky can tell Tex is offended. He looks at the three dead bodies replying, "I wasn't sure myself Tex if I was going to do it. By the time I made up my mind, it was too fucking late to tell you guys. We would have lost the element of surprise. After the other night at the warehouse, I knew you two would respond accordingly if I needed you to."

Tex and I both nod our heads telling Nicky it's cool. Then I ask, "So what's our plan from here Nicky?"

"Here's our story. We showed up to make the deal. We rang the fucking bell a couple of times and nobody answered, so we fucking left. It can't get any simpler than that."

Tex and I both nod agreeing. The plan is so simple it will probably work. If it doesn't, Tex and I will fall back on Rocco for protection.

"Do me a favor guys. Find me a shirt, some soap, and a fucking towel. I'm going to jump in the pool to clean up," Nicky says.

Nicky starts undressing while we go get Nicky what he asked for. As we're looking in one of the bedrooms, we notice six shoeboxes on one of the beds. Inside them is more fucking cash and blow! After sifting through the dresser draws, Tex and I decide on a plain white tee shirt. That way it has no relation to the person we're taking it from. We then grab Nicky a bar of soap and a towel. We walk out the cabana door to the pool where we find Nicky doing the backstroke. The two big white Cockatoos are speaking Spanish to him as he swims back and forth. I throw Nicky the soap saying, "Guess what Nicky?"

"You fucked the dead broad?"

"No, no you fucking pervert. We found six shoe boxes full of cash and blow sitting on one of the beds."

Nicky stays silent for a moment while he soaps himself up and washes his face. "How do I look? Did I get all the blood off?"

"You're clean Nicky, but you're still ugly," I sarcastically reply as Nicky gets out of the pool.

When I hand Nicky the towel he snickers saying, "He's a real pretty boy, huh Tex?"

"Yeah he is Nicky. When we were overseas, Droz was what we called a faggot magnet. The fags followed him all over the place. One rich fag even offered to buy Droz a Mercedes for some booty."

"Well did you give up some booty for the Mercedes?" Nicky asks.

I put my hand on my hip poking my butt out like a fag. Then using the fruitiest flame voice I can muster, I reply, "I would have Nicky, but he couldn't find me a pink one."

Tex and Nicky bust a gut laughing. Then Nicky says, "You would do well in prison Droz."

"Of course I would," I gayly reply.

Nicky finishes drying himself off and getting dressed. When he's done, he turns to us saying, "We'll leave the drugs and cash behind for the cops to split up. I'm taking a page out your book Droz. Just another drug related homicide in South Florida and some happy crooked cops. We'll sell the smack to Antonio's people tonight. I'll act really fucking pissed they weren't home when I showed up. When they tell me their guys got whacked, I'll say I'm sorry to hear that but where's my fucking money. If they don't have the dough with them, I'll just deduct it from my bill, and that will be that. Grab the suitcase with the cash and put it in the trunk. Then pull the car out of the garage, and I'll close it behind you. I'll lock the front door from the inside and leave with Tex through patio area. Let them think they got surprised by the pool. Pick us up on the side of the house Droz."

I pick them up on the side of the house and we leave for home.

Roratonga......

When we get back to my house, I bring a brick of hash in with me. Tex grabs some beers, and Nicky helps himself to the Oban. I go looking for my mom's old sewing box. It's very old and was given to her by her grandmother. I loved old things. If they could talk, imagine the stories they would tell. I find the sewing box in a closet and grab a large sewing needle out of it. I take the album out of "Goats Head Soup" by the Rolling Stones and head back to the living room. Tex hands me a beer and a thick water glass to smoke the hash out of. Nicky takes out a switchblade and cuts open the burlap bag holding the hashish. Its strong odor fills the room. The seal "Free Afghanistan" is burnt right into the front of the brick. Nicky looks at the brick proudly saying, "You got to love Charlie Wings. He's the only drug dealer in the world with our government's stamp of approval."

We all chuckle as Nicky slices a nice chunk of hash off the oily end of the brick. I squeeze and sniff the brick. Then I pass it over to Tex for his inspection. He squeezes it and runs its entire length under his nose. Nicky takes a sip of Oban and sarcastically says, "Hey Mr. Connoisseur, does it meet your approval?" Tex looks at Nicky like Alexa Hente in the coffee commercial nodding his head with a grin. I put the oversized pin through the album cover and stick the big chunk of hashish on top of it. I torch the chunk of hash until a piece of it starts to burn like a coal in a barbecue. If it's really good hashish, I'll only have to light it once. I get it cooking good and put the glass over the pin, trapping the smoke. When the glass is full, I tip open the bottom and suck up all the smoke trapped inside. I can't hold it down for more than a few seconds before I start coughing my balls off. My eyelids immediately get heavy. I knew right then this was the real deal!

"Don't just sit there and veg out on us Droz. Scoot that album cover down a yonder." Tex barks. I slide the album cover over to him. Tex leans over the coffee table and cracks open the glass. He deeply inhales all of the smoke built up inside it. Tex looks up at us with his cheeks bulging out of the sides of his face. Then like a volcano, he erupts coughing all over the place. He grabs his beer and downs half of it.

Nicky stares at the glass saying, "Look at that fucking hash burning under that glass. It's really fucking cooking now boys." Nicky cracks open the bottom and let it rip, emptying the entire glass of smoke. Nicky starts grunting like a pig in heat trying desperately to hold down the smoke.

"He's in trouble," Tex says.

With those words, Nicky starts coughing so violently he falls off the couch! Lying on the floor looking like he's about to die, he motions for Tex to hand him his beer. Nicky downs the cold beer and then looks up from the floor smiling. After a few minutes to recoup, we indulge again! Now we're all really fucking high, so Tex decides to tell Nicky a sailor story. As Tex starts the story, I head to the kitchen and get everybody another beer.

"Here we are Nicky, right smack in the middle of the South Pacific. We drop anchor off one of the Cook Islands named Roratonga. From the deck, you can see huge mountains with big white clouds hanging over their peaks. The island looks like the one in that old King Kong movie. It's truly one of God's little emeralds. The crew's licking their chops in anticipation of five days of hedonism on the island."

Nicky interrupts saying, "We didn't get much R&R in Vietnam. It was more like here's your mission quit your bitchen.

Hell Tex, we were lucky to get a hot shower and some hot food once in a while."

"Well that's a damn shame Nicky. Our mission was all about showing the flag under Jimmy Carter. The president wanted us to be little ambassadors and go visit places we hadn't been too since WW11."

I return from the kitchen with the beers saying, "We were more like pirates than ambassadors Nicky."

Nicky smiles as I hand him his beer. I hand Tex his, and he takes a giant gulp before continuing. "All of us swinging dicks piled into the small boats to take us to shore. As we get closer to land, it becomes obvious our ship's visit is a really big deal to these natives. They're all dressed up in their tribal outfits jumping up and down waving at us. Native tribesmen start playing their drums as we get off the small boats. I thought we all might be dinner until the beautiful native girls placed flowered leas over our necks."

Nicky and I laugh as Tex continues. "The captain has a really special oversized lea placed over his neck by the chief's wife. We find out later our Captain Wild Bill and Chief Noka Laka worked out plans for our arrival over the ship's radio. Now the chief himself, Nicky, is a big, jolly sort of fellow. His wife is just as jolly, and a bit oversized just like him. So they definitely fit one another."

Nicky shakes his head saying, "Chief Noka Laka? Now that's a fucking trip of a name there Tex."

"He looks really trippy too Nicky. He wore this really crazy head ornament. It made him look like he had wild colored bird feathers growing out of his head. The chief now tells us we're all invited to a ceremonial feast. The crew cheers, and then the captain gave the old be on your best behavior speech. After that, we follow the chief and his entourage down a beautiful cliff laden beach. When we finally arrive at the site of the feast, the sun is just starting to set. The sky over the ocean turns into a fiery, purplish red. This makes a beautiful backdrop for the small native huts and kiki torches lining the beachhead."

Nicky moves up to the edge of the couch. He is clearly engrossed in Tex's story telling. "They had three big, old boars, Nicky, being spit roasted and turned by native men. The older women were preparing all kinds of unknown foods using big, handmade, wooden bowls and utensils. While the old broads were cooking, the young girls were dancing for us Nicky. They were half-naked in their tribal outfits. They all had silky, brown skin and curvy bodies. The ones that weren't dancing walked around filling our wooden mugs with some kind of homemade wine. The chief's family sat at the front of the feast with the captain and his officers. You could tell they wanted to keep us all separated. There was no mingling going on whatsoever."

"It was like first class and coach on an airplane Nicky," I comment.

With a pissed off look Nicky shakes his head. He downs his Oban and gives himself a refill before angrily replying, "You see? You fucking see? No matter where the fuck you go in this world, there's always cocksuckers who think they're fucking better than you. I'll go out of my way to fuck people like that."

"No arguments here Nicky, the both of us feel the same way," I say.

Tex nods his head, takes another big slug of beer, and continues. "So now the food's ready and it's time to chow down. Of course the officers and the royals were served first."

Nicky angrily interrupts again saying, "Of course the cocksuckers were served first. They should all get a fucking bone stuck in their throats and choke to death."

We all laugh and high five. Then Tex continues. "Outside of the boar's meat, none of us had a clue as to what else we were eating Nicky."

Nicky laughs and says, "Now that part sounds a lot like Vietnam. One day it was their pet, and the next day it was your fucking dinner. Nothing went to waste in that fucking place. For all we knew we might have been fucking eating each other."

Tex and I shake our heads in disbelief. Then Tex continues. "When dinner was over Nicky, the real show began. The drums got louder, and men started juggling fire torches. They were incredible. They actually juggled the torches while tossing them back and forth to each other. After a while, a group of other natives began performing ceremonial sword dances. The sword dances looked really dangerous too Nicky, but no one even got a scratch. After about an hour of this, the chief silenced the drums and stood up to make an announcement. 'My honored American guests, you will now witness an ancient ceremonial dance of our tribe called Maka Rikki Laka. In the English language, this means Dance of the Virgins. It will be led by my beautiful daughter, Princess Latta.'

"The King now claps his hands together, and a group of their prettiest, young girls gather in front of their table. They bow to the chief and captain. Then they turn around towards the crew and bow too. The chief now claps his hands three times. He must have expected something to happen because he gets upset and claps even harder. Nothing still happens. The chief hollers out, 'Latta! Latta! Latta!' No answer. He turns to his wife yelling, 'Woman, where's our daughter?' She looks at her husband like she aint got a clue. The chief starts flailing his arms around wildly and berating his wife into tears. I thought he was going to belt her for sure. Getting nowhere with his wife, the captain calmly suggests something to the chief. The chief nods his head, and we form a search party to look for Latta. We search the ceremonial area first. No Latta. Then we search all the huts. No Latta. The wife now says to the chief, 'Let's check the lagoon Noka. You know how our daughter loves the lagoon on the nights of the full moon.'

"That seemed to calm the old chief down because he replies back nicely to his wife, 'Good idea my wife. I am mad, but will be happy if we find her there.'

"So now we all head to the lagoon hoping to find his daughter. When we get to the lagoon, we found Latta. She's butt naked with her tits flapping in the wind bouncing up and down on Droz's cock!"

Hysterical, Nicky falls on the floor laughing his ass off! Tex and I are laughing too, but Tex continues with the story. "The mother faints right into the captain's arms Nicky. Chief Noka Laka stands there speechless while his daughter and Droz have a screaming orgasm together. All of us Navy guys are chanting, 'Go Droz go! Go! Go! Go! Go Droz go! Go! Go! Go!'

"The tribal men all start angrily yelling, 'He's raping Princess Latta, we must stop him! He must be punished!' Finally, Droz and Latta realize they have an audience. Latta's father is beside himself with rage, and heads toward Droz with his men. The captain leads a bunch of us to head them off. Now all hell breaks loose Nicky, and it's a donnybrook! Fists and feet are flying everywhere! What a brawl Nicky! The fight went on until the shore patrol shows up and fires their guns in the air. The captain orders all of us back to the ship. The chief demands the captain to leave Droz behind to face rape charges. The captain says, 'With all due respect chief, we all witnessed your daughter pleasuring herself on top of my sailor. The two of them were so lost in passion they didn't even notice we were watching.'

"The chief starts screaming with spit flying out of his mouth. 'She was a virgin Captain! He ruined her for marriage! She can no longer perform the sacred dance! She is disgraced before my people, and he must pay for defiling her!'

"'Sorry Chief. No can do,' The captain answers.

"'I will call your president! I will have justice for Latta! You will leave my island now and never return!'

"'Okay Chief. If that's the way you want it, but I'll also be making my own report of the incident. There's plenty of witnesses Chief. If I were you, I would save my family any further embarrassments by dropping the matter.'

"Steam shoots out of the chief's nostrils and ears as he again demands us to leave. The captain pats Droz on the back as we walk away."

Nicky's still on the floor. He shakes his head exclaiming, "That story's got to go down as one of the all-time Navy classics!"

"One of many Nicky," I pat myself on the back bragging.

"Wait Nicky. That's not the end of the story," Tex says.

"You mean there's more?" Nicky raises his eyebrows replying.

"Shit yeah Nicky. Let me grab us all another beer while Tex finishes the story."

"A month later Nicky, we pull into Adelaide, Australia for two weeks of liberty. Adelaide is known as the city of churches."

"It really should be called the pussy capital of the world," I say as I return with the beers.

We all take a few chugs before Tex continues. "You wouldn't believe the amount of hot women running around Adelaide Nicky. The local newspapers advertised our arrival, so when we pull into port there are crowds of people and high school marching bands waiting for us."

Nicky shakes his head in disbelief saying, "I get fucking Vietnam, and you guys get the cruise to debauchery."

"Yeah, you got a raw deal Nicky," Tex says taking another slug of beer. Then he continues. "The captain made an agreement with the mayor of Adelaide to open the ship up for tours, so the entire crew has to take turns giving them. This tour thing, Nicky, turns out to be a gold mine for young snatch. As one of the schools is boarding the ship for a tour, we hear a sweet, little island voice shouting, 'Michael Droz! Michael Droz! It's me Latta!'

"It turns out the chief was so pissed off at his daughter, he ships her off to a Christian School in Adelaide."

Nicky looks at us both in disbelief saying, "Get the fuck out of here. Now you're bullshitting me."

I look Nicky in the eye replying, "No, no Nicky, it's all fucking true. I nail hot, little Latta again right there on the fucking ship."

Nicky jumps up hollering. "No fucking way! No fucking way you fucked her on the ship!"

Tex smiles and pours Nicky another Oban. Then he calmly says to Nicky, "Nicky, we all got laid all over the ship. Married officers who didn't want to cheat on their wives rented out their staterooms by the hour."

"What about the fucking captain? What was he fucking doing while all of this was going on?" Nicky seriously asks.

Tex and I laugh. Then I reply, "The captain, Nicky, was leading the fucking way! He was nailing two fucking broads at a time in his Captain's Quarters. Wild Bill was a fucking ass master in the first degree!"

Tex and I high five as Nicky says, "You guys got to write a fucking book or make a movie. This kind of shit fucking sells."

Nicky now reaches for the suitcase with the dough. He opens it and starts pulling out rubber banned stacks of hundred dollar bills. Each stack contains ten grand. He threw me twenty stacks. He stands up saying, "Here's your cut Droz."

"Thank you Nicky. What do you want me to do with the smack and hash in my trunk?"

"I'll take the rest of this brick and you guys can keep the rest. Bring the smack with you to my house tonight. Be there by nine and make sure you're armed."

"You got it Nicky."

With that said, Nicky leaves. Tex and I look at each other silently for a moment. Then Tex breaks the silence asking, "You think Antonio's guys are going to try and whack us tonight?"

"Nah, my instincts tell me Nicky's plan will work. If I were in Antonio's shoes, I would be hard pressed to blame Nicky without proof. It would be a big mistake going off halfcocked with a psychopath like Nicky. If I suspected Nicky, I would bide my time being friendly until I knew for sure. In any case, we'll both be prepared if I'm wrong."

FOR BETTER OR FOR WORSE...

It's almost four thirty and we're already hungry for dinner. We take a swim to freshen up and then get ready to head over to my club. Before we can get out the door the phone rings, it's Annmarie. "You miss me?" She asks in her Brooklyn accent while snapping gum.

"Of course I do Annmarie. In fact I was just thinking about you," I wink at Tex as I reply.

"Joanie and I were wondering if you want us to spend the weekend with you guys."

"Hold on Annemarie, I just stepped out of the shower and need to grab a towel."

I put my hand over the receiver asking Tex quietly, "You want to get some pussy, or do you want to go eat at the club?"

"Hmm, that's a tough one Droz. The food at the club is really good. Can't we do both?"

I think for a second and then nod my head replying, "Why not?"

I take my hand off the receiver continuing my conversation with Annemarie. "Sure Annemarie, but we got some things to do first. What time do you plan on coming over?"

"After our rendezvous with the girls, say midnight?"

"That should work. We'll be looking forward to it.

"Me and Joanie are too, if you know what I mean," Annmarie giggles replying.

"Cool. Then we'll see you girls around midnight. If we're not back yet, I'll leave the screen door on the patio unlocked for you. You and Joanie can hang out there until we get home."

"Okay Droz, but don't keep us waiting, or we'll start without you," She teasingly replies.

My eyebrows rise along with my dick as we say our goodbyes. After I hang up, I say, "These chicks are really fucking cool Tex. They don't give us any fucking hassles whatsoever. No bullshit like where are you going? What are you doing? Who are you with?"

"You're right Droz. They are cool. Let's hope they stay that way. Are we ready to go? Because I'm starving."

"First, we need to get the rest of the hash out of the trunk and put this money away." We both go outside and quickly unload the hashish. Then we drop our cut into our floor safe. When we're done, I lock up the house and we head to my club. I don't think twice about driving around with a trunk load of heroin. Why should I? I got Rocco protecting me, right? It's barely after five, and the parking lot's already half-full. Ozzie and Mickey greet us both with hugs. Maloney sees us walk in and fills two frosty mugs with draft beer. Putting them on a coaster, he cheerfully says with his big Irish smile, "How are you two hooligans doing?"

"We're loving life Mahoney."

"That's good to hear boys. That's how it should be at your age. I hope you boys brought your appetite. A couple of the fellas went swordfish fishing last night and caught a whopper of a fish. They said it dragged them up and down the coast for half the night. How about I have the cooks grill you boys up a couple of fat pieces?"

"That sounds too good to be true Tom. Are you down for some swordfish Tex?"

"Of course I'm down. I'm about starved already. Make mine a double order Tom."

Maloney laughs saying, "You got an appetite just like Billy, Tex. We also just got in a load of colossal size stone crab claws from Florida City. How about I have Jason bring you boys out a tray before dinner?"

"Stone crab claws? What about the whole crab?" Tex asks.

"The way it works Tex is they're only allowed to take one claw off the crab and then throw it back."

"Dang, they throw the little critter back in the water with only one claw? What happens when the poor fella runs into a two clawed one?"

"He runs," Tom replies.

The three of us laugh really hard as Maloney motions to Jason. Jason comes over to the bar with a big smile saying, "If you're getting the stone crab claws you have to try the mustard sauce."

"That's right Jason. The mustard sauce is fantastic boys. Get the cooks to grill Droz a big piece of swordfish and a double order for Tex."

"Okay Tom," Jason replies and goes puts in our order.

We make quick work of our first beer and Mahoney gladly supplies another. It isn't long before Jason returns with a large tray full of stone crab claws. They're sitting on a bed of ice with a bowl of mustard sauce sitting in the middle. The claws are cracked and ready to eat. Tex and I go full force at them. After a few moments, Mahoney walks over asking, "How you like them boys?"

Neither one of us can speak because our mouths are so full, so we just nod mumbling, "Mmm." It didn't take long before there was nothing left on the tray but a bunch of empty shells. We would have gotten more, but Jason comes out of the back with dinner. The grilled swordfish portions are gigantic! Tex smiles when Jason puts down his double order. The swordfish comes with a salty crusted baked potato and a fresh tomato salad. Halfway through dinner, Georgie and Billy come walking out of the back. Jason is right behind them carrying another big tray of stone crab claws. They sit down beside us, and Mahoney gets them both a frosty mug of beer. Billy picks his beer up first taking a big gulp. The thick head of his draft sticks to his Fu Manchu mustache.

"Are you enjoying your dinner boys?" Georgie asks in an upbeat tone.

"You better believe it Georgie," Tex says between bites.

"Unbelievable Georgie," I quickly add.

Georgie smiles as he casually says. "They don't serve sword-fish in prison."

Billy sucks down a crab claw adding, "You won't be seeing any of these babies in stir either. I hope the both of you are stay-ing out of trouble."

"Sure we are Billy. Why you ask?"

"We're worried about you two. This place is turning out to be worse than New York."

Georgie takes a slug of beer and then says, "Every time we turn on the news there's another drug deal gone bad and people ending up dead. On the five o'clock news tonight, there were three more drug related homicides. A father, a son, and some young girl were all brutally murdered over drugs, right Billy?"

Billy nods his head and downs his beer. He motions for Mahoney to bring him another before saying, "The news said they're all Colombians. Part of a drug cartel fighting some kind of turf war down here. You guys hear anything about that?"

"We aint heard a thing Billy. All we do is smoke a little weed, drink beer, and bang chicks," I reply.

"That's good to hear Michael. After burying your father and mother the last thing we want to do is bury you guys too," Billy replies.

My food goes down with a gulp. Georgie and Billy drop the subject after that. They probably feel they're doing their duty playing father to me. It also makes me really miss my parents.

Friday nights are really busy at the club, so Georgie and Billy politely excuse themselves. I give Mahoney and Jason a C note tip and we leave. In the car, Tex says, "Nicky's plan worked. They think the murders are part of a drug war."

"Well at least the cops do Tex. We'll see later if Antonio's people bought it."

Tex nods. We now go back to the house to take a piss and arm ourselves. In Karachi, there's a myth about the word assassin coming from the word hashish. The myth says assassins would get really ripped on hashish before heading out on their mission, so Tex and I sit down and tilt the glass a few times before leaving.

When we get to Nicky's house, he's outside waiting for us. He has a big black shopping bag in his hand. Nicky's has on a light blue "Life is a Beach" tee shirt, and sporting a big smile. "You like my fucking shirt?" Nicky proudly asks.

"I guess," I reply.

"Hell yeah I like your shirt Nicky. I want one. Where did you get it?" Tex laughs saying.

"I'm glad to hear that Tex because I got one for you and Droz."

Nicky reaches down into his shopping bag saying, "Here you go boys. I got a large one for you Droz, and I got a jumbo the fucking elephant one for Tex. I picked them up at surf shop down on the beach. Come on, put them on. We'll all look like douche bag tourists together."

We change our shirts while Nicky laughs saying, "My wise guy friends picking up the hooch tonight will get a real fucking kick out of this. I got some extra ones for them to take back to Brooklyn. I got some news too."

"Good news or bad news?" I anxiously reply.

"Let's get on the road, and I'll clue you boys in on our way to the port."

We all pile into the Lincoln and head towards Miami. "So, what's up Nicky?" I ask.

"A fucking Spanish guy showed up unannounced knocking at my door. I answer with one hand on the doorknob and the other on my pistol. He introduces himself as one of Antonio's friends named Eduardo. He asks me if he can come in. I look right and left to make sure he didn't have any other cockroaches with him. Everything looked cool, so I let the prick in. All calm like Eduardo asks me what happened to the drop this afternoon. All calm like, I put my gun in his face saying, 'What happened? I'll tell you what the fuck happened you cocksucker. I showed up with the fucking hooch like I'm supposed to, and nobody was fucking home. You Colombian dirt bags fucked me over. Now my people are up my ass looking for their fucking money. You got my fucking money Eduardo?' I shook him up pretty fucking bad. He begs me not to shoot him and to please let him call Antonio, so I let him. When Eduardo finally gets a hold of him, he starts babbling in Spanish. Then he hands me the phone with his hand shaking. Antonio says, 'Don't shoot Eduardo Nicky. You'll get paid.'

"I stay calm but pissed telling him, 'Your men left me holding the fucking bag today Antonio. What the fuck happened?'

"'I go home to be with my family and unfortunately some people see this as an opportunity to hurt me. I won't burden you with the details Nicky. Go through with what we talked about and we'll work out the dollars later.'

"That sounded good to me, so I told Antonio cool. We say our goodbyes, and I hand the phone back to Eduardo. Eduardo makes a speedy exit. Bottom-line, maybe they fucking bought it, or maybe they didn't. Ah what the fuck. You can't live forever anyway, right boys?"

The three of us nod our heads laughing, and then I say, "It was on the five o'clock news Nicky. The cops think the fucking murders were part of a drug turf war."

"Well that's good to hear. At least we fooled the cops."

When we get to the port, the security guard smiles and let us by. Again, I am amazed at how busy this place is. Cars, trucks, ships, and people are all moving about with a sense of purpose. Nicky spots his two wise guy friends from Brooklyn and tells me to park the car over by their truck. They're pretty easy to spot. They're the only two pasty looking white guys around. The three of us pop out of my Lincoln together bringing big smiles from Nicky's friends. Both men are dressed in jeans and sporting the traditional wife beater tee shirts. One of them says, "Nicky you cocksucker, I can't believe you aint fucking dead yet."

The other guy now says, "What the fuck's up with those tee shirts Nicky?"

"We're disguised as douche bag tourists. I got you guys a couple to wear on the way home. Meet my new crew members, Droz and Tex," Nicky replies smiling.

"Pleased to meet you guys, I'm Donnie and this is my best friend Joey."

We all exchange kisses and hugs. Donnie's about six feet tall with slicked back, short, black hair. He's got tattoos going up and down both arms. Joey's a bit shorter with long, black, hair pulled back tight into a ponytail. He also has tattoos and a gold-hooped earing through his left ear.

Nicky now says, "As far as being dead, the night's still fucking young. Let's see what goes down tonight with these fucking Colombians. You guys are fucking packing, right?"

"Of course we're fucking packing Nicky. You're expecting a problem with these spics, or what?" asks Donnie.

"Probably not Donnie, but you can never tell with these Spanish cocksuckers."

Joey spits on the ground and says, "You got that right Nicky. I hate dealing with all the fucking spics and niggers back in Brooklyn. They're a bunch of backstabbing motherfuckers. They'd kill their own mother for a fucking dime bag."

Everybody nods their heads agreeing. I think to myself, "Can't trust the spics and niggers? You can't trust Nicky!"

Nicky uses his favorite line now, "You got my fucking money Donnie?"

"What the fuck you think Nicky? Joey, go in the truck and get Nicky his fucking money."

Joey goes around to the back of the truck and opens it up. He pulls down a duffle bag and brings it back to Nicky. "You counted this twice, right?" Nicky asks.

"Of course you untrustworthy prick. Three times in fact. Just to be sure I didn't short you." Donnie indignantly replies.

"Who the fuck are you kidding Donnie? You counted it three fucking times to make sure you didn't overpay me you cheap cocksucker. At the price I'm giving you this pure shit for, you'll make a fucking fortune."

Donnie pats Nicky on the back saying, "No shit Nicky. Nobody got prices like you. Nobody up north got a connection like you. You told us this will be a steady thing, so we aint even going to cut it."

"Our Manhattan clients will pay top dollar for pure shit like this," Joey adds.

Nicky tells me to toss the duffle bag into the backseat. I lift the bag up and throw it over my shoulder. Four and a half million dollars is pretty fucking heavy. Nicky tells his friends to leave the back of their truck open and follow us. Nicky guides me to the same berthing area we made the last coke deal in. Antonio's men are all standing around in a group. Nicky pats me on the leg saying, "Pop the trunk. Then you guys follow me."

Nicky motions to his friends to stay put while we swagger over to Antonio's men. In perfect English, one of Antonio's men introduces himself. "Hello Nicky. My name is Hector. I will be handling this deal for you. Is that the truck you want loaded?"

"Yup, that's the truck Hector."

Hector speaks Spanish to his crew and they go to work.

"I got the smack in the trunk," Nicky tells Hector.

"Antonio told me to be expecting it."

Hector whistles to one of his men and he jogs to a parked black Camaro. He starts it up and drives it over to my car. When he gets out, he opens up his trunk and unloads the heroin from my car into his. Meanwhile, Hector's men are putting the finishing touches on the back of the truck. This time they pack it in tight with crates labeled "100% Colombian Coffee." The deal finishes without a hitch. Nicky shakes hands with Hector, and then we walk over to Nicky's friends. "We're all done," Nicky tells his boys.

They both smile and Donnie says, "If all goes as planned we'll be back next week."

Nicky nods. Then they put on their "Life is a Beach" tee shirts and leave. On the way home in the car Nicky says, "You just made yourself four hundred grand Droz. So, you like working for me, or would you prefer working for one day you'll disappear Rocco?"

"Of course I'd rather work for you Nicky. I feel like I can trust you more," I reply. Nicky nods his head smiling as I light up a joint. Let's face it. Nicky has been good to me and Tex, but he might only be being good to us because he still needs us. Then again, there's always the possibility the three of us are really becoming friends. One thing I know for sure. As long as Nicky's luck with the Colombians and the law holds up, we'll all continue to prosper greatly.

When we get back to Nicky's house, I let Tex carry the duffle bag in. "How about some black coffee and anisette," Nicky asks.

We both reply, "Sure."

We take a seat at the kitchen table as Nicky makes the espresso. When it's done, he grabs a bottle of anisette from his liquor cabinet. As I sip my espresso, I remind myself life is good and Nicky aint so bad either. Nicky pours us all a shot of anisette saying, "I propose a toast to loyalty. Remember there's no statute of limitations on murder, and we've already shared a few. If we aint going to be loyal to each other we might as well shoot it out now. Agreed?"

Tex and I nod our heads agreeing. Then we all tap glasses and down our shots. "Since we all agree how important loyalty is, I'll tell you a little story. Light up another bone Droz."

Nicky savors his espresso as I light up a bone. I pass the joint to Nicky, and he starts his story. "A while back a problem arose while we were dealing heroin for Frankie. Frankie kept his shit stashed in a warehouse by the Hudson River in Yonkers. It was business as usual until we started getting fucking complaints from our customers. They said the quality of our smack was getting worse and worse. Now this really pissed Frankie off because he knew the shit he was getting from Charlie Wings was fucking pure. The shit had to be cut up a little bit, or there would be dead junkies all over the fucking place. Even after we stepped on it, Frankie knew he still had the best smack in town. What Frankie didn't know is that somebody was fucking with it in the warehouse. When Frankie found out, he wanted blood and started accusing everybody around him."

Tex interrupts as he takes the joint from Nicky saying, "Sounds like you got a weasel in the hen house Nicky, and everybody's getting blamed for him."

Nicky chuckles and takes another shot of anisette. Then he sips his espresso before replying, "You're right about that Tex. It takes just one fucking asshole in the crew to get us all whacked. I didn't blame Frankie for what he's thinking. It's the nature of our fucking business. Deal with it, or get yourself a day job."

We all laugh heartedly at that notion! Then Nicky continues. "So anyway we're all fucking scumbags in Frankie's eyes until we find out who the real fucking scumbag is, so after Frankie cools down I get him alone and suggest we stake out the warehouse. Frankie agrees, so the next fucking night we do just that. I take Sally and Vinnie with me because I knew it aint one of them. About three in the morning, a car we don't recognize pulls up to the back door. A fucking guy gets out wearing a hooded jacket, so we can't tell who it is. He uses a key to get in. Frankie whispers he wants this cocksucker alive. We wait a few minutes and then sneak in the door behind him. Guns drawn, Frankie throws on the lights, and like a fucking cop, I yell freeze! This cocksucker thinks it's the cops and throws up his fucking hands. He got his back to us, so I tell him to turn around slowly and take off his fucking hood. It's fucking Joey, Frankie's son."

"Wow, so Frankie's boy is the weasel in the hen house," Tex says grinning.

"He sure is Tex."

"So what did Frankie do?" I ask.

"What did he fucking do? I'll tell you what he fucking did. Frankie starts yelling at the top of his fucking lungs. 'Why! Why! Why the fuck did you embarrass me like this Joey! Didn't I give you everything?'

"Joey stares down his old man saying, 'That's the problem Dad. You do give me everything. I wanted to earn on my own.'

"Frankie erupts again. 'Earn on your own! You could have asked me for a fucking job you ungrateful son of a bitch! But no! You rather rob me instead! I ought to whack you right fucking here and throw your body in the fucking river! Who the fuck else is involved!'

"The kid clams up like a good little soldier. Frankie couldn't show it, but we knew he was proud of his fucking kid for clamming up. He would have been a lot more embarrassed if Joey just rolled over on his friends. No one wants a fucking rat for a son. A fucking thief you can deal with, but not a fucking rat. That's how my old man felt."

"Mine too," I quickly interrupt. Nicky stirred up all the rotten feelings I'm battling inside me. Here I am sitting at a table making toasts to loyalty while I'm Rocco's little snitch bitch. My old man's looking down at a squealer for a son!

Nicky continues. "Now Frankie says, 'So Joey, you want to be a fucking tough guy? Your old man can play tough guy. Nicky, tie this little son of a bitch to a chair.'

"I follow Frankie's orders and grab Joey by the back of the neck. The kid fights back, so I had to rough him up a little to get him in the chair. Then Vinnie and Sally get some rope and help me tie him in. I start wondering to myself, 'How far is Frankie willing to go to get his kid to fucking talk?' I didn't have to wonder long before Frankie takes out his piece and bang! He blasts one over his kids head. This shakes the kid up. Frankie yells, 'The next one won't miss Joey! I'm fucking warning you! The next bullet goes right through your fucking kneecap! I'll ask you one more fucking time, who's in on this with you?'

"Joey starts crying and mumbles, 'Howie.'

"'Howie Rose?' Frankie asks puzzled. The kid nods. 'Who else Joey, tell me who else is involved?'"

I stay quiet wanting Nicky to continue.

"Joey starts crying harder, so Frankie hands him a handkerchief saying, 'Just tell me who else son and it'll all be over.'

"The kid takes a deep breath and says, 'Bobby Santori before he died.'

"Frankie looks at me knowing exactly what I'm thinking, so he quickly says, 'I won't do it Nicky, and neither will you. Just get it out of your fucking mind.'

"Then I tell him, 'We're all going to hell anyway Frankie. If this gets out we'll just get there a little quicker and in smaller pieces.'

"Frankie shakes his head and then unties the kid saying, 'I love you Joey. I got friends all over the world you will be safe with. You can never talk about this to anyone. If you do and your uncle Rocco finds out, he'll kill me. Do you understand that Joey?'

"The kid says, 'I understand Daddy. You know I would never want that to happen. I love you too. That's why Howie and I never said a word to anyone. Don't you worry about Howie's daddy, he's one of us.'

"'I won't worry about Howie, Joey.' Then Frankie hugs his kid while giving me a look telling me to kill Howie.'

"Then Frankie says, 'Right now I want to get you out of here Joey and away from this shit before you end up like Bobby. Okay?'

"The kid feeling relieved his ordeal is over, hugs his father and says, 'Okay.'

"Before I can even get to Howie shit happens. His mother finds dope and a syringe in his room. She takes it right to the old man demanding he find out where the fucking kid got it, so old man Rose has his boys find the kid and drag him home. He knew Howie smoked weed, but never suspected anything like this. Howie immediately rolls on his friends. He tells his father you and him were selling weed for a black guy in southwest

Yonkers named Shayne. He said Shayne fucking pressured you two into selling the smack for him."

I can't keep quiet any longer yelling, "That rat fuck Howie lied and got my best friend fucking killed! Howie fucking knew Shayne hated narcotics! I saw Shayne kill a motherfucker for selling that shit in his neighborhood!"

Nicky laughs saying, "Needless to say, Frankie and I were tickled fucking pink Howie sung that tune. It would have been good riddance for the crew if he hadn't."

"That's all well and good for you fucking guys, but it got my best friend killed!"

"Come on Droz. Calm down and face fucking reality. It was only a matter of fucking time before some young punk in his neighborhood got ambitious and took him out anyway."

Nicky puts his arm around me now saying, "Better him than you right?"

"Of course better him than me Nicky, but fuck Howie, he's a scumbag rat fuck. He got Shayne killed and ratted me out for no fucking reason."

Nicky chuckles before replying, "No fucking reason? He had a couple of good fucking reasons. You just didn't know them."

"Like what fucking reasons Nicky?"

"His biggest reason was he's a fucking junkie. Junkies will do fucking anything to protect their supply."

"You're right about that one Nicky."

"Of course I'm right. Plus all the money he's making with Joey. The dough made from selling heroin makes the weed business you guys had together expendable."

I shake my head saying, "I never suspected Howie of selling heroin and being a fucking junkie Nicky. I wasn't close enough to him to see it for myself. Shayne and I were definitely expendable."

"Glad you see it for what it is Droz. You don't have to like it, but at least you see it. Now learn from it. After Howie spills his guts old man Rose calls your father. Rose's boys grab Shayne when you two show up at the warehouse. Your father and Billy finished off Shayne by the river. Old man Rose's boys disposed of the body. Later that evening Howie did us all a fucking favor and popped one spoon too many. Case fucking closed. That's why your old man retired and got you the fuck out of Yonkers. He was afraid you would end up like Howie. He brought you down here thinking Coral Springs would be safer."

"So much for that fucking thought. It's worse down here than it ever was in fucking Yonkers," I reply.

"It's like the wild west down here," Tex adds.

"My advantage is I got Frankie and Charlie Wings fucking backing me," Nicky says.

"How the fuck did Howie know Joey anyway Nicky?"

Frankie told me they met as kids when old man Rose set up church bazaars in the neighborhood. It turns out old man Rose had a fucking warehouse right near Frankie's. Hanging out with Howie one day at the warehouse, Joey noticed some of his old man's crew coming and going from another warehouse. After a while, they put two and two together. That's when Joey stole the fucking key. He made a copy and found his old man's stash. It was that fucking simple."

"Thank you for telling me all of this Nicky. Now I know you really fucking trust me."

Nicky laughs slapping me on the back saying, "Of course I fucking trust you Droz. Why shouldn't I fucking trust you? What are you going do to me? Rat me out to Rocco?"

The three of us all laugh heartedly together as my guilt for being a rat grows bigger and bigger.

Nicky gets up from the table and grabs the duffle bag full of money. He opens it up and dumps the cash all over the living room floor saying, "There should be four hundred and fifty stacks of hundreds laying there. Each stack should have ten fucking grand in it. Count out your fucking share while I go pinch a loaf for myself. That black coffee got my fucking bowels moving."

Nicky heads to the john and we start counting. As we're counting, we hear Nicky grunting and groaning in the bathroom.

I mean he's really struggling in there. As we're laughing, Tex shouts, "Hey Nicky are you alright? It sounds like you're giving birth."

Nicky keeps grunting and we keep laughing. We hear the bathroom door swing open and Nicky yells, "I thought I'd be nice to you two cocksuckers and keep the door closed. Now let's see who gets the last fucking laugh!"

Tex and I aint afraid; after all we were on a ship sharing stalls with all kinds of foul and disgusting shit doers. Then an odor from the deepest parts of hell penetrates our nostrils! We gag and almost barf it's so bad! Tex and I start yelling, "Mercy flush, mercy flush!"

Nicky's basking in glory sitting on the bowl laughing. He now says, "I told you fucking pricks I'd get the last laugh! Back in fucking Nam they called me the fiend in the latrine."

Nicky doesn't flush until he's done. Tex and I had to open every window in the house. Nicky walks out of the bathroom proclaiming, "I feel like a new man boys. You guys done counting yet?"

"Yeah, were done Nicky," I reply still gagging.

"Good. Now that were all done with business, I think I'll call up an escort service."

"You better wait until the house airs out Nicky, or they'll charge you extra for hazardous duty," Tex says sarcastically.

Nicky laughs and grabs the phone book out of a draw. He calls us both over saying, "You want to fucking talk about hazardous duty Tex? Let me fucking show you who has hazardous duty. Whoever owns these fucking escort services has hazardous duty. They just don't know it yet. Within a fucking month, they'll be either out of fucking business, or under my control. Boy's this is what we call low hanging fruit in our business. Plus you get free fucking pussy. How many girls should I get for us tonight?"

"If you need us to start shaking them down we'll stay Nicky. If you don't, we already got a couple of chick's waiting for us back at the house," I reply.

"I don't need you boys tonight. What I'm going to do now is try out all of the different fucking services. Get friendly with the girls. It's like a fucking reconnaissance mission. Money is what talks to these broads. I'll throw cash at them, and they'll give me all the information I need to take over. The guys running these places all think they're tough guys pushing around broads and johns. They'll crumble like cheap fucking suitcases when we walk in the door. Sally and Vinnie love this shit, so we got to wait for them before we do it anyway. So you two boys go home and enjoy your steady pussy."

I didn't like the feeling I got when Nicky said that. He said it like we were pussy whipped or something, so I ask, "How do know it's our steady pussy Nicky?"

Nicky snickers replying, "Come on Droz. What do you think I was born yesterday? You got two fucking chick's waiting back at your house on a Friday night, right?"

"Right."

"Now tell the truth. It was their idea right?"

Reluctantly, Tex and I nod our heads.

"Need I say more?" Nicky smugly replies.

"You figured that one out pretty good Nicky," Tex says.

"I'll make a bet that their young too, right Tex?"

"Oh yeah Nicky," Tex replies with a big smile.

"Are they Italian?"

"Yup," I reply.

Nicky belly laughs now saying, "You two are taking a bigger risk fucking them two young Italian girls than working with me. I hope it's fucking worth it because if their fathers find out Rocco can't even help you."

Tex and I smile real wide. Then I say, "Believe me when I tell you this Nicky, it's fucking worth it. These two young Italian chicks even do each other."

"Oh no, now you guys are making me sick to my stomach. Please don't tell me you turned these poor young Italian girls into fucking perverts?" Nicky asks dramatically.

"We didn't turn them into perverts Nicky. They like to do it," Tex replies.

"Don't fucking lie to me. You both fucking encouraged it, right?"

"Of course we fucking encouraged it Nicky! What the fuck would you do?" I say.

Nicky shakes his head like he wouldn't. Then he replies, "Do what you want. You're both going to hell anyway. Being pervert child molesters just drop you both down lower in the pit."

"What are you, a fucking priest now Nicky?" I sarcastically ask.

With a very concerned and worrisome tone, Tex asks, "Just for that Nicky? Just for having some fun? We're going to be tortured more in a deeper part of hell?"

Nicky nods his head yes, and asks, "What do you think Tex? The both of you went from ordinary thieves and murderers to no good fucking pervert child molesters."

Nicky has to be fucking kidding, but Tex believes him. This will ruin the night if I can't get Nicky to say it's a joke.

"Come on Tex. Nicky's fucking kidding. Right Nicky; tell Tex you're just kidding."

Nicky frowns shaking his head before answering. "Sorry, but you both added pervert child molester to your long list of sins."

Sorrowful now Tex says to me, "Haven't we already done enough Droz to piss off the man upstairs? I don't think God will punish us anymore than we already got coming for just screwing them. When we get home, we just have to put our foot down and tell them girls to stop fiddling with each other. If they don't listen, we'll have to just stop seeing them. That's all there is to it. My momma and grandma didn't bring up a pervert."

I put both hands on my head in disbelief of what I'm hearing. Tex is brought up God fearing, and Nicky played right into it. Nicky bursts out laughing. "What's so funny Nicky?" Tex asks.

"With all the fucking sins you've already committed in your life, I had you fucking worried about two little cunt lappers?

Nicky gives Tex a playful shove now saying, "You big knuckle-head, just go and fucking enjoy yourself! It would be a fucking sin if you didn't enjoy these two horny young girls munching on each other!"

"Well damn Nicky; you really had me thinking there for a moment."

"I was just fucking with your head Tex. You only pass through this world once, and life surely aint worth living if you can't fuck who you want, right? Personally, if it was me Tex, I would consider the two teenage clam divers a fucking bonus!"

"You got that right Nicky!" Tex says as we all high five each other.

"Now back to fucking business. Did the money count out right?"

"I guess. We didn't count every stack of course, so we won't ultimately know until we do."

"I'll get you guys some counting machines from my friends back in Brooklyn. Fuck Antonio's people. We keep our money inside our own family. Take your cut and go have some fun with your little girlfriends. I'll catch up with you guys later."

"Thanks for all the dough Nicky. I never even seen this much money before I met you," Tex adds.

"I hope we all live long enough to fucking spend it Tex. You never can tell in this fucking business."

On that somber note, we all hug and kiss. Then we throw our dough in pillowcases and leave.

As we pull out of the driveway, I spark up a doobie. We both stay quiet with our own thoughts smoking the joint. I reach to turn on some tunes and Tex stops me saying, "I really like Nicky Droz, and I don't want to see him killed for what he told us tonight."

I take a deep breath pondering for a moment before replying, "I really like Nicky too Tex. He's a pirate like us. I don't want to see him killed either, but you can't serve two masters."

"Are you pulling the Bible on me Droz?"

"Well isn't it relevant here? You know exactly what Jesus said."

"Of course I do. I know it by heart. No servant can serve two masters; for either he will hate the one and love the other, or else he will be loyal to one and despise the other. You cannot serve God and mammon."

"Rocco sure as hell aint God Tex, but Nicky might certainly be fucking mammon. No matter how much we both like Nicky, my instincts are telling me to stay loyal to Rocco."

"You aint steered me wrong yet buddy. If your instincts are telling you to stay loyal to Rocco, then that's what we'll do."

"Good, that's settled. Now let's get our perverted minds on that sweet little pussy waiting for us back home. Pass that joint too, you fucking Bogart. The whole fucking time we've been talking you been bogarting that fucking joint."

Tex chuckles passing me the joint asking, "Do you think we're getting a little lazy Droz?"

"What do mean by lazy Tex?"

"I mean lazy by sticking with these two broads Annemarie and Joanie."

"Are you saying you're getting bored with these two and want to pounce on something strange for a change?"

"I don't know if I would say bored Droz. I'm just worried that we're getting lazy."

"Didn't we both just admit we like these chicks?"

"Yeah I know Droz, but just on principle alone we need a few more broads on our menu."

"You're right Tex. We'll hit the beaches together and find a few more."

"Good idea Droz, and we'll do a little fishing too.

"Hopefully Nicky and Rocco won't bother us."

"Hopefully," Tex replies.

We get home before the girls show up which is a good thing. We need to stash the cash without the girls seeing it. Annemarie and Joanie are both cool, but the less they know the better. After dumping the cash, we take ourselves a quick shower. Still wrapped in our towels we sit around the coffee table eager to smoke some more hash. Before I can cut a piece off the brick the doorbell rings. Tex and I look at each other with a big grin knowing what's coming up next. Tex says, "I aint bored Droz. I'm horny. You cut up that hash while I get the door and give these little ladies a big surprise. Watch their faces light up when I open the door."

Tex drops his towel opening the door shouting, "Come and get it!"

Holy shit its Willie! Tex embarrassingly grabs his towel wrapping it back around him. Laughing my ass off, I invite Willie in. Willie gives us both a blank stare as he cautiously walks in. I close the door behind him and take a seat on the couch next to Tex. With a look of disbelief, Willie shakes his head and then goes off on us in Spanish! Every part of his body is moving at once in a crazy tirade! He reminds me of Ricky Ricardo scolding Lucy. When he calms down, he speaks in English to us in a very disapproving tone. "This isn't funny Droz. Johnny and I were both afraid this would happen to you. So I guess this is your Navy friend I've been hearing about?"

Tex and I are in stitches watching Willie. I catch a breath replying, "Yeah Willie, this is my Navy buddy, Tex. Tex, this is my longtime friend Willie I've told you about."

They both sort of nod at each other. Then I inquisitively ask, "So what were you and Johnny afraid was going to happen to me?"

Willie raises his eyebrows tilting his head saying, "In the Navy you would become someone's butt fuck buddy. Just look at you two. You both obviously have spent one day too many out at sea together. You guys have gone from shipmates to butt mates!"

Tex puts his big arm around me proudly saying, "Oh well, no use in trying to hide it anymore Droz. There you have it Willie, our secrets out in the open. We've come out of the closet."

Willie nods his head like he knew it all along and says, "Now that your dirty little secret is out Tex, what do you have to say for yourself?"

"Well Willie, I'm glad you asked. The way you shuffle your booty around while you're talking sure did make me want to try a Cuban boy. How about you just go back a yonder and take yourself a shower. Then grab yourself a towel and join us here on the couch. We'll all get high a spell and then start to get to know each other a little better. Have you ever had yourself a Cuban boy Droz?"

"Nope, can't say that I have Tex. I'll bet you Willie here aint had himself a real cowboy either, aint that right Willie?"

Willie puts his hand on his hip poking out his booty. Then he puts one finger in his mouth and swirls it around. Swaying his hips in a provocative manner, he points his ass right at us. Then Willie touches his butt with his wet finger and imitates the sound a hot pan makes when it hits water. Acting like a real flaming faggot now, Willie replies, "I thought you boys would never ask! Tie me up and abuse me gringos! Fuck my ass till I cry, and I'm yours forever!"

The three of us are hysterical! When we finally calm down, Tex says, "Take a seat here Willie. We were just about to fire up some hash. We were expecting our girls, so that's why I answered the door naked."

Willie nods his head and waves his hand at Tex, like don't worry about it pal. Willie takes a seat on the couch and I put a chunk of hash on the pin. Tex hits it with the lighter to get it cooking. While the hashish smolders and fills the glass with smoke, Willie says, "Johnny came to see me. He told me everything. He swears he won't fuck up what you set up for him."

"Yeah, well he better not Willie, or we'll never see his ass again."

"These Hawaiians are really that bad Droz?"

"You better believe it Willie."

Willie shrugs his shoulders. As we're talking, the glass has filled with smoke. Tex pushes it over to Willie saying, "Go ahead Willie. You got the first hit. It's pretty powerful stuff, so be careful."

Willie leans over the coffee table and lifts the glass to his lips. He slowly inhales all of the smoke inside. Willie smiles as he lifts his head up from the table. His smile is quickly replaced by a look of strain and pain. Willie's eyes turn beet red. When he can't hold down his hit any longer, he coughs out a cloud of smoke. "Damn I thought my lungs were going to burst!" Willie exclaims.

Tex goes next, and then it's my turn. After my hit, I feel a warm glow permeating through my body. I lean back on the couch, and Willie says, "Damn Droz, this shit is good. That one hit got me zoned already."

"Take another hit Willie and stay a spell," Tex says.

"Man Tex, I would love too, but I have to pick up my girlfriend Mizar from her cousins baby shower. I told her I was coming by to get some weed before I get her. If I don't pick her up she'll come looking for me."

"That's cool Willie. I already bagged an ounce up for you. Let me go get it."

I bring back Willie's bag and toss it to him. "Thank you Droz, how much do I owe you?" Willie asks reaching for his wallet.

"You don't owe me a dime Willie."

"You're too good to me amigo."

"Willie, you gave me a fucking fortune in fancy clothes. If anything, you're too good to me."

We both hug. Then Willie says, "Before I forget, my father wants to invite you to Grandpa's birthday party. He'll be 84."

"Wow, God Bless him Willie. He sure doesn't look it. When's the party?"

It's on Sunday. Meet us at my house around eight. From there we'll go to the port where my father said he has something really special planned for him. Bring Tex along too."

"Cool Willie. We'll be there."

"I appreciate the invite Willie," Tex says.

"No problem Tex."

"Take another hit of hash before you go Willie while I cut you a chunk off the brick."

"Oh cool Tex. Thanks a lot man."

Tex cuts Willie a nice size chunk and hands it to him. We all hug and say our goodbyes. About five minutes later, there's another knock at the door. Tex takes a peek out the window this time, and sure enough, it's the girls. Tex answers the door boldly dropping his towel again! The girls giggle, and Joanie leads Tex by his dick into the living room bragging, "Better than a leash Annmarie."

"Whoa, whoa, slow down there baby girl! I don't want to see the other end of that thing!" Tex shouts.

Annemarie and I laugh while Joanie exclaims, "Oh, I'm sorry Tex! I didn't realize it was that fragile!"

"Ah heck Joanie, I'm just kidding with you. You can pull on that bad boy all day long if you want. I've been tugging on it my entire life, and I aint found the other end yet."

We all laugh and sit down to smoke some hash. It's the girls first time, so we break them in easy. Once they're good and stoned, we take them out on the patio for a moonlight swim. Then we cuddle with the girls naked on the steps of the pool. I gaze up at the night's sky and it's full of stars. It reminds me once again of my nights out at sea. When we go back into the house, the girls pull a big surprise on us. Instead of giving us a lesbian show like they usually do, Tex and I are both escorted separately to our rooms. When Annmarie gets me there she says, "Joanie and I decided we would do things different tonight."

"So I see."

"We thought it would be nice to be a couple for once."

"That's cool with me Annmarie."

I'm no fucking dummy. I know what's up here. Annmarie and Joanie want to see if we want them as girlfriends instead of just fuck toys. I've been starting too really dig Annmarie anyway. I'm sure Keona and Teresa Sue pursue their own emotional and physical needs when I'm not around, so tonight I will do the same.

I run my hands gently through Annmarie's hair pushing it back from her face. Annmarie's a very beautiful girl, so I stare into her pretty green eyes telling her that. Then softly brushing my cheek across hers, I whisper, "I'm glad we're alone."

Annmarie smiles wide as she caresses my body. Laying me down on the bed she begins kissing and licking me all over. By the time she works her way back to my neck, I'm very aroused. Our lips meet in a deep sensuous kiss. Then I return the favor by kissing and licking my way around her sexy little curves. I love Annmarie's curves, so I take my time showing her. When I get to her breasts, I tease her nipples by running my tongue around her areolas. Annmarie has big areolas, and now they're covered with sexy little goose bumps. When her nipples get nice and hard from my teasing, I gently suck them into my mouth. While I'm sucking on one breast I softly use the palm of my hand in a circular motion stimulating her other nipple. Annmarie lets out tiny moans of pleasure and begins pushing my head down her body. I slowly kiss and lick my way between her luscious thighs. Once there I kiss and lick her everywhere except her pussy. I brush my lips across her pubic hairs teasing Annmarie even more. Moving her hips up and down Annmarie guides my face to her pretty little snatch. I kiss her pussy like I'm kissing her lips. Then slowly use my tongue in a long lapping motion up and down her pussy. Annmarie purrs arching her back. She tries using her hands to bury my face in her sweetness, but I grab them preventing her. I continue slowly licking her like this until she begins shuddering. Then I suck Annmarie's pussy into my mouth and swish my tongue around her clit. She grabs my head letting out a sultry moan shaking in orgasm. Annmarie's really hot now, so I swirl my tongue around her swollen clit and suck it until she erupts into multiple orgasms. I rise up from between Annmarie's thighs with a wet smile. Then I move up her body putting my knees on both sides of her head. I rub my big dick all over her pretty little face and playfully slap her with it. I tell Annmarie to treat the head of my cock like she treats Joanie's pussy. When she finds the sensitive spot behind the head, she hones in. Annmarie drives me wild with her sucking and licking motions. When I can't take it any longer, I pull my cock out of her mouth and spread her legs. I slowly penetrate her inch by inch, teasing Annmarie until she begs me for more, but I don't listen. I just keep teasing her. Soon I feel Annmarie's hungry little pussy contracting around the head of my dick, so I thrust my entire length deeply into her tight wet pussy. Annmarie moans loudly shaking in another huge orgasm. Our two bodies become one as we passionately grind each other into bliss. Drenched in sweat and totally spent, we fall asleep locked in each other's arms.

DIVIDED LOYALTIES...

Annmarie and I wake up the next morning cuddled in love. Tex and Joanie were already swimming in the pool. I could tell by watching them play together their relationship had changed for the better too. Annmarie and I jump in and swim around for a while too. Then I cook everyone a big breakfast. After we're done eating, the girls clean up while Tex and I walk out on the patio to talk.

"Last night was sure different, wasn't it Droz? Tex asks.

"You can say that again Tex. I don't know if it's a good thing yet, or a bad thing. But I think they think they're our girlfriends now."

We both shake our heads in disbelief. Then Tex says, "I hope everything went right for Johnny."

"You and me both, we'll find out quick if it doesn't. Bad news travels fast."

"That's for sure Droz."

"I'll wait until tomorrow to tell Rocco about what I found out from Nicky. I'm sure he'll be calling us as soon as he finds out Bennie the Bookie got robbed."

"Good idea. That will take Rocco's mind right off of it. He'll be patting you on the back instead of sticking a hot poker up your ass."

I laugh replying, "It might be better Tex if we aint around in case things go south for Johnny this morning. Maybe we ought to take the girls to the beach."

"Sounds good to me buddy."

We take the girls down to Deerfield Beach and relax the entire day hoping the best for Johnny. We don't come home until twilight. Then we take a shower, change clothes, and head right back out to the Sweden House. A giant top of the line buffet we all thoroughly enjoy.

When we get home, I roll up a nice fat joint mixed with pakalolo, Thai Sticks, and hash. I break the weed up first and then soften up a chunk of hash with my lighter. I knead it all together and roll it up. Then I lightly run my lighter up and down the joint melting the hash into the weed. That's the key to a good hash joint. We all go out on the patio with some beers and toke up. The joint burns for over half an hour, and gets us really, really, stoned. We ended the night by going to our respective rooms like couples again.

Cuddled up sleeping, I'm awakened by the phone. I peek at the clock. It's before seven. I pick up the phone knowing its Rocco.

"Hello?"

"He stood the motherfuckers up! That scumbag motherfucker never picked up the Rossetti brothers!"

Nicky's screaming through the phone wakes up Annemarie. I put my finger to my lips letting her know to keep quiet.

"Don't fucking lie to me Droz! Is that prick with you?"

"No Nicky. Just Tex and the girls are here."

"Do you know where the fuck he is?"

"I aint heard from Johnny since we were all here together."

"You fucking better not be covering for him Droz! You better remember where your fucking loyalties are!"

"Calm the fuck down Nicky. I'm not covering for him. I aint got no fucking idea where the fuck he is. For all we know he might have gotten pinched. If he got fucking pinched holding something he would be too scared to call his father."

Nicky's silent. Then in a calm voice says, "Damn Droz, I didn't even think of that. I'll reach out to somebody and find out. If the cocksucker calls you or comes over I can count on you to do the right thing, right?"

"Of course you can Nicky; if I see him I'll even hold him for you. But don't you fucking question my loyalty again, capisce?"

There's silence on the other end again. Then Nicky sarcastically says, "Look, I'm sorry I hurt your feelings you little pussy. My cousin got me in a blind fucking rage right now."

"No apologies needed Nicky. I understand all too fucking well how Johnny can piss somebody off," I chuckle replying.

"Yeah, no shit. Let me go see what I can find out. If you don't hear back from me you and Tex meet me at my house around 9 PM Monday."

"You got it Nicky." I hang up the phone.

Then Tex walks in the bedroom saying, "Nicky's a tad bit testy this morning."

"That's his fucking problem Tex, and he tried to make it mine."

"Who was that on the phone?" Annemarie asks worried.

"Johnny's cousin Nicky."

"Why's he so mad?" Joanie asks concerned.

I think to myself, "If I tell the girls to shut up and mind their business, it will only fuel their curiosity," so I give off a great big sigh saying, "Johnny promised to meet his cousin and some of his friends last night and he stood them up."

Annemarie and Joanie look at each other. Then Joanie says, "We know where Johnny is."

"Really, where is he?" I ask surprised.

"Johnny and Stacy rented a room on the beach last night," Annmarie replies.

"You know that for sure Annmarie?"

"We both do. Stacy told us all about it last night. She said Johnny's been real nice to her."

"She thinks he's going to propose," Joanie gleefully adds while glancing at Tex.

"Don't you think that's wonderful Droz," Annemarie chimes in all bubbly and starry eyed. I look to Tex for help and he quickly says, "Don't look at me Droz, I didn't ask you that question."

"Well isn't it Tex?" Joanie shoves Tex asking. Staring at us with big puppy dog eyes, the girls await our answer. Sometimes you just have to roll with the punches, and this is one of those times, so we both hug our girls replying, "Of course we do."

The girls give us loving smooches and we head for our respective bedrooms. Then there's a very loud knocking at the door. I put my finger across my lips letting the girls know to keep quiet. I tiptoe down the hallway and peek out the window. I see two big mugs standing at my door. They looked to be in their mid-thirties dressed in classy suits.

"Who is it?" I gruffly ask.

"Am I speaking to Droz?" A gentlemanly voice answers.

"Yeah, now what can I do for you?"

"We're here to escort you and your friend Tex to Angelo Santori's house."

"Go fuck yourself. I know where Angelo lives. We'll get dressed and go over there ourselves."

"We would appreciate it if you don't make this any harder than it has to be."

My mind is racing a mile a minute. Could it be I've already out lived my usefulness? Tex storms out of the bedroom with our 45's as I think quickly replying, "Look guys, you woke us up. Give us some time to get our shit together."

"You guys have ten minutes. And please, don't try anything foolish."

Now the phone starts ringing. I pick up the phone, and it's Rocco. "Don't give my men any trouble Droz."

"Why the fuck are you sending two fucking Guidos over here Rocco?" I indignantly reply.

"I wouldn't call them Guidos if I were you Droz. Just go along peacefully, and there won't be any trouble."

"What the fuck's going on Rocco?" Rocco hangs up on me. I think quietly for a moment. Then I look at Tex saying, "If Rocco wants us dead I don't think he would knock on the door. This is about Johnny. I guess they're trying to let us know they mean fucking business. We'll get dressed and let these two mugs do their jobs."

Tex nods his head. The girls are going to know Stacy disappeared, so I turn to them saying, "Johnny's missing."

"Missing? What do you mean missing?" Annemarie asks confused.

"Is Stacy missing too?" Joanie worriedly asks.

"I don't know Joanie. I have to go over to Johnny's father's house with Tex. You both are welcome to stay here as long as you want. If we take too long, I have a spare key in my top dresser drawer. Lock up when you leave."

Tex walks in my room dressed and ready to go. We kiss the girls goodbye and head to the door. I peek out the window before we leave and see the two men standing by a brown Fleetwood Brougham. They're both shooting the shit and smoking a cigarette. We walk outside and I say, "Good morning gentlemen." They snicker and take another drag then extinguish their smokes under their $500 shoes.

"Both of you put your hands on the car so we can pat you down," One of the guys says.

We oblige. Then I say, "Those are nice suits you're wearing. If you're interested I got a connection for designer threads."

They ignore me as they finish searching us and tell us to get in the car. As we're pulling away, I sarcastically ask, "Are you two always this sociable?"

No answer. Then the guy in the passenger seat really belts one out. His fart smells so fucking bad he had to shit his pants. Tex and I start gagging. The driver quickly rolls down the windows shouting, "Madone Joey! We're supposed to get these fucking guys to Angelo's house alive!"

"Hey Franco, what the hell you want from me? It was that fucking pickled herring they gave me this morning. I think it was fucking bad."

"You always blame the fucking food Joey. Last night you let loose in the restaurant and blamed the fucking clams. I ate the clams and there wasn't a thing wrong with them. I think you got a flatulation problem Joey."

"I aint got no fucking flatulation problem Franco. Now roll up the fucking windows before you mess up my hair."

Tex and I find great humor in these two. When we pull up to Johnny's house, I see Rocco's Lincoln, a pink Coupe De Ville, and a red Porsche convertible parked in the driveway. Franco parks his Cadillac behind Rocco's Lincoln and says, "Okay fellas, get out nice and easy."

We get out of the car and they escort us to the front door. Joey rings the bell. Carina opens the door with a big smile saying, "Hello boys."

"Hi Carina, this is my friend Tex," I reply.

Carina looks up at Tex saying, "My, my, I guess everything really is bigger in Texas."

"Pleased to meet you ma'am," Tex charmingly replies.

Carina smiles at our two escorts asking, "Would you boys like some more coffee, or maybe something else to eat?"

"No thank you Mrs. Santori," Joey replies.

"Remember you can always ring the doorbell if you need anything."

"Thank you Mrs. Santori," Joey replies.

Carina lets me and Tex in shutting the door behind us. She grabs a broom conveniently located by the door and starts swinging it like a Louisville Slugger! We cover up as Carina's yelling, "I know you two know where he is! You both better not lie to me!"

Angelo comes running down the hallway hollering, "Carina, Carina, calm down, calm down! You don't want to kill them before they can tell us everything."

Out of breath from her onslaught, Carina subsides from the attack. Her anger quickly turns to tears and Angelo consoles her in his arms. He looks at us pissed off. Then he shakes his head saying, "I need this? You two think I need this?"

Tex and I look at Angelo like we don't know what you're talking about.

"The two of you follow me," Angelo gruffly says turning down the hallway with his arm around his sobbing wife. When we get into the kitchen, I couldn't help smiling when I see Rocco. Sitting next to Rocco, I figure is Bennie the Bookie, his wife, and Stacy's mother. The table's full of all kinds of Jewish foods. I see Lox and bagels of course, along with an array of smoked fish. There are also knishes, potato salad, coleslaw, and a large tray of Danishes. Oh yeah, and pickled Herring. I figure I might stay away from that. Carina and Angelo invite us to sit down at the table with them.

"Would you boys like some coffee?" Carina kindly asks like nothing ever happened.

"Sure Carina, how about you Tex?"

"I'll have a cup too Mrs. Santori."

"Oh just call me Carina, Tex. Help yourselves to some food boys," She replies graciously.

Angelo sits down at the table and smiles saying, "There's plenty of food here boys, so don't be shy. Our guests had it catered for us all the way from Miami. This is Bennie, his wife Marsha, and their daughter Sarah."

Tex and I stand up to shake hands with everyone. The three of them smile and are quite cordial considering the situation. Bennie is a short, portly man; I'd say in his mid-sixties. His wife is tall, skinny, and about the same age as Bennie. Sarah isn't bad looking at all. I can see where Stacy gets her looks from. Sarah has long, dark, curly hair, green eyes, nice lips, and a curvy body. I'd say she's in her forties, but very fuckable. Bennie looks like he aint got a fucking dime. He's wearing old clothes and wears no jewelry. This is in total contrast to his wife and daughter. Both of them have on expensive new clothes and lots of gold jewelry. As I am giving Tex a crash course on the Jew food Bennie the Bookie stands up speaking in his strong New York Jewish accent saying, "Eat boys, enjoy." Bennie is being so nice I can't help feeling we're being fattened up for the kill. While Tex and I dig in, the rest of them make small talk. Marsha and Sarah are complaining how there are no good women's clothing stores down here. Carina complains she has to drive twenty miles to get a decent loaf of Italian bread. Rocco, Angelo, and Bennie, are all shooting the shit about horses. After we clean our plates twice, Bennie asks politely, "How about a nice freshly baked Danish boys? We have cheese, poppy and prune."

"Sure Bennie, prune's my favorite," I reply.

"What kind of Danish would you like Tex?" Bennie asks.

"Hmm, they all look so good Bennie. How about I try one of each?"

Bennie laughs turning to his wife saying, "You see Marsha; I'm not the only one who can eat three Danishes."

Marsha looks at Tex smiling and then frowns looking at Bennie saying, "If you looked like Tex Bennie, I wouldn't complain."

Carina chokes on her coffee while the rest of us try not to laugh. Bennie fakes a laugh replying, "My wife the comedian, if she doesn't complain she isn't happy. Well now that everyone has enjoyed a wonderful breakfast, let's get down to why we are here. Our granddaughter Stacy along with your son Johnny is missing. There weren't any phone calls or messages left with you, right Sarah?"

"Not a word Daddy. Stacy did say she would be seeing your son Johnny last night, but that's it."

Carina looks at Angelo to say something. Angelo takes a sip of coffee and says, "Well Sarah unfortunately my son Johnny is known not to come home without calling. I tell him all the time if you're going to stay out all night, please let us know. It worries my wife sick when he does this.

Carina holds Angelo's hand for support before dramatically saying, "It does, it really does Sarah, and the little son of a bitch knows it too. I'm telling you Angelo I just can't take it anymore. This kid is going to be the death of me." Carina now bursts into tears. Her eyes are like fucking water pistols. Now she pleads with me. "Michael, your mother is watching and listening, so don't you dare embarrass her by lying. Do you know where my son and Stacy are?"

Rocco is just sitting back sipping his coffee taking in the drama. Still chewing my prune Danish I reply sincerely, "Carina, it breaks my heart seeing you upset like this, but I aint got a clue where they are. The last time I seen Johnny was Friday morning. He came by and wanted us to go to the track with him. We already had plans with a couple of girls to go to the beach, so we didn't go. I haven't heard a word from him since."

Carina's tears turn into snake venom as she gives me the evil eye saying, "Swear on your mother's grave Michael you don't know where they are."

Without blinking, I raise my right hand replying, "I swear."

Carina stands up and smacks me in the head yelling, "You're lying! I know you're lying! You see Angelo! You see! This is your fucking fault!"

Angelo pointing to his chest in disbelief replies, "My fault, how's this my fault Carina?"

"You and every rotten father like you! You teach these kids to keep their mouths shut! You don't tell me anything, and your son never tells me anything! The two of you use me like a nigger to cook, clean, and wash your dirty fucking clothes!"

"You don't have a maid Carina?" Marsha shockingly asks.

"No, I don't have a fucking maid Marsha, and I don't want a fucking maid! I just want to be appreciated!"

Carina starts really balling now as Angelo shakes and rubs his head. Then he says, "For crying out loud Carina, how in the hell did we get on this subject?"

Rocco now suggests the men go out on the patio to talk. Marsha looks down her nose at Rocco, and Bennie says he needs to use the bathroom. He'll meet us out there in a few minutes. As soon as we get out on the patio, I go on the offensive. "What's up with sending those two meatheads to my house? You guys don't trust me to come when I'm called for?"

Angelo pats me on the back replying, "Just appearances Droz, we want Bennie to think we're taking this as serious as he is. He may not look it, but he's really fucking pissed. He wanted to send his own crew to come get you. I backed him off by telling him it was my son that caused the problem, so I'll handle it. He couldn't refuse me when I put it that way."

Nodding my head I reply, "What's all the fuss about anyway? Johnny's out fucking Stacy all night, big fucking deal."

Rocco looks at me like the Grim Reaper saying, "Cut your fucking bullshit Droz. Where's Johnny, and where's the fucking money?"

"No clue Rocco. I aint seen Johnny since Friday morning," I quickly reply.

"How about you cowboy, do you know where my son is?" Angelo asks.

"Like old Droz here says Angelo, we aint seen Johnny since Friday morning."

The patio door opens, and Bennie joins us. He takes out a fat cigar and lights it. Bennie takes a few puffs to get it going and then boldly states, "Boy's I know my granddaughter and Angelo's boy robbed me of a large sum of money. More important right now is my granddaughter and Johnny is missing. This is causing an enormous amount of stress on both of our families. If there's anything either one of you can tell me that will help me find her it will be deeply appreciated."

As sincere as I can be, I reply, "With all due respect Bennie, we can only imagine how bad you feel being betrayed like that. But like we said inside, the last time we saw Johnny was Friday morning."

Bennie chews on his cigar scowling at us. Then with dead man's eyes, he says, "Play it your way boys. For now Rocco, I'll leave this in your hands. I'm sure you won't let me down."

As Bennie turns walking away, Carina walks out onto the patio all excited saying, "They just called! They just called!"

"Where are they?" Angelo anxiously asks.

"They wouldn't say. They said they were sorry, and they're getting married."

Rocco gives his brother a congratulatory handshake while Bennie puts his hands on the sides of his face letting out a loud and painful, "Oy vey!"

Rocco, seeing Bennie in obvious pain, puts his arm consolingly around him saying, "At least they're both okay Bennie."

"Did Johnny say anything else Carina?" Angelo asks.

"He did. He told me to tell you not to go bothering his friends because he didn't tell anyone what he's doing."

"See Rocco, I told you I didn't know," I say with a shit eating grin.

"Let's just hope you won't have to eat those words," Rocco replies grinning and patting me on the back.

Angelo puts his arm around Bennie merrily saying, "Let's all sit down for a cup of black coffee and a nice shot of anisette."

"Make mine a double," Bennie replies.

We all pile back inside while Carina fixes the coffee. After getting our coffee and anisette, Angelo proposes a toast. "All's well that ends well!"

After Rocco makes some more small talk with Bennie, he politely excuses himself. Before he can escape, I cut him off at the door saying, "I really need to speak with you Rocco."

"Sure kid."

"Give me a minute to rescue Tex, or he'll never forgive me."

"Meet me at my car," Rocco chuckles

When I return to the kitchen I see Stacey's mom talking up a storm with Tex, so I say, "Excuse me everyone. Rocco just asked me to run an errand with him, so I'll have to go."

"Oh, okay Michael," Carina replies.

Everyone else just keeps talking, so I say louder, "I hate to interrupt you Tex, but we have to go."

Sarah puts her hand on top of Tex's saying, "Does he really have to leave Droz? We just started a conversation about horses. I love horses, and Tex seems to know so much about them."

Carina raises her eyebrows as she pours everyone more coffee. Bennie, Marsha, and Angelo don't hear a thing and just keep talking.

"It's up to him Sarah. So what will it be Tex. Stay or go?"

Tex switches to his charming mode replying, "Well it would be kind of rude of me Droz to leave in the middle of a conversation with a lady. If you don't need me to come along, I'll just stay right here."

Sarah smiles from ear to ear while I grin saying, "Okay cowboy, I'll pick you up later."

I rush out the front door and see Rocco shooting the shit with his two gorillas. When they see me, they snicker. Then they give Rocco the traditional hug and kiss before they leave. Rocco pops the locks to his Lincoln, and I get in. As he's pulling away he says, "That was a pretty smooth move my nephew pulled. The marriage part may actually save him. He must have told you something Droz. I know my nephew. He had to brag to somebody."

Letting out a sigh I calmly say, "Johnny didn't tell me anything Rocco."

Rocco chuckles replying, "All right Droz. I'll drop it for now. So what's on your mind?"

"Nicky told me everything."

"And what do you mean by everything?"

"He told me how Shayne got killed and where your son Bobby got his dope."

Rocco's face turns to stone as he stares at the road ahead of him. Then without any emotion says, "Spit it out."

Rocco drives to the beach and parks before I can finish spilling my guts. When I'm finally done, tears trickle down his cheeks. Rocco takes out his hanky and wipes his tears. Then he gets serious saying, "Charlie and Nicky I knew were scumbag drug dealers. Frankie is the poisonous snake I didn't know about. I want you to continue what you've been doing as I plot my revenge. Your loyalty will be rewarded Michael."

"Sure Rocco, I'll do anything you want."

With that said Rocco starts the car and drives away. On the way back to Coral Springs, Rocco tells happy stories about his son. I enjoy seeing this side of Rocco. It makes me feel closer to him. Rocco is glad Nicky educated me about Charlie Wing's deep involvement with narcotics and the government; further proving his point about who are the real bad guys in our society. When we pull into his brother's driveway, all of the cars are gone. Rocco says, "Go ring the bell and get Tex. If I stop the car and go to the door Carina will make me come in again."

I hurry up and go ring the bell. When Carina answers the door she says, "Why's Rocco still in the car Michael? Tell him to come in for some coffee. In fact, how about I make you both lunch?"

"Rocco told me he's in a hurry Carina. If you could just tell Tex I'm here that would be great."

"Tex left," Carina replies laughing.

"He walked home?"

"No. Sarah took him home with her. Stacy's mom sure likes them young."

I stand there speechless as Rocco toots the horn. Carina still laughing says, "You better get going Droz. Rocco's just like Angelo. He hates to be kept waiting."

I give Carina a hug and kiss then dash to the car. When I get in the car Rocco asks, "Where's Tex?"

"You're not going to fucking believe this Rocco."

"Believe what?"

"Stacy's mom took Tex home with her."

Rocco pulls out the driveway shaking his head saying, "I don't know what this world is coming too. I just don't know anymore." I shrug my shoulders.

On the way back to my house Rocco says, "Listen. With Johnny being gone Angelo may ask you and Tex to help out."

"Not a problem Rocco. We'll be glad to help out."

Rocco nods his head as he pulls into my driveway. When he sees a car parked there he asks, "I see you have company. Anyone I should know about?"

Better to tell Rocco the truth than have him memorize the plate and find out I'm lying. "Two very beautiful, young Italian girls from Brooklyn that Tex and I really like."

"Let me guess, Annmarie and Joanie?"

"How do you know?" I reply stunned.

"Never mind how I know, and you better be wearing condoms. You're playing with fire here. If you knock these two girls up you better be prepared to marry them."

"Of course we're wearing condoms," I lie.

"Good. Alright, go see your girlfriends and cover for your buddy, and if I don't see you there, have a goodtime tonight at Willie's grandfather's birthday party."

"I will Rocco. Hey, you know about that?"

"I may or may not go. It depends how the rest of my day goes."

"Cool Rocco, maybe I'll see you later then."

"Maybe," Rocco says and pulls away.

Inside the house, the place is as clean as a whistle. The carpets are vacuumed, the beds are made, and the bathrooms sparkle. Out on the patio I see the girls lying in the sun. I open up the sliding glass door saying, "Thank you for doing such a great job cleaning the house."

"No problem," They reply simultaneously.

"How did it go?" Annemarie asks.

"Piece of cake, Johnny's marrying Stacy."

Annmarie stares at me in shock as Joanie yells out, "What?"

"I can't believe it! When's the wedding?" Annemarie exclaims.

I wave my hands towards the girls saying, "Calm down girls, calm down. Nobody knows where they are, or when the wedding is."

"They better not elope," Annemarie says.

"That would be very selfish of them," Joanie curtly adds.

"It sure would Joanie. Wouldn't that be selfish of them Droz?" Annemarie bluntly asks.

I rub my head replying annoyed, "I don't know Annemarie. Just leave me alone about this. I've been hearing about this shit all fucking morning, and I've had it for now. Whatever they decide to do is their own fucking business, and we all should just wish them the best of luck."

They glance at each other like maybe I'm right. "Where's Tex Droz? Didn't he come home with you?" Joanie asks concerned.

"He volunteered to help Johnny's old man with a few things. Without Johnny around, me and Tex will have to pick up the slack for a while."

"That's so thoughtful of him to volunteer. Isn't it Annemarie?" Joanie asks lovingly.

"It sure is Joanie. You're so lucky Tex is such a nice guy," Annmarie replies with a warm smile.

I'm thinking to myself, "He better not pull up with fucking Sarah!" The girls tell me they have to be home for Sunday dinner. I understand that perfectly, and I miss it. I remember my mom sweating over a hot stove every Sunday morning getting it ready. There would be hell to pay if you dared miss it. After they leave, I go into the garage and work out. Then I take a nice, long leisurely swim. After the sun bakes me dry, I head inside for a little snooze.

It's almost five o'clock when I get up, and Tex still isn't back yet. We need to leave around seven to be at Willie's by eight. I grab a beer out of the fridge and take a seat on the couch. Then I cut off a piece of hash and put it on the needle. Before I can fire it up, I hear a motor rumbling in my driveway. I peek out the window and see Tex slopping spits with Sarah in her red Porsche. After saying their goodbyes, Tex steps up and over the car door instead of going through it. Sarah backs out smiling as he waves goodbye. Tex puts his key in the door and with my hands on my hips, I ask, "Really? Really Tex, was this really necessary?"

Tex looking the worst for ware struggles to smile saying, "She killed me Droz. She really, really, killed me."

"What do mean she killed you? She's twice your fucking age Tex. If anything you should have killed her!"

Tex plops down on the couch shaking his head. He looks at my cold beer like a man who had been stranded on a desert island. He picks it up and downs it. After letting out a major ahh, he looks at me dramatically saying, "That there woman drained me of every damn drop of fluid in my body. I can't even move Droz. Can you please get your old buddy Tex another beer?"

Shocked and jealous at what I'm seeing I march into the kitchen to get us a couple of beers. Giving him a look of pity, I open his beer for him asking, "What in the hell did she do to you?"

Tex raises one eyebrow and gulps down half his beer before replying, "What did she do to me? The question really should be what didn't she do to me. Sarah said she aint had sex in a forever, and the woman tried to make up for it all in one day."

"Dam Tex, what luck! Will she do us both?"

"I sure hope so Droz because she's insatiable. I'm too tired to tell you the details, but I will later."

"Just so you know I covered for your ass with Joanie. I told her you volunteered to help Angelo with some things since Johnny aint around. Both girls think you're some kind of fucking saint for volunteering."

With another gulp, Tex finishes his beer. He musters up a smile saying, "I knew you would Droz. So how did it go with Rocco?"

"I'll tell you on the way down to Willie's. Go hit the rack for a while so you can get your energy back."

"Thanks Droz, I need it."

Tex uses every ounce of energy he has left to walk back to the bedroom and take his nap. I stay in the living room hitting the glass. Sitting there stoned, Rocco's words echo in my head. "Your loyalty will be rewarded Michael."

GRANDPA'S BIRTHDAY PARTY...

I come out of my stupor just in time to wake up Tex and get ready. We jump in the pool to freshen up and then go get dressed. I roll up a bunch of weed before we arm ourselves and head out the door. On the way down to Miami, I clue Tex in on everything I told Rocco and his response. It's a fairly long drive to Willie's, so we listen to tunes and toke up real good. Before I exit Highway I-95, I open up the windows to air out the car and our clothing. I turn down Willie's street, and there's a block party going on! There's got to be at least a hundred people celebrating Grandpa's birthday. Everyone's eating, drinking, and dancing in the streets. A Cuban band is jamming away on a stage. The horns and bongo drums vibrate deeply into your chest. Tables full of Cuban foods line the sidewalks. Cuban flags and banners are flying everywhere. We park where everyone else parked, which is anywhere you can. It looks like we're the only gringos at the party, so Willie spots us right away. He walks towards us with a beautiful young girl strapped tightly to his arm. I can safely assume it's Mizar. Dressed in an array of vibrant colors, Mizar is flat out gorgeous! Willie smiling proudly says, "Droz, Tex, I want you to meet the love of my life, Mizar." That puts a big smile on her pretty face.

I return her pretty smile with a smile of my own saying, "It's a pleasure to meet you Mizar."

Tex with his big bold Texas accent says, "Well it sure is a pleasure to meet you Mizar. Old Willie here just can't stop talking about you every time he's around us. Now that I've met you, I can see why. She sure is one pretty, little lady Willie. You need to put a ring on that girl's finger before somebody else does."

To Willie's chagrin, Tex is in rare form. Willie puts a look on his face like thanks a lot Tex. Mizar smiles at Tex and in her cute little Cuban accent thanks him. Then she pushes Willie away yelling! "So William, these are the gringos you tell me you stay with when you screw your whores!"

"Ay, caramba!" Willie hollers holding his head in his hands pleading. "Mizar, must you always embarrass me?"

Mizar flicks her hair back and waves her finger in Willie's face saying, "Just don't think I'm stupid William." Mizar smiles at us now politely asking, "Would you two gentlemen like something to eat?"

We look at each other and nod yes.

"Follow us," Mizar says as she leads Willie by the nose over to the tables full of food.

As we follow Tex softly says, "You got to like her fire Droz. She must be hot as a pistol in bed."

"Shit yeah Tex. Maybe Willie will let us watch through a window or something."

Tex grins nodding his head. Mizar gets us plates and utensils first. Then she begins guiding us through the different tables full of foods. She does a great job of explaining everything as she piles food onto our plates.

"Try one of these. Its Cuban style ale called hautey," Willie says as he pops open a couple of bottles for us. We both put our plates down for the moment and grab the beers. Tex takes a monster swig, and I chug down a few gulps.

"Now that's a good beer Willie," Tex says letting out a loud belch. "Oh excuse me Mizar."

Mizar smiling sarcastically replies, "Don't worry Tex I'm used to it. Just make sure you warn me if it comes out the other end. Willie never does."

Willie shakes his head as I comment, "That is a good beer Willie. Thank you."

"It's my pleasure Droz. I would like to thank the both of you for coming to my grandfather's birthday party. We'll be leaving soon for Grandpa's surprise. I still don't know what it is. My father kept it a secret."

Mizar puts her hands on her hips saying, "It's no secret Willie when none of the women are invited. We all know what you men pigs are planning to do. Your father is going to put on a cha cha girly show for Grandpa."

Willie rolls his eyes and innocently laughs. Then he winks at us saying, "I hope so."

Mizar slaps Willie on the shoulder. Then she sticks her nose in the air strutting away.

"You think you better go after her Willie?" Tex asks.

"No Tex. If I do that she'll know for sure we're all up to no good," Tex and I laugh.

"What's a cha cha girly show Willie?" I ask.

"Before Castro ruined our country, beautiful girls put on extravagant shows using a dance we call the cha cha. My grandfather loved watching the cha cha girls back in Havana."

"Sounds like we'll be having some fun tonight Willie," Tex says while chewing.

"You guys finish up your food while I go say goodbye to Mizar. When you see my father and the other men get into their cars you get into yours and follow."

"We'll be right behind you Willie," I reply.

Tex washes down his food with the rest of his beer. Then he says, "Look at all of them cute little senoritas dancing in the street Droz. Too bad we have to leave."

"I don't know Tex. Look at the mommas and poppas watching us looking at all of those cute little senoritas."

476

Tex looks across the street. He smiles waving at the parents saying, "I think you're right Droz. Not one of them parents are smiling and waving back."

"Do you expect them too Tex?"

I see Willie's dad and grandpa walking to their car. We clean our plates and head for ours. Nobody's going anywhere fast with all of the people partying in the street. I carefully maneuver around everyone trying to follow the other cars out. I count nine cars in front of us. When we finally get through the maze of partygoers it only takes us about fifteen minutes to get to the port. Willie's dad pulls up to a different entrance than the one we went through with Nicky. This entrance has a very high barbed wire fence that two men open for us. We're the last car through and the two men lock the gate behind us. After a few turns the cars in front of us start parking in a brightly lit area by the dock. There's a small cargo ship docked close by. I see men dressed in tuxedos holding musical instruments. Next to them is a group of exotic half-naked women. The girls have G-strings on and nipple pasties with red tassels hanging from them. Their bodies are elaborately adorned with beautiful colored feathers. The girls smile and wave to everyone getting out of their cars. The men all cheer and whistle, so we follow suit.

"I'll be damned Droz. Mizar was right!" Tex exclaims.

"We're at the big boy party now Tex!" I boisterously reply.

Willie rushes up to us glowing with excitement shouting, "You guys are going to love this! Come over to the wooden keg and try some real Cuban rum!"

Willie's father has a beautiful stage setup for the show. The three of us grab a little wooden mug from a stack sitting by the keg. Then we take turns at the tap. I put that cup to my lips and wow! "Damn Willie! That's the smoothest, sweetest tasting rum I've ever tasted!"

"Of course it is Droz! It's made in Cuba!"

Instead of sipping the rum, Tex downs it. He raises his eyebrows shouting, "Hell yeah Willie, that there liquor got my toes tingling!"

We wait our turn for a refill as the girls and the band take the stage. After filling our mugs with rum, we follow Willie to our seats next to his father. As soon as we sit down the band starts playing and the girls start dancing! Tits and ass are jiggling all over the stage, Oh my! Now Grandpa's on stage dancing with the girls!

"Look at old grandpa go!" Tex shouts.

Willie's dad proudly shouts, "Some things never change boys! The girls still love him! My father is eighty four years old, but today he looks closer to twenty four!"

Now the entire crowd gets on their feet, cheering grandpa on! What a sight to see! When the birthday boy has enough cha cha dancing with the girls, he joins us. After an hour or so, the band and the girls take their bows to a rip roaring standing ovation!

Willie's father excuses himself and gets up on the stage. He grabs the microphone and starts speaking in Spanish to everyone. I don't understand Spanish, but I can tell he's thanking the girls and the band for their performance. He starts clapping and then everyone gives them another standing ovation. Before the girls leave, they all take turns hugging and kissing Grandpa goodbye! After they board a bus and leave everyone heads for their cars. Willie's dad asks us to stay behind and help with the cleanup. That's when all hell breaks loose! Rifle shots ring out from the rooftops. Willie, Tex, and I instinctively hit the floor reaching for our guns. We quickly look to Willie's dad and grandpa for guidance. They're still standing stoically on the stage as cool as a fucking cucumber! They motion at us to stay out of it. Each rifle shot is followed by a blood-curdling scream that echoes off the walls of the warehouses. The three of us stand up and join Willie's dad and grandpa. As the rifle shots continue it doesn't take a genius to figure out these shots aren't meant to kill. They are meant only to maim. When the wounded men attempt to get into their cars they are shot again in their hands, legs, arms, and shoulders. Whoever's doing the shooting sure knows what they're doing. I count fourteen men crawling around on the ground in pools of their own blood. Willie turns to his father in shock asking, "What will you tell Momma and the other families when they ask you what happened to them?"

Willie's dad looks over the massacre giving no reply. The wounded men are left to painfully wallow in their own blood. A crew of men in a truck appears along with other men driving forklifts. Two men throw large bags off the truck while another man on the ground cuts them open with a machete. Then all the men pick up the bags and pour them all over the bleeding men. The men start rubbing salt in their wounds! As the tortured men scream in agony they are kicked, cursed, and spat on. When their tormenters have their fill, they pile the bodies onto palates. The forklifts lift the palates of bodies and dump them into a large cargo container. Just when you figure things can't possibly get any worse for these poor souls, they did. Four men wearing thick black gloves and carrying crates full of live rats walk out of one of the warehouses. The rats are crawling all over each other making creepy little squeaky sounds. The men walk up to Willie's dad and grandpa with the crates to show them. They both look at the live rats and nod their heads in approval. The four men walk over to the container and empty the crates of rats right on top of them. Then two guys with blowtorches seal the container from the outside. Small holes are now drilled into the sides. I cannot begin to describe the bone chilling sounds of fear and agony when the rats discover their feast. A large crane loads the container onto the cargo ship. As soon as it's loaded, the ship unmoors and pulls out to sea. On the pier, the men all kiss and hug. Willie's grandpa now speaks, "These traitors jeopardized everything we are doing for our people. Without Rocco's help, we would have never known we were betrayed by those so close to us."

"This is like a war, and anything goes," I say boldly.

Willie's dad puts his arm around me saying, "It's not like a war. It is a war, Michael. A war we must win. A war the American Government refuses to help us fight. The Cuban people love this country and everything it stands for. We're proud of our citizenship, but we've learned to distrust the government. They speak from both sides of their mouths. This is why we must take matters into our own hands. You boys go home now. It's time for Grandpa and me to reward the loyal men with their new positions. Say goodbye to your amigos Willie. You may not see them for a while because you too are being assigned a higher position of responsibility."

With that said, we all hug and kiss. We wish Grandpa happy birthday again, and Willie walks us to my car. On the way I bluntly say, "Willie, please don't invite me to anymore of your family gatherings."

"Me either," Tex adds.

"How do you think I feel? I'm just as surprised as you are. You must think my family is made up of monsters," Willie shakes his head replying.

"No we don't Willie. We believe everything your father just told us. Your family is doing what our government has failed to do. Defeat Castro and free your people."

Tex shaking his head says, "It's downright shameful and embarrassing, Willie, our government won't help your people. What are we, about a stone's throw away from Cuba? We have a Navy base there and everything, but we still let Castro live.

"It's only ninety miles Tex," Willie sadly replies.

Tex gets riled up now saying, "See that! Only ninety damn miles away, and we aint lifting a finger to help! We can go fight way off in Vietnam to stop communism, but we can't stop it in our own damn backyard! I call bullshit!"

"I call bullshit too Willie, so don't feel bad about your family. Just be proud your family is making such a difference in so many people's lives. God bless you all Willie."

"God will bless your family Willie," Tex adds giving him a hug. Willie gets teary-eyed hugging him back. Then he says, "God bless Rocco too. Without his help, we might have lost everything. I don't know what my father has in store for me, but I'll come see you as soon as I can."

"You do that Willie," I reply. Then we all hug and kiss again before saying goodbye. As we're pulling away I say, "You know Tex. Rocco knew this was going to happen all along, and he never mentioned a word to me. That's kind of fucked up of him, don't you think?"

Tex grabs a joint out of the ashtray. He lights it up and takes a big hit. He grunts a little before replying, "When you're planning something as devious as this was Droz, the element of surprise is everything. The less people who knew about it the better, you know that."

"What about them fucking crates of rats at the end Tex? What the fuck was up with that? I can still hear them little fucking bastards squeaking in my fucking head."

"That was just icing on the cake." Tex chuckles as he turns on the tunes and passes me the joint. As I become absorbed into the weed and the music, the squeaking sounds of the rats disappear.

TILL DEATH DO US PART…

The next morning we have our bacon and eggs out on the patio. Last night's already a distant memory. The sky's deep blue with big puffy white clouds floating all around it. As Rocco would say, "It's another beautiful day in paradise!"

After breakfast, we smoke ourselves a nice fat hash joint. Then Tex and I melt into our respective lounge chairs soaking up the sun. A nice lazy day with no one to bother us is just what the doctor ordered.

Later on, Tex and I go to my club for lunch. We start drinking beer and shooting the shit with the retired firemen. One story leads to another, and before you know it, its dinnertime. Boy what a life my father had!

We didn't hear from Nicky, so half past eight we leave my club and head to his house. Nicky's waiting outside for us when I pull into the driveway. I roll down my window asking, "What's up Nicky? Is everything alright?"

"Everything's great Droz. Pop the lock, and I'll clue you guys in on the way."

"Where are we heading Nicky?" I ask as he jumps in the backseat.

"A farm in Redland, it's about 50 miles southwest of here. Head south on the turnpike, and I'll tell you when to get off. The CIA has everything secured there for him."

"Secure for who Nicky?" I ask curiously.

"You guys are going to meet the big boss tonight, Charlie Wings. Sally and Vinnie will also be meeting us there with our drug profits. Spark up a joint Droz."

Tex and I give each other a quick look before I enthusiastically reply, "Fucking cool Nicky, it aint every day you get to meet a legend."

"You got that right Droz. Plus we're getting paid," Tex says with matched enthusiasm.

I spark up a joint and pass it back to Nicky. I look in the rearview mirror, and Nicky looks happy. He's all relaxed sprawled out in the backseat. Nicky hits the joint a few times and passes it to Tex saying, "The call girls down here are fucking sweet. They aren't all drugged out like the fucking whores up north. These Florida bitches are clean and wholesome. I didn't even use a rubber. I gave them some blow, and they told me everything I wanted to know. We'll be running the call girl business down here in no time."

Nicky rambles on without mentioning a word about what happened at the port. I'm sure someone working with Antonio has told him. After getting good and stoned we just listen to tunes until Nicky taps me on the shoulder saying, "Get off at the next exit. Then make your first right."

I listen to Nicky and turn down a dark two-lane road. About ten minutes later, he says, "Shut the radio and slow down. Make a left after the U-Pick-em sign. Do about twenty miles an hour from here on out."

I make the left and head slowly down the dark road. After driving a few miles two sets of headlights come on in front of us. "Blink your lights on and off three times," Nicky says.

When I do, the headlights in front of us are turned off. "Now turn your lights off and roll down the windows. Pull up slowly and stop right in front of the two trucks."

When I come to a stop, four men dressed in khaki's and polo shirts carrying small machine guns approach my car. They look inside each window, and one of the guys says, "What's up Nicky? We've been expecting you."

"What's up Kevin?"

"Same old shit Nicky, looking out for Charlie. Go down the road about another half mile and you'll see a brick farmhouse. Sally and Vinnie are already here."

"Thanks Kevin. You heard him Droz."

Kevin's men pull over to one side letting us through. I drive up the road about a half mile to the farmhouse. It's a large brick house, with a solid brick wall all around it. I counted six more men dressed the same way as Keven. Some are armed with machine guns, and others are carrying shotguns. Four of them stand guard at the wall, and the other two are perched on the porch. I park next to three brand new Chevy Vans and a big black Mercedes limousine. The limousine has diplomatic plates. The silence is getting to me, so I ask curiously, "Nicky, what's up with so many armed fucking guards? Does Charlie really need this type of protection?"

"Put it this way Droz. The CIA wants to keep him alive and out of jail. It's not like Charlie's paying these stiffs. It's all tax-payer dollars. Let's get out of the car before we spook these assholes."

We exit the car and head to the front porch. "What's up Diego?" Nicky asks one of the guards.

"What's up? You're up Nicky," Diego says slapping five with him.

"Before I let you in I got to frisk your two friends."

"These are my friends Diego. Why you want to insult me like that?" Nicky replies with an edge.

"Sorry Nicky, but we don't know these guys. I have to fol-low protocol."

Right away, my instincts tell me this aint good, but what should I do? What's their protocol if I resist? It could be deadly to resist at this point. I look at Nicky saying, "I don't like this Nicky. It doesn't feel cool."

"Don't worry Droz. It's cool. I got your back," Nicky reas-sures me.

I look at Tex nodding okay. Diego frisks us and takes our 45's. He also takes my buck-folding knife and Tex's hunting knife stashed in his boot. Diego looks admiringly at Tex's knife saying, "Ah, where I come from they call this a Texas toothpick."

"So I take it you're from Texas, hey Diego?" Tex asks.

"I was born in El Paso, but I spent a lot of time with family in Juarez."

Tex nods as Diego lets us in the door. It makes me feel a little more comfortable when Sally and Vinnie greet us. We all exchange our traditional hugs and kisses. Sally looks at Nicky saying, "Remember that thing we were talking about? You know the one with our new friend?"

"Sure Sally, what about it?"

"It's all a go for tonight"

"Beautiful Sally, I'll be looking forward to it," Nicky cheerfully replies. Then he turns serious asking, "Where's the cash Vinnie?"

"I got it in suitcases in one of the Suburban's parked outside."

Nicky nods and asks, "Where's Charlie hiding?"

"He's on the other side of the house. Come on I'll bring you over," Vinnie replies.

The house is pretty damn big. It has hardwood floors and handmade furniture throughout. After walking down a long hallway, Vinnie points us to the right. We enter a big room with a giant stone fireplace. Sitting on a big fluffy couch is a man dressed in Bermuda shorts and a flowery shirt. Talking on the phone with a New York Italian accent is the infamous Charlie Wings! Three additional bodyguards are in the room with him. They are seated at a beautifully hand carved wooden bar. Also in the room are two Spanish women dressed like servants. From talking with Rocco, I knew Charlie is around his age. Rocco has a thick solid build. Charlie is a much slimmer man, but toned. He also has a great tan. Charlie's hair is jet black, and therefore, at his age, probably dyed. When Charlie gets off the phone, he smiles walking over to Nicky. They exchange happy hugs and kisses. Charlie puts his hands on Nicky's shoulders saying, "I really missed you Nicky. I thought I lost you for good this time. How the hell did you manage to get out anyway?"

"By giving my lawyer every fucking penny I had, and then some," Nicky sadly replies.

"I'm sure you're well on your way back to prosperity. So introduce me to your new friends."

"Charlie, this is Droz and Tex. They've been invaluable to me down here."

We exchange handshakes and then Charlie says, "Everyone sit down, and lets have a drink. What will you boys have?"

"I'll take a beer," Tex replies.

"Same here Charlie," I add.

"Are beers good for you guys too?" Charlie looks at Nicky, Sally, and Vinnie asking.

"Sure Charlie, beers are good," Nicky answers.

"Consuela, Maria, can you please serve my friends here all a nice cold beer?" The girls smile and quickly fetch our beers. "How are things going with our new Colombian friends Nicky?" Charlie asks.

"Good Charlie. No complaints."

"Are they happy with the heroin we sold them?"

"Antonio flew back home for a wedding Charlie, so I haven't heard back yet. But I'm sure he'll be thrilled with the quality."

"I hear our new Colombian friends don't get along so well with their counterparts from Peru."

"Yeah well, that always seems to be the case Charlie when greed sets in," Nicky shrugs his shoulders saying.

"You're absolutely right Nicky. It's always greed. They could become a dynasty if they only learned to work together like I taught our Muslim friends in Afghanistan. They have an opportunity right now to control the sale of cocaine throughout the world. It's a way bigger market than the heroin trade. It could make them richer than all of the opium dealers put together. Anyway, I got two hundred kilos here you need to deliver to our friends in New York. They've already paid me, so let's not keep them waiting. Sammy, go into the bedroom and bring out

Nicky's money. See Nicky, I already have your cut waiting for you."

"Thank you Charlie. You've always been square with me."

"My pleasure Nicky, you're one of my most loyal and trusted friends."

Sammy walks back into the room handing Nicky a briefcase. Charlie turns his attention to me and Tex now saying, "Vinnie and Sally had nothing but praise for you two."

"When you're being paid what we are Charlie, you can't disappoint," I humbly reply.

"That's a fact," Tex adds and then gulps down his beer.

"That is a fact Tex. Maria, can you please get my friend Tex here another beer?"

"Thank you Charlie," Tex says.

"So Droz, I understand you've become Rocco's new little protégé?"

"Well, I don't think I'm his little protégé Charlie. All I did was put together a deal that is paying dividends for him. I like to think of my relationship with Rocco as more business than personal."

Charlie chuckles before replying, "You're a very wise young man Droz. It's smart not to overestimate your value in a relationship. I can see why Rocco likes you. In fact, I'm starting to like you myself. This makes the decision I made even harder."

Chills run up and down my spine as Charlie waves his hand. The two bodyguards behind the bar draw down on me and Tex with pump shotguns. I quickly turn to Nicky for help. Nicky nods to Sally and Vinnie. The three of them take out their pistols pointing them right at us!

Enraged I holler, "You dirty cocksucker Nicky! You set us up!"

With a shit eating grin, Nicky sarcastically replies, "Don't tell me you're fucking surprised Droz. How many times do I have to tell you? You can't trust anybody in this fucking business, especially me."

The three of them take delight in laughing at me and Tex. Tex looks to me for a sign of hope, and I have none to give him. Tex shakes his head grimacing accepting his fate. It's killing me inside because I know Nicky's right. I shouldn't have trusted him. I should have listened to my instincts and never gave up my gun. Instead, I made scared excuses to myself why I should. Now I'm not only going to get myself killed, but Tex too.

Charlie Wings now says, "If it makes you feel any better Droz, Nicky didn't betray you. He's just being a good soldier and following my orders. A man in my position can't afford to have any loose ends. Unfortunately, you and Tex have unknowingly become loose ends. Your friend Rocco is one of the most ruthless, cunning, and powerful men in the world. Sooner or later, he will find out what's going on. When he does he'll make the both of you talk. I can guarantee it."

"That's not true Charlie! We don't fucking rat!" I shout in desperation.

Charlie laughs at me.

"Don't fucking laugh at me Charlie! I'm telling you the fucking truth! We don't fucking rat!"

Charlie laughs even louder now while the rest of the room joins in. Their laughter is eating at my soul!

"The truth is, when interrogation is done by professionals everyone talks. It's just a matter of when," Charlie says.

"Look Charlie, me and Tex got money. We'll disappear on our own. We've been all over the world in the Navy. We can disappear in places where Rocco will never find us."

Charlie sighs and shakes his head before replying, "I'm truly sorry Droz, but I will not jeopardize my operation on you two. My men are highly trained professionals. I can assure you both they will make this unpleasant task quick and painless, so don't make this any harder than it has to be."

Charlie Wings coldly nods to his men. The two men walk slowly toward us with their shotguns pointed at our chests. Nicky, Sally, Vinnie, and the other bodyguard are right with them. As I'm being escorted to my execution my life flashes before me. I hear my father and mother's voices. All my thoughts are confused. My heart pounds faster and faster with every step I take. I begin sweating as the reality of dying closes in. Suddenly, like a bolt of lightning! Everything becomes crystal clear! I always wanted to be a gangster, and I always wanted to go out in a blaze of bullets! I got my wish! As soon as I see a glimpse of an opening, I'll go for one of their guns. When we arrive at the front door, gunshots ring out from the outside. I'm deafened by shots being fired from behind me. Instantly I feel the warm wet sensation of blood dripping down the back of my head. I guess this is what Charlie Wings meant by quick and painless. I glance back at my executioners seeing Nicky, Sally, and Vinnie finishing off Charlie's men! It's their blood on the back of my head! Tex and I are alive! Outside the door, a war is going on. I hear some men yelling in Spanish and others in English. Nicky must have made a deal with Antonio to usurp Charlie. Charlie Wings yells, "What the fuck's going on out there Nicky!"

"Everything's alright Charlie, just stay put until it's over," Nicky yells back.

Nicky puts his finger over his lips letting us know to keep quiet. Then with a demonic smile says, "Follow us back to Charlie. Stay a few steps behind and let us go in first. He'll have a fucking heart attack when he sees you're both still alive."

Sally and Vinnie can hardly contain themselves as they pat us on the back. I whisper to Nicky, "What the fucks going on outside?"

"It's a surprise," Nicky replies like the devil.

"You're sure full of surprises tonight aint you Nicky?" Tex whispers.

We quietly follow a few steps behind. When they enter the room, we hear Charlie. "I don't like what I'm hearing Nicky. I could swear I hear men yelling in Spanish. I hope for your sake this isn't what I think it is."

"For my sake Charlie, are you sure you're not hoping for your sake? Come on in guys."

Tex and I proudly walk in the room. I'll hand it to Charlie. He doesn't panic. He just stares at Nicky shaking his head in disgust. Then he grabs a bottle of booze from behind the bar and pours himself a drink. Charlie downs it in one gulp and quickly pours another. Charlie begins talking like a disappointed parent to Nicky. "How could you Nicky? How could you find it inside yourself to betray me? I treated you like a son. Today you have broken my heart."

Nicky stays silent as he walks over to the bar grabbing the bottle from Charlie. He pours himself a drink and downs it too. Then he slams the glass on the bar saying, "You aint got a heart Charlie. You just like to pretend you do."

Charlie laughs at Nicky as he pours himself another drink. In a defiant cocky tone, Charlie asks, "Tell me Nicky. Was it for the money? Do you really believe your new Colombian friends can make you richer than I can?"

"Not everything is for the fucking money Charlie."

Charlie snickers at Nicky. He downs his drink and pours himself another before replying, "Sure Nicky. You can tell yourself that. Tell yourself whatever you need to get you through the night. What do you think will happen when my friends in Washington find out your Colombian friends killed their CIA agents? Do you really think the Colombians will be able to protect you? They won't even be able to protect themselves when our military starts dropping bombs on their family's villages. From this day on Nicky, you and your friends will be sleeping with one eye open. There's no place on earth for any of you to hide. If they find you alive, you will be thrown in a prison in some God forsaken country. There you will be tortured for the rest of your miserable lives. Think about it Nicky. Think about it real hard because I'm the only one in this world who can protect you from that fate."

Charlie Wings slowly sips his drink waiting for Nicky's response. A new round of automatic gunfire begins raging outside. The men who were once yelling orders in Spanish are screaming in panic. Charlie smiles from ear to ear as he refills his glass arrogantly saying, "Sounds like reinforcements have arrived Nicky. The battle seems to have turned my friend, and not in your favor. Please don't do anything rash now Nicky. It will only make matters worse for you and your friends. Your coup has failed."

Before any of us can respond, there's a powerful explosion at the front of the house. Nicky, Sally, and Vinnie didn't move. Tex and I stand there befuddled not knowing what to do at this point. We hear men moving throughout the house speaking to each other in a very strange language. Charlie begins nervously muttering to himself, "It can't be. It can't be. It just can't be."

"Hello Charlie. Long time no see. What has it been, twenty, maybe twenty five years?"

It's Rocco! Nicky must have saved his ass by giving up Charlie Wings! Rocco the fucking rat maker! I sure feel a whole lot better inside knowing Nicky is a rat just like me. Right behind Rocco dressed in battle fatigues is Ariella, Katrina, and five other men. The language we were all hearing is Hebrew. We couldn't recognize the language, but Charlie Wings sure did!

"I think closer to thirty Rocco. Can I offer you a drink?" Charlie asks nervously.

"Sure Charlie. Why not? It just might be your last one anyway."

"Killing me would be a mistake Rocco. I can be of tremendous help to you."

Ariella speaks in Hebrew to her men and they leave the room as Charlie continues. "The CIA told me you made an alliance with the Mossad. I must say, Ariella, your reputation and work with Kidon is world renowned."

"Your reputation is also world renowned Mr. Wings, but for all the wrong reasons," Ariella smirks replying.

Charlie nods his head graciously. Then he asks, "There are two servants hiding in the bedroom Rocco. May I call them out here? I assure you it's no trick."

"They're not servants Charlie. They work for me. The girls are each equipped with a signaling device. When Nicky started escorting Droz and Tex outside the girls signaled the cartel members to start attacking your men."

The girls walk out of the back bedroom smiling. Charlie forces a smile saying, "Nothing like being taken down by the best Rocco. I salute you. Would you mind if I asked you how you pulled this all off?"

As the girls are getting everyone a beer, Katrina pats Charlie down and escorts him to a chair. When Charlie's seated Rocco replies, "It's a pretty simple plan Charlie. Our friend Nicky killed three of Antonio's people and robbed them of a million dollars. My informants fed Antonio credible information Nicky did it on your orders. The same informants tipped off Antonio that a meeting between you and Nicky would be taking place here tonight. Antonio was warned the both of you would be heavily guarded by CIA agents, so he responded accordingly. After they killed your CIA Agents, Ariella and her unit killed them. Now we use the Colombian Drug Cartel as a scapegoat for the deaths of the agents. The amount of coke and heroin that will be found here will be proof of a CIA drug deal with the Colombians that went bad. The CIA and Washington will force the Colombian government into cooperating with us to destroy the cartels. This is a positive step in trying to control the flow of narcotics into our country."

"Still trying to save the world Rocco?" Charlie asks smiling.

"It helps me sleep at night Charlie."

"Does working with a ruthless killer like Nicky help you sleep better at night too? Or did you spare his life for his part in your son's death for bringing you, me, and Frankie?"

Rocco sways his head from side to side before replying, "Maybe, maybe not Charlie, but I do believe in redemption. It came to my knowledge Nicky killed a guard in prison. This guard was a piece of shit shaking Nicky down for drug money. Dirty guard or not, Nicky soon found himself facing life in solitary confinement without the possibility of parole. That's when I had one of my people reach out to him. I gave Nicky a chance to atone for his sins, or grow old and die alone in his cell. Nicky wisely chose redemption. He confessed everything to me he knew about my son's death. Then he swore to help me rid America of narcotics. Soon after Nicky's release from prison, he recruited his childhood friends Sally, Vinnie, and Joey to help him. The three of them also swore their allegiance to me. Unfortunately for Joey Jumbo, the Peruvians gunned him down. This created a void in Nicky's crew. My Godson fueled by greed because of his gambling habit quickly wanted in. I quilled my nephew's misplaced ambitions by having Nicky recruit Droz and Tex instead."

Rocco turns to me saying, "I know what you're thinking Droz. You're thinking why did I deceive you, or why did I even need you and your friend Tex to help me if I had Nicky."

"Well of course Rocco. What do you expect me to be thinking?" I reply hurt.

With a fatherly smile, Rocco walks over to me saying, "I can tell you're upset with me Michael, and you have every right to be. But hear me out before you judge me."

"Sure Rocco. I'll hear you out," I reply with glassy eyes.

"I have big plans for you Michael. I told you when we first met you had the two things money can't buy and I can't teach, balls and instincts." I also said if you gave me loyalty I would open up doors for you that you never thought existed. I needed you to prove your loyalty to me. Now that you have, I'm fully prepared to keep my promise to you. That is if you want to still work for me."

My heart glows and tears trickle down my cheeks. Rocco acknowledges my tears by opening his arms to me. I immediately jump into them saying, "Of course I do Rocco. You're the only person in this world I will ever work for."

Rocco hugs me like a son saying the magic words I cherished hearing from my father. "I'm proud of you Michael."

Nicky now points his finger at Charlie lecturing him. "You see Charlie? That's the heart you're fucking lacking. It's all about business to you and Frankie. We always felt like fucking peons to you two."

Losing his temper, Charlie jumps up from his chair shouting, "Why you ungrateful cock sucking son of a bitch Nicky! You were nothing but a two-bit street punk until me and Frankie made you rich! Now you want to complain we didn't hug and kiss you enough? Go fuck yourself! Do me a fucking favor Rocco. Put a bullet in my fucking head so I don't have to hear this pussy faggot bullshit anymore!"

Ariella and Katrina roughly shove Charlie back down into his chair. Rocco smoothly reaches into his pocket pulling out a hammerless snub-nosed revolver calmly saying, "Okay Charlie, have it your way."

"Rocco no, no Rocco, I didn't mean it!"

Bang, Rocco fires a shot taking off a piece of Charlie Wing's ear! Charlie freaks out screaming at the top of his lungs. "Okay! Okay! I take it back Rocco! I want to live! I'll do anything you fucking say Rocco! Just please, let me fucking live!"

"Do I sense a sudden change of heart Charlie?" Rocco sarcastically replies with a sinister smile.

"Yes Rocco. Please let me live," Charlie's says solemnly.

Rocco slowly paces around Charlie's chair. As he takes out his hanky and hands it to Charlie, he asks, "I guess you would you like a chance to atone for your sins too, huh Charlie?"

Charlie holds Rocco's hanky tightly over his bleeding ear replying, "Look Rocco. Nicky's the spawn of the fucking devil. If he can redeem himself, I certainly can."

Nicky and his boys laugh. Then Nicky says, "I'm a fucking saint compared to you Charlie."

Charlie gives Nicky the evil eye replying, "We're only saints in our mother's eyes Nicky."

Rocco chuckles and says, "We both have friends in Washington Charlie. The difference is my friends want to put an end to the political careers of your friends. I will agree to let you live if you agree to betray your friends and help me bring them down."

"Just tell me how you want it done Rocco and I'll do it. After tonight, I might lose some of them friends. They might even shut me down."

Ariella interrupts. "Your friends will still need you Charlie for a new deal in another part of the world. As far as being shut down goes, you were being shut down soon anyway."

"What do you mean new deal Ariella? And what do you mean I'll be shut down anyway?" Charlie replies shocked.

Ariella looks to Rocco and he nods. "The political landscape in Afghanistan will be changing Charlie. The Russians realized the war they're waging there has become too costly to pursue. The Mujahedeen with the help of the United States has created a no win situation for the Russians. Instead of being stubborn like America was in Vietnam they have decided to pull out. When they do, the CIA will reward the Afghan warlords by turning over your entire opium trade to them. There are two Afghan brothers."

Charlie interrupts. "You can stop Ariella. I know the brothers, and they have been trying to backdoor me since day one. I always got double talk out of Washington when I complained about these guys. One of them is very popular with the people, and the other is the Afghanistan version of Nicky. Make one brother a political puppet, and let the other brother strong arm the drug trade."

"You got it Charlie," Ariella says smiling.

Rocco pours Charlie another drink. He hands it to him saying, "Our government is going down a slippery slope with these Muslim extremists Charlie. Israeli Intelligence says Muslim extremists want to restore a caliphate to the entire Middle East and drive Israel into the sea."

Charlie downs his drink and Rocco refills it as Ariella says, "They will not stop there Charlie. Extremists plan on spreading their jihad right here on American soil. The money made exporting opium will be used to recruit and train new jihadists throughout the world. Oil money will also be used to purchase modern weapons and new types of explosives. The politicians backing you in Washington Charlie are ignoring this intelligence."

With a look of reflection, Charlie slowly sips his drink. Now he stares directly at Ariella saying, "They're not ignoring it Ariella. They think they can control it. What's my next move Rocco?"

"I want all the dirt you got on these assholes supporting you in Washington. I'll make sure it gets in the hands of the right journalists. This November we'll oust these cocksuckers and put in our own people."

Charlie chuckles before replying, "I got a money trail on everybody I do business with in Washington. The only difference between a whore and a politician is how much money they get to spread their legs."

"I hope for your sake Charlie the information you give me isn't bogus."

Charlie puts his hand over his heart replying, "On my mother's grave Rocco, I give you my word I won't fuck you."

Rocco chuckles while pouring Charlie another drink. Then he says. "Through Ariella's fantastic intelligence work we have found every single offshore banking account you have Charlie. With the cooperation of my international banking contacts, your accounts are now under my control. My accountants have set up a history of direct deposits into your offshore accounts from the banks controlled by the drug cartels in Cartagena. So what do you think will happen to you if you fuck me?"

With a look of total disgust, Charlie shakes his head accepting his fate. He takes a gulp of his drink and actually manages a smile before replying, "I guess I shouldn't be too surprised Rocco. Ever since we were kids, you always knew how to figure out all the angles. You left me penniless with no one to turn to but you."

"True Charlie, but if you stay loyal you will have a future. Ariella, would you please go outside and get Diego?"

Ariella leaves the room with Katrina following right behind her. "You kept Diego alive?" Charlie asks.

"Diego is part of the setup Charlie, and he's also part of the new deal coming your way after Afghanistan."

Diego walks in the room limping with a bullet wound to his left leg saying, "Ariella is going to stay outside with her men and finish up the job Rocco. She wants to go over everything with a fine tooth comb before we leave."

Rocco nods his head. Then Charlie asks Diego, "So all of your friends are dead except you Diego. How's that make you feel?"

"You mean my acquaintances Charlie. Outside of the bullet I took in my leg for your ass, I feel pretty damn good. How about yourself?"

"My old friend Rocco here blew off a piece of my ear and took all my money, but other than that I'm good too. So Rocco, tell me how Diego plays into this."

"Well first his staged heroics saved your life. He took a bullet during the firefight and you lost a piece of your ear. Ballistics will prove the bullet Diego was hit by came from one of the Colombian's weapons."

"Okay, I get that part Rocco, but what's this new deal all about."

"Things will be changing in this hemisphere too Charlie. Our new president will seek trade agreements with our bordered countries Canada and Mexico. Thus, our borders with Mexico and Canada will become relaxed. This will quickly be exploited by the Mexican drug lords to export heroin and marijuana into the states. After what happened here tonight, any CIA ties to the Colombian Cartels will be broken. As we all know, the CIA funds its illegal wars and covert operations from the drug trade. Once the flow of illegal drug money is closed in Colombia and Afghanistan another one must be found."

"So you're telling me I better learn to speak Spanish."

Diego laughs heartedly saying, "When the Mexican people realize how easy it will be to cross the border all of you gringos better learn Spanish."

Tex laughs along with Diego and says, "You got that right Diego."

Rocco frowns and says, "We'll have that discussion another day Diego." Diego quickly nods as Rocco continues. "Soon the CIA will ask you, Charlie, to recruit Mexican drug lords who are sympathetic to our political agenda. The CIA will arm and train them to wipe out the other gangs who didn't. Mexico shares our borders. This makes protecting the flow of drugs into America simpler and less expensive than it presently is today. My sources tell me Juarez will become ground zero for these drug lords. My people make a big effort to keep tabs on everyone's backgrounds in the CIA. Diego knows Juarez and will fit nicely into the CIA's new plans. He's already seasoned in the CIA's illegal drug trade, and will soon be considered a hero for saving their infamous drug runner Charlie Wings. Diego, explain the rest to Charlie."

"My pleasure Rocco. A few months ago Charlie, I was approached by Rocco's people. They showed me pictures and let me hear recordings of Colombian cartel leaders meeting with Mexican mafia leaders. At first, I laughed at them believing it was a setup to get me to flip sides. I walked away, but curiosity soon got the best of me, so I checked out things for myself. I was shocked when I found the same photos and recordings showed to me by Rocco's people in our possession. Digging deeper I uncovered even more startling proof that Rocco's people were right. There are four international ports of entry connecting Ciudad Juarez and El Paso. This includes the Bridge of the Americas, Ysleta International Bridge, Paso Del Norte Bridge, and Stanton Street Bridge. These combined allow millions of crossings making Ciudad Juarez a major point of entry and transportation for all of central northern Mexico. My beloved City of Juarez where my loved ones still reside would become ground zero for the drug trade. There are thousands of hard working families that have spent their entire lives working and growing their businesses in Juarez. Some of these businesses have been passed proudly down for generations. They would all soon be held hostage by the Mexican Mafia. I could not and will not be a part of the genocide of my own people. I hope you understand now Charlie why I betrayed you."

Charlie reluctantly nods his head. Then he says, "I don't understand why I was kept in the dark about this."

Rocco refills Charlie's glass saying, "It's in their best interests Charlie to keep blinders on you like a horse. You were never one of them, and you never will be. You're just some scumbag drug dealer they need to make them money."

Charlie takes a swig of his drink and then replies, "It makes sense when you put it that way Rocco. I was using them, so why shouldn't they be using me? I kept them in the blind as much as I could too. I made more money for myself that way. Who do you want me to give the dirt to Rocco?"

Ariella and Diego will clue you in on your new intelligence network after we leave. In the meantime, I have a meeting set up with Frankie tomorrow. I don't want him disappearing on me before I can talk to him, so I want you to tell him everything went down as planned tonight. Droz and Tex are dead."

"That won't be a problem Rocco. He's expecting me to call him. Since you're in such a forgiving mood Rocco, what do you have in mind for Frankie?"

"I just need him to keep working the deals I have him already on, and to keep cooperating with you. Frankie doesn't know it yet, but all of his domestic and offshore banking accounts are now under my control too. He makes one move I don't approve of, and he'll be spending the rest of his life in prison. We both know Frankie, Charlie, and the prison lifestyle just doesn't suit him."

Laughing whole-heartedly Charlie replies, "You got that right Rocco. Hey Rocco, I'm going to need access to some of my money. I got people on my payroll to take care of."

"That won't be a problem Frankie. I've made arrangements allowing you to withdraw up to 100k a month. That should cover things for you. As my level of trust with you grows, so will your withdrawal capabilities. Not to mention you still will be able to earn."

"You're letting me live, you're letting me earn, and you're allowing me to take care of my people. I consider this mercy Rocco, and I will repay you with my loyalty." Charlie nods his head saying.

If you really mean that Charlie we can achieve a lot of good together. If you don't mean it, you'll be dead or in prison."

Ariella walks back into the room saying, "We're ready to leave Rocco."

"Good Ariella. Droz, Tex, you'll be coming with me. Nicky, Sally, and Vinnie, you guys will lay low for a couple of weeks. Take in some sun at the beach. Read the newspapers and you'll know what's going on. You guys have all done an excellent job so far. Soon I'll be in position to put all of my so called friends in New York in jail for the rest of their lives. Charlie, when I step out that door your new life begins. I strongly suggest you use it wisely."

"I will Rocco. You can count on it."

Both men hug and kiss. When we all leave the house, Ariella warns us not to touch anything. Then she tells Nicky, Sally, and Vinnie to get into the blue Lincoln located on their right. Ariella tells Rocco, me, and Tex to get into a black one on our left. Outside I get my first glimpse of the battle. Bullet ridden bodies are everywhere. My car is gone, and the three vans are destroyed. Charlie's limo looks like Swiss cheese. Before I can ask Nicky about my money, Ariella pushes me along saying, "No time for sightseeing Droz, just move."

Nicky, Sally, and Vinnie jump into their Lincoln. As they drive off, I wonder if they had the money. When we get into our Lincoln it quickly pulls away. One of Ariella's men drove while another rides shotgun.

"Where are we heading Rocco?"

"My place in Boca, we'll spend the night there. In the morning, I'll have my meeting with Frankie. I can't wait to see the look on his face when he sees the two of you alive."

"That makes three of us, right Tex?"

"You got that right Droz. Hey Rocco, I'm a little worried about Nicky, Vinnie, and Sally. Shouldn't we be watching their backs? After what happened tonight I'm sure Antonio will stop at nothing to get them."

Rocco grins like the Cheshire cat cheerfully replying, "No need to worry about Antonio and his family Tex. Father Mac is taking care of that for us."

"Father Mac Rocco? How in the world is he involved with Antonio?" I ask surprised.

"It's called the old poison in the communion trick. Works like a charm. It can take out entire families without any violence."

"Rocco that's horrible! I don't believe you!"

"Can I get an Amen?" Tex says like a TV evangelist.

Rocco waves his hand at us both saying, "It's the oldest trick in the book. How do you think the Roman Catholic Church became so powerful? It surely wasn't by throwing holy water on people."

Ariella's two men laugh at that one! Rocco continues. "Who knows how many royals and nobles the church rubbed out because they wouldn't see things their way? The Vatican possesses secret poisons from days of old that even today are undetectable. At first, the victims get dizzy and then they start vomiting. Everyone thinks it's from the food. That's why it's great to use at weddings and christenings. When the victims lay down to sleep it off, they fall into a coma and die. No one ever suspects the priests. Years ago, Father Mac did charity work over in Colombia. He knows all the Church head honchos. I told him to offer them more money than they're getting from the cartels. It's a no brainer for the greedy bastards, so they spiked the communion."

"The good old church Rocco, selling out to the highest bidder," Tex says.

"Well Tex unfortunately that's the way it goes, but thankfully this time it goes in our favor. Soon there will be airstrikes on their drug labs, towns, and villages. This will cripple their cash flows. Next, our government will come out and openly support the Colombian government's war on drugs. Our special forces units will then assist the Colombian Army in wiping them out."

After Ariella's men drop us off in Boca, we take showers and turn in. Rocco wakes us up early, about six thirty in the morning. He says Frankie will be here by eight. Rocco's in a really happy mood and cooks us all breakfast. Eggs, bacon, sausage, and even homemade pancakes! When we're done eating, we help Rocco clean the kitchen. Like clockwork, Frankie knocks on the door at eight. Rocco tells us to stay out of sight until we hear him talking to Frankie. Frankie knocks again and Rocco shouts out, "Hold your horses Frankie; I'll be there in a minute!" When Rocco opens the door, we hear Frankie laugh and say, "Rocco, what are you still doing in your underwear? I figured you would be up and dressed already. What are you sick?"

"A matter of fact I am. I'm heart sick Frankie."

Rocco speaks so we walk out into the living room. As soon as Frankie see's us, he bolts for the door. In one fast swoop, Rocco pulls a black tie out of his underwear and snares Frankie around the neck with it! "Are you surprised Frankie?" Rocco sarcastically asks as he tightens his grip. With even more sarcasm now Rocco continues. "Awe, what's the matter Frankie? Are you at a loss for words? Here, let me loosen the tie a little. You recognize this tie Frankie?"

Frankie's face turns crimson as he frantically cries out, "No! What did I do Rocco!? What did I do!?"

"Well you should recognize the tie Frankie. You gave it to my son for his confirmation you worthless piece of shit!"

"Please! Let me explain Rocco! It was all Charlie Wing's fault! I know where he is. Let me help you get him!"

The muscles in Rocco's arms and shoulders bulge as he tightens his grip around Frankie's neck. Rocco looks at us with devils' eyes calmly saying, "There's nothing more gratifying than slowly choking the life out of a prick like this."

Frankie struggles wildly to get out from Rocco's grip, but Rocco's way too strong. He pulls Frankie by his neck over to a mirror smashing his face right into it. The force of the blow leaves Frankie with pieces of mirror lodged into his forehead. Frankie starts bleeding from all over his face. Ever so slightly now, Rocco loosens the tie from around his throat saying, "Take a nice deep breath Frankie. I don't want you to die too quickly."

Frankie's desperately gasping for air while Rocco continues talking to him. "You were supposed to be Bobby's Godfather. You were supposed to be one of my closest friends, but you betrayed me. If you had only come to me and told me the truth Frankie, I could have forgiven you. Instead you made a fool out of me."

Rocco tightens his death grip around Frankie's neck. Frankie's eyes bulge out from his skull. It's a surreal moment watching Rocco in his tighty whities slowly strangling the life out of Frankie. It's a scene forever cementing Rocco in my mind as the stone cold killer Nicky said he is. In his throes of death, Frankie pisses his pants. When he dies the smell of shit permeates the room. Rocco shouts vehemently, "I fucking knew it! I knew this cocksucker would shit himself! It aint like the fucking movies, is it boys? In the movies, they show a Mafioso do the rope trick in his nice pressed suit. Well now, you know it's all a bunch of fucking bullshit. You need to bring a change of clothes when you do this kind of hit. Nine times out of fucking ten the cocksucker you're strangling will piss and shit all over you. Just like this prick did."

Tex and I stand there in shock witnessing the killer side of Rocco. Rocco notices us staring and says, "What the fuck are you two pussies standing there looking at? It fucking stinks in here you assholes. Go open the patio fucking doors already!"

Tex and I jump to Rocco's commands! When we're in the kitchen, Tex timidly whispers, "I guess killing Frankie got Rocco in a real foul cursing kind of mood."

"Whatever kind of mood he's in Tex, I don't know if I ever want to see this side of him again," I timidly whisper back.

"Me either," Tex whispers.

"What the fuck are you two little sissy's whispering about in there!" Rocco yells.

We quickly open up the patio doors and walk back to the living room. Looking at Frankie's dead body my curiosity gets the best of me, so I ask Rocco, "Why did you let Charlie and Nicky live Rocco, but kill Frankie?"

Rocco's sinister stare cuts right through me. I fear I might have really fucked up by asking him that question. Then Rocco bursts out laughing saying, "Boy Droz, you sure do have balls asking me that question right now. Since you got the grapefruits to ask, I'll tell you. Frankie was my son's godfather. That made him part of the family. He was also a trusted friend for many, many, years. Charlie and Nicky were never my trusted friends, or ever part of my family. Frankie broke my heart and made a fool out of me by lying to me for all of these years. For that, I could never forgive him, so I killed him. I didn't tell Charlie Wings what my real plans were for Frankie because I didn't know if I could trust him yet. I couldn't take the chance of Charlie tipping Frankie off. Charlie's loyalty will soon be tested in other ways just as yours was. You wanted Future Visions from Frankie didn't you?"

I light up like a fucking Christmas tree replying, "You know I did Rocco."

Well now, the door's open for you to get it. A chance to use that genius IQ you have. Let me give you a little hint of what the future may have in store for you. There's a secret government program going on right now called ARPANET. It's billed as an emergency communications system in case of disaster or nuclear attack. It's really being used for a mobile nukes program. We have highly trained officers with briefcase computers capable of launching our missiles from anywhere in the world through this system. It has the Russians and the Chinese scared shitless. I'm told one day it'll evolve into the future of all communications. It's supposed to have tremendous potential with the right financial backing. My friends and I can provide that backing. In time, everyone on the planet will have access to what will eventually be known as the internet. The government plans to use this internet to keep tabs on everybody. Future Visions will be in on the ground floor."

Wow Rocco! That's fucking unreal! When will you get me and Tex involved?"

"I don't know for sure yet. Meanwhile the both of you still have to help Nicky. I'm determined to bring down the drug dealing scum in New York. There's an ambitious young Italian guy working in the Attorney General's Office I got my eye on. We'll feed him enough evidence to put these bums in jail for the rest of their lives. Nothing will be more gratifying to the Italian American community than another Italian American putting these dirt bags away. It will skyrocket this guy's career into politics. You can never have enough friends in high places that owe you."

All of a sudden, there's a loud knock at the door. Tex and I quickly look at Rocco. Rocco smiles saying, "Nothing to worry about boys, it's only the cleanup crew."

Rocco opens the front door in his tighty whities like he didn't have a care in the world. Four men walk in carrying all kinds of cleaning stuff ready to go to work.

"After you guys take out the trash make sure you fill the boat up with gas."

"Sure thing Rocco," one of the men replies.

"Boys, I'm going to go take myself a hot shower and get dressed. When I'm done the three of us are going on a little vacation."

"Vacation, that sounds cool Rocco. Where are we heading?" I excitedly ask.

"We're going to your old stomping grounds Hawaii. We'll be meeting Father Mac out there. I'm anxious to see the house and boat he bought."

"That sounds great Rocco," I quickly reply dying inside.

"You don't have to ask me twice," Tex adds.

I got to get a message to Keoni to warn Johnny, so I ask Rocco, "As you know, the car you gave me is gone, so we need to borrow yours to go back to the house and pack some things."

"No need. We'll pick up what we need when we get to Honolulu. I like traveling light."

"That's cool. Well, Tex and I aint got much dough on us Rocco. It would be a good idea if we go home and get some cash for the trip. We don't want to feel like we're freeloading or anything. We also need to tell our girls we're going to be away for a while, so they don't worry."

The men cleaning up just shake their heads at that last line about saying goodbye to our girls. Rocco gives me a parental look and in a condescending tone replies, "Well that's very considerate of you Droz, but we don't have time. Our flight leaves Palm Beach International at 11:08. Call the girls when we get there. As far as cash goes, I'm sure my good for nothing godson can provide that for you." Rocco casually turns around heading for the shower singing Enrico Caruso's, Santa Lucia.

As we watch Rocco's men carrying Frankie's body out to the boat, Tex says, "I sure do hope our tickets say roundtrip on them." I nod silently.

ABOUT THE AUTHOR

I poured my heart and soul into this novel, thus a lot about who I am is contained in these pages. If it wasn't for a beautiful angel I met on the beach over 20 years ago, I would have never been alive to write it. After introducing myself to her, she asked me my occupation. I gave her a sly smile and coolly replied, "I'm a gangster." She giggled and smiled back replying, "No you're not. You just haven't met someone who believes in you yet." We've been skipping down the "Yellow Brick Road" together since.